Soldiers and Martyrs

Patriots of the American Revolution Series Book Four

Geoff Baggett

Cocked Hat Publishing

ISBN: 0997383399
ISBN 13: 9780997383393

Dedicated to my mother, Velma Ruth Williams Baggett. I cannot believe that it has almost been twenty years since she passed. Childhood abandonment and adoption marred her understanding and view of her personal identity and history. She never even knew that she had a family tree full of Patriots, martyrs, and heroes. I hope that she is smiling in Heaven as she enjoys my discoveries.

With special thanks to my wife, Kim Baggett. She is the ultimate partner, editor, splatterdasher buttoner, Colonial hair stylist, tent constructor, seamstress, and bookseller. She has endured much throughout three decades of marriage to this helpless, hopeless nerd.

As always, thanks to Steve Mallory, Debbie Mallory, and my new friend and avid reader, Shirley Ezell, for their generosity, expertise, editing, proofreading, input, and encouragement.

Cover Photography: Geoff Baggett

Cover Design by Natasha Snow - natashasnow.com

Revolutionary War Novels
by Geoff Baggett
Patriots of the American Revolution Series
Brothers and Warriors (Book One)
Partisans and Refugees (Book Two)
Frenchmen and Long Knives (Book Three)
Soldiers and Martyrs (Book Four)

Patriot Kids of the American Revolution Series
Little Hornet (Book One)
Little Warrior (Book Two)
Little Spy of Vincennes (Book Three)

Kentucky Frontier Adventures
A Bucket Full of Courage (Book One)

Creative Writing Journals for Kids
By Geoff Baggett

My Colonial Journal for Girls
My Colonial Journal for Boys

PART I

Patriots of the Piedmont
1776

1

AN ORDINARY NIGHT

April 20, 1776
Saturday Evening – Guilford Courthouse, North Carolina

The night was soft and quiet, and uncharacteristically cool for late April, even in the Carolina Piedmont. Almost every fireplace in the town belched a steady stream of gray-white smoke. The heavy, humid air caused most of the smoke to remain low in the atmosphere and hover like a hazy blanket above the rooftops of the sleepy little North Carolina village of Guilford Courthouse. No one wandered the streets after dark. It was a Saturday evening. Most respectable people in the township had already retired to the privacy of their homes.

The typical sounds of village life emanated from those homes. There was a mixture of piano music, singing, muffled laughter, passionate amorous encounters, and the occasional crying baby. In the distance, several annoying dogs barked. On the northern side of town, a very misinformed and confused rooster crowed. The freshly plowed fields and pastures beyond the edges of the township were dark and silent. It was a soft, quiet night, indeed.

Like most of the other idyllic, whitewashed frame houses along Main Street in Guilford Courthouse, an orange-yellow flicker of fire and candlelight escaped through the milky glass windows of the James Billingsley home. The dancing light bathed the tiny lawn and gardens beyond with a soft glow. Very few sounds came from the Billingsley abode. Six of the family's nine children were gone from home, either committed to the bonds of matrimony, or living on and operating the family farm. Only the youngest three remained: fifteen-year-old Martha, fourteen-year-old Walter, and the baby of the family, Basil, age nine.

The sun had been below the horizon for almost an hour, and it would soon be time for bed at the Billingsley house. James Billingsley, the master of the home, preferred going to bed early and rising early. He still held title to his farmlands near the town, but he had turned over the day-to-day operation of the farm to his oldest sons, Samuel, James Jr., John, and Henry. Even though he had personally abandoned farm life and made a home in town several years ago, Billingsley still preferred to keep "farmer's hours" in his daily life. He considered the humble schedule of country folk to be a cornerstone of his personal work ethic.

The Billingsley family customarily retired early on Saturday evenings, as Sunday was James' primary work day. Over the past few years he had devoted his life to full-time preaching. James Billingsley was an exhorter among the Separatist Baptists of Guilford County. He was an unordained lay preacher who served several small Baptist congregations throughout the region. He and another fellow exhorter, Tidence Lane, had honed their preaching skills under the strict and watchful eye of the infamous Rev. Shubal Stearns. Stearns was a former Presbyterian from the Northeast who had converted to the Baptist faith during the Great Awakening. He brought the Separatist Baptist movement to North Carolina in 1755, and preached faithfully on the frontier until his death in 1771.

James and a small cohort of other exhorters took responsibility for area churches after the Rev. Stearns' death. Now, on most Sundays, James preached at least three sermons in two or three different churches in the area. Most of the time he preached at the nearby Sandy Creek or Abbots Creek Baptist Churches. Though

James Billingsley was not theologically trained or officially ordained, his sermons were neither lectures nor boring. He was a passionate, fiery, energetic preacher. So, retiring early on a Saturday night was something of a necessity. James needed the extra rest to carry him through the exhausting physical trials of preaching the Word on Sunday.

It was a wonder that the man had not already retired to his bedchamber. On this particular night, however, he was simply too absorbed in poring over the pages of the latest *Virginia Gazette*, a newspaper published in faraway Williamsburg. He sat in his preferred rocking chair beside the front window, nursing a warm, medicinal toddy of milk, whiskey, and nutmeg as he enjoyed his weekly paper. He had been quite animated in his reading that evening, sometimes slapping his hand on his knee and proclaiming an enthusiastic, "Amen!"

The other members of the family were all gathered in the parlor for the evening, as well. In addition to the large fire in the fireplace, approximately two dozen beeswax candles adorned candelabras and candlesticks throughout the room, providing ample light for all who were gathered there. James' wife and children were slightly mystified and somewhat entertained by his strange behavior, but they chose not to verbalize their curiosity or concerns. Instead, they devoted their attention to their individual endeavors and interests. Tomorrow was Sunday. There would be no idle leisure activities, chores, or games on the Sabbath. As usual, it would be a day filled with church services, Scripture readings, seriousness, and prayer. The members of the Billingsley clan hoped to reap at least one more hour of entertainment from this pleasant evening before their father ordered them all to bed.

Mrs. Elizabeth Billingsley sat opposite her husband in a rocking chair that was identical to his. She sipped a toddy, as well, though it was not quite as "medicinal" as her husband's. She busied herself by mending several sets of wool socks afflicted with ripped, hole-infested toes. It was a very familiar weekly task in this faithful mother's life. Raising six boisterous boys provided her with an endless flow of torn, shredded items of clothing in need of repair.

The elegant young maiden, Martha, sat quietly in a comfortable, padded Queen Anne chair in the far corner of the room. Like her father, she, too, was reading. However, she did not care for the newspapers and political pamphlets that her father consumed on such a regular basis. Instead, she was enjoying, for at least the third time, the thrilling words of Jonathan Swift's adventurous novel, *Gulliver's Travels.*

Walter and Basil, the youngest of the six Billingsley boys, lay on their bellies on the floor in front of the fireplace. Each had a soft pillow tucked beneath his chest and chin. They were engaged in a fiercely competitive contest of dominoes. It was only a matter of time before some explosion of conflict between the two boys would bring an end to the tranquility of this otherwise quiet Saturday evening. It had happened far too many times before.

The sharp click of an ivory chip being deposited in victory broke the Billingsley silence.

"And that, Basil, is the final play. We have reached a stalemate. Once again, I am the victor."

"No, Walter! You did not win!" squealed Basil Billingsley, rising to his knees. "You have more dominoes left over than I do!" The headstrong, competitive nine-year-old was angry. He was on the edge of livid, actually. Basil despised losing, especially to his brother.

Their father lowered his newspaper ever so slightly and glared at them over the top of his spectacles. He considered saying something, but decided that, thus far, the developing conflict had not risen to the level of fatherly intervention. The boys' mother sighed in frustration. She knew that an explosion of anger was imminent. Margaret rolled her eyes with an air of drama that only a teen-aged sister could muster.

Walter Billingsley, five years Basil's elder, maintained a calm demeanor, but rejoiced on the inside. He, too, anticipated that a juvenile fit would soon visit the Billingsley household. He knew better than anyone the simple, yet effective methods required to elicit just such an emotional explosion out of his younger brother. He loved to watch the boy throw an emotional tantrum and then get into trouble with his parents afterwards. The corners of Walter's mouth curved upward, forming a wry, mischievous grin. Both his expression and his voice displayed a subtly condescending and patronizing tone.

"Now, Basil, if you will simply recall the rules of the game, you will realize that I am, as usual, the winner. Once again, I remind you that it is not the number of dominoes in hand that determines who wins. It is the number of pips on the game pieces. My three dominoes have a total of seven pips. Your two dominoes have a combined total of nine. Therefore, I win the game."

On the far side of the room Margaret giggled quietly. Basil's ears turned red in embarrassment when he realized that his brother was correct. The veins on his forehead throbbed. His hands began to tremble.

"Cheater!" he exploded in anger and frustration.

He jumped to his feet and kicked viciously at the dominoes that stretched in a long line on the wide heart pine floorboard in front of the fireplace. Several of the ivory game pieces launched dangerously close to the flames.

"Why! You annoying little toad!" yelled Walter as he dived to retrieve his precious dominoes from the fire.

James Billingsley could no longer tolerate the conflict between his sons.

"Boys! Stop it this instant! I will not have the two of you sullying the waning moments of this glorious day with your selfish bitterness and callous words. Walter, you will cease referring to your brother in such unkind terms. And Basil, you must learn now to control that temper of yours. If you find yourself unable to adhere to, or even remember, the rules of the game, you should stop playing it." He shook his newspaper in disgust. "I grow weary of this insufferable bickering between the two of you that invades our home every single evening. I will not stand for it anymore. Do you understand?"

"Yes, Father," answered Walter firmly.

"Yes, Father," echoed Basil with a trembling voice that was barely above a whisper.

"Very well, then." He paused and took a deep, cleansing breath. "Now, I want you all to gather 'round. Put away your games and books. I must tell you about the latest developments at our Fourth Provincial North Carolina Congress."

"Oh, Father!" wailed Martha. "Must we suffer more of your boring politics?"

"My dear daughter, the events of recent days in this colony transcend politics as usual," responded James. "Now come closer, all of you. You must hear this!"

His sons and daughter obediently crossed the room and joined their parents. Walter politely fetched a small stool for his sister. The boys, as was their custom, sat cross-legged in the floor.

Their father began, "I believe that we are on the cusp of a rebellion against England that will sweep this continent and forever change the face of the Americas."

His wife emitted a loud sigh and frustratingly dropped the sock that she had been mending into her lap. She almost glared at her husband.

"Darling, surely you do not believe that the horrid rebellion of Boston will reach us way down here in the South. We are at peace in North Carolina."

James Billingsley stared sternly at his wife. His voice dropped in tone, sounding akin to a growl. "Do not denigrate the sacrifice of our Patriots in the North, my dear. Many have shed their blood and given their lives in response to the tyranny of King George. And contrary to your claim, I submit to you that we are not at peace. As you are well aware, there have been several skirmishes between British vessels and our Colonial forces in the county of Brunswick."

She responded bluntly and dismissively, "Those were coastal disputes, James. They were way over on the Atlantic. Those events have nothing to do with us. Besides, the only real fighting going on right now is being perpetrated by George Washington and his band of malcontents in Massachusetts."

James shook his head vigorously. "No, my dear. You are absolutely wrong. Our own Royal Governor, Josiah Martin, has been forced to seek refuge on a British ship off of our coast for almost a year! The Royal government has not effectively functioned in North Carolina since then. And I just read in the *Gazette* the account of the battle at Moore's Creek Bridge."

"Another coastal dispute between the Royal Navy and some lowland outlaws and thieves," declared his wife.

"No, my dear. You are wrong! It was an actual ground battle among infantrymen. Over one thousand Whigs engaged over one thousand six hundred Loyalists up from South Carolina. Those Loyalists were men determined to intervene in the politics of North Carolina. A great battle occurred in Hanover County! And those tenacious Patriots killed almost fifty of the enemy and captured over half of the remaining combatants. I tell you … it was a battle bathed in blood and revolution, right here in our very own colony!"

The members of James' family stared numbly at him. They had heard some talk about a recent battle at a bridge somewhere to the east. Most of the men of Guilford seemed obsessed with the subject. But most of the women and children paid it little mind. Until this moment, the members of the Billingsley family had no idea of the size and scope of the battle that had taken place within the borders of their own colony.

"But why would we desire to rebel against England now?" moaned Elizabeth. "The farming is successful and pays well. Our economy is good. The Indians seem to be staying on their side of the mountains. The political environment today is nothing like it was during that horrendous Regulator Rebellion of the previous decade."

James Billingsley's jaw dropped in disbelief. "My dear, have you already forgotten that I was connected to a significant number of those Regulators? Have you forgotten that we once feared that Governor Tryon would place a price on *my* head? Have you forgotten the economic oppression that we suffered at the hands of our British overlords?"

"No, Husband, I have not forgotten. I remember that bloody battle at Alamance where some of our friends bled and died. And I remember all too well how our Baptist churches once numbered five or six hundred people in attendance, and now they number in the dozens on a good Sunday. That Regulator Rebellion served to scatter our people, kill our communities, and decimate our wonderful churches."

"I will admit that many of our Baptist brethren have fled this county in search of more freedom over the mountains or down in the frontiers of Georgia. And I know that our churches have suffered severe loss." He paused dramatically. "But I have often been tempted to follow them in search of that same freedom."

"James!" his wife scolded him in disbelief. "Surely you would not simply walk away from our precious lands and our other financial holdings." She waved her hand in a wide circle, dramatically highlighting the expanse of their majestic abode. "How could you ever leave this beautiful, stately house less than one block from our county courthouse? James, you are revered and respected in this community. This is our home!"

Elizabeth's face registered confusion, concern, and fear at the mere possibility of leaving Guilford Courthouse.

"Are we going to move over the mountains, Papa?" asked Basil excitedly. "Can we live in a log cabin? I would love to see a real bear!"

James sighed at his son. "No, Basil, we are not moving over the mountains." He turned to his wife. "But perhaps I would go, Elizabeth, if I thought that I might have the opportunity to find liberty and breathe air that is truly free."

"God forbid the notion!" she retorted.

Her children gasped. They had never before heard their mother issue such a scandalous swear.

This time Elizabeth's voice emanated from her tiny, quivering lips in the form of a growl. "I will not leave my home and my grown sons and daughters, and miss out on experiencing my grandchildren growing up, just so that you can go in search of this elusive freedom that you describe."

James smiled victoriously. "Most likely we will not be required to leave our home, my love. It seems that freedom is attempting to find its way to us."

"Whatever do you mean?" she asked, confused.

He shook his newspaper enthusiastically. "The Fourth Provincial Congress just closed its session in Halifax last week. They authorized our representatives to the Continental Congress to cast their votes for independency from Great Britain!"

"What?" she responded in disbelief.

"What does that mean, Papa?" asked Walter curiously.

"It means that the Royal Governor has been removed, once and for all. Josiah Martin is no longer Lord over North Carolina. We have a new representative government."

James beamed with pride and held up the newspaper. "And that government has issued a declaration. The words are contained in a document called the *Halifax Resolves,* which were passed last Friday, April 12. The *Resolves* proclaim that if the Continental Congress ever considers a vote on whether or not to separate from Great Britain, the North Carolina delegation is authorized to vote for separation. The text of their resolves is here in the *Gazette.* Listen to what those brave, noble men declared ..." He cleared his throat and began reading.

> "*Whereas the moderation hitherto manifested by the United Colonies and their sincere desire to be reconciled to the mother Country on Constitutional Principles, have procured no mitigation of the aforesaid wrongs and usurpations and no hopes*

> *remain of obtaining redress by those Means alone which have been hitherto tried, Your Committee are of Opinion that the house should enter into the following Resolve, to wit: Resolved that the delegates for this Colony in the Continental Congress be empowered to concur with the other delegates of the other Colonies in declaring Independency ...*"

He stopped reading, and then added, "The vote on these resolves was unanimous. Eighty-three voted for it. None in the assembly voted against it."

The Billingsley family sat in stunned silence. Even the aloof Margaret seemed captivated by the notion of an outright rebellion against England.

"Will there be a shooting war in North Carolina, Papa?" asked Margaret. "Here amongst our fields and homes?"

James Billingsley drew in a deep breath. "Perhaps one day there will, Margaret. Some of your brothers may be called upon to serve the causes of freedom and liberty."

Walter declared, "I will fight, Papa. I want to fight for freedom! I want to go with my brothers!" He held his chin high and poked out his chest in pride and defiance.

James grinned at his son and tousled his hair. But as he looked at the faces of his wife and daughter, he could see that the serious nature of the subject at hand was somewhat overwhelming to the fairer members of his family. He had pressed his discussion of politics entirely too far. He sensed that he needed to change the subject, at least for the evening.

"I did not intend to get all of you so worked up and worried about our future. I sincerely apologize if I have frightened you. Please, do not worry yourselves regarding battles and conflict on this beautiful night. Whether or not there will be a war is a matter for God to decide. It is in His sovereign hands. Anyhow ... if there is to be a war here in the Carolinas, it will probably be years from now. Indeed, such a war will likely be fought along the coast and in other distant places. I do not want you to worry about such things." He gazed apologetically at his wife and children. "Again, I am deeply sorry if I have frightened you."

James rose to his feet. "Now … it is time to retire. Off to bed, all of you. We will talk about these matters on another day."

The children all rose obediently, kissed their mother and father, and then dutifully ascended the stairs to their bedchambers. James and Elizabeth watched them lovingly and proudly. Moments later the doors to their rooms clicked shut as they prepared for bed.

James turned and knelt on the floor in front of his wife. He gently took her by the hand.

"My dear, I am deeply sorry if I have upset you with all of this talk of rebellion, war, and independency. I certainly did not intend to trouble you so."

"I am quite all right, my dear. I will confess that it is troubling, indeed. I just hope that if war does come, it will be as you say … in some faraway place. I cannot imagine violence and conflict visiting us among our beautiful, peaceful villages of North Carolina."

"Neither can I, my love. Neither can I."

2:00 AM – That Same Night

Walter bolted awake. He lay flat on his back and remained perfectly still in his bed. Something had roused him from a deep sleep. But what was it?

As he fought to overcome the disorientation of his state of slumber and the haunting darkness of the night, he realized that it was some sort of sound that had awakened him. It was a strange sound. Deep, booming, and loud. He was unsure about its source. All that he knew was that the sound was out of place. It was wrong, somehow … not a sound that one would expect to hear in the wee hours of the morning on the Sabbath.

Walter was relatively certain that the noise had its origins somewhere outside the house. Several dogs roused throughout the neighborhood, unleashing an annoying and expanding chorus of barks and howls that extended beyond the town limits to the homes in the surrounding country. That, too, was odd for the middle of the night.

Then he heard the sound again. This time he knew what it was. It was a fist pounding on the front door of his home.

"What in heaven's name?" he muttered. "Who would call at such an indecent hour?"

On the other side of the bedchamber he heard Basil's bed creak. He glanced toward the place where his brother slept. The fireplace beyond contained only a remnant of embers from the evening fire. In the dull glow of the dusky orange coals, Walter could see his little brother sitting up in his bed. The boy was grinding both fists into tired eyes.

"What was that sound, Walter? Was it thunder?"

"No. Someone is knocking on our door. I heard it twice."

"In the middle of the night?" whined Basil. "It must be something bad. Maybe someone has died and they have come to fetch Papa."

"Not likely, little brother. Those kinds of things usually wait until morning. No one makes funeral or burial plans in the middle of the night."

"Well, what is it, then?"

Walter shook his head in the darkness. "I do not know. But I am going to find out."

Walter threw back his blankets and walked toward the fireplace. He grabbed a handful of tinder from a basket on the mantle and tossed it onto the glowing coals. He leaned over and blew vigorously on the dry material, which immediately burst into lively, bright flames. He took a sterling silver three-candle stand from the mantle, removed a short beeswax candle, and lit the charred wick in the fresh flames. He used that candle to light the other two candles on his stand.

As he turned and began walking away from the fireplace, once again a fist slammed against the downstairs outer door. There were three thunderous knocks. Both boys jumped at the sound. This time the banging was accompanied by a loud, harsh voice.

"James Billingsley! I demand that you open this door! By the decree of Josiah Martin, Governor of His Majesty's Colony of North Carolina, you must reveal yourself and submit to questioning!"

They heard their father's voice bellow from somewhere downstairs, "One moment, Sir! Allow a man the time to put on his breeches, for God's sake!"

Walter began running. Basil threw off his bedcovers and, following Walter, raced toward their chamber door. Walter opened it and both boys dashed into the upstairs hallway. The top flight of the stairwell ran parallel to the rear wall of the house, just outside and to the right of their bedroom door. There was a narrow walkway that ran behind the upper flight, connecting the two rear second-story bedrooms. The boys leapt down the first short flight of stairs to the small landing where the stairs turned ninety degrees and then led down to the foyer and the front door. Their wool stockings slid across the polished wood of the six-foot-wide landing and they collided in a heap against the far wall. One of the candles tumbled from Walter's stand and fell to the floor of the landing, splashing a puddle of melted wax onto the floorboards. Walter quickly grabbed the candle, re-ignited its flame with one of his other candles, and stuck it back into the stand.

Their father's stern voice rumbled from the darkness below. "Boys, stay upstairs. Go back to bed." He sounded gruff and frightened.

Walter leaned forward and held the cluster of candles toward the source of the voice. His father was standing in the dark foyer, behind the bolted and locked door. He was wearing black breeches and stockings. His white nightshirt hung untucked over the top of the breeches. He was not wearing any shoes.

Their father growled, "I mean it, boys. Stay upstairs."

"But, Father!" groaned Walter.

"Do not argue with me, Son! Simply do as I say!"

"Yes, Father," responded Walter.

He tugged at Basil's nightshirt and led him back up the stairs. Once they were out of their father's line of sight, Walter blew out his candles and dropped down to the floor. He had just enough angle to see down the stairway and spy on the events below. Basil followed his brother's lead.

"What are we doing, Walter?"

"Shh!" Walter held his finger over his lips, forming the universal sign of silence.

The pounding resumed on the door. The flickering light of several torches invaded the foyer through the thick glass that adorned each side of the beautiful, decorative entrance. In the eerie glow of the torchlight, Walter could see the heavy wood vibrating from each blow. The invisible voice bellowed from beyond, "Open this door, in the name of the Crown!"

Elizabeth Billingsley peeked from behind the doorway to the parlor. She carried a single candle in a small brass stand. The boys' mother wore a heavy linen robe over the top of her shift. Her hair hung loosely over her shoulders. Walter chuckled a bit under his breath. He could not recall the last time that he had seen his mother's hair loose and not under the concealment of a bonnet.

Elizabeth whispered, "What is going on, James? What do these men want?"

"I do not know, Elizabeth. Please, darling, go back to bed. The voice does not sound like a friendly one."

"I will not return to bed! Not until I know what matter is so urgent that it requires our being roused from sleep in the middle of the night!"

James Billingsley sighed frustratingly at his wife's disobedience. He composed himself as best he could, stood up straight, and tried to portray as distinguished an appearance as possible. He poked out his chest with all of the pride and dignity that he could muster, and then reached out and released the locking latch on the door.

Whoever stood on the other side of that door took immediate advantage of the breech. The huge portal of thick oak exploded inward, knocking James off of his feet. Elizabeth screamed in alarm. James landed with a loud thud and a cry of pain. He skidded awkwardly on his backside across the slick, polished floor. He did not stop until his head slammed into the lower newel of the staircase handrail.

A stocky young man of average height stepped through the door. He was wearing a dark watch cloak over the top of his blue coat. An elegant black cocked hat decorated his head. Curiously, below the hat there was a stained linen cap. The man did not appear to have any hair. Six more men followed closely behind him. Three of them held torches. All of them were carrying 75-caliber British Army Brown Bess muskets. The men scattered left and right as they began a search of the bottom floor of the house.

"Be sure to search the basement thoroughly!" ordered the leader of the group.

Near the top of the stairs Basil attempted to rise. He instinctively wanted to run downstairs and protect his parents. Walter grabbed him by the arm.

"Wait!" whispered Walter.

"But Mama and Papa!" protested Basil.

"There's nothing we can do against all of those armed men." Walter paused and considered their dilemma. He quickly formulated a plan. "Basil, go to our room and get your clothes and shoes on. Slip out the back window and run to get James. Tell him to bring men and weapons. Tell him that armed soldiers have come for Papa."

Basil stared in disbelief at his brother. "But the farm is over a mile outside of town!"

"Then you had better get going right now. I will stay here and see if I can figure something out to help Mama and Papa. Now go, Basil! This is bad. Really bad."

Basil nodded reluctantly and then slipped quietly into their room. Walter could hear the boots of the men scuffing against the floorboards downstairs as they searched the house.

"It took you long enough to unlock the door! We were just about to break it down," boomed the cloak-covered man in a deep, angry voice. "What were you doing, hiding your weapons and contraband?"

James, fifty years old and slightly overweight, struggled to rise to his feet. He clutched at a rapidly-growing knot on the crown of his head. Elizabeth darted to his aid and helped him stand.

The abused, wounded man responded, "Whatever are you talking about, sir? You are speaking utter nonsense! Who are you, and what right do you have to barge into my home in the middle of the night?"

"I am Captain David Fanning of His Majesty's Loyalist Militia. I have been dispatched by order of Governor Josiah Martin to weed out the rebel leaders in this region. Your name was near the top of our list, Mr. Billingsley. We suspect that you are one of the local rabble-rousers who has been inciting rebellion against the Crown. Renegade preachers are dangerous among the citizenry. Indeed, the rebellious preaching of so-called men of God like yourself has incited these mutinous *Halifax Resolves* being passed by an unlawful rebel government. Furthermore, we suspect that your home is a repository of weapons and munitions for your traitorous band."

"Why, that is preposterous!" wailed James. "I am no rebel. I am a humble farmer and a faithful exhorter in the Baptist church. And there are no weapons in this house! But even if there were, I am a free Englishman and entitled to such!"

"Humph!" grunted the man disdainfully. "Baptist. The very sound of that word reeks of treason! You and the Papists are an abomination in this land! There is no true church but the King's Church!"

His angry face twisted into a sick grin. "You amuse me, Mr. Billingsley. I know very well who you are. I was merely a lad of fifteen years, living in Johnston County, when I was drafted into the militia during your so-called Regulator Rebellion. I spilled the blood of your kinsmen at Alamance. I remember reading about you. You preached sermons against our governor and King. You signed letters begging for clemency for your traitorous friends. Your signature is on papers in the government archives, evidence of your rebellious ways!"

At the top of the stairs, Walter felt a slight change in temperature and a rush of cool wind across the right side of his face. Basil had opened the window in their room. The cool air had entered the house and then filtered down the stairwell.

"*Good,*" Walter thought. He prayer, "*Go quickly and bring help, little brother.*"

Walter jumped when, from the bottom of the stairs, his father's voice exploded in anger. He had never heard such a tone come from his father's mouth.

"That was five years ago, you imbecile! And all I ever did was beg for the lives of some of the men involved. I abhor the use of capital punishment. Surely, sir, you are not intimating that writing a correspondence to the governor to beg for a man's life is some form of crime!"

"It is when that man is a traitor to the Crown," hissed Captain Fanning.

"Well, at least I *am* a man, sir!" responded James. "You are still behaving like a fifteen-year-old boy ... nay ... an infant! For only a spoiled child awakens grown people in the dark of night in order to stomp, scream, and have his way."

The men who had been searching the first floor and basement returned to the foyer. It was a fortuitous return, as it seemed that Captain Fanning was prepared to unleash his temper in a violent manner upon James.

One of the men reported to Fanning, "Sir, there is nothing of suspicion in the basement, kitchen, or first floor rooms."

"Very well, Sergeant."

Fanning glanced up the stairs. His eyes met Walter's. The boy rolled sideways and tried to hide himself behind the upper newel of the staircase, but it was too late.

"Sergeant, I saw movement at the top of the stairs! There may be rebel militia concealed there. Search the second floor thoroughly, but proceed carefully. Take anyone you find into custody."

The sergeant and the other men glanced up the stairs and hesitated briefly.

"Well! What are you waiting for? Go! Bring me some prisoners!"

2

THE HANGING

"Wait!" protested James. "There is no one up there except my children! You must not allow armed men to invade their chambers." He pleaded, "Please, leave them in peace!"

"If that is the case, then we shall have no problem with them, Mr. Billingsley. But I spotted eyes peering at me from the top of the stairway. One of your children may very well have been overly-curious and eavesdropping on our conversation." He paused dramatically. "Or, perhaps, there is a rebel hiding in your home … one of those so-called 'Sons of Liberty' ruffians. Whatever the case may be, we are compelled by our mandate to investigate."

He motioned to his men. Four of them stepped between James and Elizabeth and began their cautious ascent up the stairs. The first two men had their pistols drawn. The others wielded torches.

James stared in defiance at Fanning. "You said that someone was eavesdropping on our 'conversation.' Is that what you believe we are having here, sir? A 'conversation?' It seems more like a vicious, vengeful inquisition to me," declared James bitingly. He nodded toward the armed men ascending the stairs of his home. "You are on a fishing expedition, searching for some imaginary enemy. And sending armed men to rouse children from their beds is nothing short of terrorism. I shall see you brought up on charges and incarcerated for your crimes!"

Captain Fanning's face flashed an evil grin. "Semantics, Mr. Billingsley. One man's conversation is often perceived as another man's inquisition." He shrugged his shoulders dismissively. "Either will suffice in this instance. It makes no difference to me. Besides ... you, sir, are the criminal under investigation. I am the one pursuing British law and justice on this night. You are a wanton perpetrator of mutiny and insurrection!"

James responded with a loud and obstinate voice, "Horse shite! I have committed no crimes! I have been party to neither mutiny nor treason! There is no cause, legal or moral, that can excuse this violent invasion of my home. And there is no justice in terrorizing a man's family. You are a disgrace to whatever cause that you claim to represent."

Captain Fanning unexpectedly raised his right hand and struck James sharply across his left cheek. "I am shocked, Mr. Billingsley. I thought you were some type of 'man of the cloth.' Renegade Baptist clergy must hold to a standard of conduct different than that of the true men of God in the King's Church." He took a deep, irritated breath. "You will remain silent for the remainder of our time here, Mr. Billingsley. Do not speak again unless it is in response to a direct question from me. Have I made myself absolutely and unmistakably clear?"

James rubbed his burning, sore cheek and nodded. He was ashamed that he had used gutter profanity, yet he was also proud that he had stood up to this pompous bully. He glared at the invader with a stare of hatred that could have melted stone.

Walter crawled stealthily back into his bedchamber and silently closed the door. He tip-toed over to the open window and quietly closed it. He hurriedly tidied the bedcovers on Basil's bed and made it appear as undisturbed as possible. He then jumped back into his own bed and drew the wool blanket over his body. The door immediately swung open and slammed against the adjacent wall. A man stomped across the room, threw back Walter's blankets, and hauled the boy out of his bed.

The man threatened with a heavy Irish brogue, "Come with me, lit'l laddie! And don't be a-makin' any trouble, or I'll bash ya skull wit' me musket!"

"What is this about?" asked Walter, rubbing his eyes and feigning sleep and ignorance.

"Just shut your mout' and get down those stairs." The man shoved Walter in the direction of the door.

From the bedroom on the opposite side of the stairway, there came a blood-curdling scream. Somehow, Martha had managed to sleep through all of the storm of activity in the downstairs of the house. Her scream stopped for the briefest of moments when she paused to catch a breath, and then resumed with renewed vigor and volume.

A voice exploded in her room, "Shut up! You're making my brain ache with that confounded wailin'! I ain't here to hurt ya! The Cap'n just wants everybody downstairs!"

There was a sudden, odd crunching sound, followed by a dull thud. The female screaming stopped. Then a different voice ... a deep, manly voice ... began to howl with pain. There was a mixture of cursing, banging, and gasping. It sounded like a violent struggle was taking place in Martha's room. Walter prayed for the welfare and honor of his sister.

Several seconds later, the man inside her room shouted, "You insolent little bitch!"

There was the sharp crack of flesh striking flesh, no doubt an open palm slapping Martha Billingsley's tender face. The next sound to come from the room was a mournful, wailing cry. Moments later, Martha appeared in the doorway wearing nothing but her shift. Walter watched helplessly as his sister was herded roughly through the door of her bedchamber onto the walkway at the top of the stairs. She covered her swollen left cheek with her hand and sobbed uncontrollably. She immediately caught sight of her brother.

"Walter, what is happening to us?" she wailed.

The man who had invaded her bedchamber followed closely behind. He shouted angrily, "No talking!" He then placed his foot on her buttocks and gave her a mighty shove. She stumbled forward and landed in the arms of her brother, who attempted to console her.

Walter wrapped both of his arms around Martha's shoulders and whispered, "Shh. Just be calm. Everything will be all right."

The man who followed Margaret out of her room was holding an extinguished, still-smoking torch in his left hand. With his right hand, he swatted at a large spot of pine pitch and soot that covered his right cheek. His eyebrow on that side was completely scorched bare and his fur felt hat showed evidence of having caught fire, as well. A thin wisp of smoke wafted from the brim. Obviously, Martha had knocked or kicked the man's torch into his face. It was a blow and a burn that the bastard would not soon forget. Walter grinned vengefully.

Two guards forced Walter and Martha quickly down the stairs. The other two men continued their search of the upstairs rooms. Captain Fanning saw the wounded militiaman's stained and burned face and hat.

"What happened to you, Jeb?"

"Nothing, sir. I had an accident with my torch," he lied sheepishly. He attempted to change the subject quickly. "We found these two youngsters sleeping upstairs. There is no one else in the house."

Walter's parents shot him a confused look. Walter opened his eyes slightly wider and shook his head almost imperceptibly.

"Are these your children?" demanded the captain.

"Indeed, sir. This is my son, Walter, and my daughter, Martha."

"I thought that you were the father of several sons," responded Fanning.

"I am, sir, but most of my boys are of age and no longer under my roof. Some of them live on and run my farm. They each have their own homes."

"And these are the only children remaining in your care?" Fanning asked for clarification.

"Did you find anyone else upstairs, sir?" James retorted with rebellious vigor. He avoided and stretched the truth just a bit in order to avoid a bold-faced lie. "Now, sir, please leave my house immediately. Just look at my family! You have terrorized my wife and son, and you have assaulted my daughter! You have absolutely no right to invade the sanctity of my home and harass us. I will report your behavior to the constable and the magistrate first thing in the morning."

A voice echoed from upstairs, "Captain! I've found something!"

The Billingsley Farm – One Mile Southwest of Guilford Courthouse

Basil ran so hard that his lungs ached and his hands shook. He ran on the open road of the Salisbury Turnpike all the way to the farm. He could not believe that he had covered so much ground so quickly. Ahead and to his right he could see the outline of the original Billingsley farmhouse in the pale moonlight. His older brother, James, and wife, Ann, lived in the old family home. Another brother, Samuel, lived in a newer house about a quarter mile to the west, just a little deeper into the small valley.

Basil began emitting a dry, empty scream the moment that he could see the first house. The only word that he could muster was, "James!"

At least a half-dozen dogs detected Basil running toward the house and unleashed a barking frenzy in the yard. After almost a minute, there was still no light or movement inside. Basil began to cry out of frustration. He continued to attempt to call out his brother's name, but to no avail. At last, his spirit lifted when he saw a dull light appear in the window of the upper bedroom. Someone had lighted a candle.

Basil kept running until he reached the front porch of the house. The door swung open almost immediately. The barrel of a gun poked out of the darkness of the doorway. Then came a familiar voice.

"Basil? Is that you? What in heaven's name is wrong? Why have you come here alone in the middle of the cold night?" James Billingsley Jr. lowered his gun and ran to his youngest brother.

Basil attempted to respond, but he was so winded that he could not take in enough air to make an intelligent sound. As he tried to speak the sudden urge to vomit struck his throat. He fell to his knees, gagged, and expelled a puddle of clear bile onto the dry dust of the ground.

Ann Billingsley appeared at the door, cradling a baby in her left arm. "What is the matter, James?"

"It's Basil! Something is wrong with him. He has been running and cannot catch his breath. The boy is sick. Bring some water!"

Ann darted back inside the house. James knelt beside his brother and cupped the back of the boy's neck with his hand.

"Calm down, Basil. Everything will be all right. Just relax, now. Breathe."

Basil shook his head. "Everything ... is not ... all ... right." He continued to gasp for air.

"Slow down, baby brother, and tell me what has happened. Did you run here all the way from home?"

Basil nodded. He took two deep, cleansing breaths. "You must ... bring help. Men have come ... guns and torches. Many men. Soldiers."

"Soldiers are at Papa's house?" James confirmed. "Why?"

Basil's breathing steadied just a bit. "They say they are militia. Came to search the house." He paused. "They claim that Papa is a traitor to the Crown. The man mentioned Alamance and the Regulators. He said Papa's preaching is stirring up treason."

James' eyes widened in disbelief. "Did Papa send you?"

"No. The men have him ... and Mama. They were searching the house, but still had not made it upstairs before I escaped. Walter sent me to get you. He said bring men and guns. Something bad is going to happen."

"Is Walter all right?"

Basil nodded and began to cry again. "He was fine when I left him ... but I don't know how he is now. Oh, James! What have I done? I should not have left him there! Both of us could have escaped!"

James embraced the boy and held him tight. "It's all right, Basil. You did the right thing. You obeyed Walter. Do not worry. I will go immediately. I will awaken other men of the militia on my way into town."

Ann arrived with a pewter mug full of cold water. Basil drank three-fourths of it and then poured the remainder on top of his head.

James placed his right hand on his brother's shoulder. "Basil, I need you to do one more thing. Do you have the strength to make it to Samuel's house and rouse him?"

Basil nodded. "I do now." He smiled and looked at James' beautiful wife. "Thank you, Ann."

"You are quite welcome, Basil. You had me worried."

James helped the boy to his feet. "There is no time to waste, Basil. Go and alert Samuel. You can ride back into town with him. I will see you there. Tell him to send one of the hired men to fetch John and Henry. Make sure our brothers know to bring all of their guns, and all of the men they can muster."

"Yes, James."

"Tell them we may have a fight on our hands this night."

"Yes, James."

Basil hugged his brother and then trotted down the wagon road toward Samuel's house. He disappeared quickly around a turn in the path. James ran toward the front door of his home.

Ann called after him, "What has happened? Where are you going, James?"

He answered over his shoulder, "Loyalists have come for Papa. I must go to his aid."

He ran quickly inside the house and fetched his hat, knife, shooting gear, two long rifles, and two pistols. In less than a minute he was mounted bareback on his horse and galloping full-speed toward the nearby village.

The Billingsley Home – Guilford Courthouse

The captain's ears perked when he heard the positive report from upstairs. His face contorted into a wicked smile. He yelled to the man, "Come, Private, and show us the contraband!"

An excited soldier came shuffling down the steps with a fowling gun in his hand. It was an ancient-looking, smooth-bore weapon that was often used to hunt birds. Fanning's expression converted from joyful expectation to somewhat embarrassed disappointment.

"Did you find anything else, Private?"

"No, sir."

"Any powder, lead, subversive literature or correspondence?"

"Nothing, sir. Only a bunch of Bibles and church books. No ordinance of any kind."

James Billingsley smiled triumphantly. He could not resist the urge to insert a dagger of vengeance and shame into the British Loyalist.

"As you see, sir, it is just as I declared to you. There is nothing illegal, treasonous, or rebellious in this house. You have abused my family for absolutely nothing! I will see you in the gaol for your assault upon my daughter and the unlawful apprehension of my family."

Captain Fanning's nose twitched with rage. He hissed, "No, Mr. Billingsley. This is exactly the evidence that I have sought. You told me only moments ago that there were no weapons in this house!"

Young Walter could no longer hold his tongue. "You call that a weapon? That is my bird gun! It was my grandfather's! It is at least fifty years old!"

"Yes, young man. Walter is your name, correct? Walter, this is a flintlock weapon, capable of inflicting harm upon His Majesty's servants and soldiers. And your devious father swore to me, an authorized representative of the King, that there were no weapons in this house. He has, therefore, lied to his King. He is a liar and a traitor to the Crown."

"That is absurd!" protested the middle-aged preacher.

Fanning continued, "And, for your crime, you will be required to pay a reasonable penalty. One hundred pounds sterling should suffice. I will require it in coin, not currency. Pay immediately and you will suffer no further consequences for your misdemeanor."

"I do not have any money!" wailed James. "No one has that kind of money! And even if I did, I would not give it to a lowlife thief and extortionist!"

"As you wish," responded the Loyalist commander in a matter-of-fact tone. He turned and faced James full-on, staring with a gaze of finality and authority. "James Billingsley, you have been found guilty by military tribunal of the offense of lying to a government official, and of repeated and long-standing treason to the government of the colony of North Carolina, the nation of Great Britain, and His Majesty, King George III. I hereby sentence you to die for your crimes. Sentence is to be carried out immediately."

Elizabeth Billingsley began to scream and cry uncontrollably. Martha simply fainted. She fell, face-first, landing with a thud as her forehead struck the pine floorboards.

"What court has declared me thusly?" demanded James.

"There is no court, Billingsley. I am your judge. I am your jury. And now I shall serve as your executioner." Fanning drew his face close to James. The front tip of his cocked hat actually touched the elder gentleman's forehead. "Prepare to meet your maker, traitor scum!"

Fanning glanced at the wide-eyed sergeant standing beside him. "Take him outside immediately. Find a substantial tree. Secure a rope. I want to see this fat pig hanged."

"You are serious, sir?"

"Yes, Sergeant! Of course, I am serious! You will obey my orders! Take this condemned prisoner outside and prepare for his execution!"

"But, sir!"

Fanning lost his temper. He stomped his foot and shook his head as he screamed with rage. "Do not refuse me, Nathan, or I will see you hanging from the tree by his side! Now get it done!"

As he stomped for emphasis on his final word, his cocked hat tumbled from his head, taking the cap beneath it, as well. It exposed Fanning's scarred, discolored, grotesque, bloody scalp. The sergeant and the other soldiers looked away immediately. Walter could not help but stare. It was one of the most unpleasant, grisly sights that he had ever encountered on the body of a living human being.

"Good God, man! Whatever happened to your head?" asked Walter.

Fanning stooped down and grabbed the bloody cap and cocked hat from the floor. He quickly returned both to his head. "It is a skin condition, nothing more! It is none of your concern, lad."

Walter felt a sudden rise of gumption in his soul. He responded, "Too bad it hasn't already killed you." And with that, he spat a thick, mucoid lump of spittle into the man's face.

Captain Fanning did not say another word. He swiftly and skillfully whipped a pistol from his leather belt and struck Walter in the top of the skull. The boy never saw it coming. Instantly, his vision exploded in a shower of silver-blue sparkles. His legs crumpled beneath him. He was unconscious before he landed on the floor.

Salisbury Turnpike – On the Outskirts of Guilford Courthouse

James Billingsley Jr. was riding full speed and clinging for dear life to the mane of his horse. He was beginning to wish that he had taken the time to saddle the animal. But, it was far too late for second thoughts. He was almost to his father's home. He could hear the horses of six other men, good friends and compatriots all, riding close behind him. He knew that his brother Samuel, the oldest of the Billingsley children, would be only minutes behind. Samuel would likely have another three or four armed men in his party.

James mulled over the numbers of his little army as he rode. He would only have about ten to twelve men at his disposal. As long as there were no more than a dozen bandits raiding his family's home, they stood a pretty fair chance. He had no real plan for combating the threat. He simply intended to ride into the street in front of the house with guns blazing. His goal was to break the will of the raiders and scatter them into the woods.

The young man's blood boiled when the wailing screams of a woman reached his ears. But it was not just any woman. He recognized his own mother's voice, shrieking in horror and pain.

James kicked violently at the sides of his horse and yelled, "Hyah!" As he held on with his left hand, he pulled a Spanish pistol from his belt with his right hand. He glanced back over his shoulder and saw that his compatriots' hands and belts were also bristling with pistols and short muskets. James leaned forward to lay low over the neck of his horse. As the animal galloped on, he drew the hammer on his pistol back to full cock and prepared to fire.

Walter fought his way back from the world of darkness. The fog that clouded his mind was thick. He shook his head in an effort to clear his brain and focus his eyesight. There was a loud ringing sound in both of his ears. He placed both hands over them in an attempt to block the irritating sound, but it only grew louder. The piercing ring was inside his head, not a product of the outside world.

He was aware that he was lying on the floor in the entryway of the house. As he tried to climb to his knees, his left foot brushed across something soft. He turned and looked. It was Martha, still lying unconscious on the floor. She rested in an odd, twisted position. Her face was pointed toward Walter. He noticed that her forehead appeared to have a large knot. Walter checked her breathing. It was steady and strong.

Walter's hearing began to return, though it was still muffled. He could barely hear his mother's screams emanating from the front yard. He glanced at his silent, still sister. Martha would have to wait. He had to attend to his parents. He eased himself up onto his feet and staggered toward the open front door, concealing himself behind the doorframe to avoid detection. The sight that greeted him was unthinkable.

His father was dangling from the low limb of a huge oak tree. He was swinging by the neck. Walter stared in complete disbelief. James Billingsley's hands were loose and clutching at the rope that was digging into the flesh of his neck. His face was beet-red. The stricken man's feet kicked fruitlessly at the ground that was well over three feet below. At least a dozen militiamen armed with muskets surrounded the condemned man. Most of them stared at the ground, unable or unwilling to witness his throes of death. One of the men, a lad that was close to Walter's age, vomited in response to the sight.

Elizabeth Billingsley continued her endless, piercing screams. As Walter's hearing improved, the screams grew louder.

The wicked voice of David Fanning echoed across the lawn, "Shut up, you worrisome whore!"

The command was followed by a loud whack. Then the screaming stopped. His mother continued her mourning with a choked whimper. Walter stuck his head through the opening to catch a glimpse of his mother. She was on her knees, staring at her husband. Her arms were outstretched in his direction. Though her mouth quivered and moved, no more sounds came forth. She cried in desperate, despondent silence.

Walter thought, "*Surely, someone will do something! Everyone in this town must be awake by now*!"

Sure enough, as he glanced at the houses on the opposite side of the highway, he saw candles flickering. He noticed several curtains rustling and a few horrified faces staring through windowpanes. But no one intervened. Not a single door opened. No neighbors appeared with weapons to come to James Billingsley's defense. Everyone was too frightened to take any action. The members of the Billingsley family were on their own.

Walter's eyes were drawn back to his father. James Billingsley kicked two more times and then his legs locked rigid, toes pointed toward the ground. Walter gasped as his father's body made a single, final spasm. His fingers of his right hand released from the rope around his neck and his right arm dropped loosely at his side. The other hand remained in place, the fingertips still jammed between the rough rope and fatty flesh. Walter could hear the sound of fluid striking the large, flat rocks on the ground beneath him. His father's bladder had emptied itself in death, sending urine streaming down his legs and soaking the ground below.

The executioners remained at their perimeter posts, surrounding the dead prisoner. All but the dastardly Captain Fanning stared at the spectacle with some measure of disbelief. He, on the other hand, ogled with pride, primal hunger, and sick satisfaction. Walter could almost swear that he saw the man lick his lips.

James Billingsley, humble farmer and faithful Baptist exhorter, was dead. Hanged. Murdered.

Something raw and primal came to life in Walter's tender, fifteen-year-old heart. Emotions broke inside him. Forgiveness and grace melted away in an explosion of unmitigated rage. His soul splintered with a hatred so vivid and so real that he thought his heart might explode. He wanted vengeance. He wanted to kill.

In that moment of unbridled rage, Walter decided to fight, and kill, and die. But what weapon could he use? The only gun in the house had been the old fowling gun that was now in possession of the soldiers. Besides, Walter had used up the last measure of gunpowder while hunting turkeys in late March. The only knives in their home were the ones in the kitchen, located through a breezeway on the north side of the house. And they were small, pitiful little things.

The rage-driven young man ducked back inside the door and leaned against the nearby wall. "*Think, Walter*!" he scolded himself.

The boy scanned to his left, toward the family dining room. There was nothing in there that would serve as a weapon, unless he could somehow rip a leg off of the dining table and use it as a club. He dismissed that notion and scanned to his right. Like the dining room, the parlor seemed devoid of potential weapons. Walter considered wielding one of the silver candlesticks that adorned the mantle. Then ... something else caught his eye.

There, hanging from a rack on the stone wall of the fireplace, was a set of forged iron tools for tending fires. The broom and ash shovel were useless. But the poker could be an effective weapon. The three-foot-long iron stick had a wicked ninety-degree hook at its terminal end with a sharp, menacing point.

"*That's it*!" Walter exclaimed silently.

He dropped down to his knees and crawled quickly to the fireplace, keeping below the windowsills and out of the line of sight of the soldiers outside. He snatched the poker from its rack and then made his way back toward the front door. As he crawled, he noticed Martha's body give a subtle jerk. Then her arms began to shake. His sister had awakened and she was attempting to move. Walter scooted on his knees over to her and placed his hand in the small of her back.

He leaned forward and whispered into her ear, "Martha, lie still."

She lifted her head slightly and looked at her brother. Her eyes were bloodshot. Her face was discolored with bruising. She appeared disoriented and confused.

"Wha ... what ... happened?"

He held his fingers to his lips to silence her. He whispered, "You fainted. I think you hit your head pretty hard when you fell."

"I remember," she mumbled. "That man said Papa was sentenced to die."

He glanced out the front door. He hissed, "The bad men are still out front. I want you to go out the back, follow the creek, and hide in the woods. You must seek refuge at the farm. Go to James' house. Ann will take care of you. Do you understand?"

She nodded, and then whispered. "What are you going to do, Walter?"

"I have to help Mama."

"What about Papa?"

Walter didn't say anything. He stared sadly into Martha's eyes and slowly shook his head back and forth. She realized immediately what had happened. Her father was dead. Tears began to flow. She opened her mouth to cry, but Walter covered it quickly with his hand.

"No!" he whispered with authority. "You must remain silent. I want these men to forget you were even here. Martha, do as I say, all right? Go now! Head out the back, and make your way around toward the south. Go quickly to the farm. Keep to the woods. Stay off of the highway."

Martha nodded. "Yes, Walter."

He helped his sister to her feet. She was still a bit shaky and disoriented. Walter hugged her. It was an emotional, fragile embrace.

He whispered, "I love you, Sister. Now, go."

"I love you, too, Walter. Please help Mama. And be safe."

"I will do what I can. It is in God's hands. Now, get going!"

He released his sister from his embrace. She turned and disappeared quickly down the short hallway beside the stairs. Walter soon heard the rear door click open and then quietly close.

Once he knew that his sister was safely out of the house, the boy did not linger another moment. He clutched the poker, his lone primitive weapon, in trembling hands. He then marched with violent determination toward the front door.

3

IRON, FIRE, AND LEAD

Walter possessed neither strategy nor plan. He simply wanted to fight back. His heart burned for revenge.

No one noticed him when he emerged from the house, iron stick in hand. One of the enemy militiamen was standing almost directly in front of the front door of the house, fewer than twenty paces from Walter. The fellow was leaning on his musket and staring, mesmerized, at the dangling body of James Billingsley. The man was facing away from Walter and unaware of his presence.

He was the one ... the target. Walter marched on, determined to kill the man. He studied the details of his victim as he approached. The soldier wore dark green breeches and socks, a beige weskit, and a filthy white shirt. His shoes were scuffed and ragged, with a couple of strips of leather hanging loosely from their sides. Clearly, he was not a man of means, nor was he a professional soldier. He had every appearance of being an ordinary fellow ... a dirt farmer, most likely.

But this particular farmer had invaded Walter's home, abused his family, and been a party to his father's murder. He had to suffer for his poor choices.

Walter felt rivulets of tears wetting both of his cheeks. He was crying, and he hated himself for it. He felt weak, childish, and ashamed. But he could not help it. He glanced to his left and saw his mother, still on her knees at the feet of Captain Fanning. Her robe was filthy and coated with bits of debris from the ground. Her hair was disheveled. She was crying, mourning, and sorrowful. Walter wanted to embrace his mother and comfort her. He wanted to promise her that everything would be all right. But that would be a lie.

He wiped the tears from his face with his left hand. When he was a mere two paces away from his target, he pivoted his body to the right and raised the poker in preparation to take his swing. His intention was to deliver a single, deadly blow to the side of the man's skull. After that, he was not quite sure what would happen. He didn't care. He simply had to make someone pay for this horrendous crime.

Suddenly, one of the militiamen across the yard gave a shout of alarm and pointed in Walter's direction. He had been discovered. Still, Walter held the advantage of surprise. No one had expected the unconscious lad to emerge from the house with a weapon in hand. Several of the raiders grabbed at their muskets, but in their haste fumbled awkwardly with the guns as they attempted to pull back the hammers on their firelocks.

The man that Walter intended to kill spun immediately to his right. Walter caught a glimpse of the fellow's right cheek. It was red and burned, and his eyebrow was singed. His cap was also scorched and burned. It was the one particularly mean and nasty man who had struck Martha and forced her from her room.

"*Good,*" thought Walter. "*This one definitely has it coming.*"

Walter screamed a barbaric yawp of vengeance and frustration as he swung the heavy iron poker. The soldier was in mid-turn when the boy delivered his deadly blow. The hook at the end of the poker embedded in the center of the man's forehead. Walter was fascinated by the sound of it. The militiaman's skull emitted a dull, hollow "crack" that sounded much like a ripe watermelon splitting open when the rind was cut with a sharp blade.

Walter immediately released the poker. The sudden impact of the iron bar against bone, along with the violent interruption of his powerful swing, initiated an unexpected, painful vibration of the metal rod. It stung his hands so badly that they were almost numb. Though the poker had stopped moving, Walter's body did not. He stumbled awkwardly to his left and landed with a violent thud on his side. He felt the sharp jab of rocks and sticks into the soft flesh of his belly and into his ribs. He yelped in pain.

Walter flipped over onto his back so that he might witness his victim's struggle between life and death. With both hands, the man grasped the piece of metal that had invaded his brain. He did not attempt to pull it out. Instead, he stood almost perfectly still and gripped tightly to the cold iron. Walter could not help but chuckle at the man's odd stance. From behind it looked like he was playing a long, skinny fife.

Then, slowly, the man's body relaxed and dropped to the ground. He landed first on his knees and remained in a kneeling position for a mere second. Finally, his body locked in a rigid spasm and he collapsed awkwardly onto his back, his feet and lower legs folded strangely beneath him.

Walter recoiled at the sight of the man's face. His eyes were still open. A single, narrow trickle of blood ran down the left side of his nose. His empty, dead eyes stared through the canopy of tall trees toward the black, star-filled sky. But he could not see the sky. The man was dead.

Walter was confused. He thought that he would feel some measure of satisfaction in having bested his enemy. He thought that vengeance and retribution would have somehow relieved his burden of pain and grief. But, as he stared into the dead eyes of the lifeless man, all he felt was an even more profound sense of sadness and remorse.

Just beyond his dead foe, in Walter's direct line of sight, the body of his murdered father dangled at the end of a rope. His memory momentarily flashed back to the evening before. Only a few hours ago he had been sitting at his father's feet and playing dominoes with his baby brother. Now, as his dead father hung from an oak tree in his own yard, Walter lay on the ground beside the body of a man that he had just killed with his own hands. Surely, there was nothing that could ever restore Walter's youthful innocence or repair his blood-tarnished spirit.

A gunshot exploded somewhere in the clearing. Walter felt the sting of dirt and sand in his eyes as a musket ball impacted the earth less than a foot from his face. Then another shot came. Walter felt a warm splash on the right side of his head and burning pain at the top of his right ear. He tried to ignore the pain as he crawled low to the ground and sought cover behind the dead man's body. Other shots came in rapid succession. Tiny geysers of dirt, grass, and debris erupted all around him. He could hear the lead projectiles thumping against the flesh of the dead body that lay beside him. There was a sharp, metallic clang when one of the balls ricocheted off of the large brass buckle of the man's waist belt. Walter was completely pinned down and unable to move.

Suddenly, the street and lawn in front of the Billingsley house erupted in an explosion of thundering horses, shouting men, and deafening gunfire. The shots in Walter's direction had ceased. The yard, previously bathed in the glow of a half-dozen torches, plunged into a state of semi-darkness as several of those torches fell to the ground. Some were extinguished altogether. Walter peeked over the top of the body beside him to see what was happening. His heart rejoiced when he saw that his brother, James, had arrived. Even in the dim, reduced torch light he could make out the familiar shape of his brother's face. He also heard James' deep, booming voice as he shouted instructions to his compatriots.

James Billingsley, Jr., and at least a half-dozen other men, were firing muskets and pistols at the militiamen gathered on the Billingsley lawn. Their voluminous fire was having a deadly effect. Most of the enemy soldiers were unable to return fire because they had just emptied their weapons at Walter. The engagement quickly turned into a rout as one after another of the Loyalist militiamen fell dead or wounded in the overwhelming barrage of gunfire.

Soon, Walter heard more horses approaching from the southwest. Moments later his brothers Samuel, John, and Henry arrived on the scene. There were two other riders with them, laborers from the Billingsley farm. Walter immediately recognized one of his best friends, Gabriel Tate, among the new arrivals. The five men immediately joined in the fight, opening fire on the disoriented and fleeing hangmen.

The shrill scream of a woman echoed to Walter's left. It was his mother! He scanned in the direction of the scream, and gasped when he saw his mother at the edge of the tree line. The evil Captain Fanning held the helpless woman by the hair of the head. He was using her as a shield against gunfire as he made his retreat into the woods.

There was a flash of movement as a horse approached from Walter's right. He recognized the rider. It was his brother, Henry, galloping full-speed toward their mother and her captor. Henry wielded a cocked pistol. Walter watched helplessly as Fanning brought his own pistol to bear on Henry. The Tory's gun barked and immediately the horse and Henry Billingsley tumbled haphazardly to the ground, throwing up a cloud of sod and dust.

Walter screamed in protest and instinctively rose to his knees, preparing to bull-rush the officer and somehow set his mother free. As he scrambled to his feet, his right shin bumped against something hard on the right side of the fallen militiaman's dead body. Walter reached down and threw back the flap of the man's coat. Beneath the wool, lodged securely in his belt, was a primed and loaded Spanish pistol. Walter grabbed the gun, pulled the hammer back on full cock, and then ran in the direction of his mother's screams.

The boy had only taken three steps when something slammed into the right side of his head. Then the world turned black. The din of battle converted into an unsettling silence.

Walter Billingsley's final thought before slipping into total unconsciousness was, "*I must be dead.*"

❧

A sudden assault of frigid, wet cold sucked the air from Walter's lungs. His eyes fluttered open as he gasped for breath. He was immediately aware that he was soaking wet. He opened his eyes. The area around him was almost pitch-black. Brilliant stars glowed in the heavens above him. He realized that he was outside … and lying on the ground.

"There he is! I told them other boys that my old buddy, Walter, wasn't dead!"

It was the high-pitched, somewhat annoying, and often foul-mouthed voice of his good friend, Gabriel Tate. The boy hovered over him, holding an empty, dripping bucket in his hand.

Walter lay still for a moment, overwhelmed by a fog of disorientation. His head throbbed. His ear ached. It felt as if he had been clobbered over the head with a board. He surveyed the area around him and struggled to discern his whereabouts.

At long last he spoke. "Gabe. Where … where am I? What hap … happened?"

"You got wounded in the firefight, Walter. Samuel and James assigned me to look after you whilst they're takin' care of business."

"How bad is it?"

"Well, you ain't got no wounds to any of your innards, thank the good Lord. But you've got a couple of attractive new features on your head. It looks like something gave you a fine lump in the front. That should go away soon enough. And you have a cute little nibble gone off the top of your right ear. But that ear was too big to start with, so it ain't a real problem."

Walter forced a painful grin.

"But the really bad news is that you took a musket ball right on the top of your brainpan. You are one lucky arsehole. I swear, you must have a skull made of granite. The ball plowed a trough through your scalp, bounced right off of the top of your skull, and kept right on flyin'! It probably landed all the way down in Rowan County! You've got a gash up there deep enough to plant taters in." He laughed heartily at his own joke.

Walter reached gingerly toward the wound and felt the bloody depression. He was shocked that it did not hurt worse than it did.

"Am I … am I going to die?" he mumbled.

Gabriel threw back his head and emitted a very raucous laugh.

"No time soon, you hard-headed bastard. Do you truly think they'd leave me in charge of you iff'n you was dyin'?" He laughed again. "You'll heal up quick enough, I'm a thinkin'. But you're likely to have one queen mother of a headache for at least the next day or two." He paused and examined Walter's head. "I'm a bit jealous, really. You'll prob'ly be able to carry an extra roll of chewin' tobaccy in that new rut in your skull."

Walter punched Gabe in the side, and then grimaced from the sudden pain in his head.

"Take it easy there, old friend," warned Gabriel. "No sudden jerkin', or your head'll remind you that your skull bones have gone and got rearranged."

A sudden wave of memories flooded Walter's mind. He remembered the invasion of his home, the unimaginable death of his father, and the ensuing firefight. He struggled to rise.

"My family!" he exclaimed. "Where are they?"

Gabriel placed his hand firmly in the center of Walter's chest. "Stay still, dammit! Your family is fine … most of 'em, anyways."

Walter's eyes shifted toward Gabe's and conveyed a plea of desperation and a hunger for information.

"Your mama is fine, Walter. She's inside now. The doctor gave her somethin' to make her sleep, and a jigger of whiskey to chase it down. Martha is inside, too. One of Samuel's men found her on the road to the farm and brought her home. She's all bumped and scratched from runnin' through the woods, but pretty fair, all things considered."

"My brothers are unharmed?" He had a sudden surge of memory as he visualized Henry going down with his horse. "Henry! How's Henry?"

Gabe shook his head sorrowfully. "His leg is pretty tore up. He had his horse shot out from under him. The beast landed on his right leg and crushed it pretty bad. Broke it in a few places. He had some bone pokin' out through the skin. He'll likely be laid up for a while. Doc says he might not ever walk right again."

Gabe paused and stared deep into Walter's eyes.

"And I'm real sorry 'bout your pa, Walter. He was already dead when we got here. There weren't nothin' we could do for him."

Walter quickly lifted his hand to his face to conceal his emotions. Huge, swollen tears released from the outer creases of his eyes and meandered down his temples, leaving behind a wet, clean streak through the dirt and grime that otherwise covered his face.

Walter replied, "I know he was already dead, Gabe. I watched him die."

Gabe patted his friend's arm. In a rare demonstration of restraint, he offered no further comment. He just sat silently beside his wounded friend.

After a long and extremely uncomfortable silence, Walter sniffed, wiped his face, and inquired, "Where is James? I want to see him."

"He's over by the road with your other brothers, talking to the sheriff and the magistrate. Those cowardly bastards finally came crawlin' out of their warm houses after all the shootin' stopped. Now they're tryin' to act like they're in charge 'round here. James and Sam'l is givin' 'em a pretty fierce lesson or two in frontier justice."

"I want to see my brothers."

"Stay put. I'll go and fetch 'em," offered Gabe.

The young fellow jumped to his feet and trotted in the direction of the road. A few minutes later a bevy of Billingsleys arrived at Walter's side. Gabriel accompanied them. Basil descended upon Walter with a barrage of squeals and hugs.

"Slow down there, Basil. Walter's been slugged," urged Samuel. The eldest Billingsley brother peeled Basil off of his wounded sibling. The four brothers knelt in a family circle of protection and care. Gabriel hovered over Samuel's left shoulder.

"What happened to all the men who killed Papa?" Walter asked bluntly.

"Loyalist hooligans," Samuel corrected him. "Bushwhackers and robbers under the employ of King George and the disgraced governor, Josiah Martin!" He spat on the ground.

"I know what they are, Sam. Now tell me ... what happened to them?"

"Seven of them won't be waking up this morning," commented John. "Another five or six stole away into the woods. We found the horses of the dead tied off in a small cove about two hundred yards to the west."

Walter nodded slightly. "There were thirteen total, as best I could tell. Their captain and another dozen men."

Samuel nodded. "That's what we calculated."

"Did you get the ringleader ... Captain Fanning?" hissed Walter.

"That was his name?" asked James in disbelief. "I have heard of him! He has made trouble across the Carolina frontier for a few months now. They say he's a real cold-blooded character, and that he has some strange malady that affects his head and makes his hair fall out."

"That's him, for sure. Did you kill him?"

James responded, "I don't think so. The dead ones all look like plain old dirt farmers, likely from South Carolina. Besides, none of them were missing any hair. Which one was Fanning?"

"The one that had hold of Mama," responded Walter, his lip quivering.

"Oh … so he was the one that got Henry," mumbled Samuel.

Walter nodded slightly. "Will Henry be all right?"

Samuel smiled. "He'll be fine. Doc says he might carry a limp for the rest of his days, but he will still be able to swing an axe and a hoe."

James wanted to redirect the conversation. "I saw you going after Mama. You were running, pistol in hand, and then I saw you lurch and go down hard. I assumed that the fellow who had hold of Mama had shot you."

Walter shook his head slowly. "No, he had just gotten off his shot at Henry, so his powder was spent. I was too afraid to shoot. He was holding Mama so close to him. I was making a move to his left, and trying to get closer, when I felt a loud thump on my head. The next thing I knew, Gabe was dangling over me and chattering a mile a minute."

The Billingsley brothers chuckled lightly. Gabe feigned a look of offense.

"Where did you get the pistol?" inquired Samuel.

Walter remained silent for a moment, and then answered, "Off of the murderous bastard that I killed … the burnt-faced one over by the steps."

The men in the circle glanced knowingly at one another.

"I saw you taking cover behind the body when I arrived," commented James. "I was wondering what had happened. Then after the fight was done we found this one fellow punched full of musket balls, with a scorched face and hat, and a fireplace poker hitched to his forehead."

"Remind me to stay clear when it's your turn to tend the fire," quipped John.

The brothers chuckled again, a little louder this time.

Walter gave a slight grin. "It was the only weapon I could find. I didn't know what else to do."

"But how did his face get singed and his hat catch on fire?" chirped the ever-curious Gabriel Tate.

"That wasn't me. Martha gets credit for that. He was the one who tossed her out of her bed, and I reckon she gave as good as she got. She smacked his torch so hard into the side of his face that it burned his hide, hair, and hat."

The image of the dainty, fairy-like Martha snubbing out a torch in a soldier's face elicited uproarious laughter within the small circle. As soon as the laughter died down, Walter's face took on a grave look of sorrow and despair.

He spoke just above a mumble. His words were choked by emotion. "I'm sorry I couldn't save Papa." His lip quivered as more tears welled in his eyes.

"There were too many of them, Walter. What more could you have done?" encouraged James.

"I don't know." His body shook slightly. "One minute I was standing inside the front door in front of their captain. Then, the next thing I knew, I was waking up just inside the threshold. And Papa was already swinging from their rope." He paused and glanced toward the hanging tree. His voice became somewhat frantic. "Where is Papa? Who took him?"

"We cut him down, Walter," James assured him, placing his hand on his brother's shoulder. "Papa is being taken care of. Some of the ladies from the church are cleaning him up proper so that we can have a service for him tomorrow."

Walter nodded, his face displaying relief.

"Why did they do this, Walter? Why did they hang Papa?" pleaded Samuel.

Walter stared empty-eyed at Samuel. "They said he was guilty of treason. That fool, Fanning, kept talking about the Regulators, and mutiny, and treason against the Crown. He talked like a crazy man! He accused Papa of hiding weapons and insurrectionists in our home. Papa swore up and down that he was not a traitor. He told the man that he was, most definitely, not hiding weapons in our house. A few minutes later one of the soldiers upstairs got all excited when he found my fowling gun."

"Grandpa's old Fowler?" asked John in disbelief.

Walter nodded. "Then that scab-headed captain declared that Papa had lied to him. Said that he had lied to the King. Called him a traitor to the Crown … again. He demanded that Papa surrender a fine of one hundred pounds sterling in coin to pay for his so-called crimes."

Gabe whistled low under his breath. The Billingsley boys exhaled in exasperation.

"And all this was over an ancient Fowler gun?" growled James.

Walter shook his head in disgust, ignoring the wave of pain.

"No, it was more than that. I think Fanning intended to hang Papa all along. He was just looking for an excuse," replied Walter. "His men were shocked by the order, you could tell. One of them tried to reason with the man. He lost his temper and acted crazy. I said a couple of unkind words in the process, and that's when he clubbed me over the head."

"But why pick on our father?" wondered John out loud.

"Maybe because they thought he would be an easy target," surmised Samuel. "He figured that Papa, being a Baptist preacher and all, would not be likely to fight back. All of the Loyalists are probably up in arms over the recent events at the Halifax assembly. They were just out to get a little blood on the cheap."

"Well, Fanning surely wasn't expecting you fellows to show up," declared Walter. "He paid for that mistake, didn't he?"

"His men did, at least," affirmed James. He paused and then patted Walter gently on the chest. "That was good thinking, by the way … sending Basil out the window to alert the rest of us. I know our Papa is dead, but the two of you likely saved Mama and Martha."

"And God knows who else they might have intended to murder on this night," added John.

An awkward silence hovered over the group.

Gabriel Tate slapped Samuel on the back and inserted himself into the moment. "Well, you Billingsley boys can all hold hands and kiss later. How's about we get Walter inside out of the cold night and tend to him proper? Besides, it will be time for breakfast soon. I'm famished! One of you fellows is gonna have to do a wee bit of cookin'."

Waves of violence rocked the Piedmont in the coming weeks. There were several more nighttime attacks like the one on the Billingsley home. Bands of Loyalist guerillas began operations across the frontier. Acting in the name of King George, they perpetrated acts of terror and sought to thwart the efforts of independence-minded Patriots. The violence escalated as bands of Whigs carried out similar attacks against their Tory foes.

The American Revolution had begun inching its way into the South. But the fighting in the Carolinas and Georgia did not involve grand armies clad in colorful, wool uniforms. It was farmer against farmer, neighbor versus neighbor, and sometimes even friend battling friend. The fighting was sporadic in timing, but intense and brutal in its execution.

Then came the Cherokee.

Many people believed that it was a direct response to the Declaration of Independence. In July, the Cherokee war parties, encouraged by the British and often accompanied by squads of Loyalist whites, unleashed a barrage of brutal assaults upon the cabins and villages scattered across the western frontier of North Carolina. These raiding parties were indiscriminate in their attacks. Men, women, and children fell under the assault of their tomahawks and war clubs. Some of the raids were beginning to invade deeper into long-settled and pacified districts.

Something had to be done. The fledgling governments of North Carolina, South Carolina, and Virginia formulated a plan to launch a three-pronged attack upon the heart of the Cherokee Nation and destroy their towns high in the mountains of North Carolina.

In early July, General Griffith Rutherford, an influential political leader and former British Army soldier from Rowan County, issued a call throughout the Salisbury District for all able-bodied men to join his army for a grand expedition against the Cherokee. Men began streaming westward, forming companies at two frontier outposts, Cathey's Fort and Davidson's Fort. By the middle of July there were over 2,500 volunteer militiamen encamped around those outposts.

Samuel, James, and John Billingsley were about to join those men.

July 25, 1776

The Billingsley Barn - Guilford Courthouse, North Carolina

"I am going, Mother. That is final!" declared Walter.

Elizabeth Billingsley pulled vigorously on her oak wood paddle and never stopped stirring. She labored intensely over the seething cauldron of grain mash that sat in the center of the barn floor. She was attempting to release the gases and accelerate the fermentation process. The product of this pot of sour mash would soon be going into the still that she had inherited from her husband, and would eventually become the "medicinal" whiskey that people throughout the county seemed to enjoy in great quantities. Home distilled whiskey had become Elizabeth's primary source of income since her husband's death.

She used her left sleeve to wipe the perspiration from her brow. Amazingly, she remained calm and resolved, even as her impetuous fifteen-year-old shouted his discourteous and disrespectful demands.

"No, Son, you are not going to fight the Cherokee, or anyone else, for that matter. You are only fifteen years old. You are still my child, and I will not allow you join this campaign. You will remain here at home. I need you here. We are barely hanging on as it is.

Were it not for Papa's distillery, we would all likely be hungry come winter. I am already loaning three sons to take part in this foolish campaign, and I will not give them another."

"But, Mother! James and John and Samuel are all leaving to join Rutherford's army in a few days! I will remain at their sides the entire time! All of my friends are going! Surely, you see the danger of the Cherokee menace!" Walter's voice screeched with a child-like whine.

"We have a greater menace facing our family right now, Walter. Cold weather will be upon us before we know it. We have to save up some silver and fill our pantry and cellar for the long winter. No, Son. Your place is here, with me and Martha and Basil. We have to keep the farm and distillery running. We have to keep our fine house in good repair, our fires burning, and our bellies filled."

Walter fumed. "Mother, I am old enough to fight. I believe I demonstrated that fact on the night that Papa died."

Elizabeth conceded the point. "It is true, Son, that you performed admirably on that night. You were resourceful and brave. Your quick thinking spared my life, and Martha's life, and perhaps even our home. It was a man-sized thing that you did on that horrible night." She paused. "But I am not about to allow you to make a habit of it."

Walter stood three paces from his mother, his arms locked defensively across his chest. He tapped his foot out of a mixture of displeasure and nervousness.

"I'm sorry, Mother, but this is simply not your decision to make," retorted Walter in a rather bland, bold, and firm voice.

His mother stopped stirring the mash, angled her head slightly, and stared at Walter with a look of maternal disbelief intermixed with brewing chastisement.

"You had best change your tone with me, young man. It is, indeed, my decision. Do not push me, boy."

She added a measure of sternness and tenacity to her uncomfortably long and terrifying stare. Then came a grave threat.

"I will see you indentured to a wealthy landowner in the East, or maybe even way up in Virginia, before I will allow you to march off to war."

"Mother! You wouldn't dare!" Walter exclaimed in disbelief, his arms dropping to his sides.

"Just try me and see, Walter. I will sign papers that will put you in a blacksmith shop for the next ten years. Just disrespect me one more time!" Her voice calmed and tears welled in her eyes. "I almost lost you once already. I will not allow such a possibility to occur again."

She resumed stirring the bubbling mash. "You mean far too much to me, Son. And I am not exaggerating when I say that I need you here at home. The farm is not going to run itself. I know that there are capable hired men working the land, but someone must represent the family. While your older brothers are gone, that someone must be you."

"But Henry is still here, Mama. He can run the farm well enough … certainly better than I."

"Henry cannot even walk, Walter. He is bound to that confounded chair and those horrid crutches. His leg may never be healthy again." She sighed. "Yes, Henry will be managing much of the operation of the farm and making most of the decisions. But someone must put their shoes in the dirt, keep a firm hand on the laborers, and maintain a careful watch over things. Until your brothers return, that someone is going to be you. And that is all that I have to say about it!"

"It is simply unfair," muttered Walter.

Elizabeth lifted her paddle from the mash and tapped the wood on the side of the iron pot to remove the excess material. As she wiped her hands on her apron, she declared with confidence, "Get used to it, Walter. This world is full of all manner of things unjust and unfair. It's best you learn that lesson now so that you will be prepared to deal with lowly circumstance and heartbreak later."

She marched by Walter and proceeded toward the house, leaving her humiliated son alone in the barn to cope with his disappointment.

4

VISIONS OF BEAUTY

August 15, 1776

Walter loved sunsets. And the sunset on this quiet, lazy Thursday evening was particularly beautiful. It painted the entire village of Guilford Courthouse with a soft, warm, purplish-pink hue. Walter sat in a comfortable rocking chair at the western end of the front porch of his home, basking in the breathtaking beauty of the coming dusk. He nibbled, eyes closed, on a thin slice of cool watermelon. Occasionally, he would steal a peek to check the changing colors of the sky and clouds. But mostly he kept his eyes closed and relished in the peace of the moment.

Peace. It was such a beautiful, fragile, and rare commodity in 1776. It was almost impossible to believe that, only a few months ago, this beautiful home and peaceful lawn had been the location of unspeakable acts of violence and combat. The Billingsley family had been unjustly terrorized and abused by Loyalist soldiers, and James Billingsley had become an unsuspecting martyr in the growing conflict that would someday be known as the American Revolution.

The patriarch of the Billingsley family did not perish in a glorious battle alongside General George Washington in the Northeast. He did not die in an Indian raid, or even in a militia skirmish on the Carolina frontier. Instead, he suffocated in his own yard, in his own tree, in a noose made from his own rope. His body had been placed in his own soil, on his own farm, by his own sons. The entire episode was an unspeakable affront to justice and humanity. It was a night that Walter would forever remember as the utter opposite of peace.

Reminders of that night abounded in Walter's world. He still found it difficult to look upon the tree in which his father had died. The monstrous, wide oak still stood broad and proud in front of the house. Even a tattered length of the vile rope remained on the high limb above, too far out of reach to be removed.

But there were some reminders of that night that could not be ignored, avoided, or escaped. Walter's body carried the vestiges of his wounds, injuries that still ached and reminded him of the nightmarish attack. He would forever have the hairless scar on the crown of his head. He would always carry a curious notch of missing cartilage and skin on the top of his right ear. Every glance into a looking glass would remind him of those moments of violence that had transformed his life.

Walter's spirit was still wounded, as well, evidenced by the sweat-drenching, soul-searing nightmares that awakened him during the dark depths of night. Even though he managed to slay and subdue his memories during his waking hours, in his sleep they found renewed force and life.

So, Walter sought whatever solace he could find in the simple, quiet, and ordinary moments of everyday living. Magnificent sunsets like the one on this soft evening were relaxing, cleansing, and humbling. In relation to the vastness of the universe, they served to remind him of how small and insignificant he truly was.

Walter did not need much reminding of that simple, inescapable truth. Watching his three older brothers ride off toward the southwest to experience the glories of war against the insidious Cherokee foe had been humbling enough. Walter had shed buckets of tears of frustration and shame on that dark, depressing, heartbreaking day. But, over the course of the following week, his sporadic tears subsided along with his bitterness and rage.

Though he would never tell anyone, he was actually quite content, and a little bit relieved to still be at home. The weather had been depressingly hot for the past two weeks, and there had been frequent soaking rains. He could only imagine how miserable his brothers were at this very moment. They were likely hot, miserable, filthy, insufficiently sheltered, and hungry. Walter's belly was full of his mother's tasty home cooking, and he would be sleeping between the cool sheets of his own bed this night.

"*Mama is a genius,*" Walter proclaimed in the privacy of his mind. He then offered a silent, heartfelt prayer. "*Thank you, Lord, for my sweet, wise Mama!*"

His mother's nearby voice interrupted his meager prayer life. "I'm very glad that you are feeling better, Walter."

He jumped, startled by the uninvited intrusion into his solitude. He had actually forgotten that his mother was sitting a mere ten feet from him, reclining in her own rocking chair. The two of them were making the most of some rare time at home alone. Martha was visiting with a friend and Basil was busy helping Samuel's wife with some chores.

Unlike most ordinary evenings, Elizabeth was not clutching any cloth, thread, sinew, or buttons in her hands. She was neither sewing nor weaving nor mending. She was resting and, like her son, enjoying the peace and quiet of the summer sunset.

Walter responded softly, "I do feel better, Mother. It seems that every day I'm getting a little bit stronger."

"What about the headaches? Do they still plague you?"

Walter tossed his watermelon rind over the porch rail, stretched, and responded, "Only in the mornings. Most days I wake up with a dull ache in the top of my head. It usually wears off once I get up and begin to move about."

"Well, 'tis to be expected. Your poor head has suffered much abuse. I s'pose we're lucky it is made of granite."

She smiled and opened one eye to peek at her son. Walter continued to stare toward the west. He did not respond to her subtle effort at levity. She attempted to continue the conversation.

"Where are your thoughts, Son? Are they with your brothers in the mountains?"

"A little, I reckon. But I am not thinking of them or the war as much as I thought I would."

"So, are you glad to be home, then?"

Walter smiled and cut his eyes at his mother. "Yes ma'am. I am glad. It was for the best. You were right … as usual."

She closed her eyes and grinned a thin smile of satisfaction. Even mothers enjoy hearing those magical words, '*You were right.*' Walter turned his attention westward again, watching those final moments as the sun's fiery edge flickered and then dipped below the horizon.

Seconds later, Walter completed his thought, "But sometimes I do wish that I was in the mountains with Samuel and the boys. I would never want to be considered a coward. I want to do my part. I want to do my duty."

"Oh, Walter! Who would ever consider you to be a coward? Everyone in Guilford knows about how you stood up to that dastardly Captain Fanning and those Tories! Legends abound regarding your actions on that night! Son, you have the respect of our neighbors and friends." She sighed deeply, gratefully. "And you have my respect."

Walter's eyes met his mother's. She smiled tenderly, her gaze conveying the gratitude of a mother to a son who had defended her home and saved her life. Walter smiled back. Elizabeth rested her head against the back of the tall rocking chair and closed her eyes once again.

She declared, "I think you just need something else to occupy your mind besides Indians and wars."

"Like what, supposing?"

"Well … a visitor might help. Your sister will be calling on us day after tomorrow. I received a letter from her earlier in the week."

"Which sister?" inquired Walter curiously.

"Clearanna."

Walter made a disappointed face and shrugged nonchalantly. Clearanna Billingsley Hamer, known amongst the Billingsleys as "Cleary," was a little over five years older that Walter. The two siblings had never been particularly close to one another during their years of growing up in James Billingsley's household. The notion of her impending visit was not all that exciting to Walter. However, he was quite fond of her husband, William Hamer. William was a jolly, good-natured fellow, and had always treated Walter like a mature young man.

"Is William coming, as well, or is he staying in Hillsborough?"

"He will be driving the carriage and bringing Cleary to us, but will continue on southward to Mecklenburg County. Hopefully, he will stay with us for at least one night. He has business in Charlotte Town, and must be gone two weeks. Cleary will be lodging with us during his absence."

Walter chuckled. "I cannot believe William is interrupting his honeymoon and leaving his bride unattended and lonesome for the mere cause of commerce."

Elizabeth pursed her lips. "Walter Billingsley! There is no need for you to be so vulgar! You should be ashamed! You sister wed Mr. Hamer well over a year ago. They are an established, well-propertied couple. Besides, a man must take time to tend to his family's business, on occasion. I, for one, am delighted that she is coming. I have not seen my Cleary in months." Her countenance brightened. "Perhaps she has some special news to share."

"What kind of news?" inquired Walter, obviously confused.

His mother sighed, exasperated by her obtuse son. "A baby, Walter! A grandchild! I simply cannot wait to have another."

"Oh … that …," responded Walter sarcastically. He shrugged. Babies were not particularly exciting to him. Birthing a baby in wartime seemed, in his humble opinion, a bit reckless and foolish. "Whatever makes you happy, Mother."

Walter's benign pronouncement introduced a pause to their conversation. His mother fell silent, lost in the tranquility of her own thoughts of babies and grandchildren. Once again, Walter focused his gaze on the western horizon. There remained little more than a dull glow in the spot where the sun had just descended. Darkness was falling swiftly. Fireflies hovered and twinkled as far as the eye could see. Millions of crickets whistled shrilly in the nearby forests and fields. Somewhere toward the distant south, a wolf howled a hollow, lonely call.

After a couple of minutes of silence and reflection, Walter stood and announced, "I believe that I shall retire, Mother."

His mother responded from the shadow of the porch, "Very well, then. Good night, Walter. I shall follow you very soon."

"Please do not tarry long, Mother. It is not good for you to remain outside alone after dark." He stepped toward his mother, leaned over, and kissed her lovingly on the forehead.

"I will just be a moment," she promised.

"Good night, Mother. I love you."

She cupped his cheek with her right hand. "And I love you, my brave, thoughtful boy."

Two Days Later

Elizabeth was assembling the ingredients for a fresh batch of whiskey mash in the barn. She demanded ample water for her concoction of fermentation. As usual, she enlisted Walter and Basil as her laborers in the most undesirable task of water procurement. The boys had been hauling buckets and piggins full of water from the family's well since shortly after breakfast. The noon hour was approaching. It appeared that the job was almost done. They hoped so, at least.

Walter leaned forward into his load as he balanced a shoulder yoke behind his neck. His lower back ached and strained at the tremendous weight of the water. There was suspended from each end of the heavy yoke two large buckets, each containing roughly four gallons. It was his fourteenth such load of the morning. His arms, shoulders, and back were almost spent. Raw, fluid-oozing blisters stained the shoulders of his shirt. He prayed that this might be their final load.

"Do you think we're done?" whined Basil, interrupting Walter's thoughts and concentration. His younger brother labored beside him, carrying his own three-gallon piggin full of water.

"I pray so, little brother. My shoulders are telling me that we must be." He grinned.

"I'm hungry!" declared the youngest of the Billingsley boys.

"As am I. Our dinner should be ready by now. Mama went inside a short while ago to make preparations. She said that Cleary and William should be here around the noon hour."

"I hope she fixes ham. And bread! Lots of hot, fresh bread! And lots of butter!"

Walter chuckled. "I do not think that ham is on the menu for today's noon-time meal. I saw Mother preparing a pot of stewed beef and red potatoes."

"I would rather have ham," muttered Basil.

"But you will eat our mother's stew, I am quite certain."

"Yep!" answered Basil. "I could eat the south end out of a northbound sow … as Papa used to say."

Both boys chuckled, despite their heavy loads, at the light-hearted remembrance of their father. They had heard him declare his hunger with that disgusting phrase hundreds of times. Both boys had fallen into a relatively steady habit of remembering and repeating his numerous and abundant verbal quips and witticisms. It was a simple way for two young boys to honor the man and keep his memory alive.

They stumbled the final fifty yards to the barn, dutifully emptied their loads into the mash pot, and then returned the buckets and piggins to their proper places of storage.

"Let us wash up and check on Mother," Walter encouraged.

Both boys darted toward a nearby horse trough that sat near the barn, sheltered beneath the ample shade of a large pine tree.

The family kept the trough full of fresh well water for their horses and yard animals. It also made a perfect hand-washing station. Plus, all of the Billingsley boys had always enjoyed dunking their heads in the icy cold water of the trough after their labors in the hot sun.

Walter knelt beside the wooden vessel. He removed his black, wide-brimmed work hat and tossed it to his left, well away from the water. He untied the leather thong that bound his queue and allowed his long, light brown hair to fall loosely over his shoulders. Next, he unbuttoned his mustard-colored linen weskit, removed it, and cast it in the direction of his hat. Basil performed similar tasks at the opposite end of the trough. Both boys splashed ample amounts of the clean, clear water on their hands and faces. It took a couple of minutes to scrub off the sweat and grime of the morning's labors.

"I want to dunk my head, Walter!"

"Well ... what are we waiting for?"

Both boys grinned. They stood and leaned over the trough. They took deep breaths, grabbed their noses, and immersed their heads in the luscious coolness. Walter maintained his head under the water, relishing in the silence and cold. He loved the way that his long hair floated loosely in the water and tickled his neck and face. He relaxed his body and mind and hovered in the sheer pleasure of the comforting, cold wetness.

Walter felt the water move as Basil removed his submerged head from the trough. Moments later he heard his brother's high-pitched voice. It was muffled and distorted by the water, but unmistakably the shrill caw of young Basil. Walter ignored him at first, but soon a hand slapped viciously across the small of his back. Walter jerked his head out of the trough, and as he stood upright he slung his hair back in an arc over his head, spraying droplets of water into the pine needles above. He reached back with both hands and wrung the excess moisture from his loosed queue.

"What is all the commotion about, Basil?"

His brother pointed toward the northeast. They saw a black buggy being pulled by a single horse. A thin trail of dust wafted behind its wheels into the heavy summer air.

"It is a carriage! Cleary is coming!" screeched Basil. He grabbed his weskit and hat and took off running toward the house.

Walter took his time collecting his items of clothing. He wanted to display a more mature and dignified response to the arrival of the visitors than his younger brother. Besides, in all honesty, he was not that excited to have his sister back home for two whole weeks. The presence of another grown woman in the house meant more labor for him in the long run. The next fourteen days would be filled with extra requests to go, fix, find, and fetch. It was always the same when his grown sisters came to call.

Walter cradled his weskit in the crook of his arm and balanced his hat in his left hand. He slowly, coolly sauntered toward the house. He allowed his soaked, light brown hair to dangle loosely over his shoulders. As he walked, he observed the carriage turning into the Billingsley driveway. The buggy wheeled to a halt in front of the steps and his brother-in-law, William Hamer, jumped to the ground. The young man's smile beamed as he waved at Basil and Walter.

Basil screeched excitedly, "William! Did you bring me some candy from the city?"

The boy's affable brother-in-law laughed, and then reached up and removed his fancy black cocked hat with his right hand, revealing a white lump beneath. He reached up with his left hand and grabbed a small cloth sack, which he promptly tossed to the excited lad.

"Sweet, chewy taffy ... your favorite, I believe, young sire!"

Basil giggled as he caught the sack. He then ran up to his brother-in-law and gave him a boisterous hug.

Walter continued his dutiful march toward the carriage, but suddenly stopped in his tracks. A most unexpected sight greeted him. There were two women seated in the carriage! One was his sister, Cleary, whom he was expecting. But the other was a maiden unfamiliar to him. Indeed, she was the most exquisite and breathtakingly beautiful woman that had ever graced his young eyes. She had the appearance of a goddess. His mind wished him to continue walking forward, but the flutter of his heart prevented his feet from taking another step.

The young woman wore a light blue short gown with a tan flower print. The creamy color of the flowers matched her linen petticoat. Her straw hat was decorated with light blue ribbon and fresh sprigs of baby's breath flowers. Her hat curled up slightly in the back. Walter caught just a glimpse of a tiny whisper of dark brown hair peeking from beneath the brow of her bonnet. Her eyes were so brown that they appeared to be almost black. Those eyes were captivating and beautiful ... and they were focused squarely on Walter. It seemed, in fact, that the young woman was fixated upon Walter's chest.

"Walter!" wailed his sister, Cleary. "How positively vulgar! Please cover yourself immediately! We have a guest amongst us!"

Walter had forgotten about his half-dressed state. His wet shirt clung tightly to the skin on his shoulders, chest, and stomach, revealing the rippled, shapely, perfect muscles beneath. Even more embarrassing for the boy was the unkempt, wet, and loose appearance of his hair. His face turned a deep crimson as he struggled to don and button his weskit. He was so nervous that his fingers fumbled clumsily with the pewter buttons.

It took a couple of minutes for Walter to finish covering himself. As he pulled his hair into a proper queue and tied it with a strand of leather, he glanced once again at the young woman who occupied the seat beside his sister. She was still staring at him. Her lips curled on each side into a mischievous smile. Walter could scarcely breathe. The silence in the driveway was horrifyingly uncomfortable. At long last, Clearanna moved to dispel the tension.

"Walter, allow me to introduce Miss Abigail Hamer. She is exactly the same age as you, and the daughter of William's Uncle Gabriel. She is William's beloved cousin who has come to visit us from the colony of South Carolina."

"State!" barked Basil.

"I beg your pardon?" Cleary asked, confused.

"It is the state of South Carolina," her baby brother corrected her. "We don't have colonies anymore. We are the United States of America, Cleary."

"That is absolutely correct!" affirmed William Hamer as he pushed his cocked hat back from his brow and tied the team of horses to a hitching post. "Basil, your sister seems to have some unexplained difficulty with making a proper reference to our new form of independent government."

"I just forget sometimes, that is all!" declared Clearanna. "It was a slip of the tongue, nothing more. Do not even attempt to paint me as some manner of raging Tory, Mr. Hamer!"

William chuckled heartily. "Of course not, my dear. You're a tried and true American rebel, the offspring of James Billingsley, God rest his soul! Now, how about we go inside and see what type of tasty meal your mother has prepared for us?"

"Not until I finish my introductions, William. You are being rude."

"A thousand apologies, my dear." William offered his wife an overly exaggerated bow. "Please continue with the formalities."

"Humph!" she grunted at her husband, nose elevated high in the air. "As I was saying, Walter, this is Miss Abigail Hamer of the *state* …" she rolled her eyes toward her husband "… of South Carolina. Abigail, this is my next-to-youngest brother, Walter Billingsley."

Walter willed his feet to move forward. They responded slowly at first, but soon propelled him on his way in the direction of the gorgeous young lady. He walked around to the right side of the carriage, where Abigail sat, and extended to her his right hand.

"Miss Hamer, it is a pleasure, indeed. Welcome to our home." He smiled warmly, feigning confidence. "May I assist you from the carriage? Surely, you are weary from your travels this morning."

"Yes, of course, Mr. Billingsley. I thank you for your kindness."

That voice! It was so tiny … so melodic and perfect! Walter's knees wobbled just a bit as the girl's delicate voice melted his heart. She rested her left hand lightly in his right hand. She was not wearing any gloves. The warmth and softness of her flesh against his was electrifying, setting off primal responses in his members that he had never experienced before. He could smell the slightly musky sweetness of her floral perfume. It was a delicate mixture of orange blossoms and jasmine. Walter could scarcely stand it all. He felt as if his heart might explode.

Walter Billingsley was vanquished. Right there beside that carriage, in a fleeting instant in time and with a single touch, he had fallen helplessly and hopelessly in love. He decided the course of his entire life in that moment. It was a brief flash of clarity and determination. Abigail Hamer would be his bride.

Abigail stepped gracefully from the carriage. Once safely on solid ground, Walter extended the crook of his right arm to offer himself as an escort.

Walter spoke most eloquently, "Miss Hamer, please allow me to accompany you inside. We have fresh water and linens for you to freshen up. Mother will have our dinner ready shortly."

"Thank you, Mr. Billingsley." She slipped her tiny left hand inside the crook of his arm. "I am honored by your asking."

Walter led Abigail around the rear of the carriage and up the stairs onto the porch. They quickly disappeared through the front door, with Basil following closely behind.

William walked over to his wife and offered his hand to assist her from the carriage. "Well, Mrs. Hamer, it appears that your little conspiracy of romance is off and running."

Clearanna smiled broadly and gave her husband a subtle wink before kissing him victoriously on his cheek.

Two Weeks Later – Saturday - August 31, 1776

Walter Billingsley and Abigail Hamer strolled arm in arm along the dusty lane that led east toward the Sandy Creek Baptist Church. It was their final late afternoon stroll together. Abigail was leaving at first light, headed back to Hillsborough with William and Clearanna. She was scheduled to depart from there on Wednesday to return to her home in Camden, South Carolina.

It had been a magical two weeks. The two teenagers had spent almost every waking moment together. They talked, took walks, and read books. They told stories about their families and laughed. Basil was a bit hurt to be left out of all of the relational festivities. He was also frustrated by the fact that he suddenly had no older brother with whom he might play or otherwise spend time. The adults in the house had to actually pull the lad aside and explain the reality of Walter and Abigail's budding romance. It seemed abundantly clear to everyone around them that the young people had fallen deeply in love.

Walter loved Abigail. That much was certain. His heart was imprinted upon the young woman. He knew that no other could ever satisfy. But still, he refused to believe that she could entertain similar sentiments toward him. Walter, for some reason, loathed himself to such an extreme that he assumed he must be unattractive and unlovable.

Mid-way through the visit, Walter decided and declared to himself, "*She is simply being nice to me. Nothing more. I will just enjoy our time together and that will be it. Then life will go on.*"

So, on this final evening together, the young couple walked arm-in-arm and in complete silence. Walter did not quite know what to say. He was out of words. He felt as if his heart was being torn apart. The day of Abigail's departure had loomed over the entire two weeks like a foreboding, dark cloud. Walter had counted down each day with dread, wishing that he could somehow cease the earth from turning on its axis ... wishing that he could make time stand still.

But his time was up. Fourteen days were over in what seemed like an instant. Tomorrow she would be gone. Yes, his heart would ache for some time. But, surely, he would be able to find his way past the pain of having loved and lost.

Abigail's soft voice invaded the silence between them. "You have not spoken to me much today, Walter. Are you upset with me?"

He tugged her arm gently, pulling her closer to his side. He placed his left hand firmly on top of her right hand as it rested in the crook of his arm.

"Don't be silly, Abigail. How could I ever be upset with you?"

"But you are so quiet!"

"I do not want to see you go. That is all. I am sad," he responded with complete candor.

"As am I," she responded quietly.

"I am sure that you are ready to see your parents and siblings. You have been gone from Camden for several weeks now."

"Yes. I miss my mama and papa. I even miss my little brothers." She chuckled, then her face became stolid and somber. "But I fear that I shall miss you more, Walter Billingsley."

Walter stopped walking, turned, and faced her. "Do you mean that? Are you being sincere?"

"Of course, I am being sincere!" Her voice took on a disciplinary tone. "I realize we have only known one another for two weeks, but I thought that you might understand me well enough to know that I do not express my emotions callously or lightly."

Walter sighed, somewhat ashamed. "I know."

"Then you should also know with all certainty that I do not go about the Carolina countryside informing various young men of my state of emotion or affection," she scolded further.

Walter dropped his chin to his chest. "Yes, I know."

"Then why would you question me now?"

He stammered, "Oh … I don't know. It's just …"

"It's just what, exactly?" she demanded.

Walter paused and took a deep, courage-building breath. He continued to stare at the ground beside Abigail's feet.

"Look at me, Walter!"

His eyes slowly rose to meet hers.

"It's just what?" she demanded again.

He pursed his lips and took another deep breath. "Abigail, just look at me. I am the humble son of a dead preacher. I am my mother's servant. Farming, caring for livestock, hauling water, and making whiskey ... these are all that I know. I am a nobody from the far side of nowhere." He felt a tear welling in his eye. "And then here you are. Perfect, beautiful, sweet, pure, and refined. You are like some sort of angel. You are an exquisite, almost divine apparition of a young woman. Now you are leaving this place, and I shall never see you again."

Abigail took hold of both of his hands. "Oh, Walter, you are so much more than what you claim to be. You are noble and honest. You are strong and loyal. You are courageous and bold. And to top it all off, you are the handsomest man that I have ever seen."

Walter chuckled. "Now I know that you jest. Please do not toy with me, Abigail. I have a crater in the top of my head and a notched ear. Plus, my pride is wounded even deeper than my skull."

"Those are the scars of noble battle, fought in the protection of your mother and your sister. My God, Walter! Those marks are reminders of what a strong and mighty man that you are!" She stepped closer to him. Her face was mere inches from his. Walter could smell her skin. "And you are my man!"

"Do you mean it, Abigail?"

"With all my heart."

"Because I sincerely want it to be true."

"It is true, Walter."

He thought that his heart might burst wide open.

"The moment that I touched your hand I knew that I wanted you to be my wife. But the notion of it seemed too far-fetched and outlandish to even consider."

She reached up and placed her hand on his cheek. "My heart is yours, Walter Billingsley. My hand is yours for the asking."

"But we are only fifteen years old, Abigail."

"That is time, Walter. Nothing more. In three years, you will be of age. It will pass quickly."

"I will need another year, at least, to earn some more money and build us a home. I know that mother will deed me some of the farm for my own place."

"What more is an extra year when two people are in love?" she mused. "I can wait."

"What about the war?" asked Walter.

"The war is a thousand miles away. It means nothing to us."

"Still, you will be in Camden, and I will be here in Guilford. You will be over a hundred and fifty miles away!"

She smiled. "We will see one another at every possible opportunity. I will visit William and Clearanna whenever I can. You can even come to Camden and meet my parents."

"Yes, I must go to them and ask your father's permission. I must also secure a ring to mark our engagement. And we can write!" added Walter.

"Yes!" Abigail almost shouted. "We can correspond through letters! We will write wonderful, beautiful, long letters about every event in our lives. We will reveal to one another our deepest feelings and secrets. We shall make the postal carriers between here and Camden wish for another route!" she joked.

"It could work," mumbled Walter thoughtfully. "It could actually work. We can make it work!"

"Of course, we can. Such was the nature of my parents' relationship. They corresponded at a distance for almost five years before they were wed."

"Then it is settled!" declared Walter. "In four years, we shall be husband and wife!"

"But, Walter. There remains one significant problem." Abigail's eyes twinkled mischievously.

"What, Abigail? What problem? What have we forgotten or missed?"

"Walter! You haven't asked me to marry you, yet."

He immediately dropped down on one knee ... right in the middle of the dusty country road. He took her left hand and caressed it between both of his hands.

"Miss Abigail Hamer of South Carolina, would you grant unto me the most wonderful honor of consenting to become my wife?"

"Why, Mr. Walter Billingsley! I would be most pleased to become the wife of the handsomest farmer in North Carolina!"

Walter jumped to his feet, lifted Abigail in his arms, and kissed her passionately.

5

A JOURNEY INTERRUPTED

July, 1778

It had been two long, relatively uneventful, and gloriously peaceful years in Guilford County. The Billingsley family thrived and prospered.

Samuel, James, and John returned safely from their successful campaign against the Cherokee. They arrived home during the second week of November, 1776, barely three months after their departure. In reality, none of them saw any combat action. They did little more than march, make camp, and experience ceaseless hunger for the duration of their enlistments. Some of the South Carolina and Virginia militias had actually engaged the Cherokee, but not the Guilford or Rowan County regiments.

The only "action" that the Billingsley boys experienced was the burning of several abandoned Cherokee towns. The commanders of the expedition had their men set fire to a couple dozen empty huts and lodges, celebrated the conflagration as a great and strategic victory, and then promptly marched their regiments home and discharged their men.

The war remained distant during the two years that followed the campaign against the Cherokee. The Indian menace was ended on the western Carolina frontier. Most of the engagements involving the British were naval forays along the coast. The only thing that remained were skirmishes and raids with Tories, but most of those violent clashes occurred in counties to the south, closer to South Carolina. Guilford County remained tranquil and safe. So, the Billingsley family returned to its familiar routine of farming.

Those two years following the birth of the United States had been insufferably long and very lonely ones for the love-struck Walter Billingsley and Abigail Hamer. Though they corresponded regularly, per their solemn vow to one another, letters simply were not enough to satisfy the passionate souls of the young lovers. Walter and Abigail invested most of their waking moments thinking, planning, and scheming how they might arrange their next visit.

The young man and woman were desperate for one another's company. Walter yearned to see Abigail again. He desired to embrace her, smell the flowery musk of her perfume, and feel the warm touch of her hand. He needed to kiss her and once again taste the sweetness of her soft, delicate lips. Abigail longed to feel the power and strength of the sturdy embrace of Walter's strong arms.

Walter had been fortuitous enough to enjoy two visits to Camden, South Carolina, since meeting Abigail in the summer of 1776. Both of those journeys had been in the company of his sister and brother-in-law, Clearanna and William Hamer. Occasionally, William's business required such visits into his native South Carolina. But it had been eight long, torturous months since the last trip to Camden, way back in the fall of 1777. And that was entirely too long for Walter. Something had to be done. His heart could no longer endure the separation.

So, Walter embarked upon his most ambitious scheme ever. By sheer force of will and desire ... or so he thought ... Walter managed to convince his mother to allow him to travel alone to Camden. He could scarcely believe it when Elizabeth finally gave her permission for the solo journey. The boy was quite proud of himself and his ability to manipulate his mother toward such a previously unimaginable outcome.

To Walter's great surprise, it had not taken the months of begging and pleading that he had anticipated. Indeed, his mother seemed to be downright reasonable in her reaction to his request. Truth be told, Elizabeth Billingsley knew full well the depth of the love that young Walter held in his heart for the lovely Abigail Hamer. She also knew that such love could neither be constrained nor denied. So, after only two weeks of Walter's begging, cajoling, and reasoning, she finally consented to the trip.

As it turned out, Elizabeth had hatched a scheme of her own. She found a way to take advantage of Walter's enthusiasm as an opportunity for commerce and profit. Two weeks provided her with just enough time to make arrangements for the lucrative sale of eight barrels of her finest whiskey to the Blind Fox Tavern in Camden. Quality alcoholic beverages were at a premium in the neighboring state due to the ever-expanding war of rebellion against England. The well-known tavern jumped at the opportunity to obtain a large quantity of quality spirits.

So, Walter's wishes and requests were granted. He was bound for Camden! He would finally be able to visit his beloved Abigail! But, as part of the arrangement, he would first deliver his mother's cargo of whiskey and collect for her a handsome sum in gold coin.

Walter had no issues, at all, with the plan. Indeed, the notion that his mother would trust him with such an important transaction made him feel all-the-more mature. Yes, the heavy load of liquor would double the length of time for his journey to Camden. But he was willing to sacrifice an extra two days so that he might enjoy the company of his beloved.

July 5, 1778

It was the morning after the second anniversary of the declaration of independency from Great Britain and King George. Walter Billingsley was preparing to depart Guilford with his mother's load of whiskey. His younger brother, fourteen-year-old Basil, busied himself by tying a hemp rope net across the tops of the barrels.

Elizabeth hovered nervously near the wagon. The concerned mother asked, voice trembling slightly, "Walter, are you certain that you know the way?"

He smiled reassuringly. "Yes, Mother. I have made the journey twice already. I know the route well, and will enjoy excellent roads all the way to Camden."

"But you must not rush, Walter," she cautioned. "The load is heavy, even for this impressive wagon. You do not want to risk damaging your rig or the cargo. Abigail will still be there, whether you arrive in two days or four days."

"Do not worry, Mother. I promise that I will not spill one drop of your precious spirits." He took his mother's hand and kissed it. "I will not rush the journey, Mother. I know what is expected of me. You can trust me."

Her cautioning continued, "This is some of my oldest and best beverage, Walter. I have bargained a handsome sum for these barrels." She paused. "The gold from this sale is important to our family, Son."

"I know, Mother."

"It will help us survive the coming winter ... and this ever-encroaching war."

"Yes, Mother. I know." He wrapped his strong arms around her. "I will not disappoint you. I promise."

Elizabeth was on the verge of tears. "I suppose that I am something of a worrier. I always have been. The fact that you have never made such a trek by yourself only incites me to worry more. The recent Tory attacks along the border with South Carolina give me even greater pause and more cause for concern."

"The Tories have been operating more to the east, Mother ... near the coast. It has been months since there was an attack in this region." He hugged her once again. "I will be fine. The roads are all busy and well-traveled. There are suitable lodging houses along the way. I will be armed with both rifle and pistols. I can take care of myself."

Elizabeth sighed and then muttered, "As I am well aware."

Her memory flashed back to that heartbreaking, violent night of the Tory attack upon their family and home. She shook her head and attempted to drive the frightful images and memories from her thoughts. She glanced beneath the seat of the wagon at the baskets and sacks of food that she had prepared for her son. "Are you certain that you have enough provisions?"

"Enough for three men." Walter chuckled. "Mother, are you trying to make me fat? Is that your strategy to keep me at home and away from Abigail?"

Elizabeth smiled warmly and reached up to cup her son's face in her soft hands.

"You are *my son*, Walter Billingsley. Please allow me just a few more months of motherhood. You shall belong to Abigail soon enough. Until then, you are still mine." She kissed him resolutely on the cheek.

Walter called to Basil, "Is the load secure, Brother?"

Basil jumped down from the wagon. "It is, indeed. You shall not lose a precious drop of our mother's sin juice!"

"Basil!" his mother exclaimed, slapping him firmly on the butt. "I will not tolerate such callous words!"

"Yes, Mother …"

Basil subtly rolled his eyes at Walter as he handed his older brother a small cloth sack.

"What is this?" asked Walter curiously.

"Just a little something for you to give to Abigail's father. It's a pound of our best pipe tobacco. I cured it myself. It's been commiserating with a little rum and vanilla since last fall. Premium stuff. Mr. Hamer should be impressed."

"Thank you, Basil. I am certain that he will enjoy it."

"I figured that I would do my part to help you win him over. After all, you need all the help you can get." Basil laughed at his own joke.

The brothers stared at one another for a few moments. It was a strange, uncomfortable pause for both of them. They were not, exactly, known for expressing brotherly affection. Indeed, throughout their childhood they had been bitter rivals in most of their endeavors. But, both young men were growing older and wiser. Living in a fatherless home had matured both of them beyond their years.

Basil broke the silence. "Well ... you be careful out there on the road, Walter."

"I will, Brother. And you take care of Mother whilst I'm gone."

"I will. Do not fret over us. We will be fine."

Walter suddenly and impetuously grabbed his brother and smothered him with a manly hug.

"I will see you next month," Walter proclaimed.

"I'll be right here waiting on you. As will the tobacco and the corn." Basil slapped his brother good-naturedly on the back.

Walter released himself from Basil's embrace and climbed up onto the seat. He lay the flintlock rifle that his older brother, John, had loaned him in the floor beneath his feet. He adjusted the two loaded pistols inside his leather belt as he grabbed hold of the reins.

He turned to his mother. "Goodbye, then, Mother. I will be home before you know it."

"I miss you already," she mumbled through trembling lips.

Walter snapped the reins and clucked at the team of horses. The gigantic animals leaned forward and strained against the heavy load, slowly tugging the wagon into the street. Walter guided the animals down the road toward the outskirts of the small town. Elizabeth and Basil stood on the brick walkway in front of the house and watched the wagon disappear around a distant curve. As soon as his brother was out of sight, Basil extended his right arm to his mother and escorted her back inside their home.

Walter soon turned his team toward the southwest, down the dusty trail toward Salisbury. Charlotte Town, Waxhaws, and Camden waited just beyond to the south. He knew that, in just four short days, he would be in the arms of his sweet Abigail.

Camden, South Carolina - July 21, 1778

Walter and Abigail rested comfortably in a lazy swing. It was the centerpiece of the large veranda that adorned the stately home of Alexander Hamer, the father of Abigail. They sipped from cups of hot tea and waved at curious passers-by. There were many neighbors and locals who wondered about the identity of this young stranger who had seemingly won the heart of the much sought-after maiden, Abigail Hamer.

"That was a wonderful meal, Mrs. Hamer. I am grateful for your invitation to dine in your home."

"You are most welcome, Walter," responded his beautiful hostess, Mrs. Audra Hamer. "But I quite imagine that you would enjoy almost anything after two weeks of endless tavern fare."

"Yes, Madam. That is true. I must confess, though, that the meals at the Blind Fox have been most agreeable and filling. Still, one grows weary of a nonstop diet of bread, soups, and stews. Your meal was like an oasis of flavor in my bland desert of tavern food."

"As good as one of your mother's meals?" she teased.

"I hesitate to utter a comparison, Mrs. Hamer. I would not wish to sully my mother's cooking reputation."

The woman giggled warmly at Walter's statement. Clearly, she was pleased by the young man's enthusiastic response to her fine meal. She was equally pleased with his kind and courteous demeanor. Walter Billingsley was not like most of the young men his age who resided in and around Camden. Dozens of them had attempted to woo Abigail. Those lads usually came across as a bit coarse and unrefined. Walter, however, had obviously been reared as a gentleman. Audra Hamer had already decided that she approved of her daughter's choice for a future husband.

Walter was equally impressed with Mr. and Mrs. Hamer. They were kind, thoughtful people. Mrs. Hamer was, in Walter's mind, an amazing mother to Abigail. She was clearly the source of her daughter's beauty and grace. She was a refined and handsome woman, and she had been most courteous and kind to Walter during his stay in their city.

"May I fetch you some more tea, Walter?" his hostess inquired.

"No, thank you, Mrs. Hamer. I am quite satisfied. I fear that if I drink another cup, I might never fall asleep tonight."

Abigail gracefully leaned forward and placed her half-empty cup on a nearby stand. She reached for Walter's hand and interlocked her fingers with his. She loved to feel the strength in his taut, muscular hands. The warm touch of Abigail's flesh sent waves of excitement and shock throughout Walter's body. He glanced at Abigail's mother, somewhat embarrassed by his beloved's bold display of affection. The woman merely smiled. Walter sensed nothing but pride and approval in her gaze.

Abigail declared, "I only wish that Papa might have been here during your visit, Walter. I so wanted the two of you to get to know one another a bit better. He will be thrilled by your gift of fine, flavored tobacco. He positively adores his pipe."

"I wish that I could have presented it to him, personally, Abigail. I sincerely regret that he could not be here during my visit."

Walter was lying. He really did not mind the man's absence all that much. He liked Mr. Hamer well enough, but deep down he was a bit intimidated by the girl's father. That was to be expected, of course. Walter had encountered scant few fathers who were eager to surrender their daughters to mate-seeking young men.

"Did you say that he is in Baltimore?" he inquired, hoping to show increased interest in Abigail's father and somehow escape the internal guilt precipitated by his wanton lie.

"Yes. He's been gone for over a month. I miss him," she stated with disappointment. "He has business partners in the city, and there was an urgent matter that required his presence. But we expect him back early next month," Abigail explained.

Walter nodded. "That is a long time to be away. And these are treacherous days to be traveling such a great distance."

"Indeed," remarked Mrs. Hamer. "I begged him not to go, but he felt that it was necessary. Abigail and I are hoping that this will be his last trip to Baltimore. I have encouraged him to divest himself of all of his holdings and interests in Maryland. He needs to focus all of his attention on his ventures here in South Carolina."

Walter nodded knowingly, though he did not understand what the word, "divest," meant. He was relieved when Abigail redirected the conversation.

"Have you ever traveled to the North, Walter?"

"No ... I have not traveled there. I have spent the majority of my days in and around Guilford. In recent years, I have never ventured beyond the southernmost counties of Virginia, those which border North Carolina. But my family has roots in Maryland. I barely remember it, but I once lived in Baltimore."

"Really?" exclaimed Abigail, somewhat shocked.

Walter nodded. "I was born there. All of my brothers and sisters were. My grandparents lived there for decades. My parents were wed there. We emigrated to Guilford in 1768. I was just a small lad, so I barely remember living there. But every now and again I see it in my dreams. And my mother tells me stories to remind me about our old home in the city."

"I cannot believe that you never told me this before," declared Abigail.

Walter shrugged. "It never came up in our conversations, I suppose. Honestly, I rarely think about Maryland. All I have ever known is life in North Carolina."

Mrs. Hamer joined in, "Abigail tells me that your father was a minister. Did his calling take him to North Carolina?"

"No, ma'am. The opportunity for land and farming is what lured him to North Carolina. The preaching came later. My father was never actually an ordained minister. He was what we call in the Baptist tradition an 'exhorter.' He was a layman preacher, but he kept busy every Sunday. He served in churches that were unable to lure actual ordained ministers to their pulpits. There are not many ordained, educated reverends anxious to leave the cities along the coast and minister in the backcountry churches. Such is the dilemma of Baptist life on the frontier."

"And then the Tories killed him," the woman stated in a tense voice.

"Yes, ma'am. Two years ago, this April."

She shook her head in disbelief. "Such a travesty. My heart breaks for you and your family, Walter." She gazed toward the distant fields to the south. "Loyalists now roam throughout the districts of South Carolina. I have heard stories of their atrocities. But then, I also have heard of similar violence perpetrated by the Whig militias. Why is it that men feel the license to utilize the same methods of their enemies, all the while decrying the injustice of those enemies' actions?" She stared into nothingness for just a moment, lost in the complexity of her thoughts. She gave a slight shudder. "I suppose that I shall never understand the hearts or minds of violent men. I thank God that we have never had to experience such things here in Camden."

"I hope that you never do, Mrs. Hamer. But I fear that that the war moving south is inevitable … it cannot be avoided. And yes, some men are, by nature, violent. But, then again, some have violence and bloodshed thrust upon them. Sometimes the only appropriate response is to fight back."

She smiled thinly and nodded her understanding. Mrs. Hamer had heard from Abigail the story of Walter's personal battle against the militiamen who invaded his home. She knew that the young man who was sitting beside her daughter had fought and killed men in the defense of his family. She could even see the wounds on his body from the battle.

"Do you really think the war will expand in earnest into the Carolinas? The battlefields and armies seem so far away," she commented, a tremble of cautious hope in her voice.

"The Tories who hanged my father were from South Carolina. I am told that their numbers are swelling and that they are becoming bolder in their activities." He paused and took a deep breath. "Yes, I believe that the British will come. It is only a matter of time. Until then, I think that we will continue to see more and more clashes between militia armies and small bands of Tories and Whigs here in the South."

Mrs. Hamer looked solemnly and sadly into his eyes. Her gaze probed the boy's thoughts and emotions.

"I hope that you are wrong, Walter."

He squeezed Abigail's tender hand tightly. "As do I, Mrs. Hamer. I abhor the notion that your wonderful family might have to endure the trials and travails of this Revolution." He smiled at Abigail. "Besides, we have no time for wars and such. We have other plans, don't we my dear?"

"Indeed, we do, Mr. Billingsley." She leaned toward him and rested her head on his shoulder.

Mrs. Hamer confessed, "Abigail has shared those plans with me, Walter. I hope you do not mind."

"Of course not, Mrs. Hamer. I expected as much. Abigail told me that she divulges everything to you." He grinned.

"Well, you are going to have to tell Mr. Hamer sooner or later, and ask his permission, of course."

"Yes, indeed. I had planned on doing so during this visit. I was quite disappointed when I discovered that Mr. Hamer was gone."

There it was again ... the lie. He was actually quite relieved. He had rehearsed asking the man for Abigail's hand at least a hundred times between Guilford and Camden, and was not personally pleased with any of his efforts.

He continued, "I suppose that we will have to hold that discussion on my next visit."

"I believe that would be wise. Abigail has shared your time table. Two years will be here before you know it."

"Yes, ma'am."

Walter, desperately in need of a change of subject, reached for his dainty cup and took another sip of his tea. He was relieved when he heard the dull thump of horse hooves echoing down the street from the north. A lone rider trotted his mount up to the front steps of the Hamer home and eased his animal to a stop. He was young man in his early twenties, clad in a colorful green weskit and tan breeches. A brand-new, unstained brown cocked hat adorned his head. He was a rather handsome, dapper-looking young fellow. He seemed particularly pleased to see Abigail.

"Good evening, folks," the man declared, tipping his cocked hat. "How are you, Mrs. Hamer?" He nodded to Abigail. "Miss Hamer." His inflection changed slightly when he uttered the word, 'Miss.'

The woman of the house stood to her feet and walked toward the steps. "I am well, Mr. Hollowell. What brings you to our home this evening?"

"I am here as a courtesy to Mr. Craven."

"The postal rider?" she inquired.

"Yes ma'am. He had a bag full of letters and correspondences, all bound for Charlestown. Since he only had two letters for folks here in Camden today, he asked if I might deliver them so that he could get on the road and travel a few miles before sundown. I told him that I would be most happy to do so." The young man smiled flirtingly at Abigail. "I did not realize that my voluntary good deed would bring me you your home today, Miss Hamer."

Abigail stood and began to walk toward the porch rail. She pulled Walter up from the swing and dragged him along with her.

"You are too kind, Mr. Hollowell. Have you, by any chance, met my fiancé, Walter Billingsley, of Guilford County in North Carolina?"

"Good evening," Walter declared confidently, nodding to the stranger. He puffed out his chest and straightened his back in an effort to make himself appear a little taller.

"Your fiancé?" the man echoed, jaw dropping slightly. "No. I had not heard the news of your engagement." He stared stormily at Walter. "I thought this fellow was a distant family member … visiting from out of town."

"Well, he will be family soon enough." She smiled proudly. "We have not formally made our engagement public, yet. But we are, indeed, pledged to be wed."

Hollowell sniffed and gnawed at the inside of his jaw. His lips poked out in an almost comical, fish-like manner.

"I don't see a ring on your finger."

Walter answered in her stead, "Abigail cannot wear my ring until I officially have her father's consent. Unfortunately, he had to leave on business before I could petition him. But, we are pledged nonetheless."

The man sat silently on his horse for an uncomfortable moment.

"Well, then, I suppose congratulations are in order. I wish you two the very best."

It was abundantly clear that he did not wish Walter Billingsley anything resembling good fortune or favor. Indeed, if looks could kill, Walter would have been rotting in a coffin.

"We are humbled by and most grateful for your sentiments, sir," declared Walter.

Another painfully uncomfortable period of silence ensued. Mrs. Hamer sought to relieve the tension. "So … Mr. Hollowell … do you have a letter for me?"

"No, ma'am." He reached into his bag and pulled out a small square of paper that was wrapped in cord and sealed with a blob of yellow wax. He thrust it toward Walter. "It's for him." He spoke the word 'him' as if it were a squirt of poison spewing from his mouth. "It listed his location as the Blind Fox Tavern." He mumbled, "I went there first, but the proprietor sent me to your home … he said that Billingsley was your family guest."

Walter leaned over the handrail and received the note with a nod.

"Thank you, Mr. Hollowell."

A third excruciatingly awkward pause ensued.

"Will there me anything else, Philip?" inquired Mrs. Hamer.

"No ma'am. That is all. I will be on my way. I bid you all a good evening." He tipped his hat respectfully.

"Good evening to you, sir," responded Walter.

The fellow slowly turned his horse and then guided it to a leisurely pace back in the direction of downtown Camden. His dejection was evident in the way that he slumped in his saddle. The young fellow was obviously devastated that the beautiful Abigail Hamer was "off the market."

"Who is it from, Walter?" asked Abigail inquisitively.

He broke the wax seal, pulled off the string ties, and opened the letter.

"It is from my brother, Samuel," he mumbled. "It's strange that he would write me …"

Walter's lips moved as he read the words on the page. His eyes grew wide. The pallor of his face morphed from a pleasant pink to an ashen gray. When he was finished, he slowly lowered the letter to his side and stared toward the sunset.

"What is it, Walter?" demanded Abigail. "Is something wrong?"

He continued to stare, stoic and silent.

Abigail stepped forward and touched his shoulder. "Walter, are you well? Has something happened at home? Is it your mother?"

The mention of his mother snatched him from his captive thoughts. He shook his head and then turned and faced his beloved.

"No, Darling. Mother is fine." He smiled thinly. "But I must beg your leave and return to the tavern to make preparation for my immediate departure. I leave at first light tomorrow."

"Tomorrow?" shrieked Abigail. "You said that you were staying in Camden for another week!"

He took Abigail by the hand. "I know, Love. But I must go quickly to Salisbury. Time is of the essence. I must be there in two days." He turned to Mrs. Hamer. "Might I leave my wagon and team with you and borrow one of your husband's mounts?"

"Of course, Walter," Audra responded. "Whatever you need. But, pray tell, why is your departure so imminent? Why the rush?"

Abigail sobbed, "I do not understand, Walter. Why must you leave so soon? What is going on? What has happened? And why Salisbury?" Tears streamed down her perfect, pale cheeks.

"David Fanning has been captured. He is being held in the gaol there, awaiting my return. I must go and verify his identity so that he might be prosecuted and held accountable for his crimes. If I am not there in two days, he will be released."

"Who is David Fanning?" asked Mrs. Hamer, confused.

Walter replied with a stony gaze, "He is the Tory bastard who killed my father."

Two Days Later - Sundown

"He has escaped?" screeched Walter, his voice colored with rage. "How?"

The road-worn, exhausted boy slammed his cocked hat down on the desk, knocking over a cup of tepid ale and scattering the jailer's documents across the desktop and floor. A small cloud of road dust exploded out of his hat and hovered in a buff-colored cloud over the pile of papers. Walter stared with unrestrained disgust at the Rowan County jailer, his gleaming white eyes glowing against his dark, dust-coated, sunburned face.

The jailer seethed with anger. "You had better change your attitude, boy. I'll tolerate neither rudeness nor a scolding from the likes of you."

"What about from the likes of me?" challenged Samuel Billingsley, stepping forward with his rifle cradled in his left arm. "Are you going to lecture us on etiquette, or are you going to answer the damn question? Does my little brother need to repeat it?"

"No, Mr. Billingsley. That will not be necessary." He sighed. "I simply have no good answer for you, gentlemen. The man just escaped. He stole away in the darkness of night. That David Fanning is a slippery one, they say. He has escaped from at least a half-dozen jails throughout the Carolinas. Probably more."

"Escaped with the help of Tory deputies or employees, no doubt. Perhaps even Tory jailers," retorted Walter. He clenched his teeth in rage.

"Now, hold on young man! You have absolutely no right to insult me or my employees!"

"I have every right!" screamed Walter. His voice dropped to an angry growl. "I interrupted a coveted visit with my fiancé in South Carolina to return here and identify this man and see him charged for his crimes. I traveled all the way from Camden in less than two days of hard riding. You had in custody, in this very building, the man who stole my father's life. The very man who strung up my Papa in his own yard. And now his murderer is gone! Vanished! And with no reasonable explanation from you, the man in charge of the prisoners."

Walter glared at the jailer, who turned his eyes away with a measure of shame.

The boy continued his indictment of the jailer. "There are only two possibilities, as I see it. Either someone in this gaol allowed him to escape, or ... he simply disappeared like a fart on a summer breeze. Call me a lunatic, but it seems much more likely that someone in Salisbury opened the door for him and handed him his hat."

"Why, you are an insolent little prick, aren't you? How dare you question my loyalty to our country! Your charges are unfounded and egregious!" responded the jailer.

Walter leaned over the man's desk, hovering within inches of his face. "And I stand by them."

"That's enough, Walter," cautioned Samuel. "You're wasting your breath. There are other ways for us to get our satisfaction."

"How, Samuel? It's obvious that the law cannot be trusted. There does not appear to be even one jail or gallows in the Carolinas that can tame the illustrious David Fanning! Good and loyal Patriots haul him in the front door and then shite-licking Tories like this fool escort him out the back!"

"I said that's enough, Walter!" scolded Samuel. "Mind your manners *and* your tongue. Go outside."

Walter hesitated. His face registered confusion.

"Now, Walter! James and I will conclude our family's business with the Salisbury gaol."

Walter started indignantly at his brother, then exhaled in frustration. He grabbed his dust-covered hat from the desk and stormed out of the door. Once outside in the cooler night air, his emotions seemed to calm down a bit. He grabbed a drink of water from a nearby well and paced anxiously in the street in front of the jail. After several minutes of waiting, he finally gave up and decided to lie down in the back of the wagon that belonged to his brother, James. He allowed his legs to dangle at the knee from the tailgate of the wagon. In his exhaustion, he instantly descended into a fitful state of sleep.

A short while later he felt a swift kick to his right foot.

"Wake up, little brother."

Walter rolled over onto his side and saw his brother, James, staring at him and smiling from ear to ear.

"You really pissed off the jailer, Walter," declared James, spitting onto the ground.

"I rather think it was the other way around," responded Walter, stretching and yawning.

Samuel's face appeared quite suddenly over the side of the wagon. He, too, was grinning from ear to ear.

"Well, you did accuse him of intentionally letting Fanning go," responded Samuel. "That took a pretty large pair of gingambobs. I didn't know you had it in you, Walter."

"Called him a 'shite-licker,' too," added James. "I thought that was the high point of the evening."

Samuel burst into uncontrolled laughter. Walter and James immediately joined him. It took a few seconds for them to reach a state of composure.

"What did you say to that horrid little man after I left?" asked Walter.

"Oh, don't worry about him," responded Samuel. "He won't be letting any more Tory prisoners slip away."

Samuel cut his eyes at James.

"Yep! Let's just say that he is well-aware of the consequences of any more lapses in his jailhouse security."

"But what good does that do us? Fanning is long gone by now."

James slapped him good-naturedly on the knee. "Fanning will get what's coming to him, little brother. One of these days ..."

"Well, boys ... I've had enough talk about prisoners and jails. Walter, let's get you fed and home to Mother," encouraged Samuel.

James nodded. "And whilst we're eating, we expect a full and detailed update on that little lady of yours down in South Carolina."

"Sounds good to me!" exclaimed Walter.

PART II

Walter's Misfortunate War
1780

6

ROADBLOCK!

Late Afternoon - March 6, 1780

It was uncharacteristically cold, even for early March. There was a thin film of ice on the winter puddles that dotted the road between Guilford Courthouse and the Billingsley farm. The low clouds that blanketed the valley were spitting tiny whispers of fine snow.

Walter tugged the collar of his overcoat a little higher in an effort to stop the invasion of frigid air. The short ride into town had started off quite pleasant, but as darkness descended it had become breezy and bitterly cold. The winter winds were flowing freely around his neck and ushering the biting air down the center of his back. He attempted to insert his frozen hands, still holding the reins, inside the breast of his thin wool coat.

"*I should have left for home an hour ago*!" he scolded himself.

Walter was bone-tired from the day's labor. During the winter lull in farm work, he had been spending almost every waking moment making improvements on his newly-obtained land. His mother had generously deeded him twenty acres from the expansive Billingsley estate. It was an ideal piece of property upon which he might establish himself and make a home for his future bride. Walter spent the entire months of January and February clearing trees from the acreage, building fences, and burning off pastures and fields in preparation for the spring thaw. Over the past two weeks, he had begun work on their first home ... a small, one-room cottage.

The short ride back into town, though torturously cold, was quite boring and uneventful. Guilford Courthouse was deathly quiet. Its families were all inside their houses, no doubt warming themselves beside their hearths and enjoying their customary evening activities. Dozens of chimneys pumped a steady stream of smoke into the chilly winter atmosphere.

Walter's frozen spirit lifted when he turned onto the main thoroughfare and caught sight of the beautiful Billingsley home. He guided his horse into the alleyway that separated his house from the neighbor's abode. As he rode around back toward the barn and stable, he noticed the warm glow that emanated from the two small windows in the detached kitchen. He smiled. There would still be some hot tea in the kettle and a delicious stew bubbling in the warming pot. With any luck, the others might have actually waited for him to return before beginning their supper.

Walter trotted his gelding into the barn as the final glow of daylight disappeared over the western horizon. He made sure that the animal had fresh hay and plenty of water, then he trudged toward the back door of the kitchen. He could smell the yeasty tang of fresh bread wafting through the cracks that surrounded the heavy door. His mouth watered. He lifted the latch and stepped out of the unwelcoming darkness into the cheerful warmth and glow of the kitchen. A large fire crackled and danced in the fireplace. Wisps of smoke leaked from below the hearth and added their dull, gray stains to the wall and ceiling overhead.

Walter's family was gathered in the toasty room, as was usual for early evenings during the winter months. Elizabeth Billingsley hovered in front of the fire. She was stirring a pot of stew with a large wooden spoon. Basil reclined comfortably in their father's old, expansive, leather-covered easy chair. He was reading a newspaper by the light of a very bright five-candle stand. Martha sat gracefully in a straight-back chair on the other side of the candle stand, sharing in its abundance of light, and reading one of her favorite novels. The subtle aroma of honey from the beeswax candles intermingled with the tasty smells of freshly-cooked food.

"Whatever it is, it certainly smells good, Mama! What's for supper?"

His mother turned to face him and rested her fists on her hips. "It's high time you showed up, Walter! I was just about to send Basil to fetch the sheriff and organize a search party!"

Basil glanced over the top of his newspaper, grinned mischievously, and rolled his eyes in an exaggerated motion. Walter bit his lip to keep from laughing.

"I told you that I would be home around dark, Mother." He pointed to the window. "See? It just got dark."

Elizabeth turned her attention back to her steaming, bubbling pot. She retorted, "I should think that you would have returned home while there was still a little daylight left."

"I had plenty of light to feed and water my horse, Mother. Why the urgency? Did you need me for something?"

"No, Dear. I just like having you home. That's all." She paused. Her lip trembled. "After all, I do not have many more of these days left."

"Oh, Mother!" Walter marched over to the diminutive woman and effortlessly picked her up off of the floor, wrapping her in a huge bear hug. "Abigail and I are not scheduled to be wed until June 3. That is almost three months from now!"

"Walter Billingsley, you impetuous scoundrel! Put me down this instant!" She kissed him warmly on the cheek as he returned her to a standing position.

"You *are* excited about my marriage, aren't you, Mother?"

"Of course, I am, Son. It's just hard on mothers when their sons are wed. I felt exactly the same way with each of your brothers. When one of my sons goes off on his own, it's like a tiny little part of me dies." She smiled and patted his hand. "You will no longer be my Walter. You will be Abigail's Walter. Things will never be the same again for me. My small world will be forever changed, and will become just a little bit smaller. Don't you understand?"

"Yes ma'am. I suppose so."

"Well I, for one, will not miss you when you're gone!" Basil interjected. "For the first time in my life, I'll get first run at a tub of clean bathwater! Praise God!"

Walter grabbed a chunk of fresh bread from its wooden platter and hurled it at his brother. The handsome, muscular sixteen-year-old expertly snagged the airborne morsel with his right hand and, smiling victoriously, took a large bite.

Walter grinned. "So, Mother ... I ask again. What is for supper?"

"Chicken and potato stew, flavored generously with dried onions and black pepper ... just as you like it."

Walter cut his eyes at Basil. "You didn't slaughter one of the laying hens, did you?"

"No, Brother. That old, mean Polish rooster tried to give me a flogging this morning. I decided that it was time for him to take a swim in Mother's pot."

"His mistake," joked Walter.

"Yes." answered Basil. "I'm thinking about making a necklace out of his huge spurs."

"That's simply disgusting!" exclaimed Martha, closing her book and joining in the conversation. She attempted to change the subject. "Did you get much work done on your cottage today, Walter? I am eager to see your progress."

"Yes, Martha, I did. And I thank you for asking. Samuel's boy, Cassius, helped me today. Gabe Tate came out to assist, as well. We finished the frame and braced all four walls. I will begin work on the rafters and ceiling later this week. The house will be in the dry before the end of next week."

"I cannot imagine that Gabriel Tate provided much in the way of help on a construction project," commented Elizabeth in a condescending, judgmental tone. "That boy is nothing but a jester. I doubt that he has ever actually worked a day in his life."

"I like him, Mama. He makes me laugh. He is my friend," declared Walter.

"Humph!" responded Elizabeth. "Son, you need to locate some more industrious friends. Anyhow ... you will have precious little time for the likes of Gabriel Tate once Abigail is here and mistress of her home. I sincerely doubt that she will have much tolerance for him lounging around your place and inserting himself into your marriage and family life."

"I simply cannot wait for Abigail to get here!" commented Martha wistfully. "She has asked me to help arrange her furnishings and decorate the cottage. It is so exciting!"

"That will be quite the job," quipped Basil. "No doubt, Miss Hamer will have a handsome dowry and wagons filled with furniture, goods, and booty!"

"Basil! That is quite enough! It is impolite to discuss such things publicly," scolded his mother. She turned to Walter. "It is a smart plan that you have, Son ... building a simple, functional, one-room cottage. Very wise, indeed."

Walter nodded, his face displaying satisfaction at his mother's comment. "It will suit our needs for now. Someday, when we need more space, we can expand the house, or even add a stairway and second floor."

"Like next year, supposin'?" exclaimed Basil. "It won't take more than five or ten minutes before there will be a little Walter Jr. on the way!"

Elizabeth was compelled once again to admonish her son, but she decided to bite her tongue, realizing that correcting the boy would likely have no effect. She merely exhaled in frustration and shook her head.

Walter suddenly took notice of the newspaper in Basil's hand. "Where did you get the paper? How old is it?"

"There was a stack of 'em at Tolford's Store this morning. They're pretty fresh, only five days old."

"Anything interesting?"

"I should say so! The British have invaded South Carolina!"

Walter's jaw dropped. For a moment, he could not speak. Then he stammered, "When? Where? What manner of forces?"

"Almost three weeks ago. They have occupied a couple of islands south of Charlestown." He opened the paper and scanned one of the stories. "Uhh … it says here that two generals named Clinton and Cornwallis are in command, with over eight thousand troops."

"Eight thousand?" exclaimed Walter in disbelief. "And Clinton, himself, is with them?"

Basil folded the paper across his chest. "That is what the newspaper says. Why? What does that mean? What makes Clinton so special?"

"Sir Henry Clinton is the supreme commander of the British forces in North America! Cornwallis is his second-in-command! This is nothing short of a relocation of the entire war!"

Walter walked over to a nearby window and stared numbly into the darkness beyond. He explained, "Things have been stalled in the North for a year or more. The war is not going well for us. The British are now going to try and split the states. With that many troops, they can overwhelm the low country and then sweep up through the Piedmont in a matter of months … maybe even weeks. The Tories in the Carolinas and Georgia will be emboldened. Their raids and attacks will increase. Men loyal to the Crown will flock to their camps to enlist."

Walter turned and faced his mother. His countenance was grim. "Mama, the war is no longer far off in the North. It has come here … to us … to our very doorstep."

Early Morning - April 30, 1780

The news of the British incursion into South Carolina swept like a wildfire across the Piedmont and western frontier of North Carolina. Walter's prophetic vision of the Tory response proved accurate and true. Raids, skirmishes, and murders began to occur with regularity throughout the farmlands and forests of North and South Carolina. The British army surrounded Charlestown and placed it under siege. The isolated port city and the Patriot troops trapped there could not last much longer. As soon as Charlestown fell, the King's forces would be loosed upon the countryside.

Walter could wait no longer. He could not bear the thought of Abigail being witness to the cruelty and subjugation of an occupying British force. He felt compelled to go to South Carolina and fetch back his fiancé to the relative safety of Guilford County. He made all of the necessary preparations for his departure.

Elizabeth Billingsley, on the other hand, was desperate to keep her son at home. She watched with tears welling in her eyes as he loaded his provisions into the wagon. It was the same wagon that he had abandoned upon his hasty departure from South Carolina in 1778, then retrieved later that year when he returned once again to visit Abigail and reunite Mr. Hamer with his prized riding horse.

"Do you think it is wise to go right now, Walter?" asked Elizabeth. "It is far too dangerous for you to be heading south on your own. You should take one of your brothers with you."

Walter shook his head vigorously. "John is already deployed with his company, patrolling the country to the southeast. Samuel and James will, most likely, be called up very soon … as soon as Charlestown falls. They must remain free to see to their own affairs before reporting to Colonel Locke down in Rowan County. Basil needs to remain here to take care of you and our farm. Anyhow … I will not be going alone. Gabe Tate has agreed to travel with me. I will rendezvous with him at Blakeley's Crossroads."

Elizabeth rolled her eyes and exhaled in disbelief. "Gabriel Tate is a buffoon! It will be as if you were taking a small child with you!"

Walter responded tersely, "This is not the time for your insults, Mother. Gabe is my friend. He is good with both horse and gun. You must stop worrying about me. I've made this journey before. I can easily do so again."

"But why do you feel that you must go and get Abigail right now? Your marriage is more than a month away. It's just not proper, Walter. Surely, her parents will not approve of her returning here with you until you are wed!"

"The British will be on the move soon, Mother. The fall of Charlestown is imminent. Once that port is in British hands, more troop ships will arrive, and the Lobsterbacks will flood the South. Camden will be in their path." He stared numbly at the wagon seat in front of his face. "No, Mother. I cannot wait. I must depart immediately. Abigail can stay in our guest room. I am certain that her parents will approve of my removing her to a place of safety."

"I do wish you would reconsider," she pleaded. "These roads are treacherous. Tories now abound in the countryside. There have been ambushes and killings on the highways."

Without thinking, Walter snapped angrily, "Stop nagging me, Mother! My mind is made up. I must leave posthaste."

He realized immediately the harshness of his words. He took in a deep breath, turned, and wrapped his strong arms around his sobbing mother. "I'm sorry I was cross with you, Mama. Believe me, I understand your worry. But I must ask that you try and understand mine, as well. I *must* go and bring Abigail home. My integrity and honor demand that I do so."

Elizabeth was vanquished, and she knew it. She sobbed. "I understand. Just please be careful, Son. And come back to me as quickly as you can."

"I will, Mother. Please pray for us … for Abigail and me."

"Yes, Walter. Of course. I always do."

"And for Gabe."

"Him, too." She exhaled. "Lord knows he needs it."

Walter wasted no more time on goodbyes, for he felt he had no time to spare. He jumped immediately into the seat of his wagon, grabbed the reins, and slapped them sharply on the rumps of the horses. The team leapt into an almost instant trot, easily pulling the empty wagon into the roadway. Walter angled the rig toward the southeast, in the direction of Salisbury. He intended to reach that town and find a comfortable room for the night before heading south toward Mecklenburg County and the Waxhaws Fork Road. That was the well-traveled highway that would take him to Camden.

Elizabeth stood in the street and waved, but Walter never once turned around. His mind and heart were fixed completely upon Abigail. Elizabeth wept tears of despondence.

Dusk – Salisbury, North Carolina

"There it be!" exclaimed Gabriel. "Lordy, I didn't think we was ever goin' to get here! I could eat a week-old dead skunk! Let's find us a pot of somethin' hot, Walt."

Walter nodded, but declined to speak. He was exhausted ... too exhausted to talk. He was even more fatigued by the ceaseless chatter that Gabe had unleashed upon him throughout the day. He was beginning to wish that he had taken his mother's advice and left Gabriel Tate at home. Walter could not verify it empirically, but he was convinced that his friend seemed to increase in word volume as the day progressed. So, he was quite relieved to see the lights of the candles, lamps, and campfires of Salisbury.

Their ride toward the south had been a bumpy, violent experience, as well. Though the roads were relatively dry and free of mud, they contained numerous ruts, mounds, and potholes ... vestiges of the recent wet and harsh winter. Walter was also shocked at how uncomfortable it was to experience such obstacles while riding in a wagon without cargo. Due to the lighter weight of the empty rig, he felt as if he had experienced to the maximum every possible bump and dip in the roadway.

As they neared the town, they breathed deeply the sweet odors of freshly-cooked food. Both boys' mouths watered. They had not eaten since before the sunrise. Their bellies ached for a good meal.

Walter thought to himself, "*Cheer up! You will have a hot supper, a warm bed, and a little bit of silence within the hour.*"

Walter popped the reins and clucked at his team, urging them forward toward the center of town. They arrived at his favorite tavern in Salisbury, the Gray Ghost Inn, in less than a half-hour.

Finding a hot meal was easy enough. After seeing to the needs of the horses and parking the wagon securely at the local livery stable, Walter and Gabe gorged themselves on a thick, hearty elk stew and a loaf of dark, dry bread at one of the dinner tables at the Gray Ghost. Three mugs of cool ale later, both of them were on the edge of being drunk, and more than ready to find a bed.

That, on the other hand, was not so easy. All of the taverns were booked and filled to overflowing. Even the "community rooms" in the attics of the taverns ... large, low-ceilinged rooms where people simply spread blankets and bedrolls on the floor and slept beside one another ... were packed with souls. They discovered that the crowded conditions were caused by the flood of incoming armies and militias. The officers of dozens of county regiments had taken up every inch of the lodging space in town. There was simply not a single bed available for rent. The proprietor at the last tavern they visited suggested that they abandon their fruitless search and sleep with their horses in the livery stable.

Walter needed no more convincing. He and Gabe trudged back to the livery and located the stall in which the horses were secured. It was relatively clean and full of fresh hay. They returned to the wagon and fetched two blankets each, which they carried back to the stall. Each man made himself a pallet in the soft hay against the inner wall. After relieving their bladders in the street, they crawled into their nests, burrowed deep into the hay, and covered up with the blankets.

Gabe continued to chatter away about the day's journey, the crowded conditions in Salisbury, and the adventure that awaited them in South Carolina. The ale had somehow managed to loosen his lips a bit more, if that were possible. Walter did his best to ignore the voluminous words of his talkative friend.

Both horses sniffed Walter. They snorted their warm breaths in his face as they nuzzled him with their soft noses. Walter smiled at their invasive curiosity and then fell promptly asleep to the unceasing drone of Gabe's twangy voice.

Walter rose before the dawn. His bones ached from the early morning chill. He discovered that Gabe was awake, and that he had already built a small fire in an empty lot beside the livery. Walter joined his friend and warmed himself beside the flames. He shared with Gabe the cold breakfast that his mother had packed for him. There was plenty for both of them. Walter wanted to get back on the road quickly, so he decided not to waste any time in search of a hot cup of coffee or tea at one of the taverns. They washed down their salt pork, biscuits, and dried apples with tepid water from their canteens.

After a quick visit to the nearby privy to enjoy his morning constitutional, Walter gave his payment to the livery owner and hitched his horses to the wagon. Gabe filled all of their canteens and water gourds from a nearby horse trough. Minutes later, Walter led his team onto the Charlotte Highway. Gabriel was uncharacteristically quiet as he leaned forward with his elbows resting on his knees. He stared thoughtfully toward the southwest and puffed gently on his walnut pipe, wafting thin clouds of fragrant, sweet smoke.

"There's a pow'rful lot of men camped in yon field," Gabe observed.

Walter was thinking exactly the same thing. He, too, had noticed an abundance of firelight in the fields and pastures along the eastern side of the highway. There were hundreds of small campfires twinkling in the open ground between the road and the tree line that was roughly a half-mile distant. It was, no doubt, a military encampment. Salisbury had become an accidental headquarters for the American army. Clearly, the regiments from throughout the Salisbury District were answering the call and mustering at the Patriot outpost.

"Militia, most likely," answered Walter. "Salisbury is their gathering spot these days."

Gabe grunted his affirmation and continued to puff. Walter clucked at the horses and urged them forward. His mind wandered southward to Camden. He wondered what Abigail was doing this morning. He imagined that she was still reclining comfortably in her warm bed, with no plans to arise until absolutely necessary.

Unlike the Billingsley home, the Hamer household included several house slaves to handle the ordinary, mundane tasks of everyday home life. Abigail, thus far in her life, had never had any responsibilities for cooking, cleaning, or otherwise maintaining a home. Walter chuckled at the thought of it. That would all change very soon. There would be no slaves in the Walter Billingsley cottage. He prayed that his wife-to-be might make a smooth transition to life as the spouse of a humble country boy and farmer.

The presence of several men in the distance interrupted his thoughts of Abigail. There was a squad of soldiers in the road less than a quarter-mile ahead. All of them were armed. Some cradled weapons in their arms. Others wore military muskets strapped to their backs. The men appeared to have a roadblock in place.

"What the hell?" Walter muttered.

"They've got the road closed off," answered Gabe, stating the obvious. He spat over the side of the wagon. "Looks like they're usin' a couple of sawhorses."

Walter responded, puzzled, "But why? I've traveled this stretch of road at least a dozen times over the past three years. I have never seen anyone blocking the highway."

"T'will be all right. Let's just play it out," Gabe encouraged. "We're just mindin' our own business. We ain't got nothin' to be affeared 'bout from a bunch of good Patriot boys."

Walter nodded, but lowered the speed of his team. As they approached the roadblock, one of the men minding the small wooden barricade signaled him to halt. The fellow appeared to be older than the other men standing near him. Walter pulled back on the reins and soothingly urged his horses to come to a stop.

"Good morning," Walter declared flatly. "What is going on here? Why have you men blocked the highway?"

"I am Sergeant Micah Anderson of the Henry County, Virginia, militia. We are road guards, here to inspect all wagons, animals, and cargo."

"Why is a Virginny outfit down here blockin' a North Carolina highway? Did you fellers run out of good roads of your own to lord over up in Henry County?" asked Gabe condescendingly.

A rapid silence befell the group of soldiers. A couple of them stepped closer to Walter's rig.

The sergeant responded. "We are authorized and commissioned by General Rutherford to perform this duty, sir. You can rest assured of that."

"Griffith Rutherford?" asked Walter.

"That's the one," responded the sergeant.

"He's in charge of the Salisbury Militia," responded Gabe. "You said you boys was from Virginny."

"General Rutherford commands all forces in this field, sir."

Walter glanced at the other men, and then fixed his eyes on the sergeant. "I'd be grateful if you would ask your men to move those sawhorses and step aside, Sergeant. I have business down in Camden that is urgent, and I have precious little time to spare. As you can see, my wagon is empty. The only weapons and provisions that we have are for our own protection and sustenance. I assure you that we are not Tories. We are pledged to independency. So, if you would please make way ..."

The soldier shook his head slowly, deliberately. "I'm afraid I cannot do that, young man. All travelers are being diverted into our camp at this time. I must ask you to pull off of the road and report to that large tent one hundred yards to your left." He pointed at the tent.

"Why?" retorted Walter stormily.

"For inspection by the quartermaster. The army has been authorized to impress all wagons and carts for the transport of goods and all horses for the cavalry and dragoons."

Walter was confused. His mind raced. His heart rate increased. He could hear the pulse and whoosh of his blood in his ears.

"What does 'impress' mean?" Gabe asked innocently and ignorantly.

The other men at the roadblock chuckled and snickered. Walter felt the moist heat of anger gathering beneath his collar. A bead of sweat formed on his brow. He sensed Gabe tensing, as well.

Walter growled, "It means they aim to take our horses and wagon, Gabe."

"Horse shite!" snapped Gabe. "You militia boys ain't doin' nothin' but takin' advantage of the war to do a little legalized bushwhackin'. Glorified highwaymen, that's what you are! Bandits with a flag! Well, you ain't gettin' none of our stuff. Now get the hell out of our way!" He lowered his voice to a growl. "And don't make me say it again."

Gabriel tossed back the flap of his coat to reveal the two pistols concealed beneath.

A couple of the men at the roadblock whistled. One of them teased, "You ain't goin' to let this li'l tadpole talk to you like that, ere ya, Sarge?"

"Shut your mouth, Byron!" the sergeant barked over his shoulder.

Walter decided to attempt another tactic. Gabriel's indignation and outright resistance did not seem to be getting them anywhere.

Walter pleaded, "Listen, Sergeant. This wagon and team of horses are not mine to give. They belong to my mother."

The soldiers laughed out loud at Walter's mention of his mother. One of them teased, "What's wrong? You need to get home so's your mama can tuck you into bed tonight?" He paused. "Maybe I ought to ride along with you and give her a little tuckin' in later."

The men broke into uproarious laughter. Their laughter, and the insult of his mother's honor, inflamed Walter's simmering ire. He became livid. He could not allow such a wanton display of injustice and dishonor to stand.

He growled, "Sir, you and your merry band of delinquents will not take my family's wagon and horses. I will not allow it."

The sergeant sighed. He was becoming frustrated and impatient. The fact that his authority had been challenged in front of his men was a problem, and he could not let the bold insolence of these two young men go unanswered.

"Listen, boys, I have neither the time nor the inclination to stand here in the middle of the highway and argue with you. I'm ordering you to turn that rig into the field and proceed immediately to the quartermaster's tent. Captain Harris will issue you a voucher for your wagon and animals."

Walter's mind reeled. This could not be happening! He had to get to South Carolina! What about Abigail? How would he ever be able to fetch her home without a wagon and team?

"And what if I don't?" challenged Walter.

The sergeant pulled a pistol menacingly from his belt.

"Then, sir, I will be forced to physically remove you from this wagon and place you in custody for disobeying a lawful military authority. Either way is fine with me. Let's just get on with it."

Walter was outside of his mind with anguish. He was no longer thinking rationally. He cast aside the notion of his own safety. He was determined to go to his beloved Abigail.

He shouted with rage, "You will not take my property!"

He suddenly and unexpectedly snapped the reins and emitted a screeching, "Hyah!" He used the dangling ends of the reins as a whip against the backside of the horses. The animals lurched forward in an explosion of energy and speed.

Gabriel shouted, "Atta boy! Turn 'em loose, Walter! Let's ride!"

The team plowed through the squad of men that blocked the road. Two of them dove to either side and rolled onto their backs in the dust of the roadway. Two others simply sidestepped the animals and removed themselves from the paths of the oncoming rig. Walter's horses split the narrow gap between the wooden barricades that occupied the center of the road. Each of the front wheels of the wagon struck a sawhorse. Both barricades tumbled into the weeds along the edges of road. Walter and Gabe were beyond the checkpoint in a matter of seconds.

They heard the sharp crack of a pistol and felt an impact against the back of the wagon seat. Splinters and chunks of wood exploded into the air and landed on their legs and feet. Walter looked, in horror, to his right and saw a gaping hole in the wood of the seat back. A lead ball had smashed through the lumber, right between the two boys.

"That son of a bitch shot at us!" squealed Gabriel. He whipped his pistols from his belt and spun around to return fire.

"No!" Walter shouted. "Don't shoot back! We just want to be left alone and allowed to go on our way. We don't want any bloodshed."

Walter slapped the reins again and urged his team forward. He glanced back toward the roadblock and grinned when he saw the soldiers fumbling with their firelocks and attempting to load their muskets.

"Them idiots didn't even have their guns loaded and primed!" exclaimed Gabe in disbelief.

"Just be glad they didn't," Walter answered, snapping the reins again. He focused intently on the road ahead of them.

Gabriel checked behind them once again and then began to chuckle. "Lordy be! That uppity sergeant what's-his-nuts sure is pissed!"

Walter glanced back, grinned, and nodded. The sergeant was running around amongst his men, waving his pistol in the air and screaming at no one in particular. Walter returned his attention to the road in front of him, cracked the reins, and continued to urge his team forward. The horses whinnied and galloped enthusiastically, their thick breaths emitting clouds of vapor into the crisp morning air. Walter prayed that he had made a clean getaway, but soon had his hopes dashed. He heard galloping off to his left.

"Rider comin'!" exclaimed Gabe.

Walter glanced once more over his shoulder and saw a lone man on horseback. The rider was approaching through the field from the direction of the encampment. He was gaining quickly on the wagon. He would be upon them within seconds, if not for the tall split-rail fence that separated the field from the road. Walter imagined that it was too tall for a horse to jump. He took some solace in the fact that the fence provided him with a measure of security.

"That boy looks determined," commented Gabe. "We best make tracks."

"Go, girls! Go!" he yelled to his horses. He used the reins as a whip to spur them on.

The rider was almost parallel with the wagon. Walter stole a glance at the man. He appeared to be a little older than Walter and Gabe. He was hatless, and leaning forward over the neck of his horse. A sword and scabbard dangled from his right hip.

"Faster, Walter! He might commence to shootin'!"

"The horses are at top speed, Gabe! They've nothing else to give!"

Suddenly, unimaginably, the rider angled his horse toward the fence. He intended to jump the barricade! Walter was certain that the animal could not make the jump. Still, the huge animal leapt high into the air. It was pointed almost directly at the wagon. Walter could scarcely believe it. His eyes widened in amazement at how quickly and gracefully the powerful animal separated itself from the gravity of the earth.

He thought, for a moment, that the horse and rider might actually land on top of them. Instead, the magnificent animal landed perfectly beside the team that was pulling the wagon. The high chest of the cavalryman's mount slammed into the side of the horse directly in front of Walter. It, in turn, lurched sideways and pressed the tongue of the wagon in the direction of the other horse. The wagon gave a mighty lurch to the right. In that exact moment, the front left wheel struck a hard bump in the road.

"Christ, Almighty!" Gabriel Tate exclaimed as his body launched into the air.

Gabriel was tossed from the wagon and went tumbling into the high, brown weeds that lined the western side of the roadway. Walter looked back and saw Gabe roll to a stop. His friend was not moving. He spun his head around to observe his attacker. The last thing that he saw was the blade of the man's sword coming directly at his face. He felt a painful whack against his left temple. He actually heard the sound of the metal impacting the bones of his face.

Then Walter's entire world went dark …

7

IN THE ARMY NOW

Walter heard what he thought was the sound of distant voices. They seemed garbled and unintelligible, as if the men who spoke them were conversing in some strange, foreign tongue. He wanted to open his eyes and see who was speaking, but it felt as if his eyelids were clasped shut. He concentrated with all his might, focusing every ounce of energy upon opening his eyes. Finally, after a mighty and exhausting effort, his right eyelid parted.

It took a while for his misty, one-eyed vision to clear. He was staring upward at the cream-colored roof of a tent. The voices continued, but they seemed somewhat closer now. And they spoke English. The front of his skull throbbed. Walter strained to turn his head to the left, in the direction of the voices. The slight movement caused his forehead to throb all the more. He saw two shadowy figures, then one was gone … departed through a ring of bright light.

"Ahh! He is awake, at last! Back among the land of the living!"

Walter was confused. He could not comprehend his environment or location. Nothing seemed familiar. He saw the remaining dark, shadowy shape approaching him. As the figure neared, its outline became less and less fuzzy. Soon a face came into view. It was the face of an older, kindly-looking fellow. It seemed strange, but Walter could still only see the man out of his right eye. His left eye remained sealed.

"Feeling better, are we?" The man smiled warmly.

"Huh?" Walter replied.

The man cleared his throat and spoke louder, "I asked if you were feeling better!"

Walter closed his eye and tried to remember what had happened to him, but the memories were not available for his recall.

"Wha ... what happened to me?" he mumbled.

"You received a rather sharp blow to the head and then suffered a nasty fall from a runaway wagon," the man replied. "You are resting in our company infirmary."

Walter was, indeed, lying flat on his back in a small bed. He opened his eye again and glanced around nervously. There were approximately a dozen empty beds spaced throughout the large marquee tent.

"As you can see, you are my one and only patient right now. I just sent my only other customer for today on his way." The man leaned in closer to Walter and winked. "I gave him a little something to loosen his impacted bowels. He will spend the remainder of the day in the privy, I quite imagine!" The man laughed out loud at his prophetic declaration.

Walter remained confused and disoriented. The fellow continued talking.

"It's quite refreshing to have someone who is actually incapacitated and truly in need of my professional care. Most days it seems that all I encounter are silly complaints from sick-call malingerers attempting to shirk their duties for the day."

A sudden surge of memory washed through Walter's mind.

"My wagon! My horses! Gabe! He fell! Where is Gabe?" Walter inquired anxiously.

"Mr. Tate is quite all right, Walter. He is relatively uninjured. The boy suffered a few minor cuts and bruises from his fall, but is otherwise quite well. He is currently visiting with some of our allies from Virginia. I believe he is attempting to sort out a resolution to the conflict that you two have caused."

"How do you know my name?"

"Mr. Tate told me, of course. He was here about an hour ago to check on you."

"An hour ago? How long have I been out?"

"Close to six hours now. You have been sleeping quite soundly. Your body needed the rest in order to restore itself you from your injury."

"So … Gabe's not in jail, then?"

The fellow chuckled. "No, son. He is not in jail. Like I said, he is meeting with the Virginians and sorting things out. I am quite certain that he will return very soon."

Walter considered the man's words. He remembered the Virginia militiamen at the roadblock, and the way in which the one fellow had insulted the dignity of his mother. The memories continued to return to him in a steady, anger-inducing trickle.

"We did not cause any conflict!" Walter declared. "Those bastards on the road tried to take my horses and wagon from me!"

"Which they are authorized to do," answered the man calmly. "There is a war on, you know. The armies have needs that must be supplied by the citizenry from time to time. Such is the reality of wartime."

"So, they simply lie in wait along the highway and hijack unsuspecting travelers who are minding their own business? They abscond with the private property of citizens and then simply hand them a worthless slip of paper? How convenient … and utterly without honor."

Walter attempted to rise from his bed.

"None of that, now! You are in no condition to move. You are confined to this bed until I clear you for duty."

The man reached toward Walter's head. Walter tensed and instinctively moved to avoid the stranger's touch.

"It is quite all right, son. I am a physician. Dr. Horace Murrow, surgeon of the Anson County Regiment ... at your service." The doctor bowed slightly.

Walter relaxed and allowed the man to do his work. Then he had a brief flash of memory ... a vision of a sword slicing the air in the direction of his face.

Walter mumbled, "Am I cut very badly?"

The doctor grinned reassuringly as he removed the protective bandage that covered Walter's left eye.

"You were not cut, at all, Walter. Lieutenant Barnes told me that he merely gave you a firm slap with the flat side of his sword. He claims he was aiming at the back of your head, just to knock you off balance, but he said that you turned toward him just as he swung the weapon. The side of the blade got you across your left temple and eye. There is a tiny tear on your eyelid. It bled a little, but it is nothing of great concern. I have cleaned away the blood, and it should heal nicely. But, you shall have a nasty bruise and a black eye for a week or so."

Dr. Murrow held a candle in front of Walter's eyes and stared intently, then turned Walter's head both ways and examined his ears.

"What are you looking for in my ears, Doc?" asked Walter curiously.

"Bleeding. That can be a sign of a serious injury to your skull. But, no need to worry. You appear to be just fine." The doctor patted Walter gently on the chest. "Son, if you don't mind me asking, how did you get that big scar on your scalp? It looks like a bullet grazed you."

Walter nodded slightly. "It was a bullet, sure enough. A .75 caliber round ball."

"And that little crescent-shaped nick in the top of your right ear?"

Walter grinned. "Another bullet."

"You also have some deep scarring on the front of your scalp. There is a hard knot that must have been there for years, it seems."

"That was the butt of a pistol."

"Interesting," commented the doctor. "Did you obtain all of these injuries at one time, or did you manage to spread them out over a few years?" He grinned.

"I got them all on the same night … back in April of 1776. A Tory by the name of Fanning attacked my home with a band of his militiamen. They killed my father … strung him up in our yard."

"Colonel David Fanning?"

"He was only a Captain when he came to my house," Walter declared without emotion.

"So, you fought back, then?"

Walter nodded grimly. "My brothers and a few other men arrived soon after my father was hanged. We killed most of them. A handful got away … including Fanning."

"So, you are a battle-hardened soldier, then," declared the doctor. "Good for you." He patted Walter's chest once more. "Now, why don't you close your eyes and get some more rest? I will awaken you when your friend returns." He rose to his feet and began to walk away.

Walter called after him, "Dr. Murrow!"

"Yes, Walter?"

"You said a moment ago that I cannot move until you 'clear me for duty.' What did you mean? What duty?"

"In the army, of course."

"But I'm not in the army!" Walter protested.

The doctor exhaled and pursed his lips. "Yes. I'm afraid you are. In the Virginia Regulars. Or, at least, you will be soon."

"But, I'm not from Virginia!"

Dr. Murrow shrugged, smiled, turned, and walked toward his desk.

May 3, 1780 – United States Encampment – Salisbury, North Carolina
"Sergeant, you are not listening to me. You cannot compel me to join your army. You have no lawful claim over me. I reside in Guilford County, North Carolina. I cannot legally or morally be forced to serve in the Virginia Line."

Walter was standing inside the tent that served as the office for a newly-forming Virginia regiment. As yet, the unit did not even have a numeric designation. The officers and sergeants over the outfit merely referred to themselves as the Virginia Regulars. But the leaders of the fledgling regiment were anxious to fill their muster rolls. They greatly desired to march in relief of their fellow statesmen and compatriots in the besieged garrison at Charlestown.

Sergeant Thomas Armstrong, acting first sergeant in the regiment, sat behind a small field desk near a corner of the tent. A handmade sign on the desk read, "Capt. Jno Williams, Commander." The sergeant stared thoughtfully at a piece of paper in his right hand.

"It says here, Mr. Billingsley, that you were manning the reins of a wagon on the nearby highway, and that you intentionally demolished a legal roadblock and endangered several of our men. One of them was injured severely."

"That's interesting," Walter responded sarcastically. "I've been under the doctor's care for two days now, and have seen no evidence of any injured soldiers. Indeed, I have been the only patient in his infirmary. I believe that I was the only one injured in the event."

"That is what is in my report. It is the official record."

"It must be nice to be able to construct your own truth," grumbled Walter.

"Quite. Nevertheless, do you deny that you were driving the wagon in question?"

"Of course not. It is my wagon."

"Then, you admit to driving through the roadblock?"

"Yes. Your men had no right to stop me and my friend. We were tending to our own business on a public road when they stopped us and attempted to steal my personal property."

"It is not considered stealing, Mr. Billingsley. It is impressment for government use. I assure you that such action is quite legal during times of war."

"You can give it any fancy name that you might like, Sergeant, but it is robbery nonetheless. Now, if you would kindly point me to where I can reclaim my wagon and horses, I would like to be on my way. My fiancé is awaiting my arrival in Camden. I am going there to evacuate her back to Guilford. We are to be married next month."

"I'm afraid that will not be possible, Mr. Billingsley."

"What do you mean? What will not be possible?"

"None of your requests, boy. Your wagon and team are gone."

"Gone?" Walter exploded with rage. "Gone where?"

"They are bound for Camden as we speak, laden with supplies and munitions for our forces in South Carolina."

Walter seethed. "So, let me get this straight. You have confiscated my property in order to deliver cargo to the very place where I was headed?" He lost his temper and launched into a rant. "I would have been more than happy to deliver your goods for you, Sergeant. All anyone had to do was ask! But, no! That arrogant sergeant at the roadblock had to act all tough and mighty and put on a show of authority for his men. He is the one who caused all of this! I demand satisfaction for my troubles, and I demand that my property be returned!"

Sergeant Armstrong rose from his chair. He leaned calmly over the desk. "You are in no position to make demands, young man. You have broken the law and endangered soldiers in the service of Virginia. You have one of two options." He pointed stormily at a document on his desk. "You can either sign this enlistment paper immediately, or I will turn you over to the officer in charge of this encampment's brig. You will be cast into our temporary jail amongst all manner of hooligans, deserters, murderers, and brigands until you can be transported north to a prison camp in Virginia. And I'm quite sure that the local thugs would greatly enjoy the company of a nice, tender, young lad such as yourself. It's your choice. But you must make it right now."

Walter was beginning to panic.

"What about my friend? What will you do with Gabriel?"

"He will receive the same offer that I just made to you. As soon as you leave my office, I will be sending Corporal Adams to fetch him."

Walter stammered. "How … how long is the enlistment?"

"Three years, or until the end of the war. Whichever comes first."

Walter was trapped and he knew it. There would be no trip to Camden. There would be no wedding. Walter Billingsley, the farmer, was about to become Walter Billingsley, the soldier.

"I thought that we were fighting for liberty and freedom, Sergeant. But this entire affair reeks with a stench of tyranny and injustice."

"You have the luxury to wrestle with such philosophical quandaries, Mr. Billingsley. I am but a soldier. I have a war to fight, and to win. I am simply doing the very best job that I can with the resources and means that are available to me."

Walter stared numbly at the enlistment form. "May I inform my mother and my family of the situation?"

"Of course, Mr. Billingsley. We send dispatches regularly northward to Virginia each Wednesday and Saturday. Our riders go through Guilford County. They can deliver a correspondence to your family, or at least to a citizen in the community who can take it to your mother."

"And my fiancé in Camden?"

The sergeant grimaced. "I cannot guarantee that we can transport correspondence southward, but we can try. Perhaps we can send a message with a future delivery of cargo. If your training goes well, you may be able to make a delivery for us in the coming weeks. Perhaps you could make a personal visit and inform your future bride."

Walter nodded. That was, at least, a tiny bit of good news. Still, he was depressed. Anguished. Broken.

"What about my property? My family and our farm will suffer greatly from the loss of the wagon and horses."

"You will receive a receipt from our quartermaster for your wagon and animals, assigning fair market value. You will be reimbursed after the conclusion of hostilities."

"*If* we win the war," Walter responded. His emphasized the word, "if."

The sergeant nodded and echoed Walter exact inflection, "*If* we win the war..."

Sergeant Armstrong picked up a goose feather quill, dipped it in an ink well, and held it over the top of the enlistment paper.

Walter inhaled a deep breath, closed his eyes for just a moment, and uttered a silent prayer. He stepped resolutely toward the desk, took the quill from the sergeant, and then reluctantly signed his name on the appropriate line.

The sergeant extended his right hand toward Walter. "Welcome to the Virginia Regulars, Private Billingsley."

May 6, 1780 – Guilford Courthouse, North Carolina

Elizabeth Billingsley had never imagined that solitude would be a part of her life. She had, after all, raised nine children. The Billingsley home had always been full of voices, quarrels, emotions, and noise. But seven of those children had already reached adulthood. The first six were gone and living in their own homes. Walter would be out on his own soon. All that remained in her household were Basil and Martha, and it seemed that lately even they sought every available opportunity to avoid remaining at home with their mother.

Once again, Elizabeth was spending Saturday completely alone. She reveled in her silent, restful day. These increasingly common periods of aloneness pained her at first, but she had rapidly developed an appreciation for the peace and quiet of solitude. On this particular day, she had already enjoyed a light luncheon and a brief afternoon nap. For the past hour, she had been sitting on her front porch with needle, cloth, and thread, stitching a new Sunday weskit for Basil. Of course, she took every opportunity to greet and converse with the neighbors and passers-by. She also enjoyed a fresh cup of tea, flavored with just a dash of her "medicinal" whiskey.

She knew that her quiet day would end eventually. Basil was at the family farm. He claimed that he was repairing a broken fence, but Elizabeth suspected that he was secretly working on Walter's house. His older brother had departed for South Carolina without finishing the floors in his cottage, and Elizabeth had overheard Basil whispering with Margaret about the unfinished work. Margaret, too, had left mid-morning to go on a carriage ride with two of her friends. They planned to enjoy an early dinner, followed by a garden party in the afternoon.

So, Elizabeth rested, sewed, sipped, socialized, and otherwise entertained herself with her own thoughts. She had actually taken a break from her sewing, and was sitting, eyes closed, in a moment of silent prayer. She was lost in the memory of her departed husband, James. It was while enjoying these cool afternoons on the veranda that she missed him the most. But the voice of an unexpected mid-afternoon guest interrupted her quiet, leisurely Saturday.

"Good day, Mrs. Billingsley! May I join you for a spell?"

She opened her eyes and saw Daniel Jeter, a middle-aged businessman, gentleman, and widower of Guilford County, standing on the other side of her front gate. He was sporting his usual warm, contagious smile.

Mr. Jeter was a pleasant enough fellow, but Elizabeth felt a bit uncomfortable around him in recent days. The widower had been showing just a little too much personal interest in her. He went out of his way to speak to her in public settings. One morning, he offered to carry her parcels while she was shopping at Tolford's store. He had even made a couple of recent deliveries for local businessmen to the Billingsley home, all in the pretense of being "neighborly."

But Elizabeth was convinced that the man had fixed his sights upon her with a plan for courtship and marriage. The very thought of it was abhorrent to her. Yes, he was a nice enough fellow, and quite pleasant to be around. Most would even consider him to be a "good catch" for a local widow woman. But Elizabeth's heart belonged to James Billingsley, even in death. She could not imagine ever sharing a home, life, thoughts, or bed with another man. She desired to carry her love for James Billingsley to her own grave.

Still, the kindness and attention were very nice, indeed. Elizabeth decided to make the most of it, short of encouraging the man toward the notion of romance.

She smiled warmly and responded, "Of course, Mr. Jeter. Come and sit. There is fresh tea in the strainer and hot water in the pot."

"Wonderful! I don't mind if I do."

He approached the house along the brick walkway leading up to the steps. Elizabeth could not help but notice what a handsome man that he was. He was wearing a smoky blue weskit over a brilliant white shirt. His breeches were dark gray in color. His socks perfectly matched the unique blue of his weskit. His black buckle shoes appeared new, and freshly polished. He sported a perfectly tied, brand-new black cocked hat. The flowery cockade matched the blue of his weskit, as well. He carried a shiny brass walking stick in his right hand, though he had absolutely no need for one.

As he stepped up onto the porch, Elizabeth greeted him properly. "I pray that you are faring well today, Mr. Jeter."

"Oh, well, indeed, Mrs. Billingsley. And I thank you for your blessing."

"Would you like some tea?"

"Yes, please. That would be quite refreshing, especially if it were flavored with some of your delicious spirits." He winked mischievously.

Elizabeth grinned. "I think that can be arranged. Please, have a seat."

Mr. Jeter removed his hat and sat in the chair that was positioned strategically on the other side of the serving table. He rested his hat on his right knee. Elizabeth poured a cup of hot water and placed the bowl of her silver tea strainer into the steaming liquid. She then reached beneath the table and retrieved a small, gray ceramic jug, which she placed beside the teacup.

"There you go, Mr. Jeter. We can let that steep a little, and then you can add as much of the spirits as you would like."

"I thank you most kindly, Mrs. Billingsley."

A brief period of somewhat awkward silence ensued.

"'Tis a lovely day, isn't it?" Elizabeth observed, breaking the silence.

"Indeed, it is. And all the lovelier, as I am privileged to observe it from here at your side on this beautiful veranda."

"Silver-tongued devil!" she thought. *"I walked right into that one ..."*

"Are you just out enjoying the day, or did a particular purpose bring you to my home?"

"Both, Mrs. Billingsley. Of course, it is always a joy to spend time with you." He smiled, flirtingly ... mischievously ...

Elizabeth blushed. She hated the fact that she enjoyed his flirtations. She punished herself mentally for entertaining such joy at the words and expressions of a man.

"You are too kind, sir. But, beyond the joy of my company, what other purpose has brought you here today?"

He reached inside the left-hand pocket of his weskit.

"I had a curious encounter with a soldier at the courthouse. He was a militiaman from Virginia, I believe ... a dispatch rider headed north. The gentleman bore a letter addressed to you." He removed a carefully folded and sealed letter from his pocket and handed it to her.

It was a military notification. Everyone dreaded receiving such a letter. They rarely contained good news. Elizabeth received the correspondence with trembling hands, but dared not look at it. She turned the addressed side down immediately in an effort to shield her heart from the potential pain contained in the letter's words. Her heart flip-flopped from anxiety.

Her mind raced. Why would a Virginia soldier carry a letter for her? Her son, John, was the only family member who was deployed with the military at this time. Surely, John had no interaction with or service in the Virginia military. But since it was an army rider who bore the letter, it must be regarding John! There could be no other explanation.

Mr. Jeter discerned her anguish and hesitation. "Are you afraid that it is bad news? Would you like for me to open the letter and read it for you?"

"No, thank you, Mr. Jeter. It is addressed to me. I must contend with whatever news it holds. But I fear that there may be something wrong with my son, John. He is in the field with his company of militia."

"Shall I leave you to your privacy, then?" he offered.

"Do you mind?" she answered immediately … perhaps a little too quickly. She did, indeed, wish to be alone. "I would never ask you to leave, Mr. Jeter, but I am most anxious to read the contents of this correspondence, and I hesitate to do so in front of company."

He rose to his feet and bowed to Elizabeth in a most gentlemanly manner. "I understand completely, Mrs. Billingsley. I pray that it is filled with good news instead of bad. If, per chance, you need me for anything at all, please do not hesitate to send for me."

"Thank you for your kindness and understanding, Mr. Jeter."

"Perhaps we can enjoy tea and conversation another time," he responded tenderly.

She smiled hesitantly. "Yes, perhaps we can."

"I bid you good evening, then, Mrs. Billingsley. Until next time …" He nodded his head respectfully and returned his hat to his head.

She stood. "Yes. Until next time, Mr. Jeter."

He turned smartly and strode toward the steps. Elizabeth watched him as he ambled down the brick walkway and through the gate. She smiled warmly when he turned one last time to wave goodbye. She nodded politely in response.

Once he was gone, Elizabeth collapsed into her chair. She stared at back of the letter for a moment, praying fervently that it did not contain news of the injury or death of her third son. Then, overwhelmed with anxiety, she turned it over to read the address. She knew immediately who had written the letter.

"That is Walter's handwriting!" she exclaimed.

She tore into the letter. Her hands trembled as she read.

My Dearest Mother,

I am writing you to inform you of a great misfortune that has befallen me on my trek to Camden. I encountered soldiers from Virginia, encamped near Salisbury, who desired to confiscate our wagon and horses on the public roadway. I refused their orders and attempted to proceed on my way, but was apprehended and taken into custody. The army has, indeed, taken ownership our wagon and team for military use.

In our attempt to flee, Gabriel and I apparently injured one of their men. He was not injured seriously, but it was enough to cause them to regard us as criminals. In lieu of pressing formal charges against us, the military authorities gave us the option of enlisting in the Virginia Line. They demanded that we choose between jail in Virginia or service in the army. Needless to say, we are both now soldiers encamped here with the Virginians. I have been compelled into enlistment for a period of three years, or until the end of the war. I believe that we will march to Charlestown very soon.

Thus far, I have been unable to get word to Abigail. There have been no postal riders dispatched to the south for several days. Please, if you are able, write to her and inform her of my predicament. Please make her understand that none of this is of my own choosing. I simply could not endure incarceration in the North.

Please tell her that I am very sorry, and that I will contact her as soon as I am able. Gabriel is here with me as I am writing to you. He would be most grateful if you could inform his parents regarding our situation.

Pray for me, Dearest Mother, as I am greatly afraid of the fate that awaits me on the battlefield. Pray that I might see home again and that my marriage, though delayed, still awaits me in the not-too-distant future.

Your Devoted Son,
Walter

Elizabeth's hands dropped into her lap, still clasping the shocking letter.

She prayed, *"Oh, God … please watch over my boy. If it be Your will, Lord, please place your hand of protection upon him, and bring him back home to me. And watch over that boy, Gabriel Tate, as well, Holy Father. You know as well as I that he needs it …"*

May 14, 1780 – United States Encampment – Salisbury, North Carolina

Gabriel Tate stuffed another finished cartridge into a partially-filled black leather cartridge box. He examined his fingers on both hands and gingerly rubbed the tips of each one with his thumbs. The skin of his fingertips was worn thin, sore, and stained black from handling gunpowder. He glanced at Walter, who sat silently on the bench beside him, and was in the process of rolling a paper tube around a .69 caliber ball.

Cartridge rolling and working in the kitchen seemed to be the primary tasks and duties of the handful of recruits in the Virginia Regulars. Beyond the scope of menial labor, Walter and Gabe remained unfamiliar with most other aspects of military life. Sergeant Armstrong had marched them and eleven other recruits around the field beside the camp a couple of times. They carried fake guns whittled from long sticks of firewood. Gabe actually enjoyed the walking and marching. For him it was a break from the monotony of camp life. Walter thought that the entire exercise was idiotic and a complete waste of time. He merely stared at the chunk of gun-shaped firewood in his hands and wondered where his confiscated Virginia long rifle had gone.

It was a Sunday afternoon, their second Lord's Day in the encampment. Sunday mornings were better than most other days. The men were allowed to slumber in their tents and relax until well after the sunrise. For those who were interested, there were a couple of worship services conducted by preachers from the nearby community. The men gathered around campfires, wrote letters to home, smoked their pipes, and sang songs. There was even the occasional jug of rum that found its way around the campfires. Sunday mornings were very quiet and most enjoyable.

During the afternoons, however, the men were expected to return to their ordinary daily labors. For Gabriel and Walter, and most of the other recruits of the aspiring regiment, that meant rolling cartridges ... the lowliest of the low among all army tasks.

The two Guilford County friends had been working in silence for almost an hour. It was almost as if Gabriel had run out of words. Walter had been enjoying the glorious respite from Gabriel's endless chatter, but after only one hour of quiet reflection, Gabe could no longer stand the absence of conversation.

"Damn it! If this here is army life, they can all have it," moaned Gabriel Tate as he rammed another cartridge into a pouch. He nudged Walter playfully with his elbow. "Do you reckon we'll ever do anythin' else besides march around in the cow pasture and roll these God-forsaken cartridges?"

Walter shrugged. He was completely in agreement with his friend, but had reached a point beyond actually caring. Walter was heartbroken, forlorn, and depressed. He hated being compelled to remain in this encampment and serve in this army. All that he could think about was his beautiful bride-to-be, and the hopeless reality that their impending wedding would either be postponed long-term or, even worse, never occur at all. He prayed that Abigail would somehow learn about his unavoidable predicament and not think that he had jilted her or gotten "cold feet" at the prospect of marriage.

Walter had done everything that he possibly could to inform both Abigail and his mother regarding their situation. He had written letters to his mother and to Abigail on the day of their compulsory enlistment into the Virginia Regulars. He saw Captain Williams place the letter to his mother in a dispatch case headed north. He did not, however, know the disposition of his letter to Abigail. Perhaps it had been sent south, but it was equally likely that his precious letter was buried beneath a pile of papers on the officer's desk. He simply did not know.

Truth be told, he was afraid to ask about the letter. Captain Williams and Sergeant Armstrong were both in foul, insufferable moods. They each had grand plans of forming a Continental Line regiment and marching off to the salvation of Charlestown. But so far, instead of enlisting two hundred men, they had a grand total of thirteen. Recruits were not, exactly, flocking to their encampment.

Neither were there any more innocent passers-by available for capture at their roadblock. Word had spread quickly throughout the region. Because of the widely-reported confiscation of goods and property, there was no more civilian traffic along the road to Charlotte. Walter and Gabriel had been among the unlucky final few who attempted to pass through.

It still galled Walter ... everything that he and Gabriel had endured. He hated that the circumstances of his life were so far beyond his control. At night, he prayed to God and begged for intervention and mercy. More than once he proclaimed to the Lord that what had happened to them was positively, absolutely unfair.

Then he heard in his mind the words that his mother had spoken to him several years before. It was ironic, really. It was way back in the late summer of 1776. Walter's older brothers were headed off to war against the Cherokee. Walter had actually *wanted* to join the army at that time! He *wanted* to join a regiment and march off to war! But his mother had forbidden him. She demanded that he stay home and help her take care of the house and farm. And Walter had declared those exact same words to her. They were the words that he had just repeated to God in his prayer.

"*It is not fair!*"

He relived in his mind that moment when his mother wiped her hands on her apron and declared, "*Get used to it, Walter. This world is full of all manner of things unjust and unfair. It's best you learn that lesson now so that you will be prepared to deal with lowly circumstance and heartbreak later.*"

Well ... later had officially arrived. And Walter found himself up to his neck in lowly circumstance and heartbreak.

An invasive, harsh voice ripped him from his indulgence of self-pity. It was Sergeant Armstrong.

"Billingsley! Tate! Enough with the cartridges! Report to your tent and gather your belongings and supplies. You need to pack a week's worth of rations. Go ahead and take two full cartridge cases each. Pack all of your gear and prepare for march at first light."

Walter responded, "I do not want cartridges, Sergeant. I want my rifle back. Where is it?"

"Captain Williams has your rifles in his tent. Don't worry … he's been saving them for you. I reckon you two will be our sharpshooters. Go ahead and grab two or three horns of powder apiece and plenty of patches. We need all of the munitions we can carry."

He turned and began to walk back toward the regimental tent.

Gabe called out, "Where are we headed, Sarge?"

The sergeant stopped and turned to face them. "Charlestown, boys. We're going to try to break through and relieve the besieged forces there. Since we don't have enough men for our own regiment, we will be used as replacements in one of the other Virginia regiments once we arrive. Ready or not, we're headed for the war."

The sergeant turned and continued on his march toward his tent.

"Ready or not …" echoed Gabe.

"Not," declared Walter.

8

CHANGE OF DIRECTION

May 21, 1780 – Somewhere East of the Yadkin River – North Carolina

The men of the Captain Williams' tiny company of Virginia Regulars labored to climb a steep, densely forested hill. The incline was so great that the hillside was, quite literally, in their faces. It was almost impossible to locate any stable footing. The only way to successfully ascend the imposing hill was by hanging on to small trees, vines, and saplings. Four men had already slipped and tumbled out of control down the slope before crashing violently against one of the trees below. Minor injuries abounded. One man likely had a broken arm.

The men were spent. They had been slowly and progressively slogging their way through the dense, jungle-like forests of the Carolina wilderness for the past two days. The would-be soldiers were miserable, exhausted, hungry, and thirsty. They were also lost. Unbeknownst to their commander, even after six grueling days of walking and climbing, they remained less than twenty-five miles from Salisbury, and were disastrously off course from any reasonable route to Charlestown.

"These idiots don't have the first idea where they're headed," Gabriel Tate whispered to Walter. "How long you reckon we'll keep on wanderin' 'bout in these God-forsaken mountains and woods?"

Just as the final word of his question departed his lips, Gabe's left foot slipped on a moss-covered rock, causing him to fall face-forward into the dank, musty carpet of leaves on the steep hillside. He emitted a loud and resounding, "Bloody hell!" He instantly slid fifteen feet down the hillside before stopping his fall by grabbing hold of a fortuitously-positioned wild grape vine.

Walter made sure that his friend was uninjured, but did not respond to his question or angry outburst. Walter was too frustrated and angry, himself, to comment. The Virginians, ignorant of the geography and topography of the Carolinas, did not have a clue as to their current location, nor any notion of where they were going.

Walter and Gabe, on the other hand, were all-too-aware of their exact location. They were lost in the dense, unsettled forests of the Uwharrie Mountains. These were not large, imposing mountains by any standard. Indeed, they were little more than hills. But the thickness of the vegetation, combined with a never-ending network of gullies, ditches, holes, and caves, made for tedious, exhausting travel on foot.

If Captain Williams had only listened to Walter five days prior, they would not be entangled in their current predicament. Early in their journey, Walter had attempted to convince Captain Williams that the quickest route to Charlestown was to travel the roads to the southwest. That well-traveled route would take them through Charlotte Town, the Waxhaws, and Camden. It also contained the best roads, and there were plenty of water sources and supplies available for foraging. But the obstinate, prideful Virginian was not about to take the word of a backwoods lad from North Carolina.

The captain's arrogant response still rang in Walter's ears. *"Private Billingsley, when I require your assistance as guide, I will ask for it. I have a consummate and instinctive sense of direction. We shall cross the Yadkin River and then proceed on the most direct overland route toward Charlestown."* What a snobbish, elitist remark it had been. Walter's pride stung smartly for a couple of days after the exchange.

But, now it was Captain Williams who was stinging from his pride-induced foolishness. His "most direct overland route," of course, led through some of the most remote, untamed, unsettled land in central North Carolina. Now, his men were exhausted, out of food, and dangerously short of water. They could not progress much further under current conditions.

Walter cast a quick glance at the captain. The man appeared to be nearing the end of his own physical and emotional rope. He was resting against a tree and attempting to coax one more drop of water from his parched canteen. Deep in his heart, Walter relished in the man's sufferings. He wanted the hard-headed captain to experience even more affliction as a consequence of his prideful stubbornness.

Still, Walter could not stand to see his fellow soldiers endure any more of the needless hardships caused by this man's poor leadership. As the captain and Sergeant Armstrong began once again to wander toward the southwest, following a spur that would lead them even deeper into the mountains, Walter felt compelled to speak.

"Captain Williams!"

"What is it, Billingsley?" the man groaned, annoyed.

"Sir, I know that you have an instinctive sense of direction, but your instincts are about to take us deeper into these hills. If we simply follow this draw to our east, it will take us down to the Voharee Creek and fresh water."

The captain glanced suspiciously in the direction that Walter had indicated.

"You are certain of this, Billingsley?"

"Yes, sir. Absolutely certain, sir."

"How do you know?"

"Because I am familiar with this land, sir. I have been in these hills before, and I know that you are headed in the wrong direction. We need to camp by the creek tonight, and then follow it downstream tomorrow toward the Yadkin. There is a shallow ford just above the convergence of the two waterways. We can get across the Yadkin there, and then cross the flatlands and head southwest toward the Waxhaws."

The captain shook his head. He began, "But the most direct route ..."

"Christ, Almighty!" Gabe Tate shrieked, angrily interrupting the officer. "Haven't you heard a word that Walter just said? You've taken us into the middle of the God-forsaken hills of Uwharrie, Captain! There are no roads or Indian trails here ... hell, the Indians don't even come up here, anymore! The old Uwharrie Indians who used to live up here all died off. I'd venture a guess that they likely starved to death. Bears don't come up here. Elk don't come up here. Have you laid eyes on the first rabbit or possum? You prob'ly can't shake a tree and get a single squirrel to fall out! They don't even come up here!"

Several of the men snickered at Gabe's colorful illustrations given in defense of Walter's admonition.

Gabe continued, somewhat less animated, "Sir, if we keep followin' the path that you've got stuck in that Virginia head of yours, we're either gonna starve to death or still be wanderin' these hills whenever the next war comes 'round!"

The captain stared at Gabe in total disbelief. He had never been addressed thusly by a lowly private. He seemed to be unable to even verbalize a response.

"Please, Captain," Gabe pleaded. "Listen to Walter. Damnation! Listen to me! We live here. We know where we are, and we know how to get you to Charlestown. Please, sir, allow us to guide the way."

Finally, Sergeant Armstrong spoke up. "Captain, I think you should listen to these lads. I believe they know what they are talking about. They know this country. You can trust them."

Captain Williams cut his eyes at the sergeant. It was abundantly clear that he did not like being challenged by his subordinates, but he was running out of options. If they did not locate a source of water soon, there could be an outright mutiny among the men.

His countenance fell as he acquiesced and subdued his willful arrogance. He did not speak. He simply nodded his affirmation to the sergeant.

Armstrong shouted immediately, “Billingsley! Tate! Take the point. Guide us to the creek.”

The spirits of the men and their captain lifted greatly when they reached the Voharee Creek. Its waters ran swift, clear, and cold. The men lay down on the rocky bank and drank from the refreshing water until they were bloated and almost sick. A couple of them began to build fires. They did not need the captain to give an order to make camp. The men were done for the day. They had reached their campsite. Captain Williams didn’t seem to mind. He was already flat on his back and sleeping soundly beside the creek.

Walter and Gabe filled their canteens and then approached Sergeant Armstrong.

“Sergeant, Gabe and I are going to scout downstream a few hundred yards and see if we can maybe find us a little meat. The men are going to be hungry after that water works its way through them.”

Sergeant Armstrong grunted. “I thought Private Tate said that the bears and squirrels don’t even come up into these hills.”

Gabe grinned sheepishly. “I didn’t say nothin’ ‘bout the deer-critters, though.”

Sergeant Armstrong responded with his own smile. “Just make sure you boys get back before nightfall. We sure as hell can’t find our way out of here without you.”

“We’ll be back, Sarge,” Walter affirmed. “Hopefully with a nice doe for roasting.”

Two hours later Gabe dropped a fat doe in a small clearing beside the creek, about a half-mile downstream from their encampment.

They field-dressed the deer, cut a small sapling for a carrying pole, and then suspended the animal from the pole by tying leather thongs around its hooves. It took them less than an hour to reach camp. The men cheered their return. The freshly-butchered meat was suspended over a half-dozen fires within minutes. Less than an hour later the men gorged themselves on a feast of steaming, tender, smoky venison.

Their fortunes had changed dramatically, and they were looking forward to their young North Carolina guides leading them out of the dense wilderness and back to a more navigable path to Charlestown.

May 26, 1780 – Twenty Miles East of Charlotte Town

It took two more days for the soldiers to make it out of the hills and down to the banks of the Yadkin River. They forded the Yadkin just north of the point of convergence with Voharre Creek. Captain Williams ordered the establishment of an extended camp. He wanted to take some time to rest his men and replenish their rations. He dispersed his soldiers to search the countryside for provisions. Two days later, their packs and haversacks were stuffed with dried meat and their canteens were full. They continued their journey toward the southwest. Walter and Gabe resumed their duties as scouts.

Captain Williams' detachment soon entered a more densely settled area along the Rocky River. This was Mecklenburg County, a populated but harsh frontier region in North Carolina. It was occupied primarily by Scotch-Irish settlers from southern Pennsylvania. Most of those families had migrated southward to escape their memories of indentured servitude and to claim and conquer lands of their own. They hacked their meager existences out of the dense forests of Mecklenburg County. They were a hearty, headstrong lot, and they hated the British and King George with a vengeance.

Walter and Gabe continued to enjoy their roles as scouts for the detachment. They soon began to encounter small farms and cabins in the woods along the Rocky River. Oddly, scant few of the homes seemed inhabited. A few were old and, as evidenced by their unkempt states, abandoned. However, about two hours before nightfall, the scouts spotted a well-kept farm. They approached the home cautiously. They took cover behind a four-foot-high split rail fence and watched the cabin for a short while. Seeing nothing suspicious, they decided to make contact.

Walter cupped his hands to his mouth and called out, "Hello in the house! May we approach?"

They heard the sounds of excitement and sudden movement inside the home. Chairs scraped against the wood floors. Footsteps pounded. A small child cried. There were also muffled, anguished voices emanating from behind the log walls. Several minutes later the door opened slightly and the barrel of a rifle emerged, pointing in their general direction.

"What do you want?" called a deep voice from behind the door. "I don't recognize your voice. We don't take kindly to strangers 'round here. You'd best be on your way."

"He's not a very trusting soul, is he?" whispered Gabe, grinning.

Walter ignored his friend. He spoke loudly, "We are seeking information, sir. We are scouts for the Virginia Regulars, making our way south from Salisbury toward Charlestown."

"How many of you are there?" the man demanded.

"Nineteen total in our party, but only two of us are scouting forward. The others are about a half-mile behind us and headed in this general direction."

"Why are you way over here on the Rocky River if you're headed to Charlestown?" asked the man suspiciously.

Gabe chuckled and shook his head in disgust.

Walter answered, "That's a long and painful story, sir. My captain from Virginia gets all the credit. He seems to have something against marching over well-traveled roads."

"Sounds 'bout like somethin' an officer might foul up," agreed the invisible stranger. "Come on out where I can see you. Weapons over your head."

Walter and Gabe complied. Moments later a middle-aged gentleman emerged from the immaculate and splendidly-constructed cabin. He kept his rifle trained on them.

"We can leave our guns and blades here against this tree, if it would make you feel any better, sir," Walter suggested.

"I would appreciate that," the man responded. His voice reflected a reduction in his suspicion and tension.

Walter and Gabe leaned their flintlocks against a large oak tree and then placed their pistols and knives on the ground nearby. They turned and faced the man, hands high in the air. He motioned for them to join him.

"C'mon over here and let's set a spell and talk. You boys thirsty? I have some hard cider left over from last fall that still has a pretty good kick."

Gabe licked his lips and grinned. "That sounds mighty good to me!"

"You can put your hands down, now," the man declared.

The boys lowered their hands and followed their host toward two benches that sat beneath a large pine tree.

The fellow yelled toward the cabin, "Margaret! Everything's all right! Bring us out three bottles of cider! And tell the young 'uns not to fret. These boys are Virginia soldiers!" He turned and offered his hand. "Gentlemen, my name is Ephraim Farr. Welcome to my home."

Walter shook his hand and nodded. "Thank you, Mr. Farr. I'm Walter Billingsley. This is my good friend, Gabriel Tate." Gabe shook the man's hand.

Mr. Farr motioned to one of the benches. "Sit, boys. Have a rest. My wife will be along shortly with our drinks. What part of Virginia are you from?"

"We're not from Virginia," answered Gabe.

"We're actually from up in Guilford County," Walter added.

"But you said you were with the Virginia Regulars …"

Gabe grinned and nodded. "Another very long story, sir. Walter here didn't take too kindly to the army commandeerin' his wagon, and we tried to roll through one of their roadblocks. Things got a little sporty after that. Let's just say that we got volunteered for the Virginia soldierin' job."

"Oh!" responded Mr. Farr, eyes wide. "Lucky you." He grinned.

A beautiful woman, several years younger than Mr. Farr, approached from the house. She carried three corked glass bottles and a platter filled with bread and smoked pork. Walter stood as she approached. He tugged at Gabe's coat and encouraged him to follow suit. Gabe rose quickly to his feet, as well. Both boys nodded respectfully to the woman.

Ephraim Farr rose and placed his right arm protectively around her back. "Mr. Billingsley, Mr. Tate … this is my wife, Margaret."

Both boys held their hats against their chests and nodded.

"Good day, Ma'am," mumbled Walter. "We are pleased to meet you, and thankful for your hospitality."

She smiled warmly. "Not at all, boys. It is my pleasure, indeed. I am grateful for your service to our nation. I have a son in the local militia who will one day be called to serve, I have no doubt. My other sons are too young for the army, praise God. I pray that this war will end before they ever receive a call to battle." She nodded to her husband. "Do you require anything else, Ephraim?"

"No, Dear. But we need some privacy for our parley. If you could, please keep the children inside for a while, until we are finished."

"As you wish, Ephraim." She nodded to Walter and Gabe. "Gentlemen ..." She then turned smartly and walked quickly back toward the cabin.

Mr. Farr and the young men returned to their seats. Their host popped the corks from two of the bottles and handed them to Walter and Gabe. They were thirsty, so they drank quickly. Walter had drained half of the bottle without even taking time to enjoy the tart sweetness of the beverage or the tickle of the fruit ale's bubbles. He began to feel its effects quickly, though, as soon as the alcohol landed in the pit of his empty stomach. It sent waves of tingly warmth throughout his body. Gabe dug into the smoked pork and bread without waiting for an invitation. He handed a slice of each to Walter. Mr. Farr grinned at Gabe's enthusiasm.

"So, your son is in the local militia?" Walter inquired as he chewed hungrily on the meat and bread.

"He's not my son. He's my wife's oldest son from her first marriage. They had three boys before her husband was killed in a tragic accident. The lads and I never quite took to one another. They left and struck out on their own as soon as the oldest came of age." Mr. Farr's countenance clouded, and he stared blankly toward the nearby forest. "They're good boys, all of them. But they were never mine, and I was not their papa. I wish it could have been different ..." His voice grew quiet as he became lost within his regrets. There was a moment of disconcerting silence.

"What is his name?" asked Walter, attempting to alleviate the awkwardness. "We may run into one another someday."

"James Hamilton," responded Mr. Farr. "He's from right here in Mecklenburg County." It appeared that he wished to change the subject altogether. "So ... Mr. Billingsley, why is your little outfit headed south?"

"Our captain has a mind to take some action that might help relieve the besieged army there," answered Walter. "I am not quite certain what he can hope to accomplish with only nineteen men, but he feels compelled to link up with other forces there and make an attempt."

"Then, you have not heard about Charlestown?" asked Farr with a measure of surprise.

"Heard what?" asked Gabe through smacking, greasy lips.

"The city has fallen."

Gabe stopped chewing and stared wide-eyed at Walter.

"What? When?" Walter demanded.

"Two weeks ago, on May 12. General Lincoln surrendered over 3,000 men. The whole lot of them. It was tragic. The Lobsterbacks have been setting up house in Charlestown ever since, and are just beginning to move out into the low country."

Gabe slapped Walter on the arm. "Hell, Walter! That was a couple days before we even left Salisbury! We've been wanderin' these damned hills and woods for no good reason!" He sighed. "What do you figure that idiot captain of ours will do now?"

Walter shrugged. "We will head back to Salisbury, most likely. There's nothing left for us to do down in South Carolina."

"The Virginians were not all captured," Farr declared reassuringly. "There was a bunch called the Third Virginia Detachment that was still on the north side of the Santee. They never got all the way to Charlestown before the surrender. They turned around, and are headed back north right now, but they are moving slowly. There are about four hundred men, some wagons, and two cannons. A general by the name of Buford is in charge. South Carolina Governor John Rutledge escaped Charlestown and was traveling with them for a while, but he has gone on ahead to Salisbury."

"How do you know all this information?" asked Walter, somewhat surprised.

"We received word from one of his forward scouts when the fellow came through Charlotte Town a couple of days ago. Buford likely crossed the Lynches River yesterday or the day before. They are definitely headed our way, moving up through Camden. I imagine Buford has a mind to get all of his men and artillery back to the encampment at Salisbury as rapidly as possible."

Walter drained the last of his cider from the dark blue glass bottle. He retrieved his hat and gave Gabe a slight nudge with his elbow. He stood to his feet.

"Mr. Farr, we are truly grateful for your hospitality, but we cannot tarry. We must depart immediately and make our report to Captain Williams."

"Of course," responded Mr. Farr. "But you boys must take the rest of this meat and bread with you. You can share it with your friends. Do you have anything in which to carry it?"

"I do!" Gabe answered. "But I don't imagine I'll be doin' a lot of sharin' with them ungrateful Virginia boys."

He winked as he reached into his haversack and removed a large, folded linen bag. He grabbed the handfuls of salty pork and the remaining chunks of bread and stuffed them into the bag. Walter claimed just enough of the food to construct a small sandwich for himself before Gabe stuffed the remainder inside his haversack.

Walter reached to shake hands with Mr. Farr. "I am truly grateful for your hospitality and your help, Mr. Farr. You probably just saved our little contingent a lot of pain and grief."

"It is my pleasure to serve, Mr. Billingsley. I wish you and those other boys all the best. You fellows be careful out there, and take care of yourselves."

Walter nodded. "We will, sir. Thank you."

Gabe and Walter retrieved their weapons and trudged toward the forest to their east. They turned and waved to Ephraim Farr before disappearing into the thick woods.

"He seemed like a right nice fellow," declared Gabe. "Still, I wonder how he managed to snag that pretty little wife of his. They seemed a might bit mismatched."

"I was thinking exactly the same thing," responded Walter, chuckling lightly. "But I believe you are right. They are good people. I hope that they will fare well out here on this frontier. I fear that the war is coming straight for them."

"It's comin' for all of us, Walter. It's all just a matter of time ..." Gabe's voice trailed off and yielded to the peaceful sounds of the forest. After a few seconds, he shook his head to clear away the intrusion of uncharacteristically deep thoughts. "Anyways, that's enough philosophizin' for one day. We need to get back to Williams and Armstrong. They'll be aimin' to meet up with this General Buford, I'm a thinkin'."

"Yes, indeed."

"And General Buford is headin' in the right direction, in my opinion. North ... away from the British."

Walter smiled. "Amen to that!"

May 28, 1780
Third Virginia Continental Detachment Encampment
Waxhaws Meeting House, South Carolina

General Abraham Buford's little army was in poor shape, indeed. The soldiers had endured several days of rain and the ensuing muddy, almost impassable roads. The thick, sticky mud created a state of generalized misery for the men who labored incessantly to move the wagons and cannons northward. The men of the Third Virginia Detachment were filthy, waterlogged, exhausted, and hungry. It was mid-afternoon on Sunday when General Buford halted the march at the Waxhaws Presbyterian Meeting House. He ordered fires built for cooking and to dry their clothing and shoes.

His men needed little convincing to enjoy the temporary halt. The exhausted soldiers relished in the respite provided by the church and the generous people who lived nearby. Within an hour of their arrival, residents from nearby villages and homesteads appeared with carts laden with foodstuffs. The ministries provided by the people of the Waxhaws stood in stark contrast to the cool aloofness and often outright disdain that they had endured in the Loyalist-infested central regions of South Carolina.

Buford's beleaguered detachment pitched their camp in a large pasture beside the church. The tiny meeting house was a well-known and beloved place of worship near the North Carolina border. It was also popular as a meeting place for local Patriots and Whigs. Buford located his temporary headquarters inside the church building. He sent out dispatch riders to the north and patrols to the south and east. He wanted to make sure that his men enjoyed a night of safety and comfort as they rested up for their final push into North Carolina. The general was desperate to enter friendlier territory and put a safe distance between his struggling army and a pursuing force of British dragoons.

Walter and Gabe made contact with one of Buford's eastern patrols in the late afternoon. The captain had wisely sent the pair of scouts ahead to link up with Buford's lookouts. He wanted to ensure that the retreating Virginians understood that a friendly force that was approaching from the northeast. The two North Carolina boys easily located a small patrol comprised of four horsemen from Buford's camp, and informed them of the proximity of Williams' detachment from Salisbury. Two of the riders returned quickly to camp to inform their commander. Walter and Gabe escorted the other two men to meet Captain Williams.

A half-hour later, the men from the patrol led Williams and his contingent to Buford's bivouac. The beleaguered gaggle of wandering, directionally-challenged Patriots emerged into the roadway near Buford's encampment shortly before nightfall. The general, himself, was waiting for them in front of the church.

Captain Williams walked smartly toward the general, stopped two paces in front of him, and gave a crisp salute. The general returned the gesture, a friendly smile on his face.

"Captain Williams, I presume?"

"Yes, General. Captain John Williams, Virginia Regulars."

"From which regiment, Captain?"

"Well, General, we were attempting to organize a new body, to be designated the 17th Virginia regiment of the Continental Line, at our encampment at Salisbury. I aspired to be named colonel of such a regiment. However, we failed to secure an adequate number of recruits for our venture. I waited as long as I could to enlarge our muster, but felt that I could tarry no longer. I headed south with the force that I had at my disposal to join in with the army at Charlestown."

General Buford nodded toward Captain Williams' humble gathering of troops. The exhausted men stood stoically in the road just a few paces behind their commander. "So, you departed for the battle front with fewer than twenty men?"

"Yes, sir. That is all that we had, sir."

"A bold decision, Captain."

"I like to think so, sir," Williams responded, his chest growing a bit larger as it swelled with pride.

"But you are little too late, I am afraid," declared General Buford, displaying an obvious look of frustration.

"Indeed, sir. We heard about the surrender only two days ago."

The general nodded and surveyed Williams' men. "Well, no matter. You boys are in the Third Virginia Continental Detachment now. Captain Williams, I am placing you in command of your own company. We shall do all of the necessary documentation, consolidate a regiment, and then labor to increase the men in your ranks once we reach Salisbury."

"Yes, sir!" answered Captain Williams proudly.

"Find yourself a place to sleep for the night, Captain. There is ample space in yon field. The locals have been most generous with their gifts of meat, corn, and ale. There is also a plentiful supply of breads and homemade pastries. You will find stews simmering in several of our pots. Help yourself to some supper, and then get plenty of rest. You are going to need it. We will depart at first light and make our final push into North Carolina. The British are hot on our heels."

"Sir?" asked the captain, confused. "I was under the impression that the British Regulars were still confined to the low country."

General Buford shook his head grimly. "A contingent of their dragoons has dogged us ever since our departure from the regions north of Charlestown. Their mission, I believe, was to capture Governor Rutledge, whom we assisted in escaping from their grasp. They are a Loyalist force, but call themselves the 'British Legion.' There is no mistaking them. The men of the legion wear colorful uniforms of red with green facings, and upon their heads they sport pompous leather helmets adorned with ostrich feathers." He chuckled. "I suppose they are aspiring to become as arrogantly British as they possibly can." His smile disappeared. "But make no mistake, they are a formidable force ... brave, heartless, and vengeful."

"And they are in our pursuit," clarified Captain Williams.

"Indeed, Captain. Most likely less than ten miles to our rear." He looked grimly down the road to the southeast. "The British Legionnaires are the hunters, young man. We are their prey. We have been fleeing from them for days. We continue that flight in the morning."

Captain Williams snapped to attention and gave another salute. "My company will be rested and at your service at first light, General Buford."

The general smiled and reached out to shake Captain Williams' hand. "It is a pleasure to have you within our ranks, Captain. You are dismissed."

Captain Williams turned to his company. "Pitch your tents on the south side of the field, boys. Get some stew in your bellies. Then, I want you to clean your weapons and roll cartridges. We may face the enemy tomorrow."

Gabe leaned to his left and whispered into Walter's ear, "We might ought to have stayed lost in the damned woods."

Walter cut his eyes at Gabe and nodded grimly.

Walter and Gabe lay on a thick bed of pine straw inside their tiny, two-man shelter. Gabe had designed them a most luxurious bed. The dry pine needles were not only for their comfort. They were an absolute necessity to protect the young men from the damp, heat-sapping earth beneath them. The area had been subjected to copious rainfall over the past week, and the ground was thoroughly soaked. Despite the nearing of summer, the late spring night had a damp chill. But nature's offering of an endless supply of sheds from the nearby pine trees provided them with a perfect, dry mattress. It was actually the most comfortable accommodations that they had enjoyed in over two weeks.

Gabe wasted no time in taking advantage of his comfortable, warm bed. He lapsed into the unconsciousness of exhaustion moments after he burrowed into his pine nest. He purred softly in the darkness. But, despite his own exhaustion, Walter could not sleep. As the hours passed, he grew more and more frustrated at his inability to relax his mind and slumber. He tossed and turned, digging a deeper and deeper hole into his pine straw mattress. He stared at the flickers and shadows of firelight that danced gaily on the linen walls of the tent. He listened to the chorus of snores and bodily noises emanating from other nearby tents. He tried to fall asleep, but to no avail.

Walter's mind was consumed with thoughts of Abigail. How he longed to see her! He attempted to re-create a vision of her perfect face within his memories. He recalled her smell, the soft tone of her voice, and the warmth of her touch. It had been several months since he had seen his beloved, and yet she was so very near the spot where he lay! Camden was less than fifty miles to the south. But it could just as well have been a thousand miles distant, because Walter was no longer headed southward. He was now a soldier in a retreating army, headed toward the safer environs of the Patriot encampment near Salisbury, North Carolina.

Walter was frustrated to be so geographically close to Abigail, and yet so helplessly unable to fetch her to a place of safety. It was that sense of frustration that kept him awake. Abigail was in grave danger. If the British Legion was only ten miles away, it meant that Camden was now behind enemy lines. His fiancé resided in territory controlled by the British.

Walter's heart was overwhelmed with worry over her well-being. He prayed fervently for her safety, and for the safety of her family. It was those prayers of desperation that finally calmed his spirit enough to allow him to enter into the realm of a fitful, restless sleep.

9

NO QUARTER!

May 29, 1780 – The Waxhaws of South Carolina

General Buford had his men on the move early. The army broke camp shortly after sunrise and departed with empty stomachs. But, despite several hours on the road, the column had managed fewer than five miles of travel. The conditions were horrid. The men had to march single-file in the center of the muddy Charlotte Turnpike. The hump between the water-filled wagon ruts was the driest and most passable ground on the roadway. Chest-high weeds, briars, and thorns made the adjacent fields almost impassable. The soldiers labored through every step as they inched their way northward toward the safety of North Carolina.

Gabriel and Walter were near the center of the frustrated column of Continentals and militiamen. Walter marched a few paces ahead of his friend.

"How much further to Charlotte Town, reckon?" Gabe wondered aloud.

"Likely another thirty miles or so," Walter answered. "We have quite a distance yet to go."

"Christ, Almighty! It will take us over a week at this pace!"

"The road cannot be this muddy forever," responded Walter. He pointed ahead to where the narrow strip of pale mud disappeared over the top of a slight ridge. "See? There's some high ground ahead. Surely things have dried out along the ridges. The roadway looks to be a different color, and the fields open up on both sides. That ground looks tended, so we might even be able to get out of this soupy road. Perhaps we will even move into an area that has received less rain."

"Not the way our luck's been goin'," Gabe grumbled. "Just think about it, Walter! We departed Guilford a month ago to travel down to Camden and collect your woman and all of her dowry and dainties. Since then we've been bushwhacked, shot at, chased, arrested, lost your mother's wagon, been drafted into the Virginia army, gotten lost in the woods, and damn near starved to death. Now we're sloggin' our way through this mud just to get back to Salisbury and start the whole thing all over again. It's madness, I tell you!"

Gabriel shook his head in disbelief and continued his rant. "On top of all that I've got a case of foul bowels, a horrid itch in my crotch and on the crown of my head, and no more leather on the bottom of my right shoe! It's like a nightmare from one of those novels that your sister, Martha, is always readin'. Nope. This is it, Walt. We're scrapin' the bottom of life's barrel. Nothing can be any worse than this."

"You've never been such a pessimist before, Gabriel Tate. What has happened to you?"

"You and this war have happened to me, you gnashgab! I'll have you know that I blame *you* for all of this, and one day I will have my satisfaction." He poked Walter playfully in the back with the muzzle of his rifle.

Walter chuckled. "I will be sure to reimburse you for your troubles out of my first Virginia bounty payment ... if ever I receive one."

"Ain't that the truth!"

A hundred yards ahead of them a group of officers on horseback broke away from the column and trotted their animals across an open pasture to the west. They rode leisurely toward a wagon that was parked on a nearby hilltop. General Buford was leading the group. Captain Williams was one of the many officers who accompanied him. The call for a halt quickly made its way down the column.

Gabe pointed and griped, "Where are the general and all of his lackeys goin'? This is no time to be makin' a social call."

Walter squinted and stared at the hilltop to their southwest. "There are some fellows in a wagon parked up there. One of them is a small lad, I think. They are probably just after a little information from some of the locals."

"Hmm ...," Gabe mumbled. He stared jealously at the men on horseback. "I would give my left tallywag for one of those mounts."

"You'd get a lot more use out of the horse. That much is certain," teased Walter. He received another nudge from Gabe's rifle barrel in the small of his back, this one a little harder than the first.

Gabe declared, "Let's get out of this mud and rest while we have the chance."

Walter needed no further encouragement. He stepped over the wagon rut to his right and proceeded to claim a relatively clear spot in the dry grass along the shoulder of the road. The location was relatively clear of briars. He and Gabe scooped up handfuls of loose vegetation to fashion makeshift pillows with their coats, placed their rifles on the ground at their sides, and then reclined in the soft grass. Both men covered their faces with their hats and comfortably folded their arms across their chests.

One of the nearby Virginia boys chastised them. "Do you Carolina gents actually believe that we'll be here long enough to enjoy a nap? Shall I make a fire and brew us some tea before nap time?"

"That would be nice," responded Gabe from beneath the shadow of his black cocked hat. "Let me know when it's ready. I'll be sure to piss in yours and sweeten it up just a bit."

"There is no need for such vulgarity, sir!" retorted the Virginian.

"Aww ... get stuffed!" growled Gabe.

There suddenly came the sound of a disturbance from the rear of the column. Men hissed, booed, and cursed.

"What in Heaven's name is going on back there?" griped Walter. "It's hard to rest in the midst of such racket."

Gabe exhaled loudly. "I don't know, and I'm too tired to look. But the boys are worked up, that's for sure."

The sound of a horse's hooves reached Walter's ears. It was something of a surprise, since all of the mounted officers were located near the head of the column.

"Did General Buford send any patrols to the south?" asked Walter.

"Not that I know of. But, then again, we've been with this outfit for less than a day. There's no tellin' how many scouts or dispatch riders are lurkin' to our rear."

"True," affirmed Walter.

The sound of the horse drew nearer. Walter and Gabriel could hear the animal's hooves splashing in the puddles of the road. The rider, whoever he was, was making his way toward the front of the column. The sounds of curses and angry verbal protests drew nearer, as well.

Suddenly, amazingly, disturbingly, a very British voice pierced the tranquility of their moment of relaxation.

"Pardon me, gentlemen. But could you be so kind as to point me in the direction of your commanding officer?"

Gabe and Walter simultaneously snatched their hats from their faces and rose to sitting positions. A distinguished-looking fellow wearing the colorful uniform of the British Legion sat astride an impressive horse on the far shoulder of the road. His clothing was pristine. He wore a black leather helmet that had white hair from a horse's tail poking from the top. A large white ostrich feather protruded from the rear of the helmet. On his shoulders, he sported the epaulettes of a lieutenant. He wore white riding gloves and glistening black boots. The officer was an impressive sight, indeed. He held a pole across his left shoulder that was adorned with a makeshift white flag of truce.

Both Walter and Gabe stared at the fellow, mouths open wide in silent disbelief. Walter glanced in both directions toward the other men of the detachment. All of them stared similarly, mouths agape. The men were dumbfounded. No one knew what to say.

The fellow chuckled. "I say, do any of you gents actually speak the King's English?"

Gabriel Tate, of course, could not resist offering a response. "We speak it just fine, Mr. Lobsterback. Our very own American version. Who the hell are you?"

He bowed his head slightly. "I am Lieutenant Andrew Mayfair of His Majesty's British Legion." The man declared his rank with the ever-pretentious British pronunciation, '*levtenant*.'

"Nice hat, '*Levtenant*.' It's queer, though. You usually only see hair like that sticking out of a horse's arse. But, then again, I reckon it still is sticking out of a horse's arse."

The men within earshot broke out in raucous laughter at Gabe's wit. The Legionnaire's face flushed red with embarrassment and anger. Walter covered his mouth in an attempt to hide his smile.

The lieutenant growled, "I have neither the time nor the inclination to involve myself in sparring verbally with the likes of you. I have important military matters that demand my attention. Please direct me to your superiors."

"Come to surrender then, have you, '*Levtenant*?'" quipped Gabe, emphasizing once again the supercilious pronunciation.

"As if that were even within the realm of possibility," retorted the officer. He sat up straight and proud in his saddle. "Now, I say again, if you would kindly direct me to your commander, I will take my leave."

Walter pointed. "He is up there on the hilltop, parleying with the men in that wagon."

Lieutenant Mayfair gazed at the hill. "Ah! Excellent! I am grateful, sir, for your assistance."

"Any time, '*Levtenant*,'" mocked Gabe. "Maybe we can meet again sometime under less cordial circumstances. I could really use a nice pair of new boots. Been achin' for a good horse, too."

The man frowned. "Indeed. One can only hope for such an encounter. You should lie back down, you mongrel, and get some rest. You are going to need it before this day is through. God save the King!"

"You and your king can both go straight to hell," Gabe blurted.

Rage displayed on the lieutenant's face. He pointed angrily at Gabe. "I shall remember you, sir!" He turned his horse sharply to the left and rode in a trot toward the cluster of men on the nearby hill.

The Virginian who had earlier teased the North Carolina boys for lying down beside the road gazed upon Gabe with a newly-discovered sense of admiration. He declared, "I don't think that fellow was accustomed to such coarse speech, Mr. Tate. Perhaps you would prefer to piss in his tea instead of mine?"

Gabe grinned sheepishly at the soldier. "You can be sure of that, my friend." He cut his eyes at Walter. "What do you think, Walt? Is there a fight upon us?"

"I don't know. Let's hope not. We wouldn't stand much chance against dragoons in this open field."

Captain Williams soon returned with the other officers. He quickly made his way back along the column until he found the men of his company. They gathered near, anxious to hear the news. The captain appeared grim.

"We are moving on with haste, boys. The enemy is near."

"How many, sir?" inquired one of the men.

He shook his head. "We cannot know for certain. That pompous bastard claims that they have over seven hundred men on horseback ... all commanded by a Colonel named Tarleton."

The men groaned.

"He also said that Cornwallis is not far behind, in command of nine battalions of infantry. They have demanded our surrender.

They offered to parole all militia and officers, but declared that all Continental enlisted men must be taken prisoner until exchanged."

The groans grew louder. The men stared at one another in disbelief.

"What happens now? What will we do?" Walter demanded.

"We will keep moving. General Buford thinks that he's full of shite. He believes they're trying to bluff us into surrendering. He informed the messenger that we will defend ourselves to the last man."

Those frightful words pealed loudly in their ears. "*To the last man* ..." There were no more groans. There remained only a numb, out-of-body feeling of disbelief among all of the soldiers. If Buford was wrong, the enemy outnumbered the Third Virginia Detachment by at least two to one. The enemy force was comprised almost entirely of cavalry and dragoons ... soldiers on horseback. And the exhausted Patriots stood little chance of surviving a cavalry charge.

The captain surveyed his men proudly. "That is all, gentlemen. 'Twill be all right. I promise you. Gather your gear and check your weapons. Prepare to move out."

In that instant, approximately a dozen shots rang out toward the south. The boom of muskets erupted in the forests that lined the roadway to the rear. A dull cloud of white smoke rose from the trees at the back of the column.

Gabe moaned, "That doesn't sound like a by-God bluff to me, sir!"

General Buford and his officers moved quickly. The commander ordered his artillery and baggage wagons to continue northward toward Charlotte Town. He then ordered the detachment to disperse in a line of defense that traversed the Charlotte Turnpike. Over four hundred soldiers were spread roughly two yards apart across the width of the entire field. They faced the enemy to the south and prepared, begrudgingly, for the coming assault.

Captain Williams' men were located on the left flank, toward the eastern edge of the field. Walter and Gabe were roughly fifty yards from the adjacent tree line. They watched in awe as the enemy soldiers of the British Legion emerged from the forests to their south.

"What the hell is Buford doin' … sendin' the artillery on to the north?" griped Gabe. "That might the only thing that could save us in this fight!"

"He is *General* Buford to you, *Private* Tate," corrected Sergeant Anderson.

Walter declared hopefully, "The general knows what he's doing."

"Don't bet on it!" whispered Gabe.

Walter busied himself counting the enemy soldiers. He shouted to his commander, "Captain Williams, there's certainly not seven hundred of them. It looks to me to be less than two hundred!"

"But on horseback," Gabe hissed at Walter. "We cannot stand against a mounted assault. Damn it! We need those cannons!"

He glanced toward their rear and observed the last wagon of baggage as it disappeared into the trees to the north. His eyes scanned the field behind them. He saw Buford and his general staff sitting proudly astride their horses at least a hundred yards behind the line.

Gabe continued his criticism of their leadership, abandoning his whisper. "Just look at him! *General* Buford's keepin' all of his options open, I promise you that! Ready to bolt on a moment's notice!"

"That's quite enough, Private Tate!" Sergeant Armstrong scolded from his position in the line. "Keep your mind on what's in front of you, not what's behind you."

"Oh, don't worry, Sergeant. My mind is fully aware of what is in front of us right now!"

"They do not appear to have cannons, either," observed Walter optimistically.

Gabe answered, "Well, at least that's a tiny bit of good news ... such as it is."

The two young men, like the scores of other men on either side of them, stared across the field. Walter experienced an overwhelming feeling of apprehension and panic. He had never been in an actual battle before. Yes, he had fought the militiamen on the night that his father was murdered. But that was different. That was personal, and filled with fiery emotion and vengeance. Now he faced two hundred dragoons equipped with carbines, pistols, and sabers. And soon they would descend upon this open field full of frightened foot soldiers.

"How long before nightfall?" Walter whispered to Gabe.

His friend glanced at the sun. "I don't know. Three ... four hours, maybe. Why?"

"I was just wondering what time it is."

"What for? You got a fancy pocket watch that I don't know about? You need to set the time and wind it?" Gabe chuckled teasingly.

"No. Nothing like that. I was just thinking about what Abigail must be doing right now. It's probably time for tea."

"Hmm ... do you reckon the captain might give us our leave so that we could head on down to Camden and enjoy a spot of Bohea? Hot and sweet? Maybe with a dish of apple pudding, or a crispy cranberry tart?"

Walter grinned. "Would be nice, wouldn't it?"

"Damn right it would be nice. Hell! I would eat a bowl of fish guts if it was anywhere but here in this field," Gabe declared.

The two friends fell silent and continued to observe the enemy soldiers maneuvering in front of them. They appeared to be dividing into three distinct groups. Approximately thirty dragoons lined up in an attack formation directly across from Captain Williams' company. There were about as many infantrymen in the tree line behind them. The enemy remained over two hundred yards away, well out of musket range.

Walter glanced at his friend. "How much longer do you think they will wait?"

"No tellin'. But I can't see any reason why they would want to dawdle."

Suddenly, thunderously, the pounding sound of hundreds of hooves striking the earth exploded across the field.

Sergeant Armstrong yelled, "Here they come! Hold your fire until they're close, boys! If you don't think you can hit the riders, then shoot the horses!"

The British Legion rode full-speed on the attack ... straight at the thin line of horrified Patriots.

Mid-Afternoon - The Hamer Home – Camden, South Carolina

Abigail wept as she stood beside the window in the sitting room. Her afternoon cup of green Hyson tea and her crisp cranberry tart sat untouched on the service table. She groaned as she watched a platoon of crimson-coated British soldiers march past the house. She clenched a tattered letter in her hand, written two weeks prior but delivered less than an hour ago. It was a note from Mrs. Billingsley, explaining Walter's tragic circumstance and his unwilling, unexpected conscription into the army.

Alexander Hamer sipped thoughtfully from his cup of tea and studied his daughter, waiting to see how she would cope with the news. The heartbroken girl turned away from the window. Her eyes met her father's.

"Oh, Papa!" she wailed. "What will I do if something happens to my Walter? I cannot imagine living my life without him!" Her body wretched in spasms as she cried.

Audra Hamer sat her cup and saucer down on an end table and ran to her child. They embraced. She cried as well. Mr. Hamer crossed the room and wrapped his arms around both of the weeping women.

"There, there, my dears ... calm yourselves. I am confident that Walter is just fine. You must remember that he is a brave, intelligent, and resourceful young fellow. He knows how to take care of himself, and he certainly knows how to fight."

Abigail wailed even louder. She grew almost hysterical. "But, Papa! There are so many of these British soldiers! Just look at them ... flooding our village and our lands! The army at Charlestown has been captured and imprisoned! There is no one left to fight for the rebellion! Walter is doomed!"

She released herself from her mother's embrace and buried her face into her father's shoulder. She needed the strength and reassurance that can only be found in a father's strong arms. He held tightly to his beloved daughter, cooing gently and stroking her hair.

Her mother suddenly grabbed her hand and gave it a strong, assertive squeeze. "Abigail! You must cease all of this whining and crying. It accomplishes absolutely nothing. Remember the commands of Scripture, from Philippians 4:6. God's Word says, '*Be careful for nothing; but in everything by prayer and supplication, with thanksgiving, let your requests be made known unto God.*' That is what we must do, Daughter! We must pray. We must give your Walter over to the protective hands of the Sovereign Almighty."

Abigail, still grasping the letter in her left hand, wiped the tears from her face with her other hand. She sniffed and nodded. Her expression changed, almost as if she had received a revelation of sorts. She shifted her gaze to her mother.

"You are absolutely right, Mother. Everything is in God's hands. I know that. I have faith. But I feel an overwhelming sense of urgency. My heart is anguished. It is consumed with an immediacy, and a heaviness for Walter's well-being." She paused as she processed her feelings and thoughts. Then she hissed, "Something is wrong! Walter is in danger! We must pray! We must pray now! Father, will you lead us?"

"Of course, Darling. It would be my honor. Let us sit, and join hands."

"We must not tarry," Abigail urged. "Walter needs us right now."

The Hamer family sat together on the settee and prayed fervently for Walter Billingsley.

Waxhaws Battlefield – Near the Border of North Carolina

"Christ, Almighty!" exclaimed Gabe. "It's really happenin'!"

Yelling erupted along the American line. Officers and sergeants barked orders at their soldiers. Sergeant Armstrong's voice joined with the chorus of commands.

He shrieked, "Hold your fire, men! Make every shot count!"

Walter and Gabe pointed their rifles downrange. They each trained their sights on one of the oncoming attackers. The wave of men and beasts loomed closer and closer. They were a mere sixty yards away, and yet there was still no order to open fire.

"What are we waitin' for, Sarge?" Gabe demanded.

"The Captain said that we must wait until they are right upon us!"

Suddenly fire erupted from among the attacking dragoons. They discharged pistols and muskets from beside the necks of their horses. Their fire was not very accurate, but it was disconcerting to the Patriots along the defensive line. A few wounded men screamed and fell. Still, there remained no order to open fire.

Gabe stood to Walter's right. Like all of the other men, he stood in a firing position. All that Walter could see was his friend's back and a small portion of the left side of his face. Gabe appeared panicked. He was literally bouncing up and down, anxious to pull the trigger. Just for a moment, Gabe glanced over his left shoulder. His eyes met Walter's.

"This is horse shite, Walt! These idiots are goin' to get us all killed! I'm goin' to shoot!"

He turned his attention, once again, to the attacking dragoons and placed his finger inside the trigger guard of his .54 caliber long rifle. He aimed at red and green wool that adorned the chest of one of the enemy dragoons.

But Gabriel Tate never got off a shot. His head suddenly snapped backwards, violently, as an enemy musket ball pierced his skull just below his left eye. The ball severed his brain stem, liquefied his lower cerebrum, and then exited the back of his skull in a cloud of bloody mist and bone fragments. His knees buckled and he collapsed to the ground in a lifeless heap. He did not move, kick, or twitch. He lay perfectly still. His eyes remained wide open, staring their empty gaze of death directly at Walter.

Walter screamed hysterically, "Gabe!"

But it was too late. His friend was gone. Gabriel Tate was dead.

Walter was frozen. Stunned. Unable to move. Bullets whizzed past his ears. He could hear the dull thuds of lead impacting earth and flesh, but it all seemed so distant. He could not seem to remove his gaze from Gabe's empty, lifeless eyes.

Walter felt a shudder and tug against his weskit. Fibers of wool and thread flew into the air as a lead projectile tore through the loose cloth that dangled in front of his belly. The sudden proximity of the bullet to his own flesh shocked him back into the reality of the battle. He turned back toward the oncoming soldiers. They were upon him. A huge, ominous, black horse filled his field of vision. A red-clad dragoon was atop the animal, holding his dazzlingly shiny sword high in the air.

Walter did not have time to think or aim. He merely angled his rifle upward from his waist, stuck the muzzle in the direction of the horse's chest, and pulled the trigger. The flesh parted below the horse's neck. The animal emitted a horrified, shrieking snort. Walter instantly dropped to his knees and rolled to his right in an effort to avoid the huge, wounded animal. He moved just in time to escape the tumbling, haphazard fall of the stricken horse.

The poor animal screamed in pain as it lurched forward. Its front legs ceased moving, but its back legs propelled it forward. It crashed onto its chest and its neck whipped down, slamming the helpless animal's head into the ground. Its neck snapped from the impact. The attacking dragoon somersaulted, head-first, and landed flat on his back with a loud, hollow thud. He slid for a short distance, but the tall grass stopped his movement. His legs were spread wide apart, with a tight, compacted wad of thick grass wedged into the "v" of his crotch. He was obviously dazed. He attempted to lift his head to orient himself and examine his body for wounds, but he was too confused and dizzy.

Walter was somewhat dazed, as well. He had struck his head against the stock of Gabe's rifle when he tumbled to the ground. Walter cast his own spent rifle aside and grabbed Gabe's unfired weapon. He used the stock of the rifle to pull himself to his feet, then limped past the dead horse toward the stunned Legionnaire. The wounded man was quickly aware of his enemy's presence. Walter was just about to shoot the man when he heard a frantic, screaming voice to his left.

"Please! I surrender! Have mercy!"

It was Sergeant Armstrong. He was on his knees beside the still body of Captain Williams. He held his arms high above his head. A British Legionnaire sat tall in the saddle above him, holding his sword high overhead and preparing to swing.

Armstrong pleaded again, "I beg you, sir! I am finished! I am unarmed! I tell you, I surrender!"

Walter stared in disbelief as the horseman slashed his sword horizontally at Sergeant Armstrong. First, the soft flesh of the underside of his left arm erupted with blood. The blade sliced easily through the meat, and then cut perfectly across the sergeant's throat. The tip of the blade nicked the underside of the man's right arm, as well. Blood poured from the severed arteries of Armstrong's neck. He frantically grasped at the wound with his hands, pawing at the exposed flesh in a vain effort to stem the flow of blood. But it was to no avail. His lifeblood poured out onto the ground at his knees. He tumbled forward, unconscious. He would be dead within seconds.

Walter screamed with rage and raised Gabe's rifle to his shoulder. The swordsman turned in response to the nearby scream. His eyes grew wide in surprise when he saw Walter a mere fifteen feet away with a rifle aimed at his chest. Walter placed the gunsight at the base of the man's neck and pulled the trigger. The fellow tumbled backward off of his horse. He was dead when he hit the ground.

Walter scanned the center of the field. The defenders' line was broken. The battle was already lost. It had lasted fewer than five minutes. Wounded Patriots littered the battlefield. He saw one of the Virginians running toward the horsemen on the road, waving a white flag on the end of a spontoon. A dragoon shot the surrendering Patriot with a pistol at point-blank range. The stricken man and his flag of surrender tumbled into the mud of the roadway.

Walter heard the sound of galloping horses far to the rear. He turned and saw General Buford and his staff riding full-speed up the road toward Charlotte Town.

"Cowardly bastard!" mumbled Walter.

He soon heard a loud, distinctly British cry from the center of the battlefield, "Colonel Tarleton is slain! Kill them! Kill them all! No quarter! Take none alive!"

All over the field, men on horseback slashed mercilessly with their swords at wounded and unarmed men. Walter saw the enemy infantrymen on the far end of the right flank descending upon the fallen Patriots and bayoneting them as they lay on the ground. He shook his head in disbelief.

He turned his attention to the dazed soldier that had been thrown from his dead horse. He crawled on his hands and knees to the man, dragging the spent rifle beside him. Again, the fellow saw Walter out of the corner of his eye. His head whipped around in fear. Walter knelt over the man's head. He raised the stock of the rifle high in the air.

"Please, sir!" the soldier pleaded. "I am injured! Have mercy!"

Walter seethed with unabated rage. He declared coldly, "You'll get the same mercy that your friends are giving us."

He quickly and violently smashed the man's skull with rifle stock. The brass butt-plate crushed the man's facial bones, driving sharp fragments deep into his brain. The fellow's body seized for a moment, and then his knees locked and his legs became rigid. He gurgled his final breaths as the blood from his crushed face filled his throat.

Walter rose to a squat and peered over the tall grass. The reserve infantrymen of the British Legion were walking toward his position. Like the enemy soldiers on the western end of the battlefield, they, too, were driving bayonets into the wounded and dead. Walter glanced at his fallen friend. He could not bear the thought of the mutilation of Gabe's body. He crawled quickly to his dead companion and grabbed him beneath the arms. He slowly pulled Gabe's lifeless body toward the higher grass to his rear. It was an excruciatingly frustrating effort. Gabe's body was so very heavy. He outweighed Walter by at least thirty pounds. The grass was exceedingly thick.

Walter futilely encouraged his slain compatriot, trying to coax him to move through the sheer power of his words and will. "Come on, Gabe! Help me out here, buddy! I have to get you out of this field!"

But his friend's body would barely budge, and the enemy soldiers were almost upon him. Walter gave a final heave just as he reached the edge of the dense grass. He managed to burrow his own body into the thick weeds, but he could not move Gabe past him and deeper into the vegetation. Gabe's body lay on top of his own.

Above the tall grass, Walter spied horsehair sticking up from the tops of the enemy soldiers' helmets. He was about to be discovered! He could already sense the searing burn of the bayonet that was sure to come. He was desperate.

He hugged Gabe's lifeless body and whispered into his ear, "I'm sorry old friend. You know that I truly love you."

He gave one final tug and pulled Gabe's body upward just a few more inches until it completely covered his own. The dense grass around him swallowed Walter's body perfectly, miraculously. Poor Gabe simply looked as if he had been shot and fallen backwards into the weeds. Walter was perfectly concealed.

The sticky mass of Gabe's congealing brains and blood stuck to Walter's face. He could smell the filth of his dead friend's bladder and bowels, both emptied in the throes of death. He gagged, making every effort to try and control his urge to vomit. He tried not to think about the fact that his dead best friend lay on top of him. The enemy soldiers were so close that he could hear their voices. He heard footsteps only a few feet away.

"Damn it all!" a voice exclaimed. "Peter! Come here! It's Lieutenant Whitmore!"

"What's wrong with him?" a distant, distinctly Irish voice inquired.

"He's as dead as Julius Caesar!"

"The hell you say!" responded the Irishman.

"Come and see!"

Walter lay absolutely still. He tried to control his breathing. His heart was pounding so hard that he thought it must be causing the grass around him to sway. His pulse thumped in his ears.

The Irishman whistled. "Jesus, Mary, and Joseph! Would ya' look at tha! His face is crushed! How do ya tink he did tha?"

"It happened when he fell off of his horse, I suppose."

"Well, it is utterly ghastly," remarked the Irishman. "But there's nuttin' we can do for him, now. Come along. Let us get back to our grisly work."

There was a pause in the conversation. Walter lay absolutely still, wondering if the men had gone away. Then, unexpectedly, one of them spoke.

"Do you feel much shame for what we're doing right now, Peter? For killing these helpless men?"

"Aye, Michael. Much shame, indeed. But we's only followin' orders. And we'd best be gettin' back to it, before one of these fancy gentlemen decides to run us through. They care as much about you and me as they do these Colonials. You'd best take care of that rebel over there in the weeds. He's likely the one who bested Lieutenant Whitmore."

"All right, Peter."

Walter heard footsteps moving in his direction. He stopped breathing altogether.

"Damn it all, Pete! This one has a hole in his head. Must I stick a blade in him? It doesn't seem right."

The Irish fellow responded, "No, Mikey. Leave the laddie be. There's no need for us to be out here desecratin' the dead … God rest their souls. Let's move on toward the road. All these rebels are dead, anyways."

Walter listened carefully as the men walked toward his right. The sounds of their steps soon faded. He strained to hear any movement nearby, but discerned none. He waited a few more minutes, and then decided to sneak a peek. He slid Gabe's body slightly to the left and looked around, but saw nothing. He heard yelling and voices far off to the right and toward the south, in the direction of the enemy's rear, but nothing in his immediate vicinity. He also heard the creaking and popping of wagons coming down the road from the north. The British Legion had, no doubt, captured the Continentals' vehicles and supplies.

Walter lay still for a while longer and stared at the sky above him, allowing the soft breeze to creep between the blades of grass and cool his face. He was amazed at how beautiful and peaceful it all seemed. The heavens were a brilliant, crystal blue, and dotted with tiny puffs of high, white clouds. Indeed, it was so peaceful that he was tempted to close his eyes and sleep.

But Walter could wait no longer. He had to make his escape. He might not have another opportunity. He slithered clumsily from beneath Gabriel's body. He carefully and reverently removed his friend's shooting bag, haversack, and powder horn, draping each around his own neck and under his right arm. He also took Gabe's knife and inserted it into his hunting belt beside his own knife. He checked Gabe's pockets for any other personal belongings. He then crawled over to the spot where he had dropped his rifle and retrieved it from the trampled grass. Somehow, he also found his brown fur-felt cocked hat lying beside the dead horse.

Walter scurried back into the cover of the weeds. He knelt for a moment beside his dead friend. He whispered, "I'm sorry I got you into this, Gabe. I will miss you, old friend."

Walter patted Gabriel's cold hand, paused for a brief prayer, donned his hat, and then crawled toward the forest that lay fifty yards to the east. It took him several minutes to snake his way through the high grass and weeds, but he eventually reached the edge of the field. He emerged from the dense vegetation into the open, leaf-strewn forest floor. Darting beneath the canopy of the trees, he quickly concealed himself behind a fallen log. Suddenly overwhelmed by his torturous thirst, he drained the last few gulps of water from his canteen.

"Damn!" he muttered. He scolded himself in his thoughts, "*I should have taken Gabe's canteen! Billingsley, you idiot, you must flee this field and find water.*"

Walter loaded and primed his rifle, checked his supplies and equipment, and then surveyed the woods to the east. He saw no movement ... no evidence of humanity. He rose to his knees, peeked over the log to ensure that no enemy soldiers were nearby, and then silently stole away into the darkening forest.

10

YOUR WAR IS OVER

It was pitch dark. Walter slowly and carefully picked his way through the shadowy forest. He was dreadfully thirsty. He did not know exactly how long it had been since he fled the battlefield. Except for the lack of water, travel in the virgin woods had been relatively easy, even in the darkness. Thus far, the ground had displayed no major ridges or hills, but only gentle rolls and swells. The trees were large and widely spaced. He continued onward, despite the darkness. He was too frightened to stop.

His perilous nighttime journey came to a sudden, unexpected, painful end when he stumbled into a large sunken place in the forest floor. He tumbled awkwardly into the depression, falling onto his left side. His rifle smacked against a vine and sailed from his hands. He slid, face-first and arms outstretched, toward the bottom of the hole, finally grinding to a stop in the thick carpet of leaves. His left hand was submerged in water. He reflexively jerked it from the cold wetness.

A sharp click echoed in the shadows to his left. It was an unmistakable sound. Someone had cocked the hammer on a firelock. Walter's heart leapt into his throat.

"Do not move. Not one twitch. Now tell me … who the hell are you?" growled a deep, throaty voice from the darkness.

Walter hesitated. He reached slowly toward his waist and felt for his knife, but it was gone … lost, no doubt, during the fall. He did not know whether to answer or remain silent and "play dead."

"I'll not ask again. I know you can hear me. I see you moving. Who are you?" the voice demanded once more.

Walter recognized the unique twang of the fellow's brogue. He heard the distinctive accent of coastal Virginia in the man's voice. He elected to speak with candor.

"I'm Walter Billingsley, from Captain Williams' company of the Virginia Regulars."

The other fellow hesitated for a moment, then asked, "Were you in that little group that came into Buford's camp at the meeting house last night?"

Walter exhaled in relief. The man in the darkness was a fellow Patriot.

"Yes. There were nineteen of us. I was one of the scouts."

Walter heard the hollow click of the hammer lock being released. There was a shuffling sound to his left. Moments later he saw an imposing silhouette in the darkness. A strong hand snatched him by the collar of his weskit and lifted him to his feet. Suddenly, the as-yet unidentified fellow spun Walter around and wrapped his huge, strong arms around him in a vigorous hug. The fellow was massive, almost a foot taller than Walter, and weighing at least two hundred pounds. And he was obviously thrilled to see Walter, whose face was pressed so hard against the stranger's chest that he could scarcely breathe.

"I'm mighty glad to see you, Walter. I've been alone out here for quite a spell. I started to wonder if I was the only one who made it out of that field alive."

Walter chuckled and struggled to extract himself from the man's grasp.

"Pardon me, friend, but I do not know your name."

The friendly fellow declared from the darkness, "I'm sorry, Walter. My name is Thomas Whitlock. I am from Essex County in Virginia. You can call me Tommy."

Walter whispered, "I'm very pleased to meet you, Tommy. Have you seen or heard any more of our compatriots?"

"No. You are the first I've encountered. If there was anyone else in these woods, I think I would have known. I heard you coming from a mile away. You were as loud as a horny bull chasing after a herd of heifers." He giggled quietly.

Walter felt a measure of shame. He thought that he had been traveling quite stealthily.

Tommy continued, "I think we're the only ones out this way. I hope there are others who got out alive, but if they did, they likely ran another direction. Probably to the west."

Walter nodded. "There wasn't much of an opportunity for the men in the center of the field to escape. They were too far from the trees."

"That's what I thought, as well," agreed Thomas.

"Buford and his officers got away, though," Walter declared bitterly.

"Yeah. I saw that, too. He wasted no time at all." Tommy muttered bitterly, "The man simply abandoned us in that field."

"He will pay for his cowardice," declared Walter. "The army will see to that."

Tommy laughed sarcastically. "Don't be too sure about that, friend. Officers have a way of slithering out of things. Trust me. I've been in this army for almost two years. It's the enlisted fellows who always pay the price for the pride and stupidity of the men with the epaulettes."

"You're probably right." Walter's thirst beckoned him to change the subject. "Say, Tommy, do you happen to have any water?"

"That's the one thing we have plenty of. There's a spring in the bottom of this hole. The water is cold, clean, and sweet."

"You mean that's not just a puddle?"

"No, sir! It's a spring, all right. A fine one, too. There's not a hint of sulfur. That's why I'm hiding out in this hole. I stumbled onto the spot just before dark. I only went over the top once to piss and take a look around." He paused. "Do you have anything to eat?"

"Yes. I have a sack full of dried venison and hardtack."

"Could you spare some? I haven't eaten anything since yesterday."

"Me, either. I have plenty, though, and am happy to share."

"What about powder and lead?" asked Tommy hopefully.

"I have an extra bag. It belonged to my friend, Gabriel."

"He didn't make it?"

"No," Walter responded tersely. "Why? What happened you your powder and munitions?"

"My bags were cut off of me during the fight. One of those bloody dragoons slashed me across the back with his sword. He mostly got the buckle on my shooting bag, though. That buckle and the thick leather straps were the only things that saved me. They took most of the blow."

"Were you cut?"

"Just a little nick. It trickled blood down my back for a bit, but it seems fine now."

"I can check it and get you bandaged up in the daylight," Walter offered. "Meanwhile, let me fill my canteen and then we can eat and get some sleep."

"Sounds good," declared Tommy. "I'm terribly glad that you stumbled into this hole. It's horrifying to be out here alone."

Walter placed his hand on his newfound friend's shoulder. "We'll be fine, Tommy. Come daybreak, we will head north and find some friends. I know some good folk up that way."

"How? You said you were with that Virginia detachment."

"I am. I mean … I was," he stuttered. "I'm the only one left alive, I suppose. But I am from North Carolina, up in Guilford

County. We'll head north until we rendezvous with some of our army friends. If all else fails, we can keep walking all the way to my house."

"That sounds just fine to me. I'll say it again. I'm mighty glad you fell into this hole with me, Walter."

"I'm mighty glad you didn't shoot me, Tommy."

The Following Morning – May 30, 1780 – Two Hours After Daybreak

"What do you think? Should we take the chance?" whispered Tommy.

Walter stared down the narrow trail toward the two approaching Negroes. They were older men, working together to pull a small cart.

"They look harmless enough," surmised Walter. "I doubt they have any connections to the British." He grinned.

"Surely they can give us a better idea of where we are."

"Of that I am certain," declared Walter. "Let's wait for them to get a little closer."

The two lost soldiers waited until the slaves were less than twenty feet away before emerging from the undergrowth along the edge of the trail. Both of the old men jumped in fear. Their eyes flung open wide with surprise.

"It's all right," Walter stated calmly. "You have nothing to fear from us. We only need information."

"Yah suh, boss. Watcha needin' to know?" asked the fellow closest to Walter. His voice trembled slightly.

Walter explained, "We're all turned around, and need to get our bearings. We want to get to the Yadkin River and follow it up to Salisbury. We must get back to our army."

"Was you mens in dat big battle yestiddy?" asked the other Negro.

"Yes," responded Tommy.

"How you's got away from dem hoss soldiers?"

"We made our escape into the woods after the fight was done," explained Tommy.

The old man shook his head. "I didn't figger anybody gots out o' dat field. I heerd 'twas bad."

"It was," Walter confirmed. "How far are we from the battlefield? Which direction?"

"You is maybe three, fo miles out. Da battle was dat way." He pointed down the road and slightly to the right.

"Three or four miles?" echoed Tommy in disbelief. "Are you certain?"

"Yah suh. Prolly closuh to fo."

"Which way to the Yadkin?" asked Walter.

The old man pointed in the direction from which he had come. "Follow dis road 'bout a mile. You's find a crick on da east side. You kin follows it rat up to da Yakin. 'Twill take you all da way to Salisbury."

"But you ain't gotta go dat way ta finds da army," added the other slave.

"What do you mean?" asked Tommy.

"Dey's a passle of 'em camped on da fuh side o da Yadkin, 'bout thee miles nawf, jus ovah in Anson County."

"Where are they from?" asked Walter, excited.

"Randolph County, I heerd. Dat's what massa say ... dey's a whole comp'ny of militia."

Walter cast an excited glance at Tommy. "My brother, John, is in the Randolph County Regiment."

Tommy broke out into a grin. "He could be there! Let's go! It's better than traipsing all the way to Salisbury."

Walter turned his attention back to the two slaves. "We are grateful for your help." He glanced at the cargo in their cart. It was full of carrots, onions, and new potatoes. "Could you possibly share a little of the food with us? All we've had for two days is a bit of dried venison."

The older slave cut his eyes timidly at his companion. "Well. Just a wee bit, I reckon. But I ain't takin' no whip fo feedin' you. You kin have two taters, two unjuns and two carrots apiece. Dat's all. Lessen you 'uns plans to rob us wif dem guns."

Walter smiled. "No. We shall not rob you. And we are grateful for your generosity."

Walter and Tommy each grabbed their allotted vegetables, nodded thanks to the kindly slaves, and then proceeded up the road.

"We'd better stay in the trees," Walter cautioned. "The dragoons might be patrolling the area, looking for stragglers."

"You're probably right," agreed Tommy. "Let's go thirty or forty yards deep in the woods and keep the road in sight. It's pretty easy travel on foot in there, anyway."

"Agreed. Hopefully, we will sup with our Patriot friends tonight."

"Perhaps even your brother!"

"I can only hope ..."

June 1, 1780 – Early Morning
Somewhere in Anson County, North Carolina

Walter stared at the dark streak of three-day-old blood on the back of Tommy's shirt. "How is your wound? Does it hurt much?"

"Not at all, actually. The bandage has held up quite well. You would have made a good surgeon's mate."

"It doesn't take a genius to cover up a wound," Walter declared. "We will remove the dressing and put on a fresh one as soon as we find an encampment."

"If we find an encampment ..."

"Surely, it cannot be much further," Walter wished aloud.

"God, I hope you are right," Tommy responded. "I cannot bear much more of this. I'm sick from green apples and gritty potatoes. I need me some meat."

"You know we can't risk a gunshot. There are too many patrols about."

"Do you seriously believe that the British Legion has crossed the Yadkin?" challenge Tommy.

"I'm not sure. I don't think we can take any chances. But, be encouraged, friend. Today is the day!"

"You said that the day before yesterday," Tommy griped.

Their trip had not been as easy or as quick as they had hoped. After they crossed the Yadkin River, Walter and his new friend, Thomas Whitlock, stumbled through thick forests and muddy fields for a day and a half. Three rain-swollen creeks and two British Legion patrols hampered their progress. They ate by pilfering vegetables from gardens and unripe fruit from two farm orchards. They spent two unbearably miserable nights in the woods, covered only by pine boughs and dead leaves. Both men prayed that this would be the day when they would finally make contact with their compatriots from Randolph County.

"Do you think they are even here in this area, or might they have moved on?" Tommy wondered.

A shrill voice pierced the stillness of the forest. "Halt! Put your weapons on the ground and identify yourselves."

Walter grinned at Tommy. "I think they are still here."

Walter and Tommy ate with ravenous appetites. They attacked their bowls of salty beef and potato stew. They had each already devoured a half of a loaf of bread. They enjoyed gulps of tepid ale in between shoving spoonsful of the hot concoction into their mouths. A festive, crackling fire burned in the fireplace of the large kitchen. It was located in an impressive brick house, abandoned by its owners, and now employed as the headquarters of the Randolph County Regiment of militia. The room was pleasant, clean, and warm. It smelled of fresh-baked bread and fragrant tea. A half-dozen militiamen whispered and nodded at one another as they watched the two disheveled, filthy fellows eat their meal.

A short, middle-aged man entered the kitchen from the hallway. He was obviously an officer, for the other militiamen in the room all jumped to their feet. Walter and Tommy started to rise, as well, but the gentleman waved his hand dismissively and stopped them.

"Sit down! Sit down! Enjoy your breakfast, boys. I am Captain William Cole of the Randolph County Regiment, in command of this company."

Both men nodded and responded, "Captain …"

"So, which one of you is Johnny Billingsley's little brother?"

"I am. I'm Walter Billingsley. This is my friend, Thomas Whitlock."

The Captain shook both men's hands.

"Is John here?" Walter asked hopefully.

The captain shook his head and frowned. "I'm afraid not, Mr. Billingsley. He is up north of Salisbury with Colonel Francis Locke, laboring to raise more troops for our cause."

"He's gone toward home, then," Walter declared jealously.

"Yes, I believe he is working in the villages near your home. Guilford County is full of Patriots, and rich in recruits. But … enough about John. What about you? My men tell me you were with General Buford. Is that true?"

"Yes, sir." Walter's face clouded at the mention of Buford. "Have you see him?"

"Who?"

"Buford," responded Tommy.

"No, I can't say as I have," Captain Cole declared, somewhat confused.

"He likely would have appeared like a shadow or an apparition if he did come through here. He was riding so hard that he's probably in Philadelphia by now," Tommy grumbled in disgust.

The captain stared grimly and nodded, as if he realized fully the implications of Tommy's pronouncement, but he offered neither reproof nor affirmation. "We've heard stories about the battle. Was it really as bad as all that?"

"Worse, sir," answered Walter. "I am the only survivor from my small company."

"And I am the only survivor from mine," added Tommy. "We found one another in the woods in the darkness that night."

"How did you wind up amongst the Virginians, Mr. Billingsley? It seems a bit odd you are not in the Guilford Regiment."

"That is a long and maddening story, sir. My friend, Gabriel Tate, and I were pressed into their service at Salisbury. We were simply in the wrong place at the wrong moment."

"Interesting. How many were in Buford's detachment?"

"Over four hundred, all totaled," answered Walter. "My company had only joined them the evening before. We were making our way south when we received word about the fall of Charlestown. We linked up with Buford's command at the Meeting House near Waxhaws. He received our entire group into his detachment."

"We were something of a mismatched lot, sir," Tommy explained. "The detachment was made up of stragglers from a bunch of different regiments and commands. General Buford was trying to bring the entire group of men back to Salisbury when the enemy caught up with us in the Waxhaws."

"Do you know the identity and disposition of the enemy you faced?"

Tommy nodded. "It was the British Legion, dragoons under a colonel by the name of Tarleton."

"About two hundred of them," added Walter.

"How many dead among your men?"

"Most all of them, I reckon," answered Tommy. "Walter and I have encountered no one else since we made our escape."

"What about wounded?"

Walter stared numbly at the captain. "Sir, they killed most of the surrendering troops. And they executed the wounded with bayonet and sword as they lay on the ground."

The other men in the room gasped in shock and protest.

"That sounds rather barbaric and most unlikely! How do you know this?" challenged the captain.

"I observed it, sir." Walter answered angrily, his lip quivering. Silent shock engulfed the room. "One of them executed my sergeant, *after* he had surrendered, right before my very eyes. After the dragoons overran us, their infantry followed and finished off the wounded. I hid in the weeds, beneath the body of one of my compatriots."

The captain shook his head in anguish and disbelief.

"What about enemy casualties?"

Walter cut his eyes at the captain. "Very few, sir. I only saw two, both by my hand."

"I only got off one shot, sir," Tommy added. "I saw none of the enemy fall."

The captain nodded his understanding. "Very well, then. And you have been on the run ever since?"

"Yes, sir. We heard from some slaves that you were encamped somewhere in this region of Anson County. We've been in your pursuit for two days. We were hoping to join up with your regiment and, perhaps, return northward."

The captain frowned and shook his head. "I'm afraid that will not be possible. We are headed to the northwest to protect the road between Salisbury and Charlotte Town from attack by the Tories. We have received word of several ambushes along the highway. The

Loyalists have begun to assert themselves since the enemy army made its incursion toward the north. Besides, you fellows are both Continental Army. You must report back to your command."

"But we have no command, sir," retorted Walter. "Our command has been slain."

"No. He's right, Walter. I have to report back for assignment to a new regiment. It is my duty," declared Tommy.

The captain smiled grimly and nodded. "The Continentals have an encampment at Hillsborough. We have a wagon carrying supplies and dispatches that will be leaving for that camp at noon. I expect both of you to join the escort for the wagon."

"But, sir!" Walter protested.

"I do not wish to entertain your protests, Walter. I am very sorry. Truly, I am. But protocol requires that you report back to your Virginia Continental commanders, or both of you will be branded as deserters. You would not want that to happen, would you?"

"No, sir," grumbled Walter.

"Very well, then. I shall provide you with a letter explaining your situation. It will serve to verify your story. You will, of course, have to make a full report to your superiors upon arrival at the headquarters in Hillsborough."

"Yes, sir." Walter stood and shook the captain's hand. "Thank you, sir … for everything. We were almost done for when your sentries found us."

"Thank *you*, Walter, for your excellent report. The events on that field in the Waxhaws will go neither unanswered nor unavenged. Tarleton's quarter will, I believe, become the rally cry of the Patriots throughout the Carolinas. He may have awakened a hungry, slumbering beast of rebellion in our region."

"I genuinely hope so, sir."

"Well, boys, get your bellies full. Be sure to fill your haversacks and horns from our supplies. We have plenty."

"Thank you, sir," Walter answered. "Whenever you see him again, please explain my circumstance to John and reassure him that I am well."

"I shall, indeed, Walter. Good luck to you, boys."

Dusk – Northeast Anson County, North Carolina

Tommy reclined next to their small campfire. He lay flat on his back, fingers interlaced behind his head, and stared at the darkening purple sky overhead. Walter sat cross-legged beside the fire, staring into the comforting embers, and puffing gently on his walnut pipe.

"So, tell me more about your sister," pleaded Tommy.

Walter smiled. "Which one? I have three sisters."

Tommy exhaled, "I don't give a rat's arse about the old married ones. What about that youngest one? What's her name, again?"

"Martha."

"And how old is she?"

"She turned twenty last month."

"And she isn't married already? Is something wrong with her? Is she not pretty?"

"I don't know! She's my sister!"

"Well, that's just a stupid answer. Either she is pretty or she is not."

Walter exhaled. "I guess she *is* pretty. She is quite lovely, actually. And headstrong, well-read, and opinionated."

Tommy grinned. "I like the sound of her already."

"Well, then … next time you are through Guilford Courthouse, you must drop by so that I can make an introduction. You can court underneath the watchful eye of our mother."

Both fellows chuckled, and then grew silent.

"I should love to visit Guilford someday. Perhaps when this damned war is done."

"You will be most welcome at the Billingsley home. I will be sure and give you a good recommendation to Martha. And you will really like my mother, as well. She makes whiskey for a living."

Tommy's eyes opened wide with shock. "I thought you said your father was a Baptist preacher!"

"Her spirits are strictly for medicinal purposes ... until they aren't."

Tommy cut his eyes at Walter with some measure of disbelief. Both boys suddenly erupted into joyful laughter. As his laugh descended into a slight chuckle, Tommy resumed his stare toward the darkening heavens. The immediate challenges of the present overshadowed his thoughts of romance.

"Reckon when we will reach Hillsborough?"

Walter sighed. "It will take a couple of days, I imagine. We are not, exactly, making good time with this rickety old wagon."

"That much is certain," agreed Tommy. "If you can even call this glorified pull-cart a wagon. I think it used to be a wagon once, back in the French war, maybe. But it has definitely lost a bit of its lumber and luster. I fear that it may vanish into dust at any moment."

Walter grunted. "It gets the job done, in a manner of speaking. At least we are traveling with some good lads, and we are warm and well-fed."

"Indeed. I would hate to be traveling these roads alone." Tommy shuddered at the thought of it. "What do you think they will do with us once we get there?"

"They will place you in another regiment, I imagine. I am not quite sure what they will do with me."

"Why is that?" asked Tommy.

"I only signed one piece of paper when they pressed me into service. I'm pretty sure that Captain Williams had my enlistment amongst his effects. It is probably lost. There was never a muster or payroll after that."

"Damnation!" exclaimed Tommy. "They have no other record of your service? If I were you, I would pack my stuff and go home!"

"Tommy! Perish the thought! I could never do such a thing."

"Why not?"

"Because it would not be honorable. I am no deserter."

"But you were forced into service," reasoned Tommy. "Almost as if they placed a gun to your head. What was honorable about that?"

"Nothing," responded Walter. "Still, I signed their paper. I pledged my allegiance to the Continentals. I aim to follow through."

"Humph!" grunted Tommy. "You are a better man than I, Walter Billingsley."

"True. And don't you forget it," Walter teased, tossing a pebble at his friend.

A loud explosion of musket fire erupted to the west. There were at least five or six shots in quick succession. Walter and Tommy jumped with surprise and instinctively reached for their rifles.

"Stay where you are!" shrieked a high-pitched voice from the concealment of nearby trees. "You fellows are surrounded. Keep your hands where we can see them."

Walter and Tommy complied. There were twelve other men camped in the clearing with them, all assigned to the wagon. Their hands went high in the air, as well. A tall man in civilian clothing emerged from the woods, pistol in hand. At least three dozen other men, all similarly dressed, entered the clearing from various places of concealment. Walter glanced furtively in every direction. They were, indeed, surrounded.

The man with the pistol declared, "I hereby claim this wagon and its contents in the name of His Majesty, King George. You rebels are now the King's prisoners."

"Who the hell are you?" demanded Tommy.

"I am Colonel Samuel Bryan, commander of His Majesty's North Carolina Loyalist Militia." He grinned savagely. "At your service ..."

Three Weeks Later

Walter had no idea where he was. He had attempted to keep track of his direction since being captured, but the constant twists and turns of their incessant travel, especially at night, had him completely disoriented and thoroughly lost.

It had been quite a tumultuous three weeks. The fourteen men assigned to the wagon were first marched to Kimbrough's Mill on the Lynches River, where Colonel Bryan's main Tory force was bivouacked. Walter was shocked at the size of the encampment. Over eight hundred Loyalists were gathered there.

Colonel Bryan's first order of business was to attempt to rid himself of all of his prisoners. He was thrilled to have the wagon full of provisions, but clearly had no desire to babysit twenty surrendered rebels. He first attempted to turn them over to a detachment of British Legion dragoons at Anson's Courthouse, but they refused his entreaties. After a week of confinement in the Loyalist camp, a contingent of the 71st Fraser's Highlanders took charge of the growing group of prisoners. The affable Scotsmen took good care of the Americans and treated them most humanely.

That all changed, however, when a tyrant by the name of Captain Thomas Proctor took charge. He was a Loyalist, tried and true, and held nothing but disdain for his Whig prisoners. He was, in a word, an arse. He deprived the prisoners of food for several days and marched them without ceasing, allowing fewer than four hours of sleep each night. His guards mercilessly poked, prodded, chastised, and hounded the prisoners.

Walter was emotionally and physically spent. He gave up any thought of resistance. He had neither the strength nor the will to attempt an escape. He was done, as was Tommy. He occupied his mind by keeping careful count of the days. He focused his complete attention on walking ... simply placing one foot in front of the other.

Twenty-three days after their capture, Walter and Tommy stumbled alongside their fellow prisoners into the outskirts of a modest-sized town. In the center of the town, a waist-high stone fence bordered a large house constructed of similar stone. Hundreds of men were confined, under guard, inside the fence. It was a prison camp.

Walter hissed at the Loyalist guard closest to him, "Where are we?"

The guard slammed the stock of his musket into the small of Walter's back. "Shut your mouth, you filthy wretch! You will speak only when spoken to!"

Walter bit his lip in anger and continued walking. The guards took them through a wooden gate and escorted them to the front of the house.

"Halt!" shouted Captain Proctor.

A couple of the men sank to the ground, collapsing from exhaustion.

Proctor lost his temper. "Get back on your feet, you cowardly bastards! You will rest when I tell you to rest."

Neither man budged. One of them was unconscious. Proctor and several of his men began kicking the two collapsed prisoners.

The heavy wooden door of the house flung open and a British officer stepped outside onto the small porch. He surveyed the prisoners and looked upon the ongoing beatings with a measure of disdain.

"That is quite enough, Captain! You are dismissed. Leave my facility at once!"

"But, sir …"

"I said leave at once!" the officer retorted. "Your services are no longer needed. Go back from whence you came."

Captain Proctor displayed his anger openly. He did not enjoy being shamed, especially in front of his men.

"As you wish, Colonel." He bowed slightly, spun around, and stormed toward the gate. His men followed him.

The British colonel waited patiently until Captain Proctor was well outside the compound. The moment that the gate was closed, he stepped forward to the front of the porch to address the newly-arrived prisoners.

"I am glad that particular unpleasantness is done," he declared. "I apologize for any mistreatment that you have endured at the hands of that arrogant Colonial. You will not be treated thusly whilst in my charge." He grabbed the yellow facings of his brilliant red coat with both hands and stood just a bit taller. "Prisoners, I am Colonel Desmond Beecham, commandant of this prison. Welcome to Camden. Your war is over."

Camden! Walter's mind reeled. At long last, and in the most convoluted fashion, he had finally reached Camden … the home of his beloved Abigail.

PART III

Wandering Prisoner
1780-81

11

HUNGRY REUNION

Camden Prison – August 11, 1780

Walter Billingsley and Tommy Whitlock were engaged in an ongoing battle of digestive wills. The challenge was well into its second week. Each man tried to identify a food that the other might find repulsive and refuse to eat, even in their current state of hunger. The young men racked their brains daily, recalling the many dishes and concoctions that had once made them gag in disgust.

It had turned into quite a challenge. Thus far, they had not identified a single formerly despised or rejected food that they would not consume joyfully today, if given the opportunity.

"I know! I know!" exclaimed Tommy. "What about ... boiled okra?" He faked a gagging noise as he made the suggestion. "Picture an iron pot, running over with the slimy goo. And all those tiny, disgusting white balls floating in it. I'm talking about the kind of okra that slithers over your tongue and then just slides down your throat, leaving a foul coat of slime all in your mouth. Would you eat that?"

A couple of the men lounging nearby groaned in disgust. One of them, a fellow Virginian named Dawson, proclaimed, "Whitlock, you finally got me on that one! I've seen my pa's slaves eatin' that stuff mixed with 'maters. There's no way I would eat that shite … even if'fn I was about to starve!"

"What about you, Walter?" challenged Tommy.

Walter lounged in the shade near his friend, reclining against the outer stone wall of the compound. He was busy polishing something inside a piece of old cloth, and appeared to be single-mindedly focused on his task.

"What was the question, again?" Walter asked.

"Are you daft? Where is your mind, boy? I asked you if you would eat a bowl full of slimy boiled okra. Dawson said he would not touch the stuff, starved such as he is. What about you? Would you eat it?"

"I would, indeed." answered Walter, exhaling loudly. "I would swallow your boiled okra without hesitation. I might even try to give it a chew first, just so my teeth might get a little exercise." He grinned broadly as he continued his task of polishing.

"Ugh! I've hated that stuff for years," declared Tommy. "My grandfather insisted on growing it to feed his slaves, as well. Somehow, he took a liking to it. My mum made me eat that horrible slime all throughout my childhood. It felt like I was eating bowls of warm vomit."

"But you would eat some right now, wouldn't you?" countered Walter.

Tommy nodded. "I would lick the bowl clean when done and then ask for more!"

Walter and Tommy laughed joyfully. It was a rare moment of levity for the tired, homesick, hungry young men.

In actuality, they were well beyond hungry. They were approaching the early stages of starvation. In the six weeks they been held prisoner by the British in Camden, they could count the number of meals received on a single hand. Overall, living conditions within the prison had been difficult, but not unbearable. The main issue was the lack of rations. And the poor nutrition was beginning to take its toll.

It was customary during times of war that a nation would provide for the needs of its own prisoners held by the enemy. Unfortunately, the Continental Congress had precious little in the way of resources to provide for the needs of its thousands of prisoners in British captivity. And the British had absolutely no desire to share their provisions earmarked for use by their army.

So, the unfortunate detainees received only rations comprised of gifts presented by well-meaning civilians among the local populace. Unfortunately, with the British armies pillaging the area farms and fields, there was precious little left for benevolent neighbors to share.

Despite their constantly gnawing hunger, and the ensuing illnesses that hunger always caused, Walter and Tommy adjusted quickly to prison life. There were just over one hundred men under guard in the military gaol at Camden. For the most part, they were treated humanely. The commandant of the facility, Colonel Beecham, proved to be a man of his word. There were no unnecessary beatings or violence. The British troops charged with maintaining the prison camp did so with organization and discipline. Clearly, they were professional soldiers who obediently followed orders and performed their duties. It seemed that very few of them found any joy in overseeing prisoners, much less making their prisoners' lives more miserable than they already were.

Most of the men in the camp lived out of doors. They were housed within the confines of the stone wall that surrounded the house that served as the prison headquarters. There were several large oak and walnut trees that offered shade and some measure of comfort. Their captors provided ample tents and tiny wooden shacks to ensure protection from occasional rainfall. But, for the most part, the men lived and slept in the open in order to escape the oppressive South Carolina summer heat.

In recent days, the mosquitoes and biting flies had become almost unbearable. Some of the men had developed disease, including cases of ague. The British surgeon in charge of the medical care of the prisoners was dumbfounded by the unexpected appearance of ague, as there were no swamps nearby that might send forth their noxious gases to infect the prisoners. Somehow, thankfully, both Walter and Tommy had managed to avoid any of the growing number of plagues and illnesses.

The large stone house in the center of the prison, in addition to serving as Colonel Beecham's headquarters, also functioned as the barracks for the men of the British guard. The officers slept in bedrooms on the second level. The enlisted men were billeted in the tightly-packed attic. Though the attic would certainly be a comfortable place to sleep in winter, in the warmer months it was quite unpleasant. Most of the guards preferred sleeping outside during the summer heat. They created a small, walled-off area in the heavily shaded gardens in the rear of the house to serve as outdoor accommodations.

The house also served as an alternate location for housing prisoners that the British considered to be criminals or dangerous. Those poor souls were contained within the basement "dungeon" of the house, and denied all access to fresh air and daylight. No one envied the men being held there. Everyone toiled endlessly to avoid being sentenced to time in "the hole."

The British constructed gallows just outside the wall on the eastern side of the compound, but executions were infrequent. Only two men had been hanged during Walter and Tommy's period of captivity. Both had been convicted as spies, a crime which almost always culminated in a mandatory sentence of death. Otherwise, the gallows merely served as a deterrent against rebellion or other problem behaviors within the prison and town.

Walter and Tommy, like all of the other prisoners, attempted to pass the time in the myriad of ways that prisoners often do. They talked, they slept, and they played games. Contests of cards, dice, and marbles were most popular. There were three decks of ragged playing cards that made the rounds among the men. Most marble players employed musket and rifle balls as a substitute for the normal stoneware spheres.

There was also some rather remarkable ingenuity and industry within the camp. Amazingly, the British allowed the men to keep their pocket knives for everyday use during their imprisonment. Most of the men whittled sets of dice from pieces of antler or bone. They carved small statuettes and other works of folk art. Their pursuits were sometimes utilitarian, as well. Many men shaped and constructed tools, cups, bowls, and eating utensils to help make prison life a little easier.

One particularly talented fellow from North Carolina carved an exquisite set of chess pieces from limbs that he pulled from one of the walnut trees. It was his third such set, actually. Colonel Beecham heard about his first one, invited the young private to bring it to his office for a demonstration, and then promptly paid the fellow a handsome sum in silver for its purchase. He also arranged for the young man to carve a similar set for General Lord Cornwallis.

That soldier and his immediate circle of friends no longer suffered from the crippling hunger that plagued the other men. Having silver or copper coin inside the prison provided one with a great advantage. Prisoners with money could purchase food and supplies over the wall from the locals. All such transactions occurred under the watchful eyes of the guards, of course.

Walter had nothing of value to trade, nor any particular skill that could earn him a clandestine income while being held in the prison. Neither did Tommy. Walter knew without any doubt that their only hope of getting a supply of food and improving their lot was to make contact with Abigail. He needed, desperately, to get a message to the Hamer family.

Thus far, none of his efforts had been successful. He attempted to coax several of the guards into taking a message for him, but none would risk such a venture without significant recompense. They wanted to be paid, and paid well. As Walter was penniless, each of them, to a man, had balked at his entreaties.

He also attempted to lure local citizens toward the wall in order to make contact and then attempt to convince someone to pass a message to Alexander Hamer. But all of his attempts had failed. Unless one had coins or goods to hold high in the air and attract attention, no one would even approach the wall of the prison compound. Local residents intentionally passed by on the far side of the road.

Walter hoped that the tiny piece of treasure that he held in his hand would change all of that. Finally, he had something that might just lure one of the citizens of Camden within speaking distance. He polished his treasure vigorously and prayed.

Tommy kicked Walter's foot with his own. "What, in heaven's name, are you doing? You've been scrubbing something non-stop for the entire morning. What is it? A stone?"

Walter shook his head. "I am hoping that it is something that can put me in contact with Abigail."

"Well ... you have my attention now. What is it?"

Walter cut his eyes at his friend. "You must keep it a secret."

Tommy sighed, exasperated. "As if I would do otherwise! Now, tell me."

Walter glanced around to make sure no one else was looking. It appeared that they were alone. He carefully unfolded the cloth and revealed his secret project to Tommy. It was a gold-gilded coat button, rimmed with stars and sporting the number '33' in the center. It was from the uniform of a member of the British 33rd Regiment of Foot, one of the infantry units assigned to Camden.

Tommy gasped. "Where did you get that?"

"I saw it fall from the uniform of one of the soldiers that brought in that group of prisoners yesterday. I just happened to catch a glimpse of the sunlight reflecting as it fell. I ran to the spot and covered it with dust, then went back and retrieved it after they were gone."

"What are you going to do with it?"

"I'm going to use it to try and lure one of the local men over to the wall. I figure it's about the size of a guinea. Surely, when one of the passers-by catches a glimpse of gold in the sunlight, they'll not be able to resist coming over," Walter proclaimed wishfully.

"Then what?"

"Then, I will give them a note to deliver to Mr. Hamer."

"You've written a note? With what?"

"I stole a page of writing paper from the soldier's area last week."

Tommy gasped. "You went into their sleeping quarters? What if they had caught you?"

"Well, they didn't."

"But they might have!" Tommy shook his head in disbelief. "What else did you swipe? A quill and ink bottle, perhaps? Did you borrow some wax and a brass seal, as well? I suppose you have your Billingsley coat of arms tucked inside your shoe."

Walter chuckled. "No. Nothing so obvious as that. I've written a rough note with the charred end of a stick. It is crude, but the message is readable."

"What happens when your prospective deliveryman discovers that you're holding a button instead of a guinea?"

"I will promise payment from Mr. Hamer. I'm sure that he will reward their effort to deliver a message … if only we can get someone to venture over here in our direction."

Tommy teased, "Are you sure that Mr. Hamer will even give a King George penny for a letter from the likes of you?"

"Reasonably sure." Walter grinned.

Tommy cut his eyes at his friend. A hopeful look expanded across his face. "Damnation, Walter! It just might work!"

August 14, 1780

The Home of Alexander Hamer – Camden, South Carolina

Abigail reclined in the sitting room, sipping her tea and mending a pair of her father's wool stockings. She was amazed at the frequency with which he ripped the toe seams from his socks. On the previous day she accused him, teasingly, of possessing "razors on his big toes." Abigail remained convinced that a decent pedicure for her father would greatly reduce her mending responsibilities.

Sewing was not a task that Abigail was accustomed to performing. In times past, the family had always hired out such work to the local laundry woman or seamstress. But these were desperate times. Most families, even the more affluent ones like the Hamers, had been forced to develop new skills in recent months. They had little choice. The British occupation had placed a stranglehold on labor and capital throughout the region. Local citizens, especially those who favored independency, had to fend for themselves.

Abigail did not mind the work. She rather enjoyed learning how to do new things. She knew that practical skills would be advantageous for her once she began her new life as a farmer's wife in North Carolina. She had been practicing her cooking for months now, perfecting most of the dishes that Walter enjoyed. She knew that he would be very proud of her. And she ached for the day when, at long last, they would be joined as man and wife.

But where was he? That was the haunting question. No one had heard from Walter after the explanatory letter to his mother. That had been almost two months ago. Neither Mrs. Billingsley nor Abigail had the slightest notion as to the designation of his regiment or the name of his commander, much less the location where he was deployed. But, Abigail remained convinced that he was alive. She could sense his presence. She knew, beyond any doubt, that her heart would have informed her if her beloved Walter had fallen in battle. So, she waited, prepared, hoped, and prayed for the day when she would hear from him again.

"Oh, Walter ..." she whispered. "Please reach out to me. Please write to me. Please find me."

A loud knock on the front door startled her in the midst of her thoughts and prayers. She accidentally poked her sewing needle into the soft flesh of her left thumb. She instinctively stuck the impaled digit into her mouth.

Her mother's voice echoed down the stairway. "Abigail, dear, would you please get the door? I am indisposed."

"Yes, Mother!"

Abigail placed the sock, needle, and thread on the thick cushion of her Queen Anne chair, rose gracefully, and sauntered to the door. She opened the heavy portal and was greeted by the sight of a stranger on the porch. He was a common working man, unkempt and dirty in appearance. His shirt, though it had once been white, was now a dull shade of off-tan. It hung loosely over the top of his tattered blue breeches. He wore no weskit, stockings, or shoes. He had every appearance of being a rat catcher. Abigail assumed it to be his chosen profession.

The man smiled broadly upon the appearance of a beautiful young woman at the door. He quickly removed his filthy straw hat and held it respectfully against his chest.

"Good mornin', milady!"

Abigail instinctively returned the door to a partially-closed position. She spoke tersely. "Yes? What is your business here?"

"I have been hired to deliver a message to Mr. Hamer, the master of this house."

"He is not here at the moment, but will return later this afternoon. You may give me the message."

"Oh, I would love to, milady. But you see, I have been promised by the fellow who gave me this message that Mr. Hamer would reimburse me well for my troubles."

Abigail eyed the fellow suspiciously. "Indeed? Since when has one been required to pay for the receipt of a letter? I know that these are strange times, but have postal riders suddenly taken to delivering messages on the hopes that the recipients will pay?"

"Oh, I am not a postal rider, milady. I am but a humble resident of Camden, asked to perform a favor for a gentleman ... for a price, of course."

Abigail attempted to discern the man's motives. She searched his countenance for any hint of artifice. He was certainly dirty, but seemed honest enough.

"Very well. Wait here. I will fetch a half-penny for your troubles."

Abigail moved to close the door, but the fellow stealthily stuck his bare foot into the opening.

"Beggin' your pardon, Miss, but this here letter will cost you a shilling."

"A shilling?" Abigail barked with surprise. "Where is it from? Philadelphia? Was it authored by His Excellency George Washington, himself?"

"No, Miss. It is from the prison at the north end of town ... the one where the rebels are housed."

She rolled her eyes. "Why, on earth, would Mr. Hamer pay a shilling for a letter from a prison, much less from someone here in our own village?"

The man appeared confused. "The fellow who gave me the letter assured me that Mr. Hamer would pay me generously. I require a shilling."

Abigail was becoming annoyed with the filthy man. She began to sense that he was nothing more than a trickster. She decided to test him.

"Who is this fellow?" she challenged him. "Is he a local resident or businessman? An employee at the camp? My father shall desire to have words with him!"

"No, Miss. He is one of the prisoners." He teasingly held up a small, stained, folded piece of paper. "He told me to inform your father that his name was, 'Walter Billingsley.' Does that name sound, at all, familiar to you, milady?"

Abigail's eyes rolled back into her head. She fainted and collapsed in a heap on the floor of the foyer.

Alexander Hamer stared across the wall that separated him from his future son-in-law. He barely recognized the gaunt figure before him. He wanted to embrace the boy, but personal contact was not allowed by the guards. Walter, despite his lowly estate, fairly beamed with pleasure at the appearance of Abigail's father.

"Walter, I simply cannot believe it is you. We received word from your mother several weeks ago about your impressment into the Virginia Continentals. How long ago were you captured?"

"About six weeks ago, sir."

"Good God! That is right about the time we received the correspondence from your dear mother. And you've been here the entire time?"

"Almost, though it took several days of marching to get here."

"Unbelievable! And all this time you have been incarcerated only two miles from our home." He stared at the ground and shook his head in disbelief. "Where were you captured?"

"Up in North Carolina. I was in a detachment headed to Hillsborough for reassignment."

"Reassignment?" Mr. Hamer appeared confused.

Walter's head dropped in sadness. "Yes, sir. My entire company was wiped out in a battle up above Waxhaw's Meeting House, right around the end of May."

"Are you talking about Buford's defeat? The massacre? You were there?" he exclaimed in disbelief.

"Yes. Why? Have you heard of it?"

Mr. Hamer nodded slightly. "Everyone has heard about it, Walter." He looked around to ensure that no one was listening, then hissed, "Banastre Tarleton is a hated figure in the Carolinas. The rumor is that his troops executed men on the battlefield."

Walter nodded grimly. "It is true, Mr. Hamer. Every word."

"Goodness. Then the rally cry of 'Tarleton's Quarter' is justified, indeed."

"People are using those words as a rally cry?"

"Indeed, they are, Son. The injustice of the massacre at Waxhaws has served to awaken the passions of the Patriots in our land."

"Well, at least that is some good news," declared Walter.

"Something that we truly need these days," affirmed Alexander. He paused, and then peered searchingly over Walter's shoulder. "What about the young man who accompanied you on your journey … the one who was to help you collect Abigail? I cannot remember his name."

"Gabriel Tate. He didn't make it, Mr. Hamer. He fell at the Waxhaws."

Alexander stared sadly into Walter's eyes. "I am so very sorry, Son. I'm sure that you cared very deeply for him."

"Yes, sir. Very much so."

Mr. Hamer looked past Walter and surveyed the camp. "What about you, Walter? How can I help you? There must be something that I can do."

"I need food, Mr. Hamer. Everyone in this place is starving. We have to fend for ourselves and attempt to trade over the walls with local people for whatever food we can secure. But I have no goods or money to trade. I am growing quite desperate. I hate to request your help, but fear that I may starve without it. I'm not asking you to feed everyone inside the prison. I just need rations for myself and my friend, Tommy Whitlock. He is a Virginian who found me on the night of the battle. He has been my constant companion, and has helped keep me alive ever since that night. I owe him my life."

Mr. Hamer nodded. "Of course. We all owe him a great debt. I will be more than happy to help you boys." He scowled. "It angers me that our local populace has been profiteering from your predicament. Our citizens need to do something to help the Patriots in this prison. I'm going to see what I can do about it. Meanwhile, take this …" He reached into his weskit pocket, removed his coin purse, and poured the contents into Walter's hand. "Will that get you by for a day or two?"

Walter gasped. "Oh, Mr. Hamer! That will feed us for a week, at least!"

"Good. It may take me a couple of days to organize your provisions. Meanwhile, I will make arrangements to send one of my hired men with a basket of rations the day after tomorrow. Abigail will be anxious to handle all of the preparations, I'm sure." He smiled. "We will send plenty of food for you and your friend, and you may share the extra with whomever you wish. I will also post a letter to your mother first thing tomorrow. She needs to be informed of your situation."

Walter was on the verge of tears. "I cannot express to you how grateful I am, sir."

"Nonsense. It is the least I can do for my future son-in-law." He smiled warmly.

Walter's lip quivered slightly. "I am desperate to see Abigail, but . . ."

Mr. Hamer nodded and finished his sentence for him. "But we cannot bring her to this ghastly place."

"Exactly."

"Perhaps we can devise a way for you to meet at some point in the future. Meanwhile, Abigail will be satisfied enough knowing that you are safe and well-fed. I am quite sure that she will invest herself wholeheartedly in taking care of you from afar."

Walter grinned. "Thank you, sir. For everything."

Mr. Hamer grabbed Walter across the fence and embraced him.

Walter protested, "Sir! The guards!"

"To hell with the guards," Hamer responded. He hugged Walter closer.

Alexander hastened home. His wife and daughter saw him coming down the street and ran onto the front lawn to meet him.

Abigail blurted excitedly, "Is it truly him, Papa? Is it my Walter?"

He smiled and nodded. "It is, indeed. He is alive."

Relief flooded her countenance. "Oh, thank God! Thank God! Thank God! I have been outside my mind with worry."

"But is he well?" inquired his wife.

Alexander's face became grim. He shook his head. "He is starving, my darling, as are most of the men inside those walls."

Abigail covered her hand with her mouth. Her appearance converted from relief to shock. "Papa, what can we do?"

"I gave him some silver coin … enough to get him by for a couple of days. Men who have money can purchase food over the fence from the townsfolk. But I'm sure it will not be of very high quality. What the boy needs is nutritious food and drink. No doubt, he will need medicine, clothing, and bedding once the weather begins to turn colder." He paused. "He has asked for some assistance for a friend, as well."

"Is Gabriel well? I am so glad that he is with Walter," Abigail declared.

Her father shook his head. "No, Daughter. Gabriel fell in battle six weeks ago. He is dead. Walter has a new companion to whom he has grown very close."

Abigail's forlorn eyes met her father's. The anguish that flooded her soul escaped from those eyes. "Oh, Papa! No! Gabriel died because of me, didn't he? He was coming to assist me!" She exploded into violent tears.

Alexander embraced his daughter. "There, now … do not speak such nonsense. It was not because of you. He traveled with Walter because they were the best of friends. And he died because it was his time."

"What are we going to do now, Alexander?" demanded his wife.

"We're going to take care of our boy and his friend, that's what we are going to do. I have promised a care basket full of goodies day after tomorrow. I assumed that Abigail would desire to be in charge of such a project."

She pulled her head away from his chest. "Oh, yes, Papa! I will construct a picnic basket fit for a king!"

"And I am quite sure that young Walter might enjoy a little letter of encouragement from you, as well … along with some stationery and pen to write you back. Don't you think?"

Abigail wiped the tears from her eyes. She smiled warmly at her father and nodded. "I shall be up all night writing letters to my Walter!"

Noon - The Following Day

"There's a hell of a lot of them. What do you think is going on?" asked Tommy, smacking his lips and picking shreds of meat from between his teeth with a stiff blade of grass. The boys had just enjoyed a hearty helping of dried beef and stale bread, courtesy of the generous financial gift from Alexander Hamer. The swarthy fellow who sold them the food had even been so kind as to include two bottles of warm, flat ale.

Walter drained his bottle and belched. "I don't know, but it must be something big."

British troops had flooded the village of Camden overnight. Hundreds of them. Their encampments occupied virtually all of the fields and pastures around the town. The scarlet-clad soldiers milled about the streets and businesses. Some companies marched smartly in formation down the main thoroughfare of the village.

"Do you think one of the guards will tell us anything?" mused Tommy.

"I doubt it. But, I suppose we can try."

Tommy pointed to a tall English soldier who was standing guard beside the main gate. "That new kid, Private Blevins, seems like a pretty nice chap. He has spoken kindly to me a couple of times. Do you think he would be willing to share some news?"

Walter shrugged. "I don't suppose it would hurt to try."

Tommy and Walter sauntered nonchalantly toward the gate and stood near the guard. They stared past the fellow at the mass of soldiers in the street. Private Blevins eyed them suspiciously.

He inquired in his perfect King's English, "I say, can I help you gentlemen in some way? You're making me a bit leery, hovering about as you are. You should refrain from standing in the gate area. Someone might get the notion that you were planning to attempt an escape." He grinned sarcastically.

"As if that would work on a day like today," quipped Walter, tilting his head in the direction of a passing company of British troops.

"We have no notions of escape, Private Blevins," Tommy reassured him. "We were just wondering what you thought about all of these troops in the village."

"There are a lot of them. New ones, fresh in town," added Walter. "What's going on?"

The private cocked his head slightly as he evaluated the honesty of the two prisoners. He seemed satisfied with the fact that they were simply curious.

He responded, "I was told that there is a rebel army in the region, commanded by a fellow named Gates. General Cornwallis has brought his regiments up out of Charlestown to engage them. But, not to worry, I'm told they will be moving on from Camden later today."

"Which direction?" asked Tommy.

"I couldn't say," responded the guard, grinning slightly. "What use would such information be to you fellows, anyhow?"

"No use, Mr. Blevins. Like I said, we're just curious. Food is already hard enough to find around here. We're worried that this flood of new troops, pockets filled with shillings, will make finding a meal a lot more difficult for us."

Private Blevins nodded knowingly. "I see your point. But, you have little cause for concern. As I said, they should be on their way before day's end."

Walter nodded. "Thank you, Mr. Blevins."

"You are quite welcome. Now, if you would kindly return to your assigned area at once."

"Right away, sir," responded Tommy.

The two friends returned to their spot in the shade. They leaned against a tree and continued to watch the boisterous activity in the street.

"What do you think, Walter?"

"I think a fight is coming, and it might be nearer to us than Private Blevins is letting on."

Dawn – The Next Morning - August 16, 1780

Walter awakened with a start. Something had shaken him. He glanced suspiciously at Tommy, thinking that his friend must be perpetrating some sort of practical joke. Tommy was sound asleep and snoring softly. All of the other prisoners were dozing, as well.

A dull, low rumble echoed across the prison yard. The ground trembled slightly. Tiny pieces of debris rained down from the tree overhead. Walter saw a flash of light to the north. He climbed stiffly to his feet and darted to the stone wall. The streets were deserted. He scanned the British encampments in the fields to the east. The tents were still in place, and smoke wafted from a handful of extinguished fires, but there were no troops. The army was gone.

There was another explosion to the north, followed by a barrage of booms. It was artillery. Again, Walter could see the flashes. They were quite some distance away, likely several miles. But, somewhere to the north, a dawn battle raged.

Walter glanced toward the gate. Private Blevins remained at his post. He, too, stared in the direction of the rumbling cannons. He nodded cordially at Walter, who returned the gesture.

Walter sauntered back over to his tree and lay back down next to Tommy. Silently, fervently, he prayed for the American armies, and for victory.

Late Afternoon

The prisoners lined the walls and stared with curiosity and wonder at the feverish activity occurring throughout the village. They had listened to hours of artillery and musket fire. They observed dispatch riders and wagons loaded with supplies departing the village throughout the early hours of the morning. The Patriots ached for some news about the battle. Could it, perhaps, have been a victory for the Continentals?

Several wagons full of wounded Redcoats rolled into Camden during the late morning. The wagons continued to arrive in a steady stream. Each one was filled to overflowing with wounded soldiers. Many of them were brightly-clad Scotsmen. The prisoners could hear their screams of agony and fear.

Two of the local taverns were immediately converted into hospitals. Surgeons and medics cared for their wounded in homes, on porches, and in the streets. The scene was something akin to an organized form of chaos. The entire village seemed to be participating in the aftermath of the battle.

The British troops trickled back into the village and their adjacent encampments throughout the afternoon. It was obvious that the soldiers had participated in a great battle. Their uniforms were stained with dirt, soot, and blood. There were dozens of "walking wounded," injured men who had managed to return to Camden on foot.

Still, the prisoners received no word. It was almost as if they did not even exist, anymore. No one in the village paid any attention to them. There were no hopeful vendors, traders, or food salesmen. No one approached the wall to sell their wares. Every available person in the village was consumed with the care of wounded Englishmen. So, the stomachs of the imprisoned Americans rumbled. Their hunger added to the torture of their need for news from the battlefront.

The men were just about to begin claiming their sleeping spots and settling in for the dusk when a cry erupted from the vicinity of the main gate.

"Look! Prisoners!"

A huge column of captives approached from the north. There were hundreds of them.

"My God!" exclaimed Tommy. "Surely, they are not planning to bring that bunch in here. Where will we put them all?"

"I suppose we will find out soon enough," declared Walter.

Minutes later the guards opened the gate and the flood of prisoners flowed into the walled compound. Several dozen British troops took up positions just outside the wall. And the captive Americans kept coming. For over an hour they flowed into the prison yard.

Near the end of the parade of prisoners, there seemed to be a bit of commotion. Two soldiers of the British Legion were dragging one poor fellow on the ground between them. He was a very young man. His arms were tied behind his back and he was unconscious. They hoisted him up the walkway toward the prison headquarters.

A tall, filthy, skinny fellow followed closely behind the stricken lad. His breeches hung off of him in tatters. His pitiful, threadbare weskit had no buttons and hung open and loose over his blood-stained shirt. He was obviously a militiaman. His voice sounded rural and uneducated. Walter guessed that he was from North Carolina. The man shouted words of encouragement to his pal.

"You hang tough now, Jamie! Don't let these buggers get to you! You ain't done nothin' wrong! We'll be loose and out of this place before you know it, mark my words!"

One of the British Legionnaires turned and gave the filthy fellow a violent shove in the face. "Get back, you stinkin' mongrel, before I run you through!"

The skinny man whipped off his nasty hat and stuck it in the soldier's face. "You can just suck my wally, you powder-head! I got a feelin' you would enjoy that." He sneered defiantly at the British soldier. "That fellow you're draggin' is my best friend in this whole world, and he ain't done nothin' wrong. You bunch of shite-lickers are treatin' him like some kind of criminal for no reason a'tall. I hope you all fall in the dunny and drown in your own piss!"

The Legionnaire turned smartly and kicked the nasty fellow in the groin. The poor man collapsed to the ground in pain, heaved, and vomited the mucoid, bilious contents of his empty stomach onto the ground beside his face. The soldiers dragged his friend through the door of the house and then slammed it closed behind him.

"I wonder what that youngster did," whispered one of the prisoners standing behind Walter and Tommy.

"I don't know. But whatever it was, he's going into the hole, for sure," Walter declared as he darted toward the fallen militiaman. He grabbed the fellow beneath his unpleasantly fragrant arms and helped him back to his feet.

The stranger nodded. "I'm grateful for your kindness, sir."

"We North Carolina boys have to stick together," declared Walter.

"How did you know where I'm from?"

"Just a guess. You have a most distinctive manner of speech." Walter grinned. "What did your friend do to get in so much trouble?"

"Jamie? Not a damned thing! But one of Tarleton's officers claimed he recognized him from somewhere."

Walter cut his eyes at Tommy. "Tarleton was in this fight?"

The fellow nodded grimly. "Hell, yes, he was. Why? You know him?"

"Let's just say we've seen his work," answered Tommy.

"We were at Buford's defeat," added Walter.

The man grunted with disdain. "I'm damn glad to meet you boys." He offered them his hand.

Walter grinned. "I'm Walter Billingsley, from Guilford County. This is my compatriot, Tommy Whitlock. He's a Virginian."

The coarse fellow shook Tommy's hand. "Well, can't everybody be from paradise like me and old Walter, here." He grinned broadly, displaying a mouth full of decayed, dark teeth. "I'm Joel Moffatt, out of Mecklenburg County."

12

A REASON TO STAY

Guilford Courthouse – August 30, 1780

Elizabeth Billingsley sat alone in her parlor. Her cup of tea was untouched and had gone cold. She reclined silently on the settee, clutching a letter against her breast. She wept. She could scarcely believe the wonderful news. Her missing son, Walter, was alive.

She heard the rear door of the house slam closed. A voice called from the dining room, "Mother! I am home! Just in time for tea!"

It was her daughter, Martha, back from an outing with her friends. She almost floated into the parlor, such was her joy and excitement.

"Oh, Mother! I have had a simply delightful time. You would not believe who joined us for the picnic! It was positively …"

She stopped mid-sentence when she saw her mother's disheveled appearance and the tears that stained her cheeks.

"Oh, Mama! What is wrong? Why are you crying?"

He mother smiled victoriously. "These are not tears of sorrow, Daughter. They are tears of utter and complete joy."

"Tell me!" Martha urged. "What has given rise to such happiness?"

Elizabeth held out the letter toward her daughter. "It is Walter! He is alive!"

Martha's eyes opened wide with shock. It had been months since they received word from Walter. Martha had long feared that he was injured or dead. She grabbed the letter from her mother's hands and quickly scanned its words. Her lips moved rapidly as she read each line.

Martha glanced at her mother, confused. "Walter is in prison?"

"A prison of war, my dear. He was captured by Tories many weeks ago."

Martha continued to read. "Oh, my goodness! Walter was in a battle?" A tear glistened in the corner of her eye. She looked sadly toward her mother. "And poor Gabriel Tate is dead."

"Yes. It is tragic. That boy was a jester and a fool, but I never harbored any ill will against him. My heart breaks for his parents. I must inform them immediately. I will go to their home after tea."

"And I will accompany you, Mother." She scanned the letter again. "How did Mr. Hamer find out where Walter was imprisoned?"

Elizabeth shrugged. "I do not know. But, it matters not. He found him, thank God. And he is actively providing for his needs."

Martha glanced at the upper right corner of the letter. "This date is almost a month ago. It took that long for us to receive a correspondence?"

"Yes, Darling. Camden is under British control. By some miracle, Mr. Hamer managed to get the letter smuggled out of Camden by sending it through a contact in Charlestown. Apparently, it traveled by sea through the port at Jamestown. A postal rider carried it overland to us, and delivered it today."

"That was quite a roundabout, wandering route for a tiny little letter," mumbled Martha.

"Indeed. It is a miracle, in my opinion. The entire set of circumstances is miraculous."

Martha smiled and took her mother by the hand. "It is truly remarkable, I agree. So ... Walter is alive. What must we do now?"

Elizabeth's chin dropped to her chest. "There is nothing practical that we can do, Martha. Not from such a great distance. But we must pray, both for Walter and for the Hamer family."

"Of course, Mother. And we shall pray that Walter will return to us very soon."

"With his lovely bride by his side," added Elizabeth, smiling broadly.

Camden Prison - September 2, 1780

Walter, Tommy, and their new friend Joel Moffatt sat behind the trunk of a large tree in a quiet, secluded corner of the prison yard. They had claimed the obscure location because they wanted to avoid the jealous, angry stares of their fellow prisoners of war. They desired to eat in peace, which wasn't easy within the tight confines of the detention area.

Eating their life-saving parcels of food from the Hamer household had become less socially challenging, though, in recent days. There were significantly fewer prisoners than there had been throughout the prior month. The population of captives had previously swelled to over five hundred immediately following the huge battle just north of Camden. The British had slowly and steadily labored to reduce that number and remove the prisoners elsewhere.

Tommy was busy sucking every microscopic fiber of meat from a chicken leg bone. Joel was thoroughly enjoying some raw tomatoes and chunks of fresh bread. Walter nibbled on a sweet cookie as he read yet another letter from his beloved Abigail.

"Well ... don't keep us in suspense, Walter. What news does the lovely maiden, Abigail, have for us today?" inquired Tommy.

"Nothing, really. She tends to ramble on about her folks and life in her home." He grinned. "It all sounds so peaceful and ordinary. I like it."

"Any news about this damnable war?" asked Joel.

Walter frowned and shook his head. "She did mention that she has seen a lot of prisoners marching south toward Charlestown. She says that she looks for me in every group."

"Well, it won't be long now," declared Joel, spitting moist crumbs of bread as he spoke. "They've been emptyin' this place out pretty steady. I figger they'll have us all cleared outta here by the end of the week." He then lifted his leg and unleashed a thunderous, putrid fart.

"Christ, Almighty, Joel! You are the foulest man I have ever met. I swear ... one of these rats must have crawled up your arse and died!" proclaimed Tommy.

Joel cackled with joy. He took a huge bite out of a raw onion. "That ain't nuthin'! Just you wait till this here fresh onion finds my bowels! I'll singe the hairs right outta yer nose. Never mind Charlestown. You boys might not survive till mornin'!" He howled with laughter.

Walter and Tommy simply grinned and shook their heads. Joel Moffatt was a colorful character, indeed. The foul-mouthed ruffian from Mecklenburg County had won their hearts during the days following his arrival in the camp. Joel could always be counted upon for a laugh, for support, and for a word of encouragement. His language was difficult to bear, at times, as was his inability to restrain any thought that entered his brain from exiting his mouth. Still, he had already proven to be a resourceful, faithful friend.

Walter lowered his letter grimly and watched another group of twenty-five prisoners marching, under guard, through the front gate. Their destination was certain. It was a network of prison encampments near Charlestown. Rumors abounded that some men were even being placed on special prison ships in Charlestown's harbor.

"Well, I, for one, don't plan on going to Charlestown," declared Walter.

"You have reason to stay, that's for sure," affirmed Tommy. "But I doubt any of us will have much choice in the matter."

"I'll figure something out. I have to. I cannot comprehend leaving Abigail."

"Hell, you ain't even seen her yet, Billingsley! What makes you think you ever will, so long as you're kept here in this British prison?" challenged Joel.

"A fellow can hope, can't he?" retorted Walter, somewhat perturbed.

There was a commotion in the vicinity of the front gate. The tiny group of picnicking prisoners peeked around their tree of concealment. Five soldiers had entered the compound, all of them sporting the distinctive red and green dragoon uniforms of the British Legion.

"Christ, Almighty!" mumbled Joel. "That's by-God Tarleton, himself!"

Walter stared numbly at the fellow leading the procession. It was, indeed, Banastre Tarleton, the commander of the Legion.

"What do you think he is doing here?" wondered Tommy.

"It's gotta have somethin' to do with James. I reckon he's the only man left in the basement of that house," responded Joel grimly.

"What did your friend do to so enrage the British?" asked Walter. "I thought you said he was an ordinary militiaman like you."

Joel scooted his hat forward and scratched the back of his nasty head. He leaned closer and whispered, "He is, 'cept for the five British Legion soldiers him and his brothers bushwhacked back in May." He spat in disdain. "The bastards raped and murdered Jamie's bride-to-be. So, old Jamie and his little brothers sent 'em on to the hereafter."

Joel looked at the faces of his friends. Their eyes displayed their astonishment.

"It was messy, bloody stuff," Joel continued. "I'm afeered they must've found out somethin', or else they wouldn't be a treatin' him this way."

"Well, let us hope that they will let him out soon," encouraged Tommy.

"Indeed," added Walter. "I will write Abigail and ask for more rations starting tomorrow. I'm quite sure that your friend will be hungry once he is released."

"I hope you boys are right," answered Joel. "I don't know what I'd do without old Jamie. He is my one and only best pal."

Three hours later the doors of the prison headquarters building swung open. Tarleton and his British Legionnaires marched smartly down the steps and quickly exited the prison compound. A few minutes after, two guards escorted a thin, pale, gaunt man out of the door and released him into the yard. The fellow was pitiful. His clothes were stained and threadbare. He was wearing only one shoe. He covered his eyes, obviously blinded by the brilliant rays of the sun.

The high-pitched voice of Joel Moffatt shrieked across the prison yard. "Jamie!"

He ran to the disoriented man and embraced him. They talked for several minutes. Joel appeared to be very excited by the substance of their conversation. He let out a loud howl of celebration and then gave his friend another boisterous hug. A short while later, Joel escorted the pitiful, wretched creature to the comfort of the shade tree where Walter and Tommy reclined. Both men rose to meet him.

"Boys!" Joel announced with great fanfare, "This here is the friend that I have told ya both so much about. The smooth talkin' lad convinced old Tarleton that he was innocent of all charges. So, here he is!"

Walter reached out to shake the man's hand. "I'm glad you're finally out of the hole. This lout hasn't stopped talking about you since he got here. I'm Walter Billingsley."

Tommy shook his hand, as well. "And I'm Tommy Whitlock."

"Glad to meet you fellows. It is good to be out, that's for sure. I'm James Hamilton."

"Come, James, we have saved some food for you," proclaimed Tommy. "Are you hungry?"

"I'm famished. I have not eaten anything but moldy bread and water for two weeks."

"Well, we saved you some freshly-baked bread and a little pork. But I'd advise you to take it slow and easy. Don't eat too much or too fast. You might make yourself sick."

"I'm most grateful, gentlemen."

They escorted the tired, hungry lad to their picnic basket.

"That looks mighty fancy," declared James. "How do you get one of those baskets here in prison?"

"It's a long story," answered Tommy. "Walter's fiancé and her family live here in Camden. They've been keeping the three of us well-fed."

"That is simply incredible," declared James as he devoured a slice of smoked pork.

Walter pondered as he watched his new friend eat. There was something very familiar about the man's name. He was certain that he had heard it before. He shot a glance at Tommy.

"Tommy, where have I heard the name 'James Hamilton' mentioned before?"

"I don't know," his friend shrugged. "I'm sure that Joel has said it a thousand times."

"No. Joel has always called him, 'Jamie.' When I heard 'James Hamilton,' it was like a bell went off in my mind."

"I don't reckon we have met," mumbled James, his mouth full of bread. "I've lived in Mecklenburg County for most of my life."

"Mecklenburg County," echoed Walter. "Where is your place?"

"Out east of Charlotte Town, along the Rocky River. Right on Coddle Creek, actually."

"The Rocky River!" Walter repeated, smiling broadly. He looked victoriously at Tommy. "Don't you remember? When we were on patrol after getting lost in the hills? That fellow who fed us meat and hard cider?"

"I think you might have lost your mind," responded Tommy. "I was never with you in Mecklenburg County ... not that I know of."

Walter gasped. "God, Almighty! I am so very sorry, Tommy. My old friend, Gabriel, was with me back then. I can't believe that I confused you with him in my memories. I must be losing my mind, indeed."

"You confused me with your very best friend, Walter. I consider that an honor." He smiled warmly.

James and Joel glanced at one another, confused.

"What the hell are you talking about, Walter?" demanded Joel. "You've been along the Rocky River? That's right where me and ole Jamie here are from!"

Walter stared thoughtfully. "I don't remember his name, but I met a fellow with a pretty young wife who said she had a son in the militia. She looked entirely too young to be married to the man, much less have a son in the army. I could have sworn that she said her son was named Hamilton." He glanced hopefully at James. "Does that sound like your folks?"

James stared disbelievingly at Walter. "Was the fellow named Ephraim Farr?"

"That's it!" exclaimed Walter, simultaneously snapping his fingers. "Ephraim Farr!"

"Aw, hell! He is my mother's husband!"

The men erupted into giddy laughter. They could scarcely believe the circumstances by which their lives had intersected.

"Wait ... are telling me that you have actually met my mother?" James confirmed.

"I have, indeed. My friend, Gabriel Tate, and I stumbled upon their farm one day. She fed us well and told us all about her sons.

She was a lovely, gracious woman, James." Walter grinned. "Mr. Farr was kind to us, as well. He seemed like a good man."

James seemed a bit stunned. He mused with wonder, "It truly is a small world, isn't it?"

September 7, 1780

Fewer than fifty captives remained in the camp at Camden. As the number of prisoners dwindled to a more manageable level, the commandant decided to begin using them as laborers on work details outside the walls. Most of the men did not mind the new assignment. Indeed, they relished the opportunity to escape the boredom of prison.

Walter and his friends were assigned a particularly enviable task. They had been taken on a most pleasant ride by wagon to Colonel Beecham's new estate, located two miles west of Camden, to perform some clean-up and maintenance. The colonel wanted the property to be made more presentable and prepared for receiving guests. He had plans for hosting parties and balls on the expansive estate. He was in a hurry to complete the work, since he was scheduled to host his first grand ball on Sunday, a mere three days away.

The colonel had confiscated the sizable holdings of a Patriot assemblyman by the name of Thaddeus Doring. The wealthy landowner and his family had been forced to flee for their lives several days before British troops arrived, abandoning the farm and home, as well as all of their slaves and other worldly belongings. The British colonel visited the estate shortly after his arrival in Camden, and found it to be quite suitable for his tastes. He laid claim and secured a legal British deed to the confiscated house, furnishings, slaves, outbuildings, and acreage.

In addition to a large brick home, the property came with several barns, numerous sheds, a row of well-constructed servant quarters, and a handsome supply of livestock. It was a perfect location for his home, with ample opportunities for business profits and plenty of space to house his personal staff and guards.

Walter, Tommy, James, and Joel were assigned the unpleasant task of mucking out the horse and cattle stalls and cleaning out some of the more neglected barns and outbuildings. But they did not mind, at all. They relished in the sense of freedom that they gained from being outside the cramped walls of the prison yard. Three dozen red-coated troops were scattered throughout the nearby fields and pastures. A squad of soldiers manned a checkpoint on the road to the farm. The abundance of enemy troops was a vivid reminder to the laboring prisoners that they were not truly free men. Still, they quite enjoyed the work. They also enjoyed a generous mid-day meal, courtesy of Colonel Beecham and his wife, served picnic-style on the lawn in front of the house. The prisoners ate alongside their British guards. For a few precious moments, they almost forgot the fact that they were prisoners of war.

After the meal, they lounged in the shade and waited for their captors to order them back to work. All four men were napping when the call came in the form of a heavily-accented British voice.

"Get up, you lazy rebels!" It was Private Blevins, one of the friendlier British guards. "Sergeant Oliver says it's time for you gents to get back to work."

All four men groaned and began to rise to their feet.

"Billingsley! You will accompany me to the implement barn. The rest of you will return to the horse barns. The colonel wants all of his riding animals fed, watered, and brushed."

"What is needed in the implement barn?" asked Walter curiously.

"I am not certain. I only know that Colonel Beecham requested a man there."

"Very well," Walter answered, sighing. He waved good-naturedly to his friends. He teased, "I reckon I will see you fellows later. Have plenty of fun amongst the horses and cows."

"Do not toy with us, Walter," advised Tommy. "You may be spending the remainder of the afternoon sharpening axes and hoes. Perhaps you might even get a blister!"

Walter picked up a small rock and hurled it at his pal.

Tommy protested, "Private Blevins! Did you see that? This brigand has assaulted me! I could be injured!"

Blevins grinned. "Enough with the horseplay. I say, you jesters are going to get the entire lot of us in trouble with the commandant. Be gone with you! To the barns!"

The three men turned and marched off toward the main horse barn. Walter trudged obediently behind the immaculately-clad Private Blevins. As they walked, he decided to risk a conversation with the friendly lad.

"How old are you, Private Blevins? You seem a bit young for the army."

"I am seventeen. And yourself?"

"I am nineteen, just a little older than you. Actually, you are about the same age as my younger brother, Basil."

"Is he in the rebel military, as well?"

"No, thank God! He is entirely too young. Besides, someone has to remain home and care for our mother."

Blevins nodded. "Of course." He scanned the area around them to ensure that no one was observing their cordial conversation, then continued the exchange. "There are actually plenty of fellows my age serving in the King's army. It's not a bad life, really. Always a place to sleep and two good meals a day. All of my clothing is provided. It's certainly much better than my prospects were back in Yorkshire."

"Is that a city? Like our York City?"

"No, not at all. It is a county, much like your American counties or districts. It is a rural place, with many large estates, farms, and small villages."

"Is there not much work and opportunity there? Surely you could possess a farm of your own."

"It does not really work that way in England, I'm afraid. Barons and lords own all of the land. The working classes rent and farm the land. Other individuals serve the lords in some capacity. My own parents are in service."

"What does that mean?" asked Walter, somewhat confused.

"It means they serve in the lord's house. My dad and mum are personal servants in the castle of the Duke of Richmond. My father is first footman, and my mother is a lady's maid to one of the duke's daughters. Had I stayed in England, I would likely have entered service, as well."

"Is it a bad life?"

He smiled warmly. "No, not at all. Compared to work on a farm or in a stable, it is luxurious. Most all of the labor is indoors. Housing, food, and clothing are provided, in addition to a salary. My parents have done quite well."

"But it was not for you?"

Blevins shook his head. "No. The army has given me the opportunity to chart my own course in life. I wanted to see things ... experience the new world. And I am very glad that I did. America is a large, strange, and exciting place. The sheer size of it is mind-boggling to me." He glanced at Walter. "What about you, Billingsley? What is your family's business?"

Walter's demeanor clouded with a quick flash of memory ... the frightful image of his father swinging from a rope in a tree. He suddenly realized that he was speaking cordially to a man who was his sworn enemy. He felt a measure of anger and hate welling up within his heart. He attempted to suppress the feelings. He certainly did not want to project his anger upon this young man. Private Blevins had absolutely no part in the murder of his father. Walter somehow managed to set aside his anger and continue cultivating a relationship with the guard.

"My father was a farmer and a preacher," he answered curtly.

"Was he a vicar, or some form of priest?"

"Neither. My family comes from a Separatist Baptist heritage."

"I've heard of Baptists, but I have never met one before." The young soldier grinned at his confession. "I suppose you cannot be very different from us Anglicans. We all broke away from the Papists, eh?"

Walter chuckled at the lad's good-natured comparison.

"You spoke of your father in the past tense. Is he no longer living?" Blevins probed.

Walter choked back his emotion. He swallowed his bitterness and rage. "No. He died in 1776, murdered by a band of Loyalists from South Carolina."

"Good heavens! I am truly sorry, Billingsley. Was he involved in the rebellion in some way?"

"No. He was certainly an advocate for independency, but he had never taken up arms. Hell, he did not even own a gun. He was just a humble preacher, snatched from his bed during the night and hanged in a tree in front of our house."

"Ghastly." Private Blevins shook his head. "So much of this war is ruthless and uncivilized."

"As is any war, I have no doubt," Walter answered. "But it is doubly so when a people are divided against themselves."

"That much is certain." Blevins attempted to pivot away from the war and back to the subject of family. "But your mother is still well, then?"

Walter's countenance brightened a bit at the mention of his dear mother. "Quite well, indeed. She keeps busy and continues to care for my brother, Basil, and sister, Martha. My older siblings are all married and live close by. She is a strong, resilient woman."

"I am glad of that. Perhaps this ugly business will all be over very soon and you can return to assist in her care."

"Perhaps. We shall see."

The young men drew near to the implement shed where Walter would be working.

Private Blevins whispered, "By the way, Billingsley, when we are alone in our private conversations, might I call you by your given name?"

"Certainly. You may call me Walter."

"Wonderful. Then, only when we are alone, you may refer to me by my given name, as well. Just be careful not to do so in front of my fellow soldiers."

"Of course." He smiled thinly. "But I do not know your given name."

"Really?" Blevins seemed surprised. "I should think that you would have heard it before. Anyway, it is Gabriel. My father chose to name me after the archangel. But my mum and my friends have always called me Gabe."

Walter was overcome by a sense of awe and disbelief. He mumbled that familiar, beloved name, "Gabe."

"Sir, I do not understand why our yield has been so frustratingly deficient," whined the Lieutenant. "I have done everything that I know to do, but still nothing seems to increase the output."

Colonel Beecham was standing with his hands on his hips and staring stormily at the large copper distillation vessel. He appeared extremely frustrated. He wanted great volumes of alcohol to flow from the strange device, but had been greeted by little more than a trickle. The tiny glass vessel at the end of the copper tubing contained less than an inch of clear fluid.

Walter worked quietly in the background, hauling loads of lumber and wood scrap to fuel the fire that cooked the mash mixture. He concealed his smile behind his collar. He was greatly entertained by the frustration and ignorance of the two British officers. He knew exactly what was wrong. The lieutenant was using whole corn instead of flaked. His fire was not in the right proximity to the kettle. He had also likely not added any sugar to the mix. But the most obvious problem was the fact that the mash was not ready to distill. It was not finished fermenting. The yeast simply needed more time to do its work.

The colonel exhaled in frustration. "Lieutenant, I need not remind you that I am counting upon this contraption to provide beverages for my forthcoming social gatherings. Liquor is almost impossible to procure in this region, at any price. I do not want your excuses! I want whiskey and brandy! If you are unable to provide what I require, I will find someone who can. I am certain that General Cornwallis can find a position for you amongst the dragoons, if needs be."

The lieutenant comprehended the officer's threat. "Yes, sir. Of course, sir. I will endeavor to make some adjustments and satisfy your demands."

"Very well, then! Now, hop to!"

The lieutenant scurried out the door of the shed. Walter quietly continued his work of unloading a wheelbarrow full of split wood. Colonel Beecham ignored Walter's presence in the shed and knelt near the terminus of the copper condensing tube. He picked up the glass jar and sniffed the contents, then lifted the jar to his lips for a taste. Walter knew that the contents of the jar were toxic. He considered, for a moment, allowing his captor to take a swig, but his sense of human decency overwhelmed his bitterness toward his British enemy. Without really thinking about it, Walter intervened.

"I wouldn't drink that, sir!"

The colonel jumped, startled by Walter's unexpected intrusion.

"And why not?"

"The first pint from a five-gallon run is toxic. It contains poison spirits that can make you very ill. Men have gone blind from a single drink of the first vapors."

"Good God!" declared the colonel, discarding the clear liquid onto the ground. He stared at the small puddle as if it might leap up from the ground and attack him. He turned his head toward

Walter. "I am grateful for your intervention, young man. It is most unexpected, coming from an enemy, no less."

"I would not wish such sickness or death upon any man, Colonel."

"Indeed. What is your name, Son?"

"Walter Billingsley."

"Where is your home?"

"Guilford County, North Carolina, sir."

The colonel nodded. He seemed intrigued. "And how is it that you have such impressive knowledge regarding the distillation of liquor?"

"My mother operates a sizeable still. She claims that her product is for 'medicinal purposes,' but the healthy seem to enjoy imbibing as much as the ill." Walter smiled.

The colonel's normally stoic face stretched into a wide grin.

"So, tell me, Mr. Billingsley, do you have other knowledge regarding this process? Have you, yourself, operated a still? Can you diagnose what is wrong with our little project? Is the equipment faulty somehow?"

"I have helped my mother for many years, and am quite familiar with the process and the science." Walter took a step closer to the still. He tilted his head toward the copper kettle and looked to the colonel for permission to inspect it. "May I?"

"Absolutely. Please. Take a look and tell me what you think."

Walter removed the cap from the still and examined the contents. He checked the copper pot and tubing. It did not take long to confirm his suspicions.

"Your equipment is fine, colonel. It might help to have a slightly longer tube, and perhaps even coil part of the tubing inside a pail of water to cool the vapors more quickly. But the real problem is in the processing and preparation of the mash."

"Whatever do you mean?" inquired the bewildered colonel, .

"Well, first of all, the fire is entirely too close to the kettle. The mixture is scorching, which will foul the flavor of any whiskey that you manage to produce. But the biggest problem is the mash, itself. It was not prepared properly. The lieutenant has thrown in whole grains. The kernels must be cracked to allow the yeast to get to the starches inside the heart of the grain. Likewise, the wheat must be cracked and the barley crushed. Has he added any sugar to the mixture?"

The colonel looked somewhat embarrassed. "Sugar? Not that I am aware."

Walter nodded. His suspicions were confirmed.

"Adding sugar will make all the difference. Sir, what you have inside the pot has not fermented. You are not getting any alcohol because there is not, as yet, any alcohol to be had. You must have a properly mixed mash, and then monitor the mash and test the fluid with a tincture of iodine to make sure the fermentation is complete before beginning the distillation. Nature takes time. This process cannot be rushed."

The colonel stared wide-eyed at the young man standing before him. He seemed awed by the lad's knowledge. His tongue probed the soft flesh inside his cheek as he considered Walter's diagnosis. After several seconds, he nodded. The man actually appeared appreciative.

"Mr. Billingsley … may I call you Walter?"

"Of course, sir. You are my master. You may call me whatever you wish."

"Very well, then. Walter, as you well know, most of the prisoners have already departed for the harbor at Charlestown. The remainder will be moved by week's end. I doubt the experience that awaits prisoners within the camps or on the prison ships will be a pleasant one."

Walter grimaced. He did not comment. Frankly, he did not know what to say. He dreaded the day that he would have to leave Camden and join the other soldiers in one of the squalid camps that ringed the city of Charlestown.

The colonel continued, "But, Walter, it appears that you have a particular set of skills of which I am in desperate need. I own the equipment and resources to produce whiskey and brandy, but my hapless staff possesses absolutely no knowledge to accomplish the task."

Colonel Beecham paused and stared coldly into Walter's eyes. It seemed that he was searching Walter's soul for evidence of honor and truthfulness.

"Walter, I am prepared to pursue a little experiment, if you are willing. I would like to retain you here in Camden, in my service, as the master of this contraption. I would charge you with the maintenance of this device and the production of spirits for my personal use. In return, I would provide you with housing here at the farm, nutritious meals, and clothing. The conditions would be much better than what you have become accustomed to at the camp in the village." He paused. "It would be on a trial basis, of course. You would have to prove yourself ... both your integrity and your skills. Would such an arrangement be amenable to you?"

Walter's heart leapt with excitement and joy. He could remain in Camden! Yes, he would be the servant of a British officer, but the scenario would keep him in the vicinity of his beloved Abigail. He could scarcely believe it.

He nodded. "Colonel, the arrangement would be most agreeable to me. I certainly have no desire to go to prison in Charlestown. And I have every desire to remain in the vicinity of Camden."

"Oh?" responded the colonel, confused.

"My fiancé, Abigail Hamer, and her family reside here. I have not seen her since my captivity in Camden, but her father has visited and been very generous toward me and some of my friends. He has supplied us with food and medicine for the past month."

"Indeed?" The colonel seemed somewhat impressed. "Is your prospective father-in-law a Whig or Loyalist?"

"I do not believe that he has actively taken a side, though I rather suspect that he leans toward independency."

The colonel grimaced. "Well, perhaps we can reason with the man and talk some sense into him." His grimace converted to a teasing smile. "Then, can I trust your word, as a gentleman, that you would not act belligerently or make any effort to escape?"

"Sir, if I have the opportunity to remain near Abigail, I would have no reason to attempt an escape. I would happily remain here, in your service and as your prisoner, until such time as the fortunes of war dictate otherwise. I will serve you faithfully with the hope that I might somehow have the opportunity see her with my very own eyes in the coming days."

The colonel nodded in affirmation. "Very well, then. The deal is done. Perhaps I could even extend an invitation to this gentleman ... what is his name?"

"Alexander Hamer."

"Ahh! Yes! I believe that I have heard his name mentioned in the village. Most excellent. Perhaps I can extend the Hamer family an invitation to attend my gala on Sunday evening. You would enjoy the opportunity to visit with your fiancé, would you not?"

Again, Walter could scarcely believe his ears. He felt as if he might cry. His eyes swelled and turned red.

"Sir, I would be forever in your debt, and would remain your steadfast servant until you should choose to release me."

"That sounds like your word of honor to me."

The colonel reached out his hand toward Walter. The gesture provided the boy with yet another moment of amazement ... that a crimson-coated British colonel would stoop so low as to shake the hand of an enlisted Patriot prisoner.

Walter timidly extended his own hand. They shook.

"Colonel, I know that I have no right to do so, but might I ask one thing of you?"

"What is it, Walter?"

"Could I possibly have my three friends remain here to assist me in producing your whiskey?"

The colonel glanced at his feet and pondered. A doubtful look came over his face.

"Walter, retaining three helpers seems a bit extreme, to me. I fully understand your desire to protect your friends and perhaps spare them from an unpleasant and uncertain future. But, I could not be militarily justified in keeping such a large contingent of prisoners for my own personal use."

Walter was crestfallen. Heartbroken. Anguished.

The colonel continued, "However, I will allow you to choose one other man to remain here and assist you."

Walter nodded. "Very well, then. I would humbly ask that Thomas Whitlock be allowed to remain here as my assistant. He saved my life once, and has been a wonderful friend to me. I owe him a great debt."

"I shall issue the orders immediately," declared Colonel Beecham. "You and Mr. Whitlock will remain here indefinitely. Your other friends will return to the holding area in Camden until such time as they are marched to Charlestown."

"Yes, sir. Thank you, sir."

The colonel nodded to Walter as if he were a gentleman. "Welcome to your new home and workplace, Walter Billingsley. I hope that this arrangement will be profitable for both of us."

13

SWEET, SWEET ABIGAIL

Beechmont Estate – September 10, 1780

It was Sunday, the day of the first grand gala at *Beechmont.* That was the new name that Colonel Desmond Beecham had selected for his freshly acquired property. It was a suitable, but curious name. The inclusion of a portion of his own last name was clever, but the utter absence of anything that resembled a mountain for at least seventy-five miles made the "mont" portion slightly questionable. Still, it was his estate, and he was the master of it.

But the master of the estate was not happy. Not at all. He had an embarrassingly insufficient inventory of alcoholic beverages for his first-ever event. After scouring the taverns and barns throughout the region, he had only managed to accumulate two small barrels of cheap whiskey and five bottles of questionable wine. There was cider and ale aplenty, but those were the beverages of peasants. There was no way that he would stoop to serving such vulgar drinks to his refined guests.

All of the important people from the Camden and Cheraws Districts were committed to attend. He had plenty of food and wonderful entertainment planned, but the absence of alcohol would surely be a social nightmare. Indeed, if his first gala proved to be a dismal failure, precious few of the high-bred

Loyalists and British officers in the region would have any desire to return to *Beechmont.*

Walter and Tommy worked diligently to provide for their master's future needs. But the products of their labors would not be ready for several weeks, perhaps even months, into the future. It would be at least two weeks before Walter's newly-renovated still would be producing spirits, and those would require some modest periods of rest and ageing before consumption.

Walter also embarked upon another experiment for the colonel. The estate's orchards were currently producing copious amounts of ripe fruit. He and Tommy refurbished an old cider press and began juicing bushels of apples, pears, and grapes. After a mere two days of processing, the boys had over fifty gallons of the various juices bubbling in their primary fermentation buckets. Walter was determined to produce wine for the colonel. These buckets held the potential for over three hundred bottles of the sweet, fruity beverage. Colonel Beecham approved of the additional project, and was most impressed and pleased with the boys' efforts and ingenuity. But, none of Walter's labors contributed to the immediate needs of the impending party, which was only five hours into the future.

The colonel realized quite early on that he would have to procure his beverages for this first event from more distant sources. He had the foresight to dispatch a wagon and squad of troops to Charlestown the previous week for the express purpose of locating and purchasing liquor. They carried with them a significant sum in silver coin. But, it was already half past noon on the day of the event, and still there was no sign of their return.

The commandant was livid. His every hope was hanging on that still-missing wagon. His pitiful wife was apoplectic. She feared that the event would be a certain failure, and a social catastrophe from which she might never recover. She was in such a hysterical state that she had retired to her bedchamber, where she wept helplessly into her pillow.

Spirits brightened, however, when one of the guards pointed out a trail of dust on the horizon around mid-afternoon. Colonel Beecham sprinted to the second-floor balcony of the home and peered to the south with his spyglass. It was his wagon, and there appeared to be barrels contained in its bed. His shout of joy echoed throughout the lawns and fields of the estate.

Walter met the wagon on the main driveway. He was wiping his hands on a soft cloth that was draped across his shoulder. He glanced at the modest load of six ten-gallon barrels.

"What is in these barrels?" he inquired.

The sergeant in charge of the wagon retorted, "None of your damned business. What the hell are you doing here? Who let you out of the prison?"

Colonel Beecham appeared through the front door of the mansion. "He is my beverage specialist, Sergeant. And, as he is my personal agent, you will treat him with kindness and a measure of respect."

"Yes, sir." The sergeant stared coldly at Walter.

"Now, answer the boy's question. What did you procure?"

"We only managed to find four barrels of cheap whiskey and two of rum. The rum is actually pretty respectable. We got it fresh off of a ship from the islands."

"Rotgut and rum," growled the colonel. "The crude libations of the masses. Whatever am I going to do?"

Walter declared, "We can make it work, sir. 'Twill be all right. We still have plenty of fruit on the trees. Thomas and I can press several more gallons of fresh apple and pear cider to provide a sweet, fruity base for your punch bowls. We can add splashes of the whiskey and rum to give it some fire. Do you have any spices? Cinnamon, cloves, or allspice?"

The colonel nodded. "Yes, of course. We have them all. The pantry is well-stocked."

"We can disguise the mixture with those, as well … give the punch a mulled flavoring, much like a spicy wine. I think your guests will be pleased. Besides, after the first few cups, it shouldn't matter." Walter grinned.

The colonel's scowl slowly converted into a frown, and then to a subtle smile.

"Walter, do you honestly think that you can make a respectable beverage out of this swill?"

"I know I can, sir."

The colonel pursed his lips and nodded. "Very well, then. I am counting on you to save my party and my reputation. Perhaps, even, my marriage." He grinned wryly. "Let's get to it."

Walter nodded respectfully. "Yes, sir."

The colonel turned toward the soldiers from the wagon. "Gentlemen, unload the barrels beside the kitchen. I am grateful for your accomplishment, such as it is. Afterward, I need you to wash and change uniforms to make yourselves presentable for my guests."

The soldiers answered enthusiastically, "Yes, sir!" They seemed quite relieved by the colonel's positive reaction to their meager load of alcohol.

The men moved quickly to perform their assigned tasks. As Walter turned to walk toward the pressing shed, the colonel spoke personally to him.

"One moment, Mr. Billingsley."

Walter paused. His master approached and leaned his mouth close to Walter's ear.

"After you attend to the mixtures and punch bowls, you should think about taking a quick bath, yourself."

"Sir?" inquired Walter, confused.

"I received a response from Alexander Hamer shortly after supper yesterday. His family will be attending this evening's gala." He grinned scandalously. "I should think that you would desire to be freshly washed and groomed for your fiancé."

Walter's heart raced. He could scarcely believe it. He would see Abigail on this day!

"So, they know that I am here?"

The colonel nodded. "I am not certain that they would have attended, if not for your presence. I wrote Mr. Hamer a personal note the day after your assignment here and explained the circumstances to him."

Walter's mind reeled. He simply could not believe that, before this day was done, he would see his beloved Abigail. It had been such a very long time. He prayed that her feelings for him had not diminished.

"I am beyond grateful, sir. I can scarcely think, much less speak. But, surely, I cannot go anywhere near your fancy party. I have nothing to wear but these shabby work clothes."

"Not to worry, Walter. I will have suitable garments delivered to your quarters. My wife's handmaid will see to it. This evening, you shall look every bit the distinguished British gentleman." The colonel winked.

Walter scrubbed feverishly. His body was crammed into a small, wooden bathtub in the narrow yard behind his quarters. One of the colonel's slaves dumped a fresh bucket of scalding hot water over his head and back. Walter leaned back and allowed the warm sun to caress his face and chest. He sighed. He had not felt such cleanliness and refreshment in over six months.

It was actually his second tub full of water. The first one had to be dumped after only a few minutes of soaking. The wooden washtub had accumulated an instant coating of mud and oily scum from Walter's filthy body. He had not immersed his private parts in soapy water for several months. He was well overdue.

As he tasted the fresh soap on his lips and ran his fingers through his long hair, Walter only wished that he had more of an opportunity to enjoy the luxurious experience. But, he had precious little time to spare. He had less than an hour to shave, wash, and dress. Abigail was likely already on her way. He had to make haste.

One of his slave attendants, an older man named Tandy, spoke respectfully, "We needs to git you all dried off, oiled up, and dressed now, suh. We ain't gots no time to waste."

"Yes, Tandy. I know. Thank you. This hot water just feels so good." He sighed contentedly.

"I's glad you likes it, suh." The dark-skinned man smiled broadly, revealing his pearly white teeth.

Walter stood as Tandy wrapped a large towel around his soapy body. He quickly dried himself and then darted along the stone walkway toward the back door of his tiny cottage. Another slave, a fellow named Coffey, was waiting for him. The two attendants methodically rubbed sweet-smelling oils and manly perfumes all over Walter's freshly-cleaned body. Next, they quickly assisted him in dressing.

The colonel had provided a beautiful matching set of royal blue weskit and breeches, both in a fine linen. A brilliant white shirt and matching stockings, along with a pair of freshly-polished shoes, completed the outfit. Tandy tied a white silk cravat around Walter's neck while Coffey styled his hair. He pulled back Walter's long, light-brown mane to form a queue, tucking in the pigtails at the top of the gathered hair. He then braided the queue tightly and secured the bottom with a blue ribbon. He tied another ribbon at the top of the braid. The finishing touch was a dark gray fur-felt cocked hat with a blue silk cockade. Amazingly, the color of the silk was a very close match to the linen of his garments.

Once they were finished, the slaves brushed Walter's weskit with camel's hair brushes. They stood back and surveyed their work.

"You looks mighty handsome, I must say, suh," declared Tandy.

"Umm-hmm," affirmed Coffey enthusiastically. "Dem red soldiers ain't even gonna know who you is!"

Walter chuckled, then frowned. "Fellows, I don't even know who I am, anymore. One minute I'm a lowly Patriot prisoner, and the next I am being washed and dressed by servants and attending parties with the British." He looked forlornly at the two men. "I feel like a traitor."

"You is jus gettin' by, like all da ress of us," declared Coffey, shaking his head vigorously. "You doin' what you gots ta do to suh-vive. Ain't no shame in dat."

Tandy nodded. "He's right, Mistuh Bills'ley. You keep on goin'. You done well by yoself. Dis war cain't lass fuheveh."

"God, I hope not!" declared Walter. He tugged at his collar and turned to face the two slaves. "So? How do I look?"

Coffey frowned. "Jus like one o' dem."

Walter groaned with disgust.

The guests began to arrive about two hours before sunset. An exquisitely manicured lawn and gardens greeted them. Torches were positioned strategically throughout the property, ready to provide light in the darkness of the evening. Six tables that held punchbowls filled with Walter's concoction of fresh fruit juice, liquor, and spices were also spaced geometrically throughout the yard. A small, newly-constructed dance floor graced the center of the lawn, directly in front of the house. Nearby, a small orchestra played gay and celebrative tunes to greet the arrivals.

An expansive, thirty-foot-long train of buffet tables sat on the southernmost border of the lawn. It was covered with an obscene display of fine foods ... meats, vegetables, fruits, pastries, and other desserts. Twelve fancily-dressed slaves stood on the far side of the tables, shooing away insects and flies with small wooden fans.

The colonel had labored diligently to account for every situation and scenario. He thoughtfully provided for the more personal needs of his guests. He had four new necessary houses constructed, each over a freshly-dug privy. Of course, for those who needed only to pass water, he provided four male and four female attendants, each with a gold-rimmed bourdaloue ... a French urine cup. The bushes on each side of the house provided ample cover for both men and women to conceal and relieve themselves before returning to their socializing and libations.

The weather was perfect for an outdoor event. Amazingly, the air was dry and crisp. The typical humidity of the upstate had disappeared earlier in the week. The scene was set for a perfect evening ... if Walter's creative use of cheap liquor and fruit juices could pass muster with the distinguished guests.

Walter stood near the implement barn and waited. The location provided him with a good vantage point to keep watch for Abigail's arrival. It was also a perfect spot from which he could maintain a supervisory eye on Tommy's ongoing work with the whiskey still. He constantly and nervously offered Tommy gentle words of encouragement and instruction.

Tommy chuckled and shook his head. "Do not worry, Walter. I'll not ruin your still. I promise! I'm just stirring the pot every now and again and making sure the fires stay lit. Your mash will be unscathed when you are finished with your partying."

Walter tugged at the tightly-tied cravat that choked his neck. He had forgotten how uncomfortable the cursed ties were.

"I have no interest in parties, Thomas. I wish only to see Abigail," he retorted stormily.

"I know. Still, I cannot help but envy you just a bit. All dressed up and ready for the colonel's gala, and your lady coming, as well!"

"Do not envy me, brother. I am just the colonel's little monkey."

"And a fine, well-dressed monkey you are!" quipped Tommy. "Will you do a little monkey dance for a halfpenny?"

Walter tried to hide his grin, but he could not. He glanced through the door at his friend. Tommy broke out into a hearty laugh.

"If you keep teasing me, I'll not give you your surprise."

Tommy ceased stirring the pot of whiskey mash. "Surprise? What surprise?"

"There is a tub of fresh, clean water and plenty of soap behind the corn crib. I had Tandy and Coffey conceal the tub there and pour it up fresh for you. Once the party really gets going, you can steal away and get yourself a good bath." He paused. "Because you need it."

Tommy grinned. "Indeed, I do! Thank you, Walter."

"It was nothing, really. Besides, I think soap and water are going to become a bit more regular part of our lives in the coming days."

Tommy's tone became serious. "I cannot thank you enough for bringing me here with you, Walter. You kept me off of those prison ships. I shall never forget it."

"It was the least I could do, Thomas Whitlock. You are, after all, my best friend."

"More like your only friend."

Walter chuckled. Suddenly, a large carriage came around the bend to the east and crossed the small bridge that spanned the adjacent creek. Walter recognized Abigail immediately. She sat in the back seat of the carriage between her parents. His heart flip-flopped within his chest.

He chirped at Tommy, "I'll see you later."

"Have fun. I shall expect a full report in the morning!"

Walter made his way across the lawn toward the greeting area. The Hamer wagon proceeded to the drop-off point where a receiving line awaited all arrivals. As the family dismounted their carriage, their driver whispered to the herald. As soon as the family was positioned at the start of the line, the fellow announced loudly, "Presenting! Mr. and Mrs. Alexander Hamer and their daughter, Abigail!"

The Hamers slowly proceeded down the line, shaking hands and greeting the various dignitaries. Across the lawn, Walter caught the eye of Colonel Beecham. The colonel motioned subtly with his head, inviting Walter to join him at the end of the line and to stand by his side. After several minutes, Alexander and Audra Hamer reached the terminus of the receiving line. Abigail followed closely behind them. None of them gave any indication that they even saw, much less recognized Walter Billingsley. Indeed, Abigail seemed to be scanning the yard and looking for him.

Colonel Beecham bowed graciously, "Ahh! Mr. and Mrs. Hamer. At last, we meet. I am Colonel Desmond Beecham of His Majesty's expeditionary army. I welcome you to my home. I am truly honored by your presence."

Alexander bowed his head respectfully. "Colonel, I cannot believe I am saying this ... but it is a pleasure. I was most surprised by your news and your invitation." He turned to his wife. "Colonel Beecham, this is my wife, Audra."

She bowed bowed gracefully as the colonel kissed her hand.

"Mrs. Hamer, a pleasure, indeed."

Alexander reached back for his daughter and tugged her by her upper arm. "And this, Colonel, is our daughter, Abigail."

"The lovely Abigail," declared the colonel as he took and kissed her gloved hand.

She did not seem very pleased.

"Miss Hamer, I have heard so much about you. And I am quite certain that you are anxious to see this particular young man."

He stepped to his left and revealed Walter. Abigail gasped, as did her mother. The young fellow was stunningly handsome in his beautiful suit. He was scarcely recognizable to her. It was not the fact that he was dressed as a gentleman. She had always seen him properly outfitted and groomed. He just seemed so very frail and thin. But it was, most definitely, her beloved Walter.

Abigail trembled as though she might cry, then offered her hand to him. He grasped her delicate hand and lifted it slowly and reverently to his lips. He could feel the electric warmth of her flesh and taste her sweetness, even through the silk of her glove. It was a glorious moment of emotional release.

Alexander Hamer's voice destroyed the tenderness of the moment. "Good God, Walter! Just look at you! I did not even recognize you! You are a prisoner, but outfitted as a gentleman! How can this be?"

Walter did not respond. He simply ignored Alexander and stared into Abigail's tear-filled eyes. He never released her hand after kissing it. In fact, he reached out and took her other hand in his, as well. They stared lovingly, longingly at one another. The silence was almost disconcerting.

The colonel coughed slightly to break the tension and responded for Walter. "Mr. Hamer, your future son-in-law has rapidly assumed the role of one of my most effective, resourceful, and faithful workers. His allegiances and politics remain unchanged, but I will continue to hope that he will someday listen to reason." He chuckled. "Walter is still technically a prisoner of war, but he is now included among my personal staff. And I take quite good care of my staff."

The young couple continued to ignore everyone around them.

At long last, Walter finally spoke. "I think that my heart might burst, Abigail. I never thought that this day would come."

She smiled warmly. "Neither did I, Walter. Father would not allow me to visit you at that horrid prison." She cast a quick glimpse of contempt at the colonel. "But I did prepare all of your food and other necessities. Did you enjoy my letters?"

"More than you shall ever know, Abigail."

His heart skipped a beat every time he said that beautiful name. Walter was completely caught up in the enchantment of the moment. It was almost more than he could bear.

Again, Colonel Beecham came to his rescue. "Mr. and Mrs. Hamer, why don't you accompany me to the banqueting tables? We can enjoy some refreshments and talk a little politics and treason while these young people get re-acquainted."

Abigail looked excitedly into her father's eyes. He smiled and nodded.

"That will be most excellent, Colonel. Just so long as they do not wander far."

"Your daughter is quite safe, sir," responded the colonel. "I have seventy of His Majesty's troops guarding the perimeter of the estate. The grounds are open and shall be well-lit after dark. Your darling Abigail will be just fine. Besides, she will be under the watchful eye and personal protection of Mr. Billingsley."

"Of course," Alexander responded, bowing gracefully. "Come along, Darling, let us go and dine among the King's men."

Audra curtsied gracefully and bowed toward the colonel, then took her husband's arm and sauntered toward the dining area.

Walter offered his right elbow to Abigail. "Shall we, my dear?" He grinned.

She wrapped her arm inside his and gently laid her head upon his shoulder. They strolled, arm-in-arm, along the driveway … almost as if there was nothing unusual, at all, about it. They somehow pretended, at least for a moment, that there was no war, and that Walter was not a captive in the hands of a despised enemy.

The lovesick couple disappeared into the darkness of the orchard. For the next two hours, Walter's entire emotional story spilled out of him. He related, through tears of anguish, how Gabe had died. He described, as best he could, the various trials that he had endured in prison. Abigail held him close and wept with him. They stole many deep, passionate kisses and embraces. It was a glorious time. They wandered the grounds aimlessly, lost in conversation and emotion. They felt neither hunger nor thirst. All of their physical, spiritual, and emotional needs were met simply by being in one another's presence.

As their journey brought them near to the building where the whiskey still was housed, Walter asked excitedly, "Would you like to see where I work?"

"That would be wonderful!" Abigail replied.

He took her inside the shed and lit a tar-soaked torch. He showed her the still, as well as his winemaking enterprise in the far corner. She seemed quite impressed.

"So, now you are the colonel's liquor man," she declared.

Walter's countenance fell somewhat. "I know it is not very impressive."

"It is, indeed, impressive! And it is a far cry better than a squalid prison camp or ship in Charlestown harbor!" She squeezed his hand tightly. "I am very proud of you, Walter Billingsley. Life has dealt you a horrible blow, and yet you have not only persevered. You have excelled. In so doing, you have saved your very life. And that means the entire world to me."

"I have only survived this ordeal because of you, Abigail. I would not desire to live, otherwise. Without you, I would have no reason to go on."

"Oh, please, Walter!"

"I mean it, Abigail. You are my everything. You bring cause and meaning to my life. Just seeing you on this night … it is almost more than I can fathom."

A single, huge tear formed in his right eye and traced a path down his gaunt cheek.

"I've just about had enough of all this fatalistic talk," Abigail scolded him. "We are together now. Our fortunes have changed. We must make the most of it."

Walter wiped his face. "You are right. I know you are. I'm sorry that I am acting like some blubbering fool."

She caressed his cheek with her hand. "You are *my* blubbering fool." He turned his head and kissed the palm of her hand.

"Well … I, for one, have had enough of your wine buckets and whiskey machines. Where are your quarters?" she demanded.

"Tommy and I have a small cottage back behind the big house. It is quite clean and comfortable. We are just happy to have a roof over our heads and a comfortable bed in which to rest."

"You must show me!" Abigail begged.

Walter shook his head. "No, Abigail. I cannot take you there. It would not be appropriate."

"Nonsense," she responded. "You are my fiancé, and I demand to inspect the place where my beloved rests his weary head at night."

"But what would your father say?"

"What Father does not know will surely not hurt him. Come, now. Show me your humble cottage."

Walter deliberated for a short moment, but quickly relented. How, after all, could he refuse any request from his sweet, sweet Abigail?

Alexander and Audra Hamer bowed gracefully to one another and slowly exited the crowded dancing floor. They meandered toward their seats at the host's table.

Colonel Beecham stood as they approached. "You two seem to be enjoying yourselves. You are not finding our Loyalist company too unpleasant, I hope."

Alexander smiled warmly. "Not at all, Colonel, I am surprised to say. You have been most gracious, and have truly outdone yourself with the evening's festivities." He took a sip from his punch cup. "And this punch is absolutely delicious. The taste is so magical that I must be careful not to overindulge."

"I must give credit to your Walter for that punch, Mr. Hamer. He perfected the recipe. That lad took several gallons of substandard liquor and transformed it into a veritable elixir."

"Really?" responded Alexander. "I should have thought that this recipe would have been quite expensive."

The colonel shook his head. "On the contrary. There were simply no quality spirits to be had in the entire district. Walter has saved both the party and the day."

Audra Hamer glanced furtively around the perimeter of the house. She appeared concerned. She whispered, "I wonder where Abigail and Walter have gone, Darling. They have been away from us for an exceptionally long time."

"Not to worry," reassured the colonel. "I saw them only moments ago. They had been walking amongst the orchards. I believe that they were headed in the direction of Walter's distillery barn. I'm quite sure he is giving her the full tour of his work and accomplishments."

"I do hope you are right, Colonel. I should not want them to do anything that might appear untoward. I abhor the notion that my daughter could be the subject of any idle talk."

Alexander took her hand. "Do not worry, Dearest. Mr. Billingsley is a man of honor. I am certain that they are only reacquainting after such a long time of separation. Let us leave the young people alone. They have many months of news to share and only a few hours to do so." He turned to Beecham. "Wouldn't you agree, Colonel?"

"Absolutely, Mrs. Hamer. Your daughter is in Walter's most capable hands."

Walter lit a candle. The dull glow illuminated the tiny room.

"Well, this is it," he declared.

"It is small, indeed," remarked Abigail.

"Yes, but it meets our needs. We each have a bed and a closet. Not that we need a closet," he joked. "I only have one set of tattered clothing."

"But what about this fine outfit that you are wearing now?"

"It is on loan from Colonel Beecham. I am not sure who the actual owner is. I will return it in the morning."

She sniffed deeply. "It smells clean in here. Like fresh soap and perfumes." She smiled.

"That is because I enjoyed a bath today. The colonel had his slaves attend to me quite nicely. I received a double dose of clean water. Believe me, I needed it!"

She covered her mouth and feigned embarrassment. "Mr. Billingsley! How dare you mention such things as bathing to a fragile young lady!"

Walter's face turned crimson red from her pretend reprimand. He smiled so widely that he felt his face might break. He was so happy that his cheeks actually ached.

Abigail turned and continued to inspect the room. "And where is Mr. Whitlock?"

"I am not certain. He spoke earlier about going to a gathering in the quarters of the women's servants. I think he has his eye on one of the colonel's maids."

"So … he will not be back anytime soon?"

"I doubt it," answered Walter. "Why? Are you anxious to meet him?"

"Not particularly, though I would like to meet him sometime soon. Tonight, however, I prefer to give you *all* of my attention."

She turned and faced him. Her gaze was captivating. Her eyes danced. Her cheeks blushed a bright red. Then, without warning, she tumbled into his arms and began to kiss him passionately. Walter hesitated to respond at first, but quickly reciprocated. He could not help himself. She smelled and tasted so very good. He wrapped his arms around the small of her back and lifted her mouth higher toward his. The young man could not impede his body's physical response to her feminine stimulation. The evidence of his excitement pressed firmly against her belly. She did not seem to mind. She had, after all, initiated the encounter.

Then, just as suddenly as she had descended upon him, she stopped kissing him and pulled away. Walter's eyes were glazed. His heart pounded so loudly that Abigail could hear its beating through the wall of his chest. Her heart thumped, as well. She felt a burning inside her that seemed to bore its way through her bosom and deep into her belly. Both of them were breathing heavily. A bead of perspiration had formed on Walter's forehead.

"Abigail … Darling … I am so sorry! I do not know what came over me. You must certainly feel violated. Can you ever forgive me?"

Abigail reached her right hand toward his face and placed her forefinger over his mouth to silence him. She turned toward the door. Walter was certain that she was going to leave the room, but she did not. Instead, she grasped the iron bolt and slid it sideways into the hole in the door facing.

"Abigail, what are you doing?"

She did not answer. She simply turned and faced her fiancé. She reached behind her neck and tugged on the decorative ribbon that secured the collar of her long gown. Then, she slowly began to undo the buttons on the back.

"Abigail! Have you lost your mind?"

"I will need some assistance with the bottom buttons, Walter. And I certainly must have your help in removing these stays."

Walter wailed in shock and disbelief, "Abigail!"

Again, she placed her finger over his lips. She whispered, "I intend to claim you as my husband this very night, Walter Billingsley."

"You *have* lost your mind!" he hissed. "Abigail, you must stop it right now. You must not tease me. It is not fair."

"I am not teasing you, Walter. I fully intend to finish what I have started."

"But, Abigail …"

"You do love me, don't you, Walter?"

"You know that I love you. With all of my heart and soul, I love you."

"And we are destined to be husband and wife?"

"Of that I have no doubt," he answered.

She stepped to him and pressed her body against his. "Then I declare, right here and now, before the eyes of no one but our God, that we *are* husband and wife."

Walter chuckled uncomfortably. "I'm not sure how a reverend would feel about that … *or* my mother … *or* your father!"

"I do not care about what any of them think. I love you, Walter Billingsley. You have been my husband, in my heart, for many months now. My soul is bound to yours. And now I must bind my body to yours. I shall wait no longer to have you."

"But, Abigail! It does not seem right!"

"It *is* right, Walter. What is absolutely wrong is the fact that we have been prevented from getting married for so long. But, tonight, we will end this injustice. Tonight, I give my person … my body … to you, as my husband."

Walter stared deeply into her perfect eyes. It was clear that she was serious. He wanted to fight against her plea. He wanted to respond rationally to her words. His mind was telling him to slow things down, but his body longed to consume the beautiful woman standing before him.

"Again, I ask. You do love me, don't you?"

"You know that I do. How could you even ask the question?"

"Then take me, Walter. Make love to me. Make me your wife. I am burning inside, and can wait no longer."

Walter paused, kissed her gently on the nose, and then reached for the candle stand. He lifted it from the table and brought it close to their faces. They smiled at one another, and then simultaneously pointed their lips toward the candle and blew, plunging the cottage into darkness.

14

THE SHIFTING WINDS OF WAR

Beechmont Estate – The Next Morning

Walter whistled a happy tune as he and Tommy walked from the servant's kitchen toward the distillery. The pewter mug full of tea that he carried in his right hand was so hot that it almost scorched his fingers, but he did not seem to care. His mind still reeled from the joy and indescribable pleasure of the previous evening.

Tommy, however, did not seem to share Walter's high spirits. His wide-brimmed round hat was pulled down low over his eyes and he rubbed both of his temples with the tips of his forefingers. He winced when Walter finished whistling his first tune and then immediately commenced with another.

"My God, Walter! Will you please cease that piercing, shrill racket?"

He grabbed his forehead as it contracted in pain from the volume of his own voice.

"What's the matter, Tommy? Did you make a few too many trips to the punchbowl last night?"

"Humph!" Tommy grunted. "As if I had an invitation to sample the British lord's punch! All that the servants had available for refreshment was a keg of rum and a few bottles of musty wine. I'm afraid that I do not run with the same social crowd as you, Mr. Squire Billingsley."

"But I take it that you had a fine time … for your headache indicates that you did not go thirsty. And I noticed the pristine condition of your bed this morning," responded Walter, grinning. "Did you sleep where you fell, or did that bath make you popular amongst the maids?"

Tommy smiled broadly, despite his throbbing headache. "One of them, in particular, but a gentleman never tells." He cut a quick glance at Walter. "How about you, Mr. Billingsley? Your bed appeared well-traveled. How was your evening?"

"I shall never forget it," Walter declared. "I still cannot believe that I was able to see Abigail. It seems surreal."

"So … are your feet sore, then? Did the two of you dance into the night?"

"We danced only a little. We spent most of our time talking and catching up."

Tommy's face broke into a wry, taunting grin. "So … is that what you call it? Because I'm thinking that maybe you have some sore members other than your feet."

"Whatever do you mean?" retorted Walter, somewhat horrified.

Tommy took a deep breath. "Well … I came back to our cottage a couple of hours after the party had started. I intended to fetch my tobacco sack. But something strange was going on inside." He glanced teasingly at Walter. "It sounded like someone was beating a sack full of cats in there, such was the commotion."

Walter's heart skipped a beat. His smile melted. He was mortified by the notion that anyone knew about his private, intimate moments with Abigail. He cut his eyes at Tommy. His friend stared back at him, eyes twinkling. Tommy patted his shoulder enthusiastically.

"Don't worry, Walter. Your secret is safe with me. Besides, I saved your arse last night and you did not even know it."

"What?" Walter responded stormily. It was the only word that he could manage. His shame was multiplying with every syllable that escaped from Tommy's lips.

"I found Mr. Hamer wandering around near the servant's quarters. It seems that he had not seen his little girl for quite some time, and was growing concerned. He was searching for the two of you."

"What did you tell him?" inquired Walter trepidatiously.

"Let's just say that I convinced him that I had just spoken to you, and that the two of you had gone for a stroll along the creek." He grinned victoriously. "I assume that he located the two of you before the night was done."

"He did, indeed. I was wondering about his strange inquiry regarding our expedition along the creek." Walter frowned, then spoke with deliberation and authority. "I am grateful for your interdiction of Mr. Hamer, Tommy. Truly, I am. But I will not tolerate any lascivious comments or the sullying of Abigail's honor. She is the love of my life. I will not be teased."

Tommy draped his arm across Walter's shoulder and tugged him close. "And I shall never speak of it again, my friend. As I told you before, your secret is safe with me."

"I really appreciate it, Tommy. Sincerely, I do."

"You are most welcome. But, I am happy to declare that I am not quite so honor-bound as you. So, allow me to captivate you with a tale of my darkness adventures with a lovely maid by the name of Ellen!"

"I thought you said that a gentleman never tells," chided Walter.

Tommy raised one eyebrow. "Unlike you, Mr. Squire Billingsley, I am no gentleman. So, here goes …"

Walter grinned as Tommy expounded upon his amorous exploits of the prior evening.

Guilford County – September 25, 1780

Samuel and James Billingsley sat astride their horses in front of their mother's home. Elizabeth and Martha stood, arm in arm, on the brick sidewalk. The brothers had come to say their farewells. They were dressed and equipped for the field. Pistols, blades, and tomahawks filled their wide leather belts. Each carried a rifle cradled across his lap. They were going to war. All of the Rowan and Guilford County regiments had been called up.

"When will you be back?" asked Elizabeth Billingsley, choking back her tears.

James shook his head. "I do not know, Mother. The current enlistment is for three months, but it may be extended. Colonel Locke has not received any orders from the district commander as of yet. We have simply been summoned for muster."

"What about John? Where is he?" demanded the concerned mother.

"John is with the Randolph Regiment, and remains encamped to the east, in Anson County. Do not worry about him. He is far from the British. He has only Tories to keep him occupied." Samuel attempted to smile reassuringly.

"Mother, have you heard anything else from Walter?" asked James, deflecting her attention away from their current military deployment.

She shook her head. "Nothing since the letter from Abigail. However, I am certain that Mr. Hamer is taking quite good care of him."

"I doubt that he is still in Camden," growled James. "We hear that most of the prisoners from the battle are now on ships in Charlestown Harbor." He stared at the ground. "Many men will perish on board those death boats."

"I still cannot believe that, of all the Billingsley brothers, Walter is the only one who has actually faced the enemy in battle!" declared Samuel somewhat jealously.

"It is foolish to envy your little brother, Samuel. He is, after all, in British captivity," his mother corrected him. "I am quite thrilled that the rest of you have remained safe and close to home."

"I do not truly envy him, Mother. I am simply confounded by the irony of the circumstance," groaned Samuel defensively.

Elizabeth's rebuke and Samuel's overly defensive response injected an awkward pause into the conversation.

Samuel sought his escape. "Well, Mother, we must be off. Colonel Locke and the regiment are awaiting us at the Salisbury muster ground."

"Do you truly believe that the British are coming?" inquired Elizabeth, trembling.

"They are marching on Charlotte Town as we speak. Our spies tell us that the army is being led by Cornwallis, himself," responded Samuel.

"And Tarleton's dragoons," added James. "The invasion of North Carolina has begun. There is also word of a large force of Tories that has departed Charlestown. Likely, they are part of this same campaign."

"So, then, the real war is upon us," Elizabeth declared.

"I am afraid so, Mother," James answered.

"Then God help us all," she prayed.

"Amen to that, Mother," echoed Samuel.

"I shall help look after your families," promised Elizabeth.

"As will I!" chimed Martha.

"They will be fine, I am quite sure," Samuel mused. "We have some of the hired men remaining on the farm, as well as Henry. He has declared that he will arm the slaves, if needs be."

Elizabeth wiped a tear from her eye. "You must allow me pray for you before you go."

She walked between her sons' horses and reached up with both of her hands, placing them on the knees of her boys. Martha joined her and held tightly to her arm as the sobbing mother prayed emotionally and fervently for her sons. When she finished, each of them leaned over the pommel of his saddle and kissed her on the cheek. They immediately turned their horses, snapped the reins, and galloped southward toward the military encampment at Salisbury … and toward war.

Beechmont Estate, Camden – October 11, 1780

Walter had come to the belief that he had formed a special, though unusual, relationship with Colonel Desmond Beecham. But, something had changed. The colonel's inexplicable fury made that truth abundantly clear.

The encounter began innocently enough. Walter needed the colonel's permission to procure an additional ton of corn for winter whiskey production. He arrived at the officer's study unannounced, as was customary. Walter's position involved frequent consultations with the commandant. But, on this particular morning, he received an onslaught of emotional wrath and verbal abuse from the man. The British officer completely lost his temper upon Walter, for no apparent reason, and then summarily dismissed him and ordered him to stay out of his house.

Walter responded obediently, of course. But, truth be told, he was quite upset. Thus far, the colonel had been quite magnanimous in his dealings with Walter, as evidenced by his invitation to the Hamer family to visit his estate. Furthermore, he had arranged for the Hamers to make another visit to *Beechmont* in early November. Walter was greatly anticipating the event. But, the verbal lashing that he had just endured had not only been unexpected. It had also been quite discouraging. And to Walter it felt transformational. He wondered if the life of relative comfort to which he had grown accustomed was about to change.

Walter buttoned the collar of his wool coat high beneath his chin in order to protect his neck from the bitingly cold morning air. The weather had taken a rather dramatic turn within the past week. The pleasantly cool days of September had been overtaken by an uncharacteristically bitter and frigid cold snap during the first week of October.

Walter stomped down the stairs of the house and turned toward the direction of the barns and outbuildings. As he trudged back to the distillery shed, he noticed several of the guards eyeing him with an air of suspicion. Some even gazed upon him with outright disdain.

Yes … something significant had happened, there was no denying it. But, since Walter had absolutely no way of obtaining any news about the war or the world beyond the fences at *Beechmont,* he could only wonder.

Arriving at the distillery barn, he jerked open the door and stomped inside, leaving the hinged portal flapping in the breeze behind him. Tommy was stooping over a newly-constructed oak barrel, pouring a jug of raw whiskey through a funnel into its opening. He stood up and stared, annoyed, at the open door. Walter shuffled to a nearby corner and plopped down in a straight-back chair. It was located beside the toasty heating stove.

"What are you doing, Walter? Shut the bloody door! It's freezin' out there!"

"Sorry, Tommy."

Walter rose, walked across the room, and pulled the door closed. He returned to his chair, grabbed the teapot from the top of the stove, and poured some hot water into a cup. He tossed in a pinch of loose tea leaves, and then sat back in his chair, closed his eyes, and folded his arms across his chest.

"What's the matter with you?"

Walter sighed. "Beecham just chewed a few pounds off of my arse … for no apparent reason. I only went to see him about getting another wagon load of corn. Before it was over, I got banned from the house."

Tommy grinned and resumed emptying the jug into the oak barrel.

"So, then ... colonel fancy-breeches is angry with his pet, eh?"

Walter shot an angry look at Tommy. "That was quite unkind and uncalled for."

"Why? It is true, isn't it?" Tommy stood up straight and sat his jug on an adjacent work table. "Now you know what a yard hound feels like."

"I do not appreciate the comparison," growled Walter.

"Well, you needed to hear it, I'm a thinkin'."

Tommy walked over to the stove and sat down in his own chair.

"May I be candid with you, Walter?"

His friend answered bitterly, "I quite think you have been doing so already."

"Very well, then. I do not want to sugar-coat it, so I will just let you have the full load. Walter Billingsley, you've been getting a bit too chummy with the colonel these past couple of months. What started out as a good thing for us has transformed into something else. Lately, it just seems wrong."

"Are you calling me a traitor?" Walter demanded, an air of disbelief in his question.

"No, Walter. I'm not saying that your behavior is traitorous. Just inappropriate." Tommy leaned back in his chair and interlocked his fingers behind his head. "Maybe, old friend, you needed this reminder of the fact that he is, indeed, the enemy."

Walter stared at his friend with a look that bordered on rage. Tommy faced down the angry stare with a warm smile. He raised his foot and gently nudged Walter's knee.

"C'mon now, Walter. Don't get all pissy. Medicine always tastes foul when it hits your tongue. You just have to hold your nose and swallow it."

Walter looked away, and then closed his eyes again. He wanted to be angry with his friend, but he knew that Tommy was right. He had allowed the colonel's influence over him to become entirely too pervasive. It was all because of Abigail, of course. The commandant held such absolute power over him, and possessed the ability to grant him access to his beloved. Somehow, Walter had allowed that power to conquer his good judgment. He suddenly felt convicted … and very dirty on the inside.

"My God, Tommy. I *am* a traitor, aren't I?" Tears welled in his eyes.

"No, Walter. You are, most definitely, not a traitor. You are a survivor. But you must learn to keep your distance. And you must not allow this business with Abigail to hold such sway over you." He sat up and leaned closer to his friend. "You must keep your wits about you, Walter. Remember that this arrangement is not permanent. I sincerely doubt that we will remain on this grand estate forever. Something will happen. Something *will* change."

Walter opened his eyes and stared with kindness at his friend.

"I think something *has* changed, Tommy. It's not just the colonel. The guards were eyeing me quite dubiously on my way back from the estate house."

Tommy slapped Walter on the knee. His eyed widened mischievously. "Perhaps our red-coated friends have suffered a setback. Let us go and investigate! The house maids will surely know something!"

October 17, 1780

The British had suffered a setback, indeed. The flood of retreating troops through the Camden District provided undeniable proof. The fields and pastures around Camden, including the grounds of *Beechmont*, were littered with tents full of cold, hungry, muddy, disheartened British soldiers.

It took a couple of days of clever eavesdropping to discover what had happened. But, the news was definitely worth the wait. Ten days prior, a force of over 1,100 Loyalist troops had been soundly defeated by a band of frontier militiamen on an obscure hilltop approximately ninety miles to the northwest of Camden. The place was called King's Mountain. It was a humiliating, lopsided loss for the King's men. Almost five hundred were killed or wounded. Most of the remainder were captured. Few escaped.

What Walter and Thomas had not been privy to beforehand was the news that Cornwallis' army had launched a successful invasion into North Carolina back in September. Cornwallis was victorious in a skirmish at Charlotte Town, and had taken control of most of Mecklenburg County. They had begun to expand their patrols into the surrounding counties, as well. It appeared that Cornwallis was unstoppable, and would continue his invasion onward through Salisbury and points northward. He seemed on the verge of slicing North Carolina down the middle, with Virginia as his next target.

However, the loss at King's Mountain signaled the end of his North Carolina incursion. His western flank was completely exposed, and the "Overmountain Men" of the Carolina and Virginia mountains threatened to surround his army at Charlotte Town. His only viable option was retreat.

And so, the beleaguered British army retraced its route southward. Cornwallis halted the retreat at Camden to resupply and give his tired, decimated, sick army time to recover and lick its wounds.

Interestingly, the defeat at King's Mountain was not the only disappointment suffered by the British and their Loyalist American allies. There had also been a rapid increase of raids by partisan forces throughout South Carolina. A renegade American colonel by the name of Francis Marion was wreaking havoc in the low country. Somehow, he always managed to make his escape into the forests and swamps, and thus avoid capture. The Patriots in the Carolinas began to refer to him as, "The Swamp Fox."

Lately, the radius of Marion's engagements had been expanding into the Camden District. His men regularly inflicted damage and casualties upon the British. Even when his raids seemed relatively ineffective, the rapidly declining morale of the Loyalists in the region could neither be concealed nor denied. The constant harassment was taking its toll. And the quiet, hidden Patriots scattered throughout the state were starting to rise up. The ranks of the rebel militias were swelling. Some Loyalists had even turned their coats and changed sides.

It seemed that the winds of war, which had been at the backs of the British invaders for many months now, were slowly and deliberately beginning to change to the favor of the American rebels.

Camden Village – December 5, 1780

"Billingsley! The colonel wishes to see you!"

Walter turned and glanced at the open door of the distillery barn. Corporal Gabriel Blevins, recently promoted to his new rank, stood silhouetted against the sunlight that streamed through the door.

"What does he want, Corporal?"

"The colonel does not make his business known to me, Mr. Billingsley. I am simply here to fetch you to his office."

"So … His Grace is allowing you back into his inner chambers?" teased Tommy.

Walter shrugged. He placed his bucket on the ground and turned to follow the corporal.

Tommy proclaimed sarcastically, "Give the colonel darling all my best wishes!"

Walter waved his hand dismissively as he stepped through the door. Once they were outside and out of earshot, Walter whispered, "What is this about, Gabriel?"

Blevins glanced around them to make sure none of his compatriots were watching, and then responded, "We are in need of supplies from the depot at Camden. I convinced the colonel to allow you to drive the wagon for me and accompany me into town."

Walter was shocked. "Why, pray tell?"

Gabriel leaned closer. "Things are not going well for the Crown in his region, Walter. There have been many skirmishes and raids. Losses have been significant. There was a terrible defeat at Rugeley's Mill yesterday … over one hundred Loyalists troops were captured. The ranks of the enemy are swelling, and their actions growing bolder. We appear to be surrounded by our foes. I fear that we may not remain here in Camden District much longer."

Walter pondered the implications of the corporal's report. If the British, indeed, abandoned their outpost in Camden, he would be most certainly be carted off to a prison ship in Charlestown harbor … or worse.

"But, why me? Why am I going to town today?"

Blevins asked reverently, "You would like to see Abigail again, would you not? It could be your final opportunity. I believe that the colonel realizes this."

A dull pang of dread struck Walter in his chest. He nodded subtly. "Indeed, I would. But, the colonel has treated me with a large measure of disdain for the past month. I cannot imagine that he is the author of any favors on my behalf."

"I believe that the colonel carries some regrets for his treatment of you as of late. He would never admit it, of course. Still, I believe that your assignment to this task is a clandestine attempt to provide you with a small measure of recompense."

Walter glanced sarcastically at the corporal.

"It is a gift, Walter. Accept it with humility and gratitude."

Walter nodded. The two men … enemies, but friends … marched solemnly toward Colonel Beecham's home.

Walter eased the wagon to a stop in front of the quartermaster's warehouse. He was shocked by the changes in the village since his time of captivity in the prison. The military presence around Camden had grown exponentially. There were checkpoints along all of the roads entering the town. Corporal Blevins and Walter endured a thorough interrogation at one of those checkpoints before being allowed to pass. Thousands of troops were encamped in the fields. Soldiers marched throughout the streets. Others trained with their weapons on a vast shooting range located behind the local church. The entire town was a beehive of military activity.

Corporal Blevins nudged Walter. "Here is the colonel's requisition. Give it to the quartermaster. He will fill the order and have his men load. Now, turn around."

Walter complied. Gabriel tucked another paper inside the ties on the back of Walter's cocked hat.

"What is that?" Walter asked.

"Your identification papers … just in case anyone asks. They identify you as a loyal servant of the King. They carry Colonel Beecham's personal seal. He thought it would be best to insure your security whilst in town."

"That was most magnanimous of him," declared Walter flatly.

"It is all for your well-being, Walter. You are going to be by yourself for a short while, and we would not want you to get shot, hanged, or quartered during my temporary absence."

Walter's eyebrow raised. "No … we wouldn't." He paused. "Where are you going?"

"I am going to visit Mr. Hamer's home to schedule a meeting for you and Abigail. I shall return for you as soon as the arrangements are made. I will take you to their home after the wagon is loaded." He paused and thumped Walter on the forehead. "You will not attempt an escape, will you, Prisoner Billingsley?"

Walter rolled his eyes dramatically. Corporal Blevins grinned and then leapt from the wagon. Walter locked the brake, climbed down from the seat, and marched confidently into the warehouse, requisition in hand.

The shadows of Alexander and Audra Hamer, and their guest, Corporal Gabriel Blevins, were visible through the curtains of a nearby window. They had vacated the house to give Abigail and Walter a small measure of privacy. Despite the cold, they were conversing over a cup of tea on the veranda. The young lovers' time alone would be brief. Walter and Corporal Blevins had to depart within the half-hour in order to return to *Beechmont* before supper.

Walter and Abigail embraced one another on the settee inside her mother's parlor. They kissed passionately. Tenderly, Abigail withdrew from the kiss and placed her head upon Walter's shoulder.

"Abigail, you are absolutely radiant. You have never been lovelier than you are right now."

"And you taste wonderful, Husband," she declared.

Walter's face blushed crimson. He glanced at the window and hissed, "Shh! Woman! Someone will hear you!"

"I do not care," she declared. "We are one flesh. You are mine now, Husband. My mate for life ... no matter what may occur." She hugged him tightly and sighed contentedly. "I simply cannot believe that the colonel arranged for our meeting today. Perhaps he will allow us to have such moments as these on a regular basis."

Walter lifted her face from his shoulder so that he could look into her eyes. He took her hands in his and breathed a deep, cleansing, preparatory breath. He was frowning.

"Walter, what is wrong? You seem anguished."

"My love, I fear that this may be the last time that we will be able to see one another for a while," he declared.

"Why?" she moaned. Tears formed in the corners of her eyes.

Walter removed his handkerchief and dabbed a huge tear that meandered down her cheek.

"Darling, the situation here has become quite tenuous for the British. They have suffered several setbacks and defeats, and seem on the verge of evacuating Camden District. If they do, then I will likely be sent elsewhere. I doubt that they will release me or give me parole, especially after so many months in captivity."

She sniffed. "Papa told me that the fortunes of this war have turned in our favor. I know that there are many more soldiers here and in the nearby fields than ever before."

Walter nodded. "They are training new recruits and increasing their forces. They could be preparing for a major battle, or for a retreat back to the coast."

"Where would they send you … if you had to go?" she asked, her bottom lip trembling.

"Charlestown, I imagine."

"Oh, no!" she wailed. "Not to those horrid prison ships! I have heard such dreadful stories!"

Walter's chin dropped to his chest. He proclaimed hopefully, "Perhaps I will not go to a ship. Maybe they will keep me in some kind of camp. I do not know. Or, Colonel Beecham could keep me with him. We cannot be certain. But understand this, Abigail … whatever happens, I will come back for you. I will return to Camden and we will be properly wed, and then we will go home to Guilford and begin our life together as husband and wife."

"There is no life to begin, Walter. My life started the moment that I saw you standing over that watering trough … with that long, wet hair draped over your shoulders and water trickling down your naked chest." She shuddered with pleasure and grinned.

"You are a bold, shameless young woman, Abigail Hamer."

"As well you should know it, Walter Billingsley."

She leaned forward and kissed him again, and then collapsed into his embrace. Moments later, the front door clicked quietly. Walter glanced in the direction of the sound. He saw the face of Corporal Blevins peeking through the partially opened entrance. The soldier opened the door fully and stepped into the entryway.

"Walter, I am so very sorry to interrupt. However, we can tarry no longer. The hour grows late, and we must obey the colonel's orders."

Walter nodded. He hugged Abigail with one final, powerful embrace. He stood, without speaking, and followed Blevins through the door, closing it behind him. Abigail covered her face and wept, anguished that she may never see her man again.

Beechmont Estate - January 4, 1781

That was, indeed, the last embrace that Walter and Abigail would enjoy before his departure from Camden. The news came quite suddenly, and with little warning.

The Patriots were on the move in South Carolina. General Daniel Morgan was marshaling his forces west of the Catawba River. British spies described the formation of an army of almost two thousand militiamen, along with uniformed soldiers of the Continental Line. Those same spies declared that the army was moving on the British fort at Ninety-Six, a strategic outpost in the western districts of South Carolina, and a major command center for the British occupiers. The fall of Ninety-Six would be nothing short of catastrophic.

The response of the British was swift and decisive. Their forces in the Camden District were preparing to march to relieve the outpost at Ninety-Six. The Royal North Carolina Regiment, Loyalists under Lieutenant Colonel John Hamilton, provided the bulk of the troops for the Camden contingent. Brigadier General Charles O'Hara's Coldstream Guards, newly arrived in the Carolinas, joined the detachment, along with a regiment of Hessians. Local Loyalist troops were organized and deployed into makeshift companies.

Colonel Beecham and his contingent of guards were ordered to join the mobilizing army posthaste. This caused *Beechmont* to enter into a state of generalized frenzy. The colonel worked feverishly to organize his affairs and prepare the estate for his long-term absence. Since all of his troops would be mobilized with the army, he had to make plans to leave his properties under the supervision of civilian employees.

Walter and Thomas had heard all of the rumors, and could easily discern the consternation and panic among their captors. They chose to conceal themselves in the distillery barn and await their fates. They hoped that, if they could simply "lay low" and keep quiet, they might be forgotten and left behind at the estate grounds along with the other servants and civilians. Such an outcome would provide the best opportunity for escape once the army departed.

But, it was not to be. Walter and Tommy were carrying cases of brandy into a newly-constructed storage room inside the barn when Corporal Blevins arrived. A wisp of snow floated through the open door. Winter had descended upon South Carolina with a vengeance. Blevins closed the door quickly behind him and darted over to the stove to warm his hands. His countenance appeared anguished.

"What is wrong, Gabriel?" Walter demanded.

The red-coated soldier frowned. "You are coming with us."

"What?" exclaimed Tommy. "Why would the colonel wish to take two prisoners with him to a battlefield?"

"It is General O'Hara who issued the order. He wants all available prisoners with the army in case we enter into an engagement. I believe that he has a desire to maintain you as candidates for prisoner exchange, should a battle occur."

Walter shook his head. "That is simply absurd. What good are two lowly privates in a prisoner exchange?"

"It is not just the two of you. There are sixteen others currently held in Camden. Most are rebel militia. I have been tasked to command a contingent of twenty guards to keep watch over the lot of you." He smiled. "I do not mind the assignment. It keeps me from the battle. And, besides, Walter ... you need to think positively. This could, after all, lead to your release."

"I suppose so. The only thing that I know for certain is that it takes me away from Abigail." He exhaled in frustration as he looked at his distillery. "And I cannot believe that it actually grieves me to leave this barn and equipment. None of it is mine, yet I feel such a deep sense of ownership over it all."

Tommy placed a reassuring hand on Walter's shoulder. "We have invested much sweat and toil in this little project, Walter. It is quite natural to feel some measure of sadness as we leave it behind. Still, it is Beecham's still and Beecham's liquor. We were nothing more than free labor. Try not to forget that." He glanced at Blevins. "When do we depart, Corporal?"

Blevins grimaced. "Within the hour."

"Good God!" exclaimed Tommy. "Why so soon?"

"Your rebel army is on the move. The troops from Camden town will be marching through here soon. We will fall in behind and join them. So, dress warmly and put on your walking shoes, lads. It is going to be a cold, long, hard way to Ninety-Six."

15

MY ENEMY, MY FRIEND

Near the North Carolina Border - January 17, 1781

Dawn approached. Walter and Tommy huddled silently beside their vigorously crackling campfire. Tommy had just added a handful of pine needles to help revive the previous evening's embers. The tents of the British soldiers in the meadow to their east were empty. A dull haze of smoke from their extinguished campfires hovered over the silent, abandoned field. The army had marched out toward the west at least an hour previous. All that remained in the massive British encampment were the prisoners and their small contingent of guards.

It was still relatively dark, but a dull, purplish glow was beginning to form in the eastern sky. The leafless trees reached upward toward the faint luminescence of the coming light, giving the appearance that they were attempting to glean a measure of warmth from the as-yet invisible sun.

The other prisoners remained fast asleep, huddled beneath their threadbare blankets beside the fading coals of the previous evening's fires. Frost glistened in the moonlight on top of their bedding and hats. Most of the guards were asleep, as well, nearer to the edges of the small clearing. A minimal contingent of sentries remained on post at the periphery of the prisoner encampment.

Walter marveled at the ability of his captors and fellow prisoners to sleep in such conditions. The biting, inescapable cold and the torturous knots of pain in his stomach prevented him from getting any rest. He had not received a single bite to eat in four days. He took a little solace in the fact that his British captors had not received any rations, either, during that same period of time. The enemy troops were every bit as cold and starving as were their hapless prisoners. But, despite the parity, their common sufferings did not make Walter feel any less hungry.

The British army had diverted toward the northwest, rather than following the original plan to march to the fort at Ninety-Six. Lieutenant Colonel Banastre Tarleton was in command of Cornwallis' forces, and his dragoons of the American Legion were leading the way for the British troops. Tarleton was determined to engage the rebels and annihilate them, once and for all. The British army had been marching incessantly for five days. The soldiers enjoyed less than three hours of sleep each night. They were physically and emotionally spent. Still, Tarleton did not care. He marched them onward in the rabid pursuit of his enemy.

Walter removed his ragged shoes in the pre-dawn darkness. They were shredded by almost two weeks of non-stop walking. He thrust his tortured feet toward the warm fire. His toes were so cold that he could not bend them. As he looked at the silhouette of his feet in the light of the fire, he noticed that both of his big toes were exposed through gaping holes in his wool stockings. He chuckled at the sight, but soon winced in pain as the feeling began to creep back into his frozen extremities. The invading heat felt like hundreds of tiny blades slashing at his flesh. But, on the other side of the pain, there was tremendous relief. Walter sighed in satisfaction at the tiny measure of comfort afforded by the humble fire.

Tommy's whisper invaded Walter's rare moment of luxury. "Where do you reckon the British are headed?"

Walter shrugged. "Who is to know? I have no idea whether or not our compatriots are near. It is peculiar, though, that they left most of their equipment in the camp."

"That is what I was thinking," agreed Tommy. "They seemed to be in quite a hurry."

"Perhaps they have gone hunting and will bring us back a haunch of venison," Walter mused wishfully.

"If you are going to dwell in fantasy, Walter, you should pursue loftier visions. At least wish for some beef, bread with jam, and hot tea. Something besides venison …"

Walter declared, "I would take just about anything right now, to be honest. The priority of a satisfied palate is far below that of my aching, empty belly."

"I suppose you are correct," affirmed Tommy. "Not that it matters. I fear that we may never eat again."

Walter shook his head. "This confounded marching cannot last forever. The British have to stop, replenish, and rest sooner or later. They cannot possibly continue on at such a feverish pace. Surely, their men will revolt if something doesn't change."

Tommy nodded thoughtfully. "Have you noticed the disdain that the foot soldiers appear to display toward Tarleton?"

"Most definitely. I doubt that there is a single infantryman among them that has any love for Tarleton and his Legion. I have heard some of their bitter, hateful comments."

"Perhaps there will be a mutiny," Tommy mused wishfully. "That would be a sight, wouldn't it?"

There was a rustle and the dull sound of boots crunching the frozen soil behind them. A low, calm voice invaded their private conversation. "That is not very likely, gents."

It was Corporal Gabriel Blevins. He knelt beside their fire and raised his hands to warm them near the flames.

"Do you think there will be a battle today, Corporal?" asked Walter.

"I have no idea. I certainly hope not. My personal desire is that we will turn around and march back to Camden. I miss my bed." He grinned.

"As do we all," agreed Tommy. "Along with Mrs. Williford's cooking."

"You will get no argument from me on that particular subject," Corporal Blevins quipped. He stood and stared toward the soldiers' encampment in the adjacent field. "You fellows remain here and keep quiet. I am going on a scouting mission."

"What kind of scouting mission?" asked Tommy.

"I am going to see if I can find us some food. Surely, something has been left behind in that camp."

"Why, Corporal Blevins! Are you intending to pilfer that encampment for rations?" challenged Walter, feigning indignation. He whispered playfully, "Are you sure you don't need any help?"

"I'll be just fine on my own on this particular mission." He grinned broadly. "I shall be back in just a bit." He cradled his Brown Bess musket in his left arm and ambled toward the empty encampment.

Once the British corporal was out of earshot, Tommy muttered, "That is one hell of a good man. It's too bad he's on the wrong side."

Walter nodded vigorously in agreement. "I just hope nothing happens to him in this war. Perhaps he will stay here when it is all over."

Tommy chuckled lightly. "I reckon that depends on the outcome, doesn't it?"

The deep, thunderous boom of a cannon shattered the silence of the morning. It was some distance away, but close enough to cause the limbs on the trees to rattle and creak as they rubbed against one another. Three more hollow booms followed in rapid succession.

Walter stared toward the southwest. He could see faint flashes in the sky above the trees, no doubt the explosions of artillery.

Several seconds later more dull booms echoed through the trees. He muttered, "Well, it appears there *will* be a fight this day."

Tommy stared numbly into the fire. He whispered, "Let us pray that it favors our cause."

Corporal Blevins succeeded in his mission. He procured a large sack of flour and a small bag of sugar from the quartermaster's tent. He also managed to scrounge a box of fragrant tea. A half-hour later the guards and prisoners were cooking flat biscuits in their pans. They sprinkled generous pinches of sugar on the biscuits and then gobbled them voraciously. They followed their humble meal with copious amounts of steaming tea.

The combination of the dense bread and hot liquid caused their stomachs to fill and distend. It was a satisfying sensation that neither the prisoners nor their guards had experienced in many days. It lifted their spirits tremendously. Walter and Thomas reclined lazily beside their fire. The combination of their full bellies, general lack of rest, and comforting warmth lured them into a deep, satisfying sleep.

Mid-Morning – The British Encampment

A loud cry in the forest roused Walter from his slumber. The sound seemed strangely out of place. Walter was disoriented. His sleep was so deep that he had forgotten where he was. It took only a wisp of frozen air and the odor of campfire smoke to remind him. He groaned unhappily, sat up groggily, and rubbed his heavy eyes with his fingers. The sight that greeted him in the nearby British encampment caused him to gasp. He stared in disbelief at the carnage and confusion.

Walter kicked his friend in the thigh. "Tommy! Wake up! Look at this!"

Tommy groaned, "Leave me alone, damn you. I have not slept this well in days."

"But look! Something has happened! The camp is in disarray!"

Tommy rose quickly to a sitting position and joined Walter in observing the enemy encampment. The sight that greeted him was most unthinkable.

Dozens of stunned, powder-stained soldiers straggled into the camp. There were no companies marching with flags and colors. There were no drummers playing, sergeants barking orders, or officers on horseback. Even the shrill cries of the bagpipes of the Scottish regiments were strangely absent. There were only stragglers, appearing singly or in twos. Most of them had no weapons. The only sounds that filled the encampment were the mournful wails of the wounded and dying.

"Where are the rest of them, Walt? There's not a hundred men in that camp right now. Where's the other thousand?"

Walter grinned. "Perhaps fortune *has* favored our cause this day."

In reality, the Patriot cause was reborn on that frigid morning in the rolling hills of South Carolina. The United States of America rediscovered hope that day. The Battle at Cowpens had been nothing short of a one-sided rout. The British suffered almost three hundred and fifty men killed or wounded. Over eight hundred were surrounded and captured. The Patriot losses were light in comparison. Fewer than one hundred and fifty men of General Daniel Morgan's American army had been killed or wounded. They won and controlled the field of battle, and even managed to capture two of the enemy's cannons.

The previously undefeated Lieutenant Colonel Banastre Tarleton was vanquished. He had arrogantly marched his exhausted, starving army directly down the throat of a superior and better-deployed force. Though he, himself, managed to escape the battlefield unharmed, his men paid a dire price for his folly.

It was a major turning point in the war in the South, so important that it caused General Lord Cornwallis to leave the comfort of his winter house and take to the field in pursuit of General Daniel Morgan and his army. Cornwallis wanted his prisoners back. He intended to teach an unforgettable lesson to these upstart rebels who dared stand in opposition to the King's army.

The North Carolina Wilderness – February 9, 1781

Walter was exhausted, as usual. Well-fed, but exhausted. The British army had just enjoyed a satisfying meal of fresh beef, requisitioned from a nearby settlement. The hot, delicious meal had done much to brighten the spirits of both the British soldiers and their prisoners. Still, though their insides were full and warm, their outsides remained under assault from the relentless onslaught of the winter chill. The men wrapped themselves in their wool coats and blankets and drew near to their fires.

Walter huddled beside his campfire and prayed. He prayed fervently that his American compatriots, somewhere in the darkness to the northeast, would reach the Dan River and make their escape into Virginia. But it seemed to him that the odds were not in favor of his countrymen. The British were moving quickly, and seemed to be gaining ground every day.

The British had been on the march since their lopsided defeat at Cowpens on January 17. They were in a foot race against the American forces. Cornwallis' newly reinforced army of over 2,500 men was attempting to cut off the retreating Americans before they reached Virginia. If he could only overtake the armies of Generals Daniel Morgan and Nathanael Greene, he believed that he could deal a final, crushing blow to the rebel forces in the south. Much to the chagrin of Walter Billingsley, they forced their small contingent of prisoners to accompany them on the arduous journey.

The British army had maintained a creeping pace for the first few days of the march. The sheer volume of Cornwallis' wagon train slowed the column considerably. They slogged and crawled along muddy roads, across overgrown fields, and through swollen creeks at a speed of less than one mile each hour.

Cornwallis grew more and more frustrated. He decided to take drastic measures when his force reached Ramseur's Mill in North Carolina. It was there that he decided to abandon and set fire to the lion's share of his wagons. He retained only enough to haul critical supplies of food and gunpowder, and to carry the wounded and sick that were unfit for marching. It was a shocking decision, but it increased their speed considerably. Now, two weeks later, it seemed that the British were within striking distance. Walter heard several of the guards mention that their scouts had actually seen the fires of the enemy.

Tommy nudged Walter. "Do you think they'll make it?"

Walter continued to stare at the fire, captivated by the dancing flames.

"I don't know," he responded blankly. "Hell, I don't even know where we are. I am so completely disoriented. We've been running in circles, it seems, for days now. We could be in Virginia, for all I know."

"We're definitely not in Virginia," Tommy declared. "We would need to cross the Dan River first, and it is sure to be swollen from the recent rains. I heard one of the guards mention something about Moravians."

Walter's head jerked in surprised. He stared, wide-eyed, at Tommy. "What about the Moravians?"

"He said we're close to some of their towns, I think. Just a couple miles to the east."

Walter's mind reeled. The Moravian villages of North Carolina were well-known. Bethabara, the first of the settlements, occupied a hilltop fewer than fifteen miles to the northwest of Salisbury. Less than twenty miles to the east was Guilford Courthouse ... and Walter's home.

"My God, Tommy, we are less than two days walk from my house!"

"Horse shite!"

"Sincerely. My father traded with the Moravians on occasion. I rode to Salem with him many times. I cannot believe that we are so close." Walter stared into the darkness of the surrounding trees.

"Don't go getting any wild ideas, Walter. There are too many crimson coats and muskets surrounding us right now. You wouldn't make it a hundred yards into those woods before you got a ball in the back."

"But I am so close to home!" Walter hissed, frustrated.

"I know. And I understand. But you have to be smart. You have to bide your time and wait for the right moment. And when that moment comes, I'll go with you. I am quite fed up with following Cornwallis all over God's green earth."

"Well, it's not exactly green right now," teased Walter. "More like, God's gray and brown earth." Both men chuckled. Walter glanced at his friend. "But how will we know when it is the right time?"

"Don't worry, Walter. We will know." He grinned broadly. "And don't forget ... I desperately want to meet that pretty sister of yours. Martha is going to fall helplessly, hopelessly in love with me ... she just doesn't know it yet."

Walter smiled and slapped his friend on the knee. Tommy erupted into joyful laughter. After a few moments, Tommy ceased his chuckling and gazed into Walter's eyes with a stare of sincerity and intensity.

He declared, "I have every intention of making my escape with you, Walter Billingsley."

February 15, 1781
Halifax County, North Carolina - South Bank of The Dan River

Walter could not help but smile at the naked arses that shined white on the opposite bank of the Dan River. The sight of those pale backsides and dangling genitals would be forever etched into his memory, as would the blood-red face and screeching tantrum that their naked display elicited from General Lord Cornwallis.

The British commander was, indeed, livid. His forces reached the Dan River shortly after daybreak. He watched helplessly as the final boatload of enemy troops disembarked on the distant bank. The Americans on the far shore then proceeded to taunt and insult their enemies. They waved, whooped, and yelled. A few of the more boisterous among them dropped their breeches and exposed their arses in their vulgar act of victorious defiance.

Then, they performed their ultimate insult in full view of the British. They attacked the bottoms of the boats that lined the bank of the river with axes and tomahawks and then released them into the current to sink. The British watched helplessly as each vessel disappeared below the surface of the frigid waters.

The race to the Dan River was over. The British had no way to cross and continue their pursuit. General Daniel Morgan had outrun and outsmarted his British foes. The Patriot rebellion would, indeed, continue.

Near the Haw River - March 12, 1781

The rebel fires were still hot and smoldering. Several pots of soup and stew were hanging on their iron tripods throughout the abandoned encampment. Tents remained pitched and in place. Blankets and equipment were strewn across the ground. The pursuing British had, once again, missed entrapping their enemy ... this time by a margin of three hours or less. The Americans had, obviously, abandoned their headquarters and fled with great haste. This time, it was General Nathanael Greene who had eluded Cornwallis' trap.

The British had been wandering the countryside of the Carolina Piedmont for an entire month. Though his original intent was to retreat to Wilmington in order to replenish and rebuild his army, Cornwallis never reached his destination. After a brief respite in the vicinity of Hillsborough, Cornwallis was lured back into action in order to pursue the army commanded by Nathanael Greene. Greene's scouts and dragoons maintained a constant harassment of Cornwallis' army, engaging him through numerous raids and skirmishes. Cornwallis was determined to locate and utterly defeat this pestering foe.

But, this would not be the day. Frustrated and exhausted, the general ordered his army of over 2,000 troops to make camp. It was less than three hours before sunset, and the abandoned rebel tents, equipment, and food located at the current site made it a perfect place to bivouac for the night.

Walter, Tommy, and the other tag-along prisoners assumed their regular location on the outskirts of the gathering of enemy troops. Like their captors, they quickly set about the tasks of building fires and cooking a meager meal. The captives had precious little to work with. Supper this night would consist of a starchy gruel of corn meal flavored with a thin slab of highly questionable salt pork. The meat had a foul odor to it, but once immersed in the large pot of water and grain, the smell seemed to dissipate somewhat. Frankly, Walter and the other prisoners didn't care whether or not the meat was spoiled. They merely wanted to satisfy their hunger.

Walter was adding sticks to the fire and Tommy was stirring their porridge with a newly-whittled wooden paddle when Corporal Blevins approached.

He barked, "Whitlock! Billingsley! I need you to come with me!"

"What for, Corporal?" inquired Tommy. "We are just about to eat our supper."

The corporal paused. "Well, go ahead and fill your bellies, then. But make it quick! We need more firewood for the King's soldiers. I volunteered the two of you for the job."

"Why us?" wailed Tommy. "You Redcoats should be collecting your own firewood. There's damned near two thousand of you in this field and only eighteen of us! It doesn't seem right!"

The corporal exhaled in irritation. "Are you quite finished with your whining? Eat your porridge and then meet me at the large oak near the latrine. You have five minutes, so make it fast." He spun and stomped stormily toward his tent.

Walter shot a curious glance at Tommy. "What was that all about? What's wrong with him?"

Tommy shrugged. "He sounds like he has his arse up over the top of his shoulders. I'm not sure why he's decided to take it out on us."

"He doesn't seem like himself," commented Walter, staring at departing corporal.

"No, he doesn't," Tommy agreed. "But, then again, you have had at least one or two of the King's men turn against you in times past, haven't you?"

Walter pursed his lips. "I suppose you're right. I just never suspected that Gabe would ever act in such a way."

"Oh! So, it's Gabe then, is it? Careful you don't get a bit too chummy with the enemy, again, Walter. You should remember how that turned around and took a bite out of your arse the last time you tried it."

"I know. You are absolutely right," agreed Walter, exhaling his displeasure.

Tommy grinned broadly and slapped two ladles full of porridge into Walter's wooden bowl. "I'm right, as always, and ne'er you forget it! Now, eat up whilst you still have a chance. Then,

I reckon we'll be His Majesty's highly-trained firewood-gathering specialists."

Walter nodded as he shoveled a spoonful of the gruel into his mouth. He grimaced at the foul taste of the soured pork.

&

"We shall proceed this way," declared Corporal Blevins, pointing to his left.

Walter and Tommy groaned and continued their trek. They had been gone from the camp for almost a half-hour, and had traversed a rather large expanse of forest.

"Reckon what was wrong with the firewood we already passed up, Corporal?" complained Tommy. "Whatever we find out here, it's going to be twice as difficult to haul back to the camp."

"Just keep moving, Whitlock," the corporal ordered.

Walter and Tommy were walking several steps in front of the British soldier. Tommy eyed Walter questioningly. Walter shrugged and shook his head. Moments later they approached a huge, dark gray boulder in the center of the forest floor.

Corporal Blevins commanded, "Gentlemen, please go around back of that rock."

Tommy glanced at Walter again, wide-eyed this time. He whispered, "What the hell is going on Walter? Is he going to shoot us?"

"Don't be silly. The corporal harbors no ill will toward us."

The men kept walking until they reached the far side of the gigantic rock.

The corporal declared, "That is quite far enough."

Walter and Tommy spun around to face their captor. Corporal Blevins knelt down and placed his musket on the ground.

"Please join me, fellows."

He motioned for them to sit. He then reached into his haversack and removed two hunting knives and extended them, handle first, toward Walter and Tommy. The two prisoners glared at the corporal and then looked at one another, thoroughly confused.

"Please, gents, take them." He wiggled both knives at them.

"What is this about? What are you doing?" Walter demanded.

"What does it look like? I am assisting you in your escape." He grinned.

"What?" exclaimed Walter. "You're joking!"

"Not at all, Walter." He pointed over his left shoulder toward the southwest. "Your comrades are somewhere over in that direction, likely only four or five miles away. If you leave now, you should be able to link up with them some time before morning."

"Why are you doing this?" hissed Tommy.

"Because I like the both of you, and I do not wish you to be harmed by any of my fellow soldiers. Consternation is building within the camp. They are tired of pursuing your rebel friends. I have heard a few of the men mention the notion of executing the lot of you. Granted, they said so under the influence of rum. But, they could just as easily stand you against a tree and shoot you with a rum-encouraged finger. I could not bear the notion of something so inhumane and criminal happening to the two of you. Therefore, I am setting you free."

"Why the knives?" asked Walter.

"They are the best that I could do on short notice. You must admit that it would look most odd for me to leave camp with three muskets." He smiled warmly. "I simply did not want you to be completely unprotected and without any resources, at all. Anyhow, if you move swiftly enough, you should have muskets in your hands before supper tomorrow."

"I don't know what to say, Gabe," muttered Walter. "Words are not enough to express my gratitude."

"Just make it through this war, Walter. That is gratitude enough for me." He paused. "We are reasonably close to your home, are we not?"

Walter nodded. "A day and a half of walking. Maybe less. I live at Guilford Courthouse."

The corporal gasped slightly, and then stared at the ground. "Walter, you had best find your way home and bypass your compatriots altogether. That is what I would do if I were you."

"Why?"

"Because we are bound for Guilford Courthouse, as well."

Walter's mind raced. "Why? What is happening in Guilford?"

"We received word from a Loyalist spy that the rebel army is forming there. There are thousands of them. It is certain that there will be a great battle close by."

Walter stared, anguished, at the corporal. Thoughts of his family immediately consumed him. He could not imagine his sweet mother being caught up in the violence and carnage of a great battle. He had to get home and warn her.

"What will happen to you?" asked Tommy. "You cannot just walk into the woods with two prisoners in tow, and then return with none. Someone will figure it out."

"True. I cannot come out of this episode unscathed. That is why one of you must strike me and bloody me up just a bit."

Walter nodded knowingly. "I understand. What do you want us to do?"

"One of you needs to find a weapon … preferably a large stick … and hit me in the back of my head. It needs to be a vigorous enough blow to injure me and draw blood, but still remain short of cracking my skull."

"So, you'd rather we not use a rock," quipped Tommy.

"That would be most unpleasant." Gabe smiled again.

The three men stood. Walter shook Corporal Blevins' hand.

"Gabe, if things do not go your way in this war, please consider staying here in America. You can have a good life here. There is land for the claiming and fortune for an honest man who will work hard." He paused. "And you're welcome in my home and by my fire any time."

"Same goes for me," chirped Tommy, shaking the soldier's hand, as well.

"I've already been thinking about such contingencies," confessed the corporal. "I sincerely wonder if I will ever return to England, no matter the outcome of this bloody conflict."

"Well, then, Gabriel ... until we meet again," declared Walter.

"Indeed. Until we meet again. Now, which one of you is going to do the deed?"

"It had better me be," responded Tommy. "Walter likes you too much. He might try to kiss you instead of hit you in the head."

All three men chuckled lightly.

Tommy pointed at the rock. "Just turn around and rest your hands on that boulder. It'll help you steady yourself."

Corporal Blevins retrieved his musket and leaned it against the rock as Tommy searched the forest floor for a suitable limb. He finally located what he was looking for. It was a three-foot long piece of oak, roughly two inches thick. The limb was old and dry, and would be much softer and lighter than a heavy, green limb. Tommy showed it to Walter. His friend nodded in approval.

"Are you ready?" asked Walter.

"I think that I shall never be ready for this," Gabe responded, trembling slightly.

"All right, then," declared Tommy. "On the count of three." He took a deep breath. "One!"

He reared back, and then quite suddenly swung the makeshift club at the soldier's head. He cried out, "Two!" just as the wood made contact with Gabriel's skull. The corporal's semi-conscious body slumped to the ground, landing in a heap against the boulder.

Walter gasped in surprise. "You told him on the count of three!"

"It's better the way I did it. He was relaxed. It was more of a surprise," Tommy explained.

"Well, check him! Make sure you didn't kill him!" ordered Walter, somewhat irritated.

Tommy knelt down and placed his hand in front of Corporal Blevins' mouth.

"Is he alive?" Walter demanded.

"He's fine. Still breathing." He rolled the soldier onto his belly. "And he's got a nice, bloody welt. That white collar on his coat will be nice and messy. They should believe him now."

Walter nodded. "Well, we'd best be going, then. He will wake up in just a bit."

"After you, sir," Tommy quipped. "Take me to Martha!"

Just After Dawn – The Following Morning

Walter and Tommy concealed themselves in a thicket beside a narrow road. Walter did not know which road it was. Far too many trails traversed the forests in this particular part of North Carolina. The exhausted young men decided to wait until first light and observe the road. Hopefully, a local citizen might pass by and inform them of their location. Meanwhile, they hunkered down behind a large fallen log and waited.

The boys had traveled hard throughout the night. They had a very difficult time navigating the rugged terrain. There was scant moonlight, and the forests were thick. It had been virtually impossible to maintain their bearings in the dark. They simply tried to walk as straight a path as possible, with the hope that the might somehow discern their location after sunup.

Tommy dozed fitfully under a shallow covering of dry leaves. Walter maintained watch over the road. It was less than an hour after sunrise when Walter heard sounds of movement. The noises were coming from his left. He recognized the sound of the steel rims of wagon wheels grinding against stones in the road. Soon he heard voices. He gave Tommy a swift kick in the foot.

"What?" grumbled his friend. "Stop pestering me!"

Walter whispered, "Wake up, Tommy! Someone is coming!"

Tommy was awake and upright in an instant. "Are they friend or foe?"

"I'm not certain. They're still a bit far off. Maybe we will know something after they come around that curve."

Men appeared around the bend a few minutes later. There were about twenty of them, all dressed in everyday clothing. All were armed with rifles and muskets and carried an assortment of bags, blades, and supplies. There were three men on horseback and a single wagon at the rear of their column.

"Militia," declared Walter.

"Yes. But whose?" grumbled Tommy. "There's twenty of them, and all of them armed to the teeth. All we have is two skinning knives."

"We cannot take any chances," declared Walter. "We'll let them pass, and then go ahead and cross the road and keep moving. We're bound to come upon a house sooner or later. Agreed?"

Tommy nodded and winked with his left eye. He whispered, "Good plan."

The two men concealed themselves behind the log, peering cautiously through a thick cluster of bushes. They maintained a close watch on the militiamen.

Quite unexpectedly, and much to Tommy's horror, Walter jumped suddenly from behind the log and screamed, "Mr. Searcy! Is that you?"

The men on the roadway instantly fell to the ground and aimed their muskets in Walter's direction. One of the men on horseback turned and pointed his mount in Walter's direction. He held his reins in his left hand and a pistol in his right. The fellow squinted at Walter, his face tense with apprehension. Then, almost immediately, the muscles in his face relaxed and displayed an expression of recognition.

"I know that you're a Billingsley, but which one are you?"

"Walter, sir."

"Walter? But I heard that you'd been captured down in South Carolina. What are you doing up here?"

"It's a long story, Mr. Searcy."

"It's Captain Searcy now, Son."

"Excuse me, Captain. Anyhow … my friend and I … stand up, Tommy!" He reached down and tugged Tommy out from behind the log. "My friend and I have been hauled around by the British for a couple of months now. We were with a group of sixteen other prisoners, but made our escape last night."

"How in the hell did you manage that?" the captain asked incredulously.

"One of our guards helped us get away. He became our friend during our time in captivity, and he took us out in the woods and set us free last night."

The captain raised one eyebrow. "How very un-British of him."

"He was a different sort of fellow." Walter smiled, then changed the subject. "Have you seen my brother, John, recently? I believe he serves in your county's regiment."

"No, Walter. He hasn't served this year. He was with Captain John Arnold for three months back in the autumn. I think he went home right around Christmas time."

Walter was greatly disappointed. He desperately desired to see one of his brothers.

Tommy asked, "Where are you headed now, Captain?"

"West of Guilford Courthouse. The army is forming there to make a stand against the Redcoats."

Tommy nodded. "We heard the same thing from the corporal who helped us escape."

"Really?" The captain shifted his weight in his saddle. "Well … I suppose you fellows had best come along with us, then."

"I was thinking of returning home, Captain. I am so close," Walter responded hopefully.

"You need to defend that home first, Walter. If the British take the field at Guilford Courthouse, I doubt that you'll have much of a home to return to. You need to fall in with my company and join the fight."

"We don't have any weapons, Captain," explained Tommy.

"Not to worry. We have several muskets and plenty of lead and powder in the wagon."

"What about some food?" asked Walter. "We haven't had much to eat over the past couple of months."

"We'll get your belly full when we stop for dinner mid-day."

"Do you happen to have any shoes, Captain Searcy?" asked Tommy. "Ours are in really bad shape."

The captain grinned. "You fellows are a might bit needy, aren't you?" He winked. "Maybe we can work somethin' out. I think we might have a couple of pairs of half-boots. We took 'em off of some Tories, so they might have a little stench to them. Jump in the wagon for now. There is some hard tack and water in there. Help yourselves to breakfast. We'll let you ride till dinner. Whilst you're riding you can dig around and see if you can find some new leather for your feet."

"Yes, sir!" Walter responded enthusiastically.

Both young men darted to the rear of the wagon and climbed into the bed. The rig immediately lurched forward and resumed its journey toward Guilford Courthouse. Walter and Tommy each inhaled three slabs of hard tack and drained two canteens of water. Minutes later, despite jostling about amongst the supplies and numerous boxes of cargo, they fell sound asleep.

16

BATTLE AT GUILFORD COURTHOUSE

Mid-Day – March 15, 1781
One Mile West of Guilford Courthouse

"I cannot believe that I am this close to home, yet still unable to go there! I can practically smell my mother's cooking!" groaned Walter, staring toward the northeast, his eyes tracing the familiar route of the Salisbury Road toward his hometown. Were it not for the cluster of heavy woods on the right side of the road, he might even be able to see the chimneys of his house.

"I don't care about your mama's cookin', but I surely would like a whiff of your pretty sister." Tommy grinned mischievously.

Walter kicked his amorously minded friend in the side of the leg. He turned and faced the opposite direction. He joined his comrades standing vigil over the field to their west. The men peered between the rails of a long, stout wooden fence that ran perpendicular to the Salisbury Road and extended north and south on each side of it. This fence was the forward defensive position of the North Carolina militia. The two recent escapees were deployed with several hundred North Carolina men along the length of the fence. Walter and Tommy's contingent were mid-way across the field on the southern side of the highway.

Tommy spat through the fence into the tall grass beyond. "I don't like it, Walter. How, in God's name, did we wind up in the first line of this fight?"

"We're just lucky, I guess," Walter quipped.

"If we are, it would be a first," responded Tommy. "The last time we were in a line like this, it was with Buford in the Waxhaws."

Walter nodded subtly. "How well I remember."

"And that didn't turn out so well for us, Walter."

"I reckon you're right about that. But we made it, didn't we? We're here now, still alive and fighting. And if we can only make it through this day, we might even be able to sleep in an actual bed tonight." Walter cut his eyes at Tommy. "Though I am quite sure Mrs. Billingsley will require you to take a thorough and vigorous bath before you climb into any of her beds."

Tommy grinned. "Walter, there's not enough water in this county to get us sufficiently clean for sleeping upon white sheets. But, I would surely like to give it a try."

Walter closed his eyes and daydreamed of home. He could almost smell the fresh-baked bread in his mother's kitchen. He fantasized about the sensation of cool, soft linen sheets rubbing against his tired, bruised body. He imagined his mother and sister, at this very moment, reading in the parlor and conversing after their noon meal. The normalcy of the vision was almost more than he could bear.

"Perhaps the British will not even come. Maybe there will be no fight today. The spies could have been mistaken," Walter declared wishfully.

"Let us hope so," mumbled Tommy.

One Hour Later

The artillery barrage lasted for almost a half-hour. The explosions of cannon fire were the most frightening thing that Walter had ever experienced ... and he had suffered more than his share of terror and fear during his short time of service in this war of revolution. The first few shells landed fifty yards short of the fence, but the expert British artillerymen quickly adjusted fire and redirected the projectiles toward their targets.

All that the Patriot soldiers could do in response was hide. The North Carolina militiamen lay low to the ground in their attempt to avoid the deadly slivers of white-hot iron unleashed by the detonating cannon balls. However, not all of the Patriots could escape the wrath of the barrage. Screams of horror and pain erupted along the line. The cannon fire was beginning to take a toll. All the while, as the front line of the American defenses huddled to escape the merciless barrage, the immense British army numbering over 4,000 men formed on the battlefield in neatly organized brigades and regiments.

Tommy screamed, “My God! Look, Walter!” He pointed toward the road.

Walter looked in the direction indicated by his friend. Less than twenty yards away, an entire section of the fence was gone. Moments ago, five or six militiamen had occupied that position. Now, all that remained of them were fragments of clothing and flesh scattered over the ground and hanging from the shredded limbs of a nearby tree.

Then, quite suddenly, the deafening cannon fire subsided. The din of the barrage was immediately replaced with the sounds of dozens of drums thumping in the field. There were bagpipes wailing their mournful song directly in front of Walter and Tommy’s position. And Walter could almost swear that he heard shouts in German to their left front.

He peeked between the lower timbers of the fence. A different form of terror gripped his heart. The field before him was a sea of red, white, and yellow. There was one portion of the army to his left that was clad in a curious combination of blue and yellow. Dozens of flags fluttered lazily in the slight breeze.

"Ready up, boys! Here they come!" shouted Captain Searcy. "Use the fence to steady your aim. Remember, you all are Carolina frontier boys. Aim small. Choose your targets careful and proper. Shoot 'em in the gullet. Make every shot count. We will hold this spot for two shots. When I give the order to retreat, go toward the left flank. Colonel Lee and his Light Horsemen will cover our retreat. We'll join up with the Virginny boys. Understood?"

"Yes, sir!" responded his men excitedly.

"Good. Now remember, men. This fence is pretty good cover, and those Lobsterbacks are prancin' around out there in the open. They make for nice, fat targets. Once you take your first shot, take the time to reload proper. Don't leave your ball hangin' half-way down the barrel. And don't forget to pull your rammin' rod! Some boys get all caught up in the frenzy of the fight and wind up shootin' their rod downrange or blowin' up the end of their gun barrel."

Walter tried to imagine how anyone could forget to pull their ramrod. He shook his head in disbelief.

The captain continued, "Hold your fire until I give the order! We're going to hit 'em before they get their guns to their shoulders. After the first shot, reload quickly and then we'll hit 'em with a second volley. After that, we retreat. Remember ... our job is to kill them. That is all! We are not here to hold this fence. We are here to reduce the enemy!"

Several of the men near Walter stood so that they could fire over the top of fence, but he chose to kneel and fire between the rails. He wanted to present as low a profile as possible and utilize the upper rails of the fence for cover. He rested his left hand on top of the center rail and cradled his new musket. It was a .69 caliber Charleville, a gift from his French allies. The iron was shiny, polished, and brand new. The weapon was unfamiliar to him. Still, the function was the same as every other flintlock, so Walter had mastered priming and loading the weapon in relatively short order. He had his first load tamped down tight and his pan primed and ready. He intended to make his first shot a good one.

The British infantrymen marched steadily toward the fence. They halted approximately fifty yards in front of the North Carolina militiamen. They were preparing to fire. Somewhere on the north side of the road a small field cannon boomed. The ball exploded in the center of a company of British troops, flinging bodies and limbs high into the air. Behind the Carolina boys, the Virginians cheered.

"Get ready, gentlemen! Full cock and take aim!" barked a voice from behind the line. It was General John Butler, the commander of the militia from the Hillsborough District.

Across the field a loud and distinctly British voice ordered, "Make ready!"

The enemy soldiers lifted their muskets high and cocked their hammers. It was the exact moment that the North Carolina troops had been waiting for.

Captain Searcy and dozens of other captains along the line of eight hundred militiamen screamed simultaneously, "Fire!"

The wall of lead tore into the British lines. For as far as Walter could see in either direction, the front row of enemy soldiers crumpled and fell like stalks of wheat. Dozens, perhaps hundreds, lay dead or dying in the high grass. The second line of the British formation fired quickly at the American position, but their fire was largely ineffective. The covered, concealed positions of the North Carolina sharpshooters resulted in minimal casualties.

"Reload quickly, boys!" shouted Captain Searcy.

Another American cannon boomed, once again decimating a cluster of the exposed British troops. Then two more cannons belched fire and death from behind the Patriot line. Their fire was having a devastating effect upon the British. More cheering ensued in the rear.

Along the North Carolina line, the Patriot militiamen feverishly tore at their cartridges and primed their pans. They hurriedly poured the remaining powder down their gun barrels, and then quickly crammed the paper wadding and balls into their muzzles and tamped the fresh loads with their rods. The entire process seemed to take forever, but in reality, less than thirty seconds had transpired. Amazingly, the highly skilled and trained British troops reloaded and unleashed another round of shots at the American line before the Patriot troops could even complete the reloading process. But, thankfully, their fire was once again ineffective.

"Make ready!" screamed General Butler. The captains echoed his order.

The cannon fire from behind the North Carolinians intensified. Explosions rocked the field in front of Walter and Tommy, sending geysers of earth, grass, blood, and flesh high into the dazzlingly blue sky. A dull haze of powder smoke began to form over the field. In several places the grass caught fire.

Like all of their fellow compatriots, Walter and Tommy cocked their firelocks and aimed at the enemy lines beyond the rails of the fence.

"Look! Along the road!" yelled Tommy.

Walter glanced to his right. His heart sank. Several dozen green and red-clad dragoons thundered westward on the packed earth of the roadway. At the head of the mounted assault was none other than Lieutenant Colonel Banastre Tarleton. He held his sword high in the air and pointed slightly forward. It was clear that he intended to slice the Patriot defenses down the middle.

The captains all along their defensive line shouted simultaneously, "Fire!"

Once again, a wave of searing lead tore into the British lines. Hundreds more men fell, either dead or writhing in agony.

Captain Searcy urged his men. "That's it, boys! Retreat! Rally on the Virginians!"

Walter and Tommy wasted no time obeying their captain. They had absolutely no desire to remain behind such meager cover. They fled. Walter glanced over his shoulder as he ran. The British were already at the fence. Many of the enemy soldiers were either climbing over the obstacle or pulling the rails out of the posts for ease of crossing. A thunder of gunfire soon erupted from behind them, just as they were reaching the edge of the woods in which the Virginians were concealed.

"God, Almighty!" screamed Tommy as the enormous lead projectiles slammed into the trees and ground all around him.

Walter and Tommy dived forward into the forest. Shredded leaves and limbs rained from overhead, ripped from the tall oaks and hickory trees that populated the woods. The scene almost had the appearance of green snow. The fresh spring foliage quickly painted the brown forest floor, coating the hard-packed leaves of the previous autumn with a thin layer of bright green.

Shouts emanated from the woods, "Get down! Hit the ground! You're in our line of fire!"

Walter and Tommy immediately dropped and lay still. The explosions of the muskets of the Virginians were deafening. Walter covered his ears, but he could still hear the projectiles screaming over his head. Smoldering fibers of burning paper wadding floated down from above.

More shouts ensued. "Get up! Keep moving!"

The North Carolina militiamen all scrambled to their feet and sprinted another twenty yards deeper into the trees, utilizing the precious moments afforded to them as the Virginians reloaded. More British lead tore into the earth around them. Walter heard metal hitting meat in close proximity. Several of the fleeing militiamen fell. One man dropped lifeless in Walter's path. He simply jumped over the fellow's still body. He quickly concealed himself behind a fallen tree.

He screamed, "Tommy!"

"Over here!"

Walter scanned to his right. He saw his friend crouching low behind a small elm tree. His hands were empty.

"Where is your musket?"

Tommy pointed toward the field. "I lost it when we went down."

"Well, find another one as quickly as you can! You can't throw rocks at the Redcoats!"

Another round of deadly gunfire belched forth from the forest. The Virginians were returning fire. Walter quickly reloaded his gun and then peeked from behind his tree. The British line was roughly sixty yards from the woods and progressing steadily in his direction. Walter took careful aim at a British sergeant who marched near the left flank of his company. He fired, and the sergeant fell. Walter concealed himself again and reloaded his Charleville.

"Found one!" exclaimed Tommy. He huddled against his tree and clutched an old British Brown Bess proudly against his chest.

"Did you get lead for it, as well?" Walter yelled over the din of the battle.

"No! Why?"

"Because, you dalcop, that Brown Bess is a .75 caliber! Your little Charleville round balls are going to ramble around inside that huge barrel!"

"Can't I just add some extra wadding?"

"I suppose it's better than nothing at all," griped Walter, shaking his head.

He turned to fire again, but another barrage of British lead screamed through the trees, decimating both foliage and flesh. A piercing, other-worldly scream filled the woods. Walter looked behind him. Fifteen yards deep into the woods a man was writhing on the forest floor. He lay exposed in a patch of open ground between two large walnut trees. Walter turned and fired once more at the attackers, then rushed to the man's aid. He slung his musket over his shoulder as he ran.

He yelled, "Tommy! Come quick!"

His friend darted to his aid.

"We have to get him behind cover. Grab his arm!"

Something tugged at the left shoulder of Walter's threadbare coat. Fibers of cloth and thread hovered in the air around his head. Walter glanced quickly at his shoulder. A British ball had ripped through the thin fabric that covered his flesh. If it had been just a half-inch lower, it would have found meat. Walter prayed a quick prayer of thanksgiving as he and Tommy labored to pull the screaming lad behind a large tree. They finally reached the safety of its huge trunk.

Walter tried to distract the boy as he examined his wound. "What is your name, friend?"

The boy stuttered from the pain. "Edward … Tuck. But … my friends … call me Ned."

Walter frowned as he examined the boy's wound. There was a gaping, oozing hole in the left side of his belly, just below the ribs.

"Where are you from, Ned?"

"Halifax … County … right on … the border of … Carolina."

"I know it well," responded Walter. He patted the boy on the shoulder. "I'm going to turn you over just a bit, Ned, and look at your back. I want to see if the ball went through."

Ned nodded. Walter lifted him gently onto his right side. The back of the lad's coat was soaked in blood. Walter glanced knowingly at Tommy, who shook his head grimly.

"Ned, my name is Walter Billingsley. I'm from right here in Guilford County. Now, listen to me. I'm going to put a bandage on this wound." He ripped the left arm off of his coat, rolled it into a wad, and placed it over the hole in his belly. "We need some pressure on it to stop the bleeding. You're going to be just fine. I want you to just calm down and rest easy behind this tree. I have to get back to the fighting. But don't you worry … Tommy and I are not going to leave you on this field."

"You … pr … promise?" Ned whined.

"I promise. We will be right here beside you. When the call for retreat comes, we're taking you with us."

"All … all right. I'm mighty … grateful."

"Meanwhile, you need to push on this bandage with your hand as hard as you can."

"I … will … Walter. And th … thank you."

Walter smiled. He glanced at Tommy, and then toward the oncoming British. They were just entering the edge of the trees.

"Let's go, Tommy! We need to find cover!"

The two friends darted toward their right, where there was a cluster of limestone boulders protruding from the forest floor. They were not large, only about two feet in height, but they would provide excellent cover.

"Behind those rocks!" exclaimed Walter, pointing. He led the way. Tommy was ten feet behind him.

The two friends had almost reached the rocks when the earth beneath them rumbled and exploded. Walter's body lifted from the ground and went flying through the air. It was the strangest of sensations. He felt a scorching fire in his feet and legs. Tree branches slashed his face and neck. And then suddenly, violently, he came to an abrupt stop when his head impacted against a tree. Walter slid, face first, down the rough bark of a gigantic hickory. Gravity pulled him quickly back to the ground. He landed hard on his chest. He lay still on the dirt-strewn ground, stunned and disoriented. He could no longer hear the sounds of battle. There was only a loud, high-pitched whine echoing in both of his ears. His limbs were numb, and he could not move them. But, somehow, he managed to lift his head.

Twenty feet away he saw Tommy. His friend lay on the ground facing Walter's direction. His eyes were wide open and staring at Walter, but there was no more life in them. There couldn't be … because the entire lower portion of Tommy's body was gone. There was nothing below his belly. His bloody bowels lay in a gelatinous heap beneath his wide-open torso.

Walter screamed, "Tommy!" And then his world turned black as he lapsed into unconsciousness.

Walter opened his eyes. He was staring at a low ceiling. He heard the dull rumble of distant thunder, and the high-pitched dripping of water as it landed in puddles. He raised up on his left elbow and looked around. The floor beside him was littered with wounded men. Most appeared to be militia. There were a handful of Continentals, as well. On the far side of the room he spied several red coats. They were the enemy wounded, isolated from the Patriots and under guard.

A voice shouted from across the room, "Doctor Edmonds, that fellow with the head injury is awake!"

An older gentleman appeared at Walter's side almost immediately. "Ah! Walter! Awake at last! We feared that you may have slipped into a permanent slumber."

Walter was confused. He had never seen this man before.

"Sir … how do you know my name?"

"Your brothers told me. I am Dr. Enoch Edmonds, surgeon in charge of this ward."

"My brothers?" Walter exclaimed. The shout sent a wave of pain through his head.

"I suggest that you remain calm, Walter. You have had a serious blow to the top of your head. And from what I can see, it is not the first time. You have a scar up there that appears to be several years old. What was it? A musket ball?"

Walter nodded. He did not care to elaborate. He was growing weary of waking up in hospitals and explaining himself to doctors. He had experienced this same exact circumstance many months before at Salisbury. The result of that encounter had been forced impressment into the army. He did not wish to repeat anything that vaguely resembled the outcome of that encounter.

"Which of my brothers are here?" he demanded, changing the subject.

The doctor pointed across the room. "Samuel is over there in the far corner. He is sleeping soundly. The poor lad took some iron fragments in his back. From the cannon fire, you know."

"Will he live?"

"Samuel will be just fine. His wounds were mostly superficial. Lots of blood, but not particularly deep. The fragments were quite easy to remove. He'll be on his way home in a couple of days."

The doctor pulled the blanket off of Walter's legs. "You took some of the same in your legs, I am afraid. I got most of it out. There are a couple of pieces in the muscle of your lower left leg that were a bit too deep. But, your body should close them off with time. Everything looks pink and clean. There is no bloody pus or foul smell."

"My head hurts badly," Walter complained.

"As well it should. It looks like you tried to use it to chop down a tree. And it appears like you attempted to sand that tree smooth with your face," he teased. "But, the cuts and scrapes will heal soon enough. And the knot has gone down quite a bit. You may keep a headache for quite some time, but you're young and strong. You will heal quickly. Count your blessings, boy. None of your innards were hurt. Heart, lungs, guts, and liver are all untouched. There's many a man inside this building who cannot claim the same."

"How long have I been sleeping?" asked Walter, scanning at his surroundings.

"Almost three days. Your body needed the rest. We are bivouacked at the Troublesome Iron Works, about fifteen miles west of the battlefield. General Greene ordered us to remain here long enough to see to our wounded and get resupplied."

Walter contemplated the doctor's words. The memory of the wounded lad, Ned Tuck, leapt into his mind. He also recalled his promise to help remove the boy from the battlefield.

"Doctor, could you check on the disposition of a young man that I encountered in the woods during the battle? He was wounded in the belly. It was really bad. He was a pitiful, frightened thing. His name was Ned Tuck, from Virginia, as I recall. Do you know if he lived?"

"Walter, I don't normally know the identities of most of our wounded, but I am quite familiar with young Ned." The doctor grinned.

"Oh? He is alive, then?"

The doctor nodded vigorously. "He is, indeed. In fact, his father left with him today. The brave man rode from his home in Virginia and only arrived yesterday morning. He miraculously located his son and made arrangements for his transport. They departed at first light this morning. His father was pulling him on a horse litter behind his pack mule."

"In this horrid weather?" objected Walter, looking outside at the pouring rain.

"He was anxious to get his boy home, as you can imagine. But, there's no need for you to worry. Young Mr. Tuck was well covered and warm, and in his father's most capable hands."

"That is truly wonderful news, indeed." He paused as his thoughts shifted back to his own situation. "You said that I have brothers here. Which of my other brothers besides Samuel is nearby?"

"James is at his company's campsite. I sent an orderly for him. He should be here soon. I think the Rowan County boys can survive for a little while without their captain." He smiled warmly.

Almost on cue, James came bursting through the door. He sprinted to Walter's mat.

"Walter! You hard-headed little cuss! How the hell are you?"

"I have a raging headache, but the surgeon says I'll live." He immediately unleashed a barrage of questions. "How is mother? How are our brothers and sisters? Did the British get into the town? Did our homes survive the battle? Who won?"

James knelt down and hugged his brother gently. "Everyone is just fine. I checked on them all yesterday. Mother is worried sick over you, of course. The battle was pretty much a draw. The British took the field, but they had so many killed and wounded that they had to withdraw immediately after. They reached the outskirts of

Guilford Courthouse before they pulled back. They did not shell the town, thank God."

"So, then, Mother is truly well? She did not experience the violence of the battle?"

James shook his head reassuringly. "There might be a few musket balls in the walls of the house and barn, not no more than that. We were lucky. Besides … Mother has other battles to attend to in her life."

"Whatever do you mean?" demanded Walter, confused.

James grinned mischievously. "Would you believe it? Mama has had to fend off a suitor in recent days."

Walter's left eyebrow rose in surprise. "You're *not* being serious."

James guffawed. "Indeed, I am! Old man Daniel Jeter has a mind to snag our mother as a wife. She's kept him at bay for several months now, but he is a persistent old fart."

"Let us hope she stays the course," Walter declared, chuckling.

"Now, tell me, Walter … how, in God's Name, did you come to be here in this battle in Guilford County? The last word we got was months ago, when you were in the prison at Camden. I could scarcely believe it when I saw the Virginians haul you into this hospital. I thought that I was imagining things."

Walter took a deep breath and then carefully recounted his saga of the past year, from his forced recruitment at Salisbury, to his interment at Camden, and finally to his escape and participation in the recent battle. He, of course, included the deaths of his friends Gabriel Tate and, more recently, Thomas Whitlock. He left out all of the more intimate elements of the story that pertained to Abigail. When he was finished, James simply stared at younger brother with a gaze of admiration.

"That is quite an amazing story, Walter. I'd say that you have been the victim of a rather steady stream of bad luck."

"It's not been all bad," Walter confessed. "There have been some good moments. Certainly, my luck has turned out better than that of my two dead friends."

James nodded grimly. "Well, I reckon you have had enough of this war. You've certainly done your part. I am going to secure discharges for both you and Samuel and then take you home."

"You can do that?" asked Walter, somewhat in disbelief.

"I have General Butler's ear. I've been his scout for several months now. It shouldn't take much effort. Besides, both of you are wounded and unfit for travel. We'll get you rested up and fed, then head for home in a couple of days."

"Thank you, James." Walter's chin began to tremble. He was on the verge of joyful tears.

"There, now, little brother. Everything will be quite all right. We'll get you healed and fattened up so that you can go down to Camden and fetch your woman." He winked. "I'll be back later this afternoon. First, I'm going to see if I can get you moved over to where Samuel is resting. The two of you can catch up on things and pass the time together."

"That sounds wonderful! I want to hear all about home. Samuel can fill me in on all the local news and gossip."

"I will get everything arranged." He patted Walter on the chest. "I love you, little brother. It brings me great joy to see you alive and safe."

"I love you, too, James. Now, please … get me home."

James smiled. He stood and walked to a nearby desk and spoke briefly to the doctor, who nodded his affirmation of James' requests. Moments later Walter's older brother pulled his coat over the top of his hat and ran outside into the rain. Walter rolled over onto his side and laid his head on his forearm. He instantly fell fast asleep.

Troublesome Iron Works - March 21, 1781

"You must always keep this paper in a safe place, Walter," ordered Captain James Billingsley.

"Why? It is only a piece of paper."

"It is your proof of service," chimed Samuel. "It might come in handy someday. Like ... if we were to ever get paid for serving in this damned war. Since you're not on any muster or payrolls, this will be the only document that you will ever have. So, guard it wisely."

"I will."

James patted both of his brothers on their shoulders. "You two stay with the wagon. I'm going to fetch some bread and meat, and a couple of bottles of rum. We will leave for home in just a bit."

"I'll be sure to keep a sharp eye on Walter. He's prone to wandering off and getting into trouble," Samuel teased.

Walter tapped his makeshift crutches against the floor beneath the wagon seat. "I shall not run off this time. I promise."

James grinned, turned, and marched toward the commissary tent.

Walter carefully folded the parchment and then removed his dark gray cocked hat. He inherited the new hat from a fellow at the hospital who had shared a mat near him. The boy's name was Daniel Pearson, and the two had become fast friends. The poor lad died from fever the previous afternoon, but before he passed, he presented his prized hat to Walter as a special bequest. Daniel was yet another in a rapidly growing list of dead friends and brief relationships in Walter's life. And Walter was growing weary of watching his friends die.

He reverently tucked the paper inside the liner, then leaned back against the rear of the wagon seat and rested his weight on his elbows. He stretched his face toward the sun, allowing its life-sustaining light to warm his cheeks. He was, most definitely, ready to depart the darkness and death of this hospital encampment and return home to his mother.

A curious voice called from across the road, "Walter! Walter Billingsley! Is that you?"

Walter turned in the direction of the voice. His heart leapt with joy when he saw the man who had called his name. A tired-looking, red-coated soldier lay beside the road on a tattered gray blanket. He was propped up on his right elbow and waving vigorously with his left hand. Walter could scarcely believe his eyes. It was Corporal Gabriel Blevins, his former captor, and the man who had set him free.

He cried out, "Gabriel! Oh, my God!"

17

I SHALL NEVER BE THE SAME

Walter descended quickly and clumsily from the wagon.

"Where are you going?" challenged Samuel.

"To see an old friend."

Walter hobbled on his rickety crutches toward the place where his former captor lay. The sight of a bloody bandage stopped him in his tracks. The corporal's left leg was gone below the knee. Filthy, crusty rags encased the bloody stump.

"Oh, Gabriel, no! Your leg!"

"I am quite all right, Walter. My wound was so severe that your surgeons had to amputate my leg. But, they say that I shall live." He smiled reassuringly.

Walter approached his former enemy and lowered himself to the ground by the man's side. It was a most difficult and awkward maneuver to perform without assistance. He inspected Gabriel's leg.

"What happened to you?"

Gabriel frowned. "A rebel musket ball hit the very center of my leg and decimated the bone. The appendage was practically severed by the shot. There were only a few inches of skin and a miniscule amount of flesh holding my leg together. It was beyond hope, so they removed it immediately."

"When was the last time anyone changed that bandage?"

Gabriel glanced at his stump. "The day before yesterday, I think. I was in a bit of a stupor, I'm afraid. My memory is somewhat clouded. The rebel doctor said that I had a raging fever for the first three days after I arrived. They claim that I am now past the worst of it."

Walter nodded. "Well, that is good. What about Colonel Beecham? Was he in the battle?"

"Yes, he was, indeed. He survived. I saw him depart with his regiment."

Walter was a bit torn emotionally by the news of the officer's participation in the battle. He certainly did not wish evil upon his former captor, but neither did he wish him well. He decided to focus his thoughts and conversation upon Corporal Blevins.

"What are you doing out here beside the road, Gabriel? This ground is soaking wet!"

"Your Continental Army gentlemen are preparing to take us all to a prison camp in Virginia. I believe we will be traveling with a group of Marylanders."

"But, how on earth did you wind up in *our* hospital? It seems a bit odd."

Gabriel sighed. "General Cornwallis abandoned the field shortly after the battle. He took the ground, but at a great cost. We lost an enormous number of troops, as I am quite sure you have already heard. I was among a group of the more severely wounded. The general ordered that we be left behind for treatment by your surgeons. I assume that he believed we had a better chance if we were not moved."

"Well, it appears that the general's strategy worked for you."

"Indeed. Though, I am a bit worried about this impending prison camp. I am not certain as to the quality of medical care that will be available there."

Walter's heart broke for the young man. He reached out to him and squeezed his hand in a most affectionate manner.

A scolding voice called to him from the vicinity of the wagon. "Walter! What the hell are you doing?" It was James.

Walter turned and smiled. "Just talking to an old friend."

James stomped over to where Walter was seated. He stared at the two men, thoroughly confused. "But, Walter! He is a British corporal! What is the meaning of this?"

"Gabriel, this is my big brother, Captain James Billingsley. James, this is Corporal Gabriel Blevins of His Majesty's 7th Regiment of Foot. He was my guard at Camden ... and the man who set me free."

"Truly? This is James?" asked Gabriel, smiling in disbelief. "How fortuitous that you managed to find one another after such a huge battle." He struggled to reach out his hand. "It is a pleasure to meet you, Captain. Walter has told me much about you and your family."

James' eyes widened. The storminess on his face cleared somewhat. He nodded to the Redcoat, but maintained his emotional distance. He made no effort to shake the soldier's hand. Gabriel, somewhat embarrassed by the rejection, lowered his outstretched arm.

James growled through clenched teeth, "My family is in your debt, sir." It seemed as if the words tasted to him like a bitter poison.

Gabriel smiled. "It was my pleasure, Captain. Walter and I formed a most unusual relationship during our time together this past year. Some might even call it inappropriate, I quite think. It was that friendship, and the conviction of my conscience, that provoked me to set him and Thomas free." He gave a small start. "Oh, wait! Walter! Where is Thomas? Is he near?" He scanned the area in search of Walter's friend.

Walter shook his head slowly and frowned. "He didn't make it, Gabriel. He perished in the battle. An exploding cannon ball killed him instantly."

"Oh. I am so very sorry to hear that. He was a good chap. So very clever and entertaining, yet wise, as well."

"Indeed, he was," affirmed Walter. He reached up to his brother, who helped pull him to his feet. Once he was secure on top of his crutches, Walter took a deep breath and declared resolutely, "James, I want Gabriel to be placed in the back of our wagon. He's coming home with me."

James stared at his little brother as if there were three extra eyes on his forehead. "What? Are you outside your mind?"

"No, I most certainly am not! This man saved my life. I owe him a debt that I can never repay, but I intend to start trying right now. I want him in that wagon with me and Samuel. Mother and Martha will help see to his care."

"But he is a British soldier! He is the enemy!" screeched James in exasperation. "Surely, you are not suggesting that we bring him into our mother's house!"

Gabriel tugged at Walter's leg and pleaded, "Walter, you needn't do this."

Walter turned to him. "You would like to go with me, wouldn't you Gabriel?"

"Of course. Nothing would please me more. But ..."

"Well, then, shut up and let me make your case." He stared his brother coldly in the eyes. "You claim that you have General Butler's ear. Well, then ... take care of this for me. Make it happen. Secure the corporal's parole. Explain who he is. Remind the general that this is the man who helped me escape. Tell him that he has officially changed sides, for God's sake! Tell him that Corporal Blevins will swear his oath. Whatever it takes. But, I want it done. And I'm not leaving this encampment unless this man is by my side."

James shook his head vigorously. "The general will not allow it. I am quite certain of the fact."

"Convince him," demanded Walter, awkwardly crossing his arms over the tops of his crutches.

James exhaled, exasperated, and then turned and trudged toward his commander's tent.

Guilford Courthouse – May 16, 1781

"Do you need anything, Gabriel? Anything at all?" Elizabeth inquired. "I can fix you some more tea. Or, perhaps you might like a book?"

Gabriel Blevins smiled. The young man was sitting up in his bed. There was a half-filled cup of tea on a nearby table, along with some stationery, pen, and ink. Two beautiful, fresh strawberry tarts lay on an elegant saucer next to his cup of tea. He was holding a recent newspaper in his hands, and was peering, transfixed, at the most recent news.

"No, thank you, mum. I am quite comfortable and content. As always, I am most grateful for your hospitality and kindness. As your enemy, I do not deserve any of it."

"Humph! You are no enemy in this house, Gabriel Blevins. And I will hear no more talk of it!" She wagged her finger in his face as only a mother can do. "You are welcome here for as long as you would like to stay." She ceased waving her corrective finger and then patted the young man's hand.

Elizabeth Billingsley was the happiest that she had been in years. Her house was full, once again. Her beloved Walter was home, and he had even brought a guest with him. She was a bit confused when James showed up at her door with a British soldier. But, once she learned how Corporal Blevins had helped Walter escape from his captivity, allegiances and nationality were of no consequence. She welcomed the foreign soldier into her home as if he were one of her own sons. The fact that he was in need of medical care and constant attention made the man's presence all the more pleasurable to her.

Elizabeth cast a quick glance at Walter, who was seated in a spindle-back side chair next to Gabriel's bed. He grinned and winked at his mother.

"All right, then," she declared. "I will leave you two to your talk of news and war. But I shall return within the hour with some hot soup and steaming bread."

"That sounds absolutely delicious," proclaimed Gabriel. "I shall anxiously await your return."

Elizabeth grinned happily and sauntered out of the room. The hems of her layers of petticoats swished as she walked. As soon as she entered the hallway, she began to hum a joyful tune.

"You mother is a jewel, Walter. Frankly, I do not know why you ever left home." He chuckled. "I fear that I shall weigh half a ton by the time I am ready to get out of this bed and attempt to walk again."

Walter laughed, as well. "She loves to dote over you, that much is certain. It's best that you just allow her to have her way. Do what she says and eat whatever she places in front of you, and she will eventually leave you alone."

"Who says I want to be left alone? Her kindness is so overwhelming, she makes my own mother seem like a sergeant in the British army!"

Both men laughed heartily. Walter was beginning to feel more like himself again. He noticed that laughter no longer made his head throb. That was definitely a good sign. The trauma to his head had been severe. The lump on his skull had diminished gradually, and a pestering headache lingered for almost four weeks. Thankfully, it had subsided significantly over the past few days. It recurred only when Walter attempted some form of strenuous physical activity.

The wounds on his legs had been a bit more problematic. Some of the deeper cuts festered during the wagon journey home and took on a bit of an odd color. He fought a significant fever for the first week after he returned home. Thankfully, his mother's devoted and expert care saved both of his legs and, most likely, his life.

Elizabeth treated the dangerous, infected wounds three times a day by dousing them with several ounces of pure alcohol from her whiskey still. For the deeper wounds, she actually parted the skin and poured the clear, fiery liquid deep into his flesh. Walter wailed in agony each time she did it, but she knew that it was absolutely necessary. She did not want mortification to set in and result in the loss of one or both of his legs ... or worse.

Walter's wounds slowly responded to the daily therapy. Once his fever broke, the larger holes in his skin and flesh sealed themselves and scabbed over. After that, he was on a quick road to recovery. He had actually been out of the bed for over a week now, and was beginning to get back into the habit of working around the house. Still, his favorite moments each day were his bedside conversations with Gabriel.

"Well," Walter urged. "What news is there of the war? I have not had the opportunity to read the latest paper."

Gabriel glanced at the date in the upper right corner of the meager, thin newsprint. "If this week-old rebel propaganda is to be believed," he winked at Walter, "General Lord Cornwallis has departed toward the east and appears to be moving northward into Virginia."

"That is what I have heard, as well. There is much talk among the locals about your old commander's movements in the field."

"At least the great battle is done and he has departed this place," declared Gabriel. "I quite prefer the peace and tranquility of your charming little community. It reminds me somewhat of home ... only much hotter."

Walter grinned. "Do you think you will ever return to your home?"

"I don't know. I haven't decided. Though, lately, I am leaning towards making a place for myself here in America. I daresay there will be little use for me in England. I cannot imagine that there could be any demand for a footless footman." He smiled at his own clever joke, but then his smile morphed into a flat frown. "I suppose everything will depend on how this blasted war plays out."

Walter slapped him on his healthy leg. "Well, as my mother said, you will always be welcome here. I'm certain that we can find a place for you amongst our family enterprises." He rose from the chair. "In the meantime, you just focus on healing and getting well. We shall have you up and about in no time, at all."

"How will you entertain yourself for the remainder of this lovely day?" Gabriel inquired.

"I am going out to the farm to visit with my brothers. Henry needs some help with the horses. Samuel is our true horseman, but he is still recuperating. His lovely wife, Mary, is doing an excellent job of nursing him back to good health. I am anxious for you to meet her, as well as all of my brothers' wives and families. I also have two sisters that you have not met."

"I look forward to meeting all of them, of course. What about your brothers in the service? Where are they?"

"James and John are both with their regiments. Cornwallis is gone, but some Tories are still making trouble here in Guilford and Randolph Counties. That bastard, David Fanning, has led several raids on homes over the past month."

"And he is the one who murdered your father?"

"That's him," Walter responded. He pointed at the tree that filled their view outside the second-story window. "He killed Papa right there … in that tree."

"Ghastly!" declared Gabriel. He didn't know how else he could respond. As a formal enemy, he felt somewhat responsible for the actions of his comrades in arms, even though he played no personal part.

"Well, that was a long time ago," declared Walter. "We must live in the here and now. We cannot change the past, but we can certainly chart a better course for the future."

"How very philosophical of you, Walter. Almost poetic. I may even write that down."

Walter picked up the linen napkin from Gabriel's table and tossed it at his friend's face. "I'll see you later, you old Redcoat."

Gabriel snatched the napkin from his face and grinned. "How about you send that lovely sister of yours to read to me for a while? I very much enjoy Martha's company."

"Not likely!" declared Walter. "Even a one-legged Englishman is too much of a charmer to unleash upon my unsuspecting sister. I shall send Basil, instead."

"God save me from that boisterous lad," mumbled Gabriel.

Walter laughed as he ambled from the room.

June 25, 1781

"It is time, Mother. I cannot and need not wait any longer." Walter stood, arms crossed, beside the silent, empty fireplace in the parlor. "I have written numerous letters to Abigail, but have had no response. I fear that my correspondences have not made it through to Camden. Therefore, I must go there myself."

Tears stained Elizabeth's cheeks, glistening in the candlelight that illuminated the room. "We have been through this before, Walter. And I remember quite vividly what happened the last time. You wound up a soldier in the army, and a prisoner, and a wounded veteran of two battlefields. I absolutely beg you not to go."

"It is not the same this time, Mother. The British are gone to Virginia. The highways to Charlotte Town and Camden are much safer now than they were before."

She continued her protest. "The Tories are still roaming the countryside, wreaking mayhem throughout the counties of the Piedmont. David Fanning remains on the loose!"

"Our own Patriot militias now control the region, Mother. The Loyalists are few and far between. Most have sensed the shifting tides of this war and have already switched sides. Anyhow, I shall not go alone. Basil will accompany me."

"As shall I, Mrs. Billingsley," declared Gabriel Blevins from his seat beside the window. "Together, we will return to Camden and fetch Miss Abigail back to her new home."

Elizabeth shook her head grimly. "I still do not like it. We have not heard a word from Abigail since last year. Her family may not even be in Camden, anymore. They could be refugees in Charlestown, or perhaps even in Georgia or British East Florida!"

"That is why I must go, Mother. I must find her and see to her welfare."

"And if she is gone … what then?"

"Then, I shall look for her until I find her. She is the love of my life, Mother. I cannot imagine living without her. Surely, you must understand that."

Elizabeth shuffled toward the parlor window and stared at the silhouette of the huge oak tree in which her husband had died. The leaf-heavy limbs swayed in the gentle evening breeze.

"Yes, Walter. I understand that very, very well."

Camden, South Carolina - July 3, 1781

"Are we almost there?" groaned Basil.

"We are, indeed!" declared Walter. "It is just down this street, and right at the second corner."

"Camden certainly appears to be different," observed Gabriel. "I have never before seen it like this. I suppose this is what it must have appeared like before the arrival of my countrymen."

The primary change in Camden was that none of the activity in the streets was military. Instead, there were citizens engaged in commerce, numerous social gatherings, several wagons being loaded or unloaded, and dozens of people conversing in the street. Normalcy. It was peaceful. It was nice.

Walter's countenance clouded just a bit as they rode past the stone house that had once served as his prison. There was a new sign posted beside that gate that read, "Hospital." Men wearing various bandages and wraps reclined in chairs beneath the shade trees of the yard. There was much activity as people entered and exited the doors of the large stone house.

Walter grumbled, "Well, at least they have put the old prison to good use."

"Indeed. A most worthwhile utilization of that facility," agreed Gabriel. "It is good to see it as a place of healing, rather than a place of interment."

"That is where you were held prisoner?" asked Basil. His face betrayed a sense of awe.

"For part of the time. I spent most of my days under guard at a nearby farm."

Gabriel mused, "I do wonder whatever became of *Beechmont*."

"I don't care," declared Walter. "Perhaps it has reverted back to its rightful owner. Anyhow, I have other business to address." It was obvious that Walter did not want to engage in any more discussion of that particular period of his life.

He guided the wagon around the turn that led to Abigail's home. His heart skipped a beat when he spied the white clapboard house. It seemed a bit more weathered than usual, but appeared to still be occupied. He brought his wagon to a stop in front of the gate and pulled back on the brake.

"I hate that we have arrived unannounced," observed Gabriel. "It seems most improper."

"Abigail won't mind!" chirped Basil. "I know she'll be really happy to see Walter!"

"And it's not as if we had any choice," added Walter. "Lines of communication have been tenuous, at best."

"Shall we go with you, or remain with the wagon?" asked Gabriel.

"Just stay here. This is all about Abigail and me. Let me have my reunion, and then I will call you fellows up to the house."

Gabriel smiled warmly. "Go, then, and enjoy your reunion."

Walter climbed down stiffly from the wagon. He stomped a couple of times to encourage the blood to flow back into his aching legs. After that, he wasted precious little time. He was desperate to see his beloved. He darted up the steps, grabbed the brass door knocker, and pounded vigorously.

Several agonizing seconds passed before he heard the locks and latches on the inside of the door clicking and popping. The heavy oak portal swung open, revealing Audra Hamer … Abigail's mother. She looked very different from the last time that Walter had seen her. Her clothing was dingy and unkempt. Her hair was greasy and ungroomed. Her pallor was almost gray and ghostlike. She did not appear to be well. The woman took one look at Walter, then instantly her eyes rolled backward in their sockets, and she collapsed unconscious onto the threshold.

Alexander Hamer was livid. His face was crimson red and his temples throbbed. He attempted to lift his wife from the floor. Walter reached to help him, but Hamer violently slapped his hand away.

The master of the house roared, "Keep your vile hands off of my wife, you dishonorable son of a bitch!"

Walter was aghast. He was thoroughly and completely confused. What could possibly be the cause for such behavior and language?

"Mr. Hamer, what have I done to you? I don't understand! I escaped my confinement a few months ago, but I was wounded in battle in North Carolina. I have only recently recovered my health. I have written several letters to Abigail, but have received no response in return. So, I have come to get her and take her to our new home."

"We received your letters. I burned them! All of them! I did not wish my daughter to have any contact with such swine as you!"

"But, Mr. Hamer! Please make me understand! What have I done?"

"You took my daughter's innocence, that's what you did! You stole her honor and her purity away from her. You ruined her. It broke my wife's heart. And I know when it happened!" His shrieking voice lowered to a deep, guttural growl. "It was on that night of the party at Beecham's estate. You had your friend cover your tracks for you whilst you raped my little girl and utterly devastated her virtue. I hate you! I only wish you had died on that battlefield, wherever it was!"

Gabriel and Basil appeared in the doorway behind Walter, drawn to the house by the screaming and commotion. Walter cast a confused glance at both of them. He knelt beside Alexander and sought to calm him.

"But, Mr. Hamer, you have it all wrong. I did not rape your daughter. I could never do such a thing! Abigail is my life! She gave herself to me. We pledged ourselves in secret as husband and wife, with every intention of being formally wed after my release. Don't you see? I could never harm your daughter. I love her with every ounce of my being!"

"You did her the gravest of harm! You brought shame upon her, and upon her family, and upon this house! I hate you! Now, leave here! Immediately!"

Walter stood upright and clenched his fists. Defiance swelled in his chest. "I will take no more of your abuse, sir. Yes, I will go … but not without Abigail … not without my beloved. Now, fetch her to me immediately!"

Alexander burst forth in heaving sobs. He pulled his unconscious wife to his breast and buried his face in her hair. Walter turned to Gabriel and Basil. Their spectating eyes were wide with confusion.

"Mr. Hamer, please. Just get Abigail for me, and I will go. You never have to see me again, if that is truly what you wish."

Alexander stared at Walter, hatred filling his spirit and gaze. "Do you not understand, Walter? She is gone!"

"Gone where? Just tell me where she is and I will go to her!"

Hamer spat uncontrollably and screamed, "No, Walter! Are you so incredibly daft? She is gone! She is gone forever! My daughter is dead! My precious little girl is rotting in a grave, and it is all because of you!"

Walter's legs began to falter beneath him. He swayed and almost fell backward, but Basil caught him. He did not faint, but his senses seemed to have departed him. He was awake, but not awake. His eyes were open, but he was not there. His mind no longer functioned. He could not speak.

Gabriel tugged at Basil's arm. "Take him to the wagon, Basil. I shall follow shortly."

Basil nodded and led Walter out the door. The dazed young man did not resist. He allowed his little brother to lead him, almost as if he were some sort of feeble-minded old man. Gabriel closed the door behind them, and then approached Mr. Hamer.

"Sir, please explain to me. What happened? When did Abigail die? How did this horrible thing occur?"

The heartbroken father wiped the tears and mucus from his mouth and nose with his coat sleeve. He attempted to compose himself.

"It was four days ago. She bled to death during childbirth."

"Childbirth?" repeated Gabriel in a shocked tone.

"Yes. Childbirth." He pointed mockingly at the closed door behind Gabriel. "She died giving birth to Walter's bastard son!"

"Oh," Gabriel responded timidly. "And the child?"

"He died, as well. It was a breech birth. The boy was stillborn." Tears began to flow again. "We buried him with our Abigail."

"Where?"

"At the church cemetery."

"I am so very sorry for your loss, Mr. Hamer."

The despondent father nodded. "Can you please help me move Mrs. Hamer to the sofa?"

"Of course."

Gabriel steadied himself by grabbing the door facing with his left hand. He reached with his right hand and helped Mr. Hamer lift the woman from the floor. Alexander suddenly realized that Gabriel was wearing a wooden peg below his left knee.

He stammered, "That is quite sufficient. Thank you. I can move her the rest of the way. Please just go, and leave us to mourn in peace."

"As you wish." Gabriel bowed slightly toward Mr. Hamer, and then made a hasty exit from the home.

Walter stared numbly at the pile of fresh dirt that covered Abigail and his unseen son. He held his cocked hat against his heart. He did not weep. He merely stared. Gabriel and Basil stood one pace behind him. They did not speak, either, for they did not know what to say.

After several minutes of uncomfortable silence, Walter turned and faced his brother and his friend. He pronounced, "My friends are dead. My Abigail is dead. My son is dead. My life is ruined. I shall never be the same." He placed his hat on his head. "You fellows had best keep your distance. Everyone I care about dies. I am cursed."

Gabriel stepped toward him and placed his hand firmly on his shoulder. "Nonsense! Truly, what happened to Abigail was unspeakably tragic. You shall miss her terribly. But, Walter, life goes on. You have survived this horrible conflict. The Almighty must have wondrous plans for you. You *must* persevere! You *will* prosper." He gave Walter's shoulder a gentle shake. "And you shall love again … someday."

"No, Gabriel. I shall never love again. Abigail was my entire life. She was my mate. There can be no other for me. I will take my love for her to my lonely, cold grave."

He collapsed against his friend and wept.

PART IV

Over the Mountains

18

QUAKERS

October 19, 1781 – The Blue Ridge of North Carolina

Walter Billingsley rested his horse in the pleasant glade that lay at the terminus of the narrow, steep mountain trail. The cliffs of stone that surrounded the trail yielded to a tiny clearing surrounded by a vast sea of towering trees. It was a beautiful, high meadow … an oasis amongst the upper ridges of the Carolina mountains. The break in the timbers provided a stunning glimpse of the surrounding peaks. To the southwest, Walter observed a towering ridge that reached high up into a shroud of low clouds. To the north and west, more diminutive mountains framed the dull, gray sky.

He surveyed and evaluated the clearing. It would be an excellent place to make camp. There was no water source nearby, but the travelers had already filled all of their canteens, leather water bags, and small barrels from a fast-flowing creek earlier in the afternoon. They had water aplenty for the evening, and would surely cross another creek in the morning. If they stopped early and made camp for the night, the extra daylight would provide an excellent opportunity for some of the men to get in some hunting. Fresh meat would be a welcome treat.

Walter stroked his horse affectionately on the neck. "What do you think, Patches? Shall we stop here for the night?"

The horse snorted in affirmation, blowing a conical cloud of vapor from her warm nose into the cool, crisp mountain air. Walter could almost swear that the animal had nodded her head, as well. He grinned.

"All right, then. You're the boss, girl."

The horse nickered and pawed at the ground with her front right hoof.

Walter dismounted slowly. Once firmly established on his aching feet, he stomped in an effort to stimulate the circulation in his legs. He leaned backward, coaxing a series of sharp cracks from the bones in his spine. His lower back, just above his buttocks on the right side, was torturing him. The pain reached below his back to elicit a burning tingle that extended all the way down his right leg. He removed his brown wool, fingerless gloves from his right hand and fished a bottle of rum from his haversack. He took a long, scorching drink. He prayed that the strong alcohol might be enough to dull the pain.

The nagging discomfort in his lower back was a relatively new development for Walter ... just another amongst many medical maladies that plagued him as a result of his numerous injuries before and during the war. The frustrating back pain usually afflicted him during long periods of standing or sitting still. Riding a horse, obviously, qualified for the latter. Two weeks in the saddle had unleashed a torrent of torturous aches and shooting pains in his back and legs.

Despite the relief provided by dismounting his horse, and the instant burning of the rum in his empty belly, the pain unleashed by the inflamed nerves in his back continued unabated. Walter knew that he needed to stay off of his horse for a while. He needed to rest. He needed a bed, actually, but there were no such luxuries to be found in the raw wilderness of the remote mountains of North Carolina. Like most recent nights, he would have to settle for another bedroll beside a campfire.

Walter took another swig of his rum, popped the cork back into the bottle, and then surreptitiously returned it to his haversack. He glanced over his right shoulder and observed the single-file line of pioneers following him up the trail through the narrow gap. Some rode horses, but most walked. It seemed clear to Walter that physical exhaustion was beginning to take its toll on the entire group. Hearty as they were, these pilgrims could use a break. An early halt and a hot meal would do wonders for the weary travelers.

Walter grinned as he watched them laboriously clawing their way up the steep hillside. They were an odd group, indeed. All were members of the Society of Friends, often called Quakers. Members of this sect were known for simplicity in life, focus upon the family, plain dress, an avoidance of war and conflict, industriousness and capitalism, an adamant rejection of slavery, and the utter avoidance of alcoholic beverages. They also had a curious habit of using ancient, King James versions of second person pronouns in their daily conversation. Walter had never heard such enthusiastic and repeated use of words like "thee," "thy," and "thou."

Six families of the Society of Friends were "answering the call" to depart their community in Guilford County and establish a new meeting house in Sullivan County, on the edge of the distant Indian Lands. There were over fifty of them altogether. Though there were a couple of elderly grandparents amongst the group, most of the entourage was comprised of young families blessed with numerous children. Their spiritual and practical leader was a fellow by the name of William Sumner.

Walter had been greatly surprised when Mr. Sumner approached him and offered him a job as scout and guide for their westward-migrating group. His initial instinct had been to decline the offer. But, as he contemplated the possibility of a journey over the mountains, he realized that it might provide an opportunity for a fresh start. He desired to flee his old life in Guilford County. He wanted to get away from the constant doting of his mother, the concerned stares of his brothers, and the awkward conversations with his sisters. Ultimately, what he really wanted was to escape the painful memories of Abigail and his dead son. Three months had passed, and he could still smell the dank earth that covered his beloved's grave. Every hour of every day he entertained visions of what his son might have looked like. He longed to swaddle the baby boy in his arms, caress his tiny hands, and hear his cries.

But, the only cries that Walter Billingsley ever heard were his own. He was a tired, bitter, and broken young man. And he needed a fresh, new life in a place where he might flee the memories of his indescribable loss. He hoped that guiding the migrating Quakers might offer him the perfect opportunity for an escape, with payment in silver as a useful bonus.

Walter's brothers encouraged the journey, as well. James, John, and Samuel had already filed North Carolina patents for lands over the mountains. They charged Walter with scouting out those lands and preparing them for future settlement. They planned to move westward and join Walter as soon as the war was over, and as soon as they could disentangle themselves from property and life in Guilford and Randolph Counties. With the increased interest in westward migration, it seemed that many Americans were in search of new beginnings.

The war still raged in the East, but the tide had turned greatly in favor of the United States. The news reached Guilford Courthouse only two days before Walter and the Quakers departed the Piedmont. American forces had surrounded Cornwallis at Yorktown, in Virginia. Amazingly, General Washington had also arrived at Yorktown with his army from the North. The French appeared, as well, and blockaded the British from the sea. Victory, which for so long had seemed a foolish impossibility, now seemed inevitable. If the British ever would surrender and abandon their claims in America, the westward migration would begin in earnest. The Billingsley brothers planned to be on the leading edge of the pioneer wave.

The Quakers agreed to allow Walter to bring his one-legged English friend, Gabriel Blevins, on the journey as an employed guide and assistant. Indeed, they seemed somewhat intrigued to have the disabled former British soldier in their midst. They were quite impressed that the two former enemies had formed such a powerful bond of friendship despite the cloud of war that hung over them. They inferred that the unique relationship between Walter and Gabriel was both a demonstration and justification of their own passionate philosophy of pacifism.

Mr. Sumner had reluctantly agreed to allow Walter and Gabriel to retain their weapons, even their pistols and blades, so long as they were not used in violence against their fellow man. Many of the Quaker men carried rifles for hunting, but claimed that they could never raise them in anger against another person. Walter was somewhat amused by their convictions, and wondered whether they would actually hold true in the face of an onslaught of tomahawk-wielding Cherokee warriors.

What Walter had not expected was the almost instantaneous fondness and respect that he would develop for the Quakers. He had long known about their villages in and around Guilford County for most of his life, but had not experienced any personal interaction with the people. He was delighted to discover that they were simple, quiet, and interesting folk. They never spoke an unkind word about anyone. They worked diligently at their daily tasks without complaint. Their families were large, industrious, and loving. It seemed that all of their relationships were marked by warmth and kindness.

The Quakers treated Walter with the utmost respect and patience, almost as if they were privy to the pains that he suffered and the secrets that he bore. Walter realized that he was regarded as a "heathen" to these odd folk, and that they had all taken him on as something of a spiritual and emotional "project." But, he did not mind. They never probed him for information. Instead, they merely responded with love and patience to whatever thoughts or feelings that Walter chose to reveal. They never passed judgment upon him, nor attempted to make him feel guilty for anything in his past. They also tolerated his moodiness and obviously excessive drinking without comment or complaint.

Mr. Sumner, the leader of the Quakers, crossed the meadow and capably drew his horse alongside Walter's. "Dost thou intend this to be a temporary halt, Mr. Billingsley?"

Walter choked back his urge to laugh. That queer word, "dost," elicited a chuckle from him almost every time he heard it.

"No, sir. This is where we will camp for the night."

The Quaker leader stood tall in his saddle and peered toward the trail that exited the far side of the clearing. "It seems a bit early to be stopping for the day. We still have at least three hours of daylight remaining. I should not desire to waste it. Could we not cover more ground before nightfall?"

"Yes, sir. But I doubt that we will find a finer resting spot for miles. We could continue on until dark, but we would likely have to camp on a steep hillside somewhere on that next ridge. As you well know, tying one's self to a tree to avoid rolling down a mountainside does not make for a good night's sleep."

Mr. Sumner grinned knowingly. "That much is certain. Dost thou still believe that we shall reach our destination before the snows of winter set in?"

Gabriel appeared beside Walter. He had been the last rider in the rear of the column of pilgrims, providing security against potential attack from the south and east. He listened silently to the exchange between Walter and the Quaker leader.

"Of that I have no doubt, Mr. Sumner. We are no more than a week or ten days from the settlements on Big Creek. The snows are well over a month away," Walter promised reassuringly.

"Very well." The Quaker leader nodded respectfully to Walter and then turned his horse toward the center of the clearing. He cupped his hands to his mouth and proclaimed, "Friends, we shall camp here for the evening. Let us cook a nourishing meal and enjoy a restful night's sleep on this rare spot of flat ground."

The people did not respond with outward emotion or enthusiasm. Such was not acceptable among the Society of Friends. Instead, they simply nodded and attended to their families' tasks and needs. They quickly dispersed throughout the meadow and began to establish their encampment. Clearly, they were quite satisfied with the early halt in the day's travel.

Mr. Sumner turned once again to face Walter. "Mr. Billingsley, I shall confer with thee after our supper." He clucked at his horse and guided the animal in the direction of his family.

Gabriel stared intently at Walter. He was greatly concerned. He could tell that something was wrong with his friend.

"Is your back still afflicting you?" Gabriel queried.

Walter nodded. The rum had not had any impact upon the pain. He needed something stronger. He reached inside his haversack and, once again, removed his bottle of rum. He took a small paper packet from his leather pouch and pulled back the flap that sealed its opening. He then poured the contents of the packet, a reddish-brown powder, into the rum and swirled it around. Once satisfied that the powder had dissolved sufficiently, he lifted the bottle and took a deep drink.

"Is that what I think it is? Surely, Walter, you are not mixing powder of opium with your rum. Is the pain truly that bad?"

"I would appreciate it if you would mind your own business, Gabriel."

"But, Walter, I am only trying to ..."

Walter snapped, "I said mind your own damned business!"

His words had not only been harsh, but exceedingly loud. Several heads turned within the camp. Women reacted to the foul language with looks of distress. Gabriel's chin dropped to his chest. He maintained his silence and waited for his friend's temper to calm. Guilt and shame descended quickly upon Walter's spirit.

"I'm sorry, Gabriel. I am just hurting and sore and foul, and I shouldn't have taken my frustrations out on you. I sincerely apologize."

Gabriel smiled knowingly. "I understand, my friend. Pain can often compel us to do and say things that we do not intend." He paused. "And not all pain is physical, you know."

Walter nodded. He wanted to change the subject. He could tolerate being a "wounded pet" to the Quakers, but had no desire for similar treatment from his friend.

Walter tilted his head toward the hillside trail. "Did you see anything unusual today?"

Gabriel removed his black floppy hat and rested it on the pommel of his saddle. "Well … I feared for a moment that a family of squirrels may have been plotting to attack our column, but I gave them a stern look and they returned to their foraging." He grinned.

"You're probably more in danger of being abducted by the Martin girls than anything else," teased Walter. "I've seen young Caroline watching over you quite intently. I believe she has some designs upon you, Gabe. I worry that you might become a Quaker and a husband before we reach Captain Kyle's fort."

Gabriel grinned wryly and then chuckled. He would be lying if he claimed that he did not enjoy the attentions of the lovely Caroline Martin. Yet, he also realized that romance with a member of the Quaker religion was somewhat outlandish, if not totally out of the question. They seldom married outside the sect, and when someone dared do so, there were dire societal and relational consequences.

"You should be careful in your predictions, Walter. You musn't pretend that you have not noticed the special attentions that Miss Mary Sumner has been showering upon you."

"Mary?" retorted Walter. "William's little girl? Hell, Gabe, she is but a child! No more than eleven or twelve years of age!"

"Indeed. But, she is a pretty little thing, and well on her way to blossoming as a young woman. In a couple of years, she will be prime age for marrying, and it seems to me that she has her mind set upon you. Save your pretense, Walter Billingsley. I've seen you looking."

Gabriel grinned teasingly as he leaned comfortably across the pommel of his saddle and gently stroked the neck of Willow, his trusty mare. The former British soldier was a handsome, striking figure on horseback. He wore a new buckskin coat and breeches. A flintlock pistol adorned his leather waist belt, and a .54 caliber Virginia rifle lay comfortably across his lap. Multiple straps from his bags and haversacks formed an impressive "X" across his broad chest. The black fur-felt floppy hat completed his mountain man appearance. The only thing missing was the lower portion of his left leg. His breeches dangled loosely over the scarred stump below his knee. The wooden peg that substituted for his leg and made it possible for him to walk was tied securely to the side of his English saddle.

Walter's face clouded. He neither liked nor appreciated his friend's good-natured teasing. His heart remained shattered and bruised by the death Abigail Hamer. A flood of repressed memories cascaded through his mind and overwhelmed his spirit. An emotional storm brewed. Gabriel had delved into a sensitive matter, and had taken his teasing comments a little too far.

"I'll not tolerate such callous talk from you, Gabriel. You should know better."

"Oh, Walter! I only wish to lift your spirits! Surely, you know that I am jesting."

"About matters of which I will not abide any measure of levity," Walter responded abruptly.

Gabriel nodded, defeated. "I'm quite sorry, Walter. I shall tread more carefully with regard to romance and affection when I am in your midst."

"See that you do. There are no such things remaining for me in this world, Gabriel. My love lies buried in a church yard in Camden." He took a long, scorching gulp from his rum bottle and then wiped his lips on the sleeve of his gray wool coat. The opium powder caused his lips to tingle and become numb. He enjoyed the sensation.

"Of course." Gabriel smiled warmly at his friend. He made a mental note of the barrier that he had unintentionally crossed, and resolved himself to avoid any repeat in the near future.

Walter took a deep breath. He was obviously ready to move on to other matters. "We need meat, Gabe. I'm leaving the camp in your charge and going in search of venison."

"Nonsense! You must stay off of that horse and rest your aching back. I shall leave our shelter cloth with you. Whilst you put our encampment in good order, I'll fetch back some fresh meat. I can recruit that young squire, Ezekiel Martin, to join me."

Walter grinned suspiciously. "I'm certain you will. Just as I am equally certain of the fact that Ezekiel's handsome, blonde-haired sister has everything to do with your enthusiastic choice in hunting partners."

Gabriel grunted, his face flushing slightly. He reached around and untied the linen tarp from the rear of his saddle. He then lifted the cloth and, with unquestioned intentionality, dropped it on Walter's head.

"I shall expect this shelter to be erected securely and a warm, crackling fire awaiting me when I return. Hop to, you rebel escapee."

He winked, and then turned his horse toward the Martin family's camp. Walter chuckled and gave Gabriel's mare a hearty slap on the rump.

"Hurry back with my supper, you Redcoat deserter!"

Walter turned and began to unbuckle the saddle from his horse. Before constructing a shelter and fire, he had to attend to the needs of his mount. Patches whinnied with delight as he loosened the leather straps beneath her belly. She turned her head and rooted her nose beneath Walter's elbow, demanding some tasty oats for supper.

Gabriel proved a worthy provider, as was usual. Everyone in the high meadow heard the two distant gunshots less than an hour after he and Ezekiel Martin departed on their hunting excursion. The preparations throughout the camp continued with excitement.

Everyone knew that the two hunters would return soon with fresh venison for the group.

After feeding and watering Patches, Walter carefully selected a more isolated spot for the tent that he and Gabriel would share. He preferred to leave some distance between himself and the Quakers whenever possible, so that he might imbibe in solitude and peace. He chose a small island of open ground off of the main meadow, on the western edge, just inside the high canopy of hardwoods. Leaning his flintlock rifle against an ancient red oak, he set about the task of constructing the shelter.

He used his tomahawk to cut several low, reasonably straight limbs for poles, and quickly converted the rectangular linen tarp into a simple lean-to. He employed a half-dozen iron stakes and short ropes to sturdy the structure. Since there seemed to be no danger of rain during the night, he did not bother to cover the shelter with boughs of evergreen. The linen would suffice to keep the moisture and dew off of him and Gabriel throughout the night. He unrolled two large tanned buckskins and suspended them for windbreaks on each end of the lean-to. There was a hint of a breeze, which could potentially turn quite frigid during the night. The supple buckskins would provide an excellent wall to fend off the autumn's chilly winds.

Once the shelter was erected and complete, Walter prepared to build a fire. He pushed a mound of dry leaves inside the lean-to to provide the soft base for a makeshift mattress. The relocated leaves exposed an open spot for a fire ring. He gathered rocks, tinder, and sticks and used his flint, steel, and char cloth to ignite a campfire immediately outside the opening of the shelter. After the fire was established and blazing, he spread a thick wool blanket on top of the mattress of bedding leaves. The layer of wool would help insulate their bodies from the heat-sapping forest floor. He tossed his other wool blanket into the far-left corner of the lean-to. He planned to cocoon himself inside the scratchy cloth and remain comfortable and warm throughout the night.

In preparation for Gabriel's venison, Walter tapped two wooden y-shaped sticks into the soft ground on either side of the fire to hold an iron cooking spit. Lastly, he located a small, flat rock. He carefully placed the stone against the coals and then removed a small teapot from his snapsack. He filled the pot with water and scooted it close to the fire. He placed a tin full of black tea, a small cloth sack of dark sugar, and two stoneware mugs near the teapot. He and Gabriel would enjoy some delicious, steaming tea with their supper.

With all of the campsite preparations completed, Walter rested beside his cheerful, comforting fire. He sat, cross-legged, just beneath the top flap of the lean-to. He puffed contentedly on his long-stemmed pear-wood pipe and sipped steadily from his opium and rum cocktail. One hour later, he was feeling quite dazed and pain free when Gabriel and the Martin lad arrived at the camp, dragging two large does behind their horses. Walter didn't bother to rise and join in the meat preparation. A gaggle of Quakers had already descended upon the carcasses. They would skin and butcher the beasts with expert hands.

A half-hour later, just as the final glow of daylight concealed itself below the western ridge, Gabriel approached the lean-to. He carried a long, thick, bloody piece of venison backstrap draped across his left hand.

"I see that you claimed us a fine, tender cut," observed Walter. His words were slightly slurred.

"And I see that you have been indulging liberally of our meager supply of rum," Gabriel scolded.

He knelt beside the fire and rinsed the venison with water from his canteen.

Walter responded, "There was nothing left for me to do. Our shelter is complete, your bed is made, and yonder boils water for you to enjoy a nice spot of tea. Anyhow, my pain is gone … that is all that matters to me."

"And it will return in the morning," countered Gabriel. "No doubt it will be accompanied by a fresh pain in your head. But, one lives and learns, I suppose."

"Right now, I'm beginning to feel a little bit of fresh pain in my arse," declared Walter, offended. "I left my mother behind in Guilford County, Mr. Blevins. I do not require a replacement."

"As you wish. Just keep your vomit on your side of the lean-to, if you please."

Walter exhaled loudly. "If I must."

He tossed a small stick at Gabriel's head. It bounced off of the brim of his hat and landed safely in the campfire. Gabriel glanced at him and smiled. He retrieved an iron spit from its leather case and forced its sharp point through the length of the backstrap, then dropped each end of the spit into the awaiting wood cradles. The meat hovered tantalizingly over the fire. Walter tossed him a salt horn. Gabriel poured a handful of the flavor-enhancing granules into the palm of his hand and then rubbed the salt over the exterior of the meat.

"That should cook up quite nicely," declared Walter. "I like my venison to remain hot and pink in the middle, by the way."

"As do I," answered Gabriel. He rubbed the remnants of salt on his buckskin breeches and then joined Walter on the soft, blanket-covered bed of leaves. He sighed. "If only we had a bottle of red wine to accent the meal. Something nice and sweet." He closed his eyes and licked his lips as he savored the memory of the fruity taste of wine. "Say ... I wonder whatever happened to all of that wine that you and Whitlock bottled back at *Beechmont.* As I recall, you stockpiled several cases in the distillery barn. I remember you processing wagons full of grapes, blackberries, apples, and pears. I was rather looking forward to sampling your pear wine. It should all be nicely aged by now."

"I doubt that it ever knew any age, Gabriel. It was probably commandeered by our Patriot armies the moment they reclaimed Camden, along with all those barrels of whiskey and brandy. I can imagine the great delight of the local militiamen when they made the discovery." He chuckled lightly. "No doubt, it was guzzled 'round campfires much like our very own, likely with a haunch of venison much like this one."

"Indeed." Gabriel stared contentedly at the fire. "Still … it would be nice to have a nip of red wine with our meat right now, wouldn't it?"

Walter grinned. "I certainly would not complain."

Gabriel reached for the handle of the spit and gave the meat a slight turn. He wanted to sear the flesh and seal the juices inside the loin. The water in the nearby kettle was steaming, so he poured a generous splash into both of their cups and then sprinkled a spoonful of tea into his bamboo tea strainer. He dangled the strainer in the first cup and observed the leaves as they became soaked and then fell to the bottom of the strainer. He returned to his seat beside Walter.

"You may have the first brew, Mr. Billingsley. I'll allow it to steep for a minute, and then use the leaves in my cup, as well."

Walter nodded silently and continued to draw on his pipe. A thin cloud of fragrant, gray-white smoke filled the lean-to. There were several minutes of uncomfortable silence. Gabriel soon rose and moved the strainer to the second cup. He picked up the first one and handed it to Walter.

"Thank you, Gabe." Walter took a sip. "Delicious. Nice and strong."

"I shall have to let mine steep a bit longer, I'm afraid. You received all of the best flavors of the brew." He smiled.

More silence ensued. Gabriel could not stand it any longer. The increased discomfort and awkwardness between the two friends was becoming most frustrating to him. He had hoped that Walter's spirits might improve as time and distance separated him from Abigail's untimely death. But, as the days progressed, his friend seemed to withdraw inwardly more and more. And now he was not simply drinking rum in response to his physical and emotional pain. He had turned to the narcotic opium to somehow numb his aches and his grief.

Gabriel leaned forward and added a cluster of small sticks to the campfire. He took a silent, deep breath. "I am truly sorry that

I offended you today, Walter. It was not my intention. I do not wish for our friendship to suffer."

"Think nothing of it, Gabriel. It is I who should apologize to you. I am the one who is proving to be the challenge in our friendship. I know that I am moody and mean, and I hate myself for it. You have been nothing but kind and generous towards me. I have no right to take my hurts and frustrations out on you."

"I can take it. After all, that is what friends are for."

"I suppose," Walter responded softly.

"Walter, you do consider me your friend, don't you?"

Walter responded quietly but firmly, "Indeed, I do. You are my best and only friend." He paused briefly. "All of my other friends are dead."

"Then, surely you know that, as your friend, I cannot stand idly by and watch you do harm to yourself."

"Yes. I know."

Gabriel endured yet another long, deliberate pause.

"The powder of opium concerns me greatly, Walter. I know you expressed earlier today that I must mind my own business. But, I consider you to be my business ... and I think you should cease using that devilish substance. I have seen what it can do to a man."

"It is only to ease my back, Gabriel. The pain is unbearable."

"I have heard similar claims before."

"What are you saying to me?" demanded Walter, a little louder.

"I am saying that I have my doubts as to the real reason why you are medicating yourself with a dangerous drug. Indeed, you may not even truly understand the reason. You are simply hurting ... hurting in body, spirit, and soul. And you want to make it all stop."

"It is because of my back, Gabriel. Nothing more. You should stop trying to create issues and drama where they do not truly exist."

"Is that what I am doing, Walter? Am I concocting things? Are you claiming that a broken heart is not the true source of all your ills?"

"I do not know what else I can say to you, Gabe. Yes, I miss Abigail. I long for my dead son. I imagine his cries in my dreams. I wonder how different my life might have been had I not violated the laws of God. I wish that things had been different. I wish that I had been a better man … a moral man." Tears welled in his eyes. He pulled his hat down low in shame and concealed his face inside the collar of his coat.

"Walter Billingsley, you are one of the finest, most honest, and most moral men I have ever known. I am honored to be counted as your friend."

Gabriel leaned forward and grabbed his mug of tea. He removed the strainer and tossed the spent leaves into the darkness beside the lean-to, then took a sip of the warm liquid. Walter did not respond to his friend's heartfelt declaration. The two men sat, in silence, and stared into the comforting flames. Gabriel could not see it, but beneath the folds of his coat, Walter smiled.

A scream echoed in the darkness. Walter assumed that someone in the encampment was experiencing a nightmare. He drifted once again toward a restful slumber. His belly was full of meat and rum, and he was toasty warm inside his thick wool blanket. He silently prayed that the sunrise of morning was still many hours away.

There was another piercing scream. Then came the sounds of shouting men. Suddenly, the forest to the south erupted with the tell-tale cries of Indians. Their high-pitched, "Yip! Yip! Yip!" was unmistakable.

It was a Cherokee raiding party.

Walter rolled frantically from beneath the shelter, almost landing in the coals of the smoldering campfire. He kicked Gabriel solidly in the thigh.

"Gabe! Wake up! Indians! It is an attack!"

Walter stared in the direction of the screams. There was scant firelight remaining in the meadow. Only embers remained in most of the campfires. Then, suddenly, there was a shower of sparks as a cloud of coals rained down on one of the linen tents. Someone had kicked embers from a fire pit onto the shelter. The cloth ignited within seconds. More screams ensued.

"What do we do?" wailed Gabriel. "These Quakers will not fight back!"

Walter retrieved his rifle, pistol, and tomahawk. "Grab your weapons and follow me, or they will slay everyone in this party!"

Gabriel frantically fumbled with his wooden leg in the darkness as he attempted to secure it to his fleshy stump. Walter sprinted toward the tents of the Quakers, rifle at the ready. Gabriel would have to catch up whenever he could.

As Walter ran toward the attack, he heard a deep voice pleading in the darkness, "Ezekiel, no! Please, my son! Thy everlasting soul!"

His pleas were followed by the loud report of a musket, and a fearsome, painful, wretched squeal. Someone from amongst the Quakers had just shot an Indian!

Walter encountered his first Cherokee warrior as he approached the burning tent. The man was facing the flames, seemingly mesmerized by the destruction. He neither saw nor heard Walter approaching from the rear. Walter drew his tomahawk from his belt as he ran. The warrior heard Walter when he was only two paces behind him and turned in reaction to the sound of footsteps. But, it was too late. Walter buried the blade of his tomahawk deep into the man's skull, just above his right eye. The Indian collapsed, writhing, to the ground.

Walter heard renewed screaming from his left, near the northeast edge of the tree line. He could see a tent in the faint moonlight. The pale linen shook violently. From beneath the cloth there came the horrified wailing of young girls. Walter took off running in that direction. As he neared the tent, he heard perverse laughter intermixed with the frightened screams. He swung the razor-sharp blade of his tomahawk downward across the smooth linen, slicing open the roof of the tent. He tripped on a root and tumbled haphazardly through the opening in the cloth, dropping his rifle with a thud on the hard ground.

Walter landed inside the tent in the midst of an unspeakable horror. One of the Indian savages was atop a young girl. Her shift was ripped open below the waist. The native was violently thrusting against the maiden, raping her. Another young girl huddled, whimpering, against the far wall of the tent. The Indian ceased his horrible crime for only a split second as he stared, confused, into the unexpected invader's eyes. Walter's pale face was the last vision that the Cherokee's brain processed before the jelly of his cerebrum exited the back of his skull. Bloody goo exploded against the wall and roof of the tent.

The roar of Walter's .75 caliber British flintlock pistol was deafening. The flash illuminated the inside of the tent with a blinding yellow light. Burning, acrid gunpowder smoke filled the enclosure of the tent. The Indian's helpless victim screamed, pinned beneath the weight of his dead body. The other girl in the corner screamed, as well. Walter tucked his still-smoking pistol back inside his belt and attempted to survey his surroundings. But, he couldn't see anything. He remained blinded by the flash.

"Who is in here?" he demanded loudly.

"Mr. Billingsley? Is it truly thee?"

"Yes, it is I. Who are you? Who remains inside this tent?"

"It's me ... Mary Sumner, and my sister, Abigail."

Abigail! That beautiful name ... the name of his beloved. The very mention of her magical name elicited an overwhelming wave of emotion throughout Walter's spirit. He immediately entertained images of his own sweet Abigail suffering beneath the violent thrusts of a savage rapist. He was overwhelmed, angry, and confused. The sound of her name had frozen him in place. He was paralyzed by grief and recollection.

Outside the tent another shot rang out. It sounded like a pistol. The pain-filled screams of another wounded Indian filled the encampment. Those horrid shrieks of agony pulled Walter from the paralysis of his mournful memories back into the realm of the living. Moments later a rifle cracked, erupting with a dull flash in the clearing outside the tent where Walter lay.

Little Mary Sumner called out to him, "Mr. Billingsley! What must we do?"

"Come to me, child. Come to my voice."

The frightened girl crawled across the layer of wool blankets that coated the ground beneath them. She lunged toward Walter. He caught her with his left arm. He pushed the dead Indian off of the girl's older sister with his right foot. With his other arm, he peeled Abigail Sumner from the floor the tent. Both girls wrapped their arms tightly around Walter's neck as each buried her head against his chest. They sobbed softly. Mary gently stroked Walter's long hair with her soft, warm hand. He struggled to his feet, burdened by the weight of the girls. He stepped through the torn wall of the tent into the darkness and fresh air beyond. A dull, orange glow emitted by two fire-engulfed tents illuminated the entire camp. Walter could see bodies strewn across the ground and two other collapsed tents, both smoldering and belching clouds of smoke.

He called out, "Gabriel!"

"I am here!" responded the familiar British from the woods beyond the burning tents. "I believe it is over. They are gone."

19

FRONTIER RANGERS

Daylight – The Next Morning

Most of the women and children were sleeping. They huddled together inside the handful of undamaged tents and shelters. Mrs. Sumner and her children dozed soundly inside Walter and Gabriel's lean-to. Mary and Abigail had been most reluctant to abandon the confident protection of Walter's strong embrace. He finally convinced them of their safety and their need to rejoin their mother and siblings. He doubted that he would ever forget Mary Sumner's loving hug and vigorous kiss on his cheek. She bestowed both upon him as he delivered her into the waiting arms of her mother.

The glow of dawn allowed Walter and Gabriel to survey the carnage in the camp. It had been a costly, bloody raid, indeed. Two men, five women, and four children were dead, all mercilessly slain with knives, tomahawks, and war clubs. All but three of the dead had been scalped and partially mutilated. Their murders were heinous, personal, face-to-face crimes. The viciousness of the attack, and the fact that it had been perpetrated against women and children, were almost unimaginable to both Walter and Gabriel.

The Cherokee raiders did not, however, escape unscathed. In addition to the two Indians that Walter killed, Gabriel downed another with a pistol ball near the Quaker tents. He killed a second with a well-placed rifle shot into the forest. They found the body of that particular Indian one hundred yards south of the camp. The warrior managed to stumble an impressive distance before collapsing and bleeding out.

But, incredibly, it was the fifth dead Indian that was the true source of confusion and consternation amongst the Quakers. That native's body lay beside the burned-out tent of Owen Martin. He was the father of the lovely maiden, Caroline. Ezekiel Martin, Gabriel's hunting partner, was his oldest son. Tragically, Owen Martin's wife lay dead inside the smoldering tent.

However, it was not his dead wife that was the object of his emotion and attention. Instead of attending to her lifeless body, he was unleashing a relentless and scathing sermon upon his son. The boy sat stoically on the ground, cross-legged beside a small campfire. Tears streamed down his cheeks. His father stood over him, Bible in hand, railing against the boy's devilish violence and his impending damnation. Four other men stood nearby. They held Bibles in their hands, as well. Each prayed fervently and out loud. Their dull mumbles were hauntingly spooky and incredibly strange to Walter.

He approached the spectacle slowly. He could scarcely believe what was transpiring before him. Ezekiel glanced at Walter. Their eyes met. Walter could feel the brokenness and shame in the boy's spirit. He smiled warmly at the lad and nodded. Ezekiel nodded back. The momentary distraction sent his father into a bit of a rage. He struck the young man in the side of the head with his Bible. Ezekiel stared longingly at Walter. His eyes begged for intervention.

"Boy, thou shalt focus thy attention upon me and me alone! The fate of thy very soul hangs in the balance. Beelzebub hath his hooks sunk deep into thee and is tugging thee toward the abyss! I must rescue thee from his wicked grasp!"

Walter could not tolerate such treatment of the boy. He could not understand how these men could be standing idly about, praying, reciting Scripture, and preaching while the bloodied and roasted bodies of their loved ones lay unattended.

"What the hell is going on here?" he demanded, stepping between the man and his son.

"This is no concern of thine, Billingsley. Thou wilt kindly step aside and cease intervening in matters of our families and our faith."

Mr. Martin glowered at Walter. It was a strange sensation to him. He had never seen the Quakers display such emotion or animosity. Walter stared back, unimpressed by the man's attempt to dismiss him.

"Everything that occurs in this camp is my business, sir. I am your guide and commander, and I demand to know why you are berating this boy." He pointed at the man's burned-out tent. "You should be caring for the bodies of your loved ones. We have graves to dig this day. Those Cherokee raiders may, indeed, return. We have precious little time for your foolishness. This is neither the place nor the moment for one of your idiotic hellfire and brimstone sermons."

Mr. Martin pointed accusingly at his son. "My son hath taken the life of another! He hath slain one of the red men! His eternal soul is in peril, Mr. Billingsley. We must rescue him. We must beg God to spare him and return him to our fold. Surely, thou seeth that this must be our priority."

Walter stared at the man in abject disbelief. He spat on the ground as a demonstration of his disgust. "Mr. Martin, the only thing that I see is a boy who acted bravely and did right by his family being browbeaten by a bunch of stinking cowards."

Gabriel emitted a low whistle of disbelief. He knew that his friend was priming for a fight ... and that it was going to be very ugly.

"Cowards, sir?" Martin's pride was wounded, though he would never admit it.

"Indeed. Cowards. Who else would let a bunch of savages kill, maim, and rape their women and children whilst they simply stood and watched?" Walter challenged.

"Thou simply faileth in understanding our doctrine, Mr. Billingsley."

"Oh, I understand it just fine, Mr. Martin. I simply see it for the stupidity and cowardice that it reveals."

Walter's nostrils flared. He could feel his pulse in his temples. He was frustrated, tired, and angry. He could smell the sickly sweetness of burning flesh that still hung over the camp. The stench of death was overwhelming. These grown men had an obligation to tend to their dead and to their distraught families, yet they seemed intent upon haranguing and heaping shame upon this brave lad … when all he had done was shoot the man who murdered his mother.

Walter's rage and indignation were intense. The pain in his back was flaring from the absence of alcohol and opium. He was somewhat shocked at how little tolerance he bore for these men that he had previously held in such high regard. Whereas before he had respected and even revered their pacifism and peaceful approach to life, now he interpreted it as wanton weakness.

"Mr. Billingsley, please understand. Our Lord, Himself, declared in the Gospel of Matthew, in chapter five, verse thirty-nine, '*But I say unto you, that ye resist not evil: but whosoever shall smite thee on thy right cheek, turn to him the other also.*' This doctrine governs every aspect of our daily lives."

Walter responded sharply, "I also seem to recall our Lord declaring in the Gospel of Luke, *'He that hath no sword, let him sell his garment, and buy one.*"

Martin shook his head most vigorously. "Thou art misinterpreting that passage, Mr. Billingsley. The prophet Micah declared, *'They shall beat their swords into plowshares, and their spears into pruning hooks: nation shall not lift up a sword against nation, neither shall they learn war anymore.*'"

"Talk about misinterpreting a passage!" declared Walter. "That is a prophecy that describes events far into the future!" He pointed at the burned body of the Martin's wife. "And, besides, this is not a matter of 'nation against nation.' This is about murderous savages and thugs laying waste to your own families."

Martin continued to shake his head. "Mr. Billingsley, thou must surely understand that not even killing in self-defense is acceptable in the life of a true man of God."

Walter exhaled, disgusted. "I recall my Papa teaching from the prophet Nehemiah. When he and the exiles rebuilt Jerusalem, the Word of God says, '*Everyone with one of his hands wrought in the work, and with the other hand held a weapon. For the builders, everyone had his sword girded by his side.*'"

"I can see thou art a man who hath at least a rudimentary knowledge of God's Holy Word." Mr. Martin nodded somewhat respectfully. "But, still, our doctrine is inescapable. It has been the sentiment of our Lord from the beginning of time. Yea, he hast even declared in the commandments, '*Thou shalt not kill.*'" The man emphasized each and every word of the simple commandment.

Walter pointed, once again, at the smoking body of Martin's wife. "And yet, the Psalmist wrote, '*Deliver the poor and needy: rid them out of the hand of the wicked.*' And King Solomon indicted cowardice in the strongest terms. He said, '*A righteous man falling down before the wicked is as a troubled fountain, and a corrupt spring.*'" He stared coldly at the preaching Quaker. "I can do this all day, Mr. Martin, but I have no more tolerance for it. This meadow reeks with the stench of your cowardice and foolishness."

Owen Martin exhaled in frustration. "I must again insist that thou interferest not in matters of our doctrine and faith, Mr. Billingsley!"

Walter ignored him. He stared into the eyes of the lad, Ezekiel. "Zeke, do you understand what you did?"

"Aye. I killed that Indian." He glanced at the dead native who lay twenty feet to his right.

"And why did you do it?"

"Because he killed my mother. And because my sisters were in danger."

The Quaker men erupted into a fresh round of mournful prayers. One of them mumbled the word, '*vengeance*,' with great drama and emotion.

"And do you feel that your actions were justified?" Walter continued.

The lad paused and thought carefully. He sat perfectly still for a moment, staring at his father's feet. He then looked again at Walter and nodded.

"Would you do it again?"

"Aye. I would."

"And do you desire to endure any more chastisement from these men?"

"No, sir. I prefer to bury my mama and my sister."

"Very well, then. Come, and we will do what needs to be done. We shall leave these fopdoodles to their judgments and preaching." He reached his hand to the boy in order to help pull him up from the ground.

"Mr. Billingsley! Thou must refrain from interfering ..."

Walter whipped his pistol from his belt and instantly pulled the hammer back to full cock. He thrust the barrel into Owen Martin's face.

Gabriel, who had been standing silently near Walter, exclaimed, "Walter! No! Not that!"

Walter cast a quick, reassuring, glance at his friend, and then returned his attention to the anguished Quaker.

"I've had just about enough of the likes of you, Mr. Martin. Your boy is welcome to camp with Mr. Blevins and me until such time as we reach our destination. I will consider him under my personal care until that day. Meanwhile, you will leave him be, or you shall answer to me. Do you understand?"

Martin stared blankly at Walter. "I understand." He paused. "I understand that thou believest that a gun maketh thee stronger than me."

"Excellent! Then you do understand, indeed." He released the hammer and returned the pistol to his belt. "Let's get on with it, then. Blevins, Ezekiel, and I will stand guard whilst the rest of you folks attend to your dead." He nodded to Ezekiel. "Grab your gun, Son. Let's go have some breakfast before we go on patrol. We must verify that these Indians are gone."

The young man fetched his ancient trade musket from its perch beside a nearby tree and quickly joined Gabe and Walter as they walked toward their lean-to on the far side of the meadow. The Quaker men stood silently, mouths agape in utter disbelief.

October 30, 1782

Kyles's Fort – At the Mouth of Big Creek – Sullivan County

The mountains were ablaze with the colors of autumn. A deep cold snap descended upon the high ridges three days after the deadly Cherokee raid, and the cold accelerated the color change on the towering mountain trees. The entire scene was beautiful beyond anything that Walter or Gabriel had ever seen. The captivating beauty of the scenery, the decline in the steep grade of the mountains, and growing ease of travel helped Walter put most of the memories of the massacre behind him. Still, he was anxious to reach his destination, complete his mission, and separate himself from his employers.

Walter led the Quakers through the main gate of Robert Kyle's fort during the mid-afternoon. The large fortress was located at the mouth of Big Creek in the Carter Valley, and surrounded by a huge grove of hickory trees. It was an impressive fort, and teeming with all manner of business and activity. Walter and Gabriel decided immediately that they would stay and make the fort their home … at least for a while.

Walter did not take the time to share any lengthy farewells. Truth be told, he was glad to be rid of the Quakers. The earlier respect that he had once held for them was gone. After their deadly impotence during the Cherokee raid, he only felt disgusted disdain toward the unreasonable pacifists. Ten days had passed since the raid, and Walter could still scarcely believe that the men had not resisted the attack, even as their own wives and children were being raped, murdered, and scalped.

Once everyone was safely inside the fort, Walter and Gabe met quickly with William Sumner to accept their final payments in silver for service as guides. Sumner seemed a bit emotional at their parting. He handed Walter a small leather bag full of coins.

"I have enclosed the amount that we agreed upon, with a humble bonus. I am truly grateful for thy services, Mr. Billingsley. And I can never repay thee for the salvation of my family. Thou delivered my girls from the jaws of death. My precious Mary will not cease talking and blabbering about thee. Thou art something of a hero in our household." He smiled warmly.

Walter nodded humbly. "I am truly glad that I made a difference, sir. I only wish that your friends entertained similar sentiments."

"Our doctrine is a good and righteous one, Mr. Billingsley. Our ways are not as thine, it is true. I still abhor the violence and death of that horrible night. But I realize, also, that the application of our doctrine of non-violence is not always so simple as it may seem. Thou opened mine eyes to that truth." He shook the Walter's hand. "Thou art always welcome in my home, Walter Billingsley … as art thou, Mr. Blevins."

Gabriel shook the man's hand. The two scouts nodded respectfully, turned, and headed toward the makeshift tavern located in the southwest corner of the fort. Curiously, young Ezekiel Martin trailed along behind them, musket still in hand. He carried several bags around his neck and a rather fat snapsack over his right shoulder.

Walter turned to the lad. “Where are you going, Ezekiel?”

“I’m going with thee,” the boy declared hopefully.

Gabriel eyed the boy skeptically, and then glanced at Walter. “Are you certain that is what is best for you? Surely, your father will be disappointed.”

“My father has not spoken to me since the day of the attack.” The lad stared at the ground at his feet. “I fear that he hates me … or at least hates what I did. But, I certainly cannot live with a man who will neither acknowledge nor speak to me.”

Gabriel cut his eyes at Walter. Walter winked subtly at his friend, then asked, “How old are you, Zeke?”

“I will be sixteen in December, sir.” He stared expectantly at Walter.

Walter sighed. “Do not call me, ‘sir.’ I am only twenty years old, myself. Well, it sounds to me like you’re old enough to choose your own path. If you want to ride with us, I am fine with it. How about you, Gabriel?”

“I have no objections.”

“Very well then,” Walter declared. “We shall be a threesome from now on. But I have to warn you, Zeke … my friends and accomplices tend to die at a young age. Gabriel, here, is the only survivor, and even he has managed to get his leg blown off.”

The boy’s eyes glazed with fear. Walter paused dramatically, and then burst out laughing. Gabriel joined him. Ezekiel stared, confused.

“Well, Walter, what is our first order of business?” inquired Gabriel, still chuckling.

“We locate Mr. Kyle and see what prospects are available hereabouts. We need a roof over our heads, and some semblance of a job. At least we have a little silver to get us started,” Walter declared, patting the lump in his coat pocket.

Ezekiel scanned the fort. “I wonder about the cause of all of this celebration. These people surely seem excited.”

The lad was right. The fort seemed to be caught up in a generalized state of euphoria. Despite the relative earliness in the day, there was much music, dancing, drinking, and merrymaking.

Walter exhaled. "There is only one way to find out, I suppose. Let's head for the pub. Captain Kyle will most likely be there."

"I have never been to a public house," declared Ezekiel, somewhat aghast.

"Then, you are most assuredly in for a treat," teased Walter as he led them toward a large cabin to their left.

The front door of the tavern was open. The sounds of fiddle music, dancing, and singing echoed through the opening. The three young men stepped inside. The room was filled with a relatively foul mixture of odors. There was the pungent sharpness of ale and rum, the stench of filthy bodies and armpits, and distinctly unpleasant notes of vomit and urine. A haze of tobacco smoke filled the room. Ample light shined through the cracks between the logs in the walls. Ezekiel stared, open-mouthed, at the spectacle of humanity inside the tavern.

Walter led the group toward a makeshift bar. A plain, homely teenaged girl stood behind the counter, pouring drinks and accepting money.

Walter dropped a Spanish silver one-half Reale coin on the rough wood surface. He nodded to the girl. "Three ales and two cups of rum, if you please."

"You'll be a needin' another one of them tiny coins for that big order," she declared.

"Spirits are a bit expensive in Sullivan County, aren't they?" observed Walter, tossing a second coin onto the counter.

The girl scooped up the silver and deposited it in her apron. "Liquor's hard to get 'round here, Mister. It's the mountains that make it so expensive. Papa has to have it hauled all the way down from Martin's Station."

"Is Captain Kyle your father?" Gabriel inquired, smiling at the girl.

She eyed him suspiciously. His thick British accent seemed to trouble her. She cut her eyes at Walter. "Where'd you find him? We don't serve no British up in here."

"Oh, you don't need to worry about Corporal Blevins. He's my prisoner of war, and sworn to serve me." Walter winked at the girl.

She rolled her eyes and sat the order of drinks on the bar. "I'll go and get Papa in just a bit ... as soon as I get caught up on these drinks. Find yourselves a seat, iff'n you can."

"Thank you, Missy," Walter declared. He handed Ezekiel a mug of ale and pushed another mug toward Gabriel. He tossed back one jigger of rum, and then prepared to drink the second.

"Hold on!" Gabriel protested. "I thought the second rum was for me!"

"Not likely," answered Walter, downing the fiery liquid. He pushed both cups toward the rear of the bar. "By the way, Missy, what is the cause of all of this celebration?"

The girl shouted from the other end of the bar. "Ain't you heerd? The war is over."

"Excuse me?"

She strolled back in their direction. "Yes, sir. Some folks brought a newspaper down from Martin's Station. Just arrived this mornin'. Some fancy-pants named Cornball, or somethin' like that, surrendered the whole Redcoat army in Virginia."

"You mean General Cornwallis?" Gabriel clarified.

"That's the one. General Washington was there, too. And all the Frenchies. They showed up by the boatful. The British is all leavin' now ... goin' to some islands, they say."

"And you are certain of this information?" Gabriel asked, somewhat in disbelief.

"They got the paper over there next to the fire. Go and read it for yourself." She turned and walked toward a small window behind the far end of the bar. She called through the opening, "Papa! Some strangers is here to see you! One of em's British!"

The little girl's shrill declaration caused the celebrations to cease. The fiddle squealed to a halt. Singing and dancing stopped immediately. Every eye in the establishment was fixed upon Walter, Gabriel, and Ezekiel. Several men fingered the pistols and knives in their belts. Walter stared wide-eyed at Gabriel. His British friend thought quickly, then raised his mug high in the air.

"A toast, ladies and gentlemen!" His British accent sent a shock wave of consternation through the room. "To the victorious armies of His Excellency General Washington! God save the United States!"

The crowd erupted into a rowdy chorus of laughter and "Huzzahs!" The celebrations resumed immediately. Liquor flowed liberally. Drunk men smoked pipes and sang songs. Several of them walked up and shook Gabriel's hand and slapped him affectionately on the shoulder. The young Englishman became an instant celebrity. He smiled mischievously at Walter.

"Well, I suppose there is no going back for me now," Gabriel remarked, once the frontier well-wishers had dispersed.

"I suppose not," affirmed Walter. "Welcome to your new home, Gabriel Blevins. I reckon you are now a citizen of these United States."

Gabe grinned, lifted his mug, and drank to his own toast. "It is good to finally be home."

December 21, 1781 – On Patrol in the Mountains

It was shortly before the dawn. Walter and Gabriel were slumbering happily inside their familiar lean-to. The men had pitched their shelter on a narrow mountain bluff that overlooked a large, wooded ravine. It was a perfect, defensible spot. There was a high, vertical rock wall to the rear of the shelter that protected the scouting party from attack from behind. There was only a single, narrow trail that allowed access to the campsite. The three men blocked that trail with boulders and fallen timbers the previous afternoon. It was as secure a location as could be found in the Cherokee-infested mountains of what would someday become east Tennessee.

Ezekiel Martin was on last watch, reclining against a large rock situated near the edge of the bluff, and maintaining a lonely vigil over their humble encampment. He hunkered in the darkness, well away from the glow of the campfire. How he longed to be near that fire! The December air was frigid. He smoked his pipe to stay awake and sipped from a cup of steaming hot, extra sweet tea. At least his hands, lips, and innards would remain warm. His shiny new long rifle lay at the ready across his lap. The lad had learned his frontier lessons well. Despite the relatively secure location of their camp, one must never be too far away from his rifle ... especially in this more remote, untamed portion of Sullivan County.

Though his Quaker father would certainly not be pleased, Ezekiel was developing into a gifted soldier and scout. He was inquisitive, quiet, and thorough. He had afforded himself most bravely and effectively in two recent skirmishes with the Indians. Indeed, the boy saved Gabriel's life with a well-placed rifle shot only four days prior. Ezekiel loved his new life in the forests, and he was thrilled and honored that his compatriots trusted him enough to sleep soundly under his watchful care.

The three men were on a long-range reconnaissance patrol near the southwestern tip of the Carter Valley. Captain Robert Kyle had employed them as Indian spies the moment that he met them. For the past six weeks, they had been patrolling the frontier to keep watch over the movements of their Cherokee nemeses, alert settlers to the presence of Indian hunting and war parties, and make regular reports back to Captain Kyle. The captain, in turn, reported to Colonel John Sevier, who was the commander of all American forces in the region.

The rowdy celebrations over the war's end did not last very long at Kyle's Fort. They were tempered by an increase in raids and the occasional murder along the frontier, all perpetrated by roaming bands of warring Cherokees. Throughout November, the scene that Walter and his group of Quakers witnessed in their mountain encampment had been repeated at almost a dozen homesteads and outposts throughout Sullivan County, especially along the more remote frontier valleys on the western edge of the Blue Ridge. It seemed that the British had failed to inform their native allies that the war was over.

Walter Billingsley and his team had been tracking a band of about twenty Cherokee warriors for the past three days. Thankfully, it appeared that the group of raiders had turned toward the south, back in the direction of their own settlements. Walter and his crew discovered signs of the retreat shortly before nightfall the previous day. Their plan for the coming daylight was simple. As soon as the sun was up, they would follow the raiding party and verify their retreat, then return northward, scouting as they went, and make their report to Captain Kyle at his fort in the place known as the Hickory Grove.

Ezekiel heard the rustling of movement from the direction of the lean-to. He glanced over his shoulder and saw Walter crawling from beneath the front flap of the linen shelter. Ezekiel smiled. The glow of the campfire revealed Walter in an uncharacteristically disheveled state. His queue had come undone during the night. His long hair was a frizzy mess, sticking out wildly in every direction.

Walter sat beside the fire and stared numbly at the flames for several seconds. Soon, he poured himself a cup of tea, tucked his pistol into his belt, and then scanned the perimeter in search of Ezekiel. When it became evident to Ezekiel that he was too well-concealed for his friend to spot him, he emitted a low whistle. Walter fixed his gaze upon the source of the sound. He took out his clay pipe and stuck it in his mouth, then grabbed his coal tongs and fished a small, glowing coal from the fire. He began walking in Ezekiel's direction.

"Mornin', Zeke. Anything to report?" whispered Walter as he sat down beside his friend.

Ezekiel merely shook his head and took another sip of tea.

"Horses are all right?"

Ezekiel nodded and expelled a cloud of tobacco smoke from his nostrils. Their mounts were tied to a sapling in a small clearing about half-way up the trail to the bluff. They could not move the large animals any further without risking a fall. Ezekiel had checked on them every half-hour during his watch. They dozed happily in the darkness.

Walter smiled. "You got any more tobacco on you?"

Ezekiel reached into his haversack and pulled out a small linen bag. He handed it to Walter.

"Hold this for me." Walter carefully handed him the tongs and coal.

He dipped the bowl of his pipe into the sack of tobacco and filled it to the top, tamped the shredded leaves with a small stick, and then retrieved the coal tongs from Ezekiel. He quickly and expertly lit his pipe, drawing deeply on the sweet, fragrant smoke.

Walter shivered. "This cold is damnable. I wish we could sleep under a roof tonight."

"That gets my vote," Ezekiel declared softly.

"Maybe in a week or so," promised Walter, stretching. "I slept well this night, though."

"I can tell." Ezekiel chuckled lightly.

"Huh?" Walter responded, confused.

"Thy hair looks like thou spent the night in a windstorm."

Walter reached up and felt of his hair, then grinned. He removed a leather thong from his pocket and pulled his wild mane back into a makeshift queue. "I shall brush it after breakfast," he declared.

Ezekiel grinned warmly. He stared intently into the darkness to the south. "Dost thou believe the heathens are truly gone, Walter?"

"Well, they were headed in the right direction. We will know later this morning. If their trail goes cold at the lower Holston, we will know that they have crossed and gone back home."

"What is the plan, then?"

"We will follow them southwest to the river, then raft across and cut back to the east. We'll check the Davidson outpost first. They are the furthest out on the southern frontier. I cannot, for the life of me, understand why they insist upon being so far out and isolated." Walter shook his head judgmentally. "After that, we will follow the buffalo trail back north toward the Holston and establish camp. We'll patrol that area for a day or two, then we will cross the river again and swing up toward Bean's Station. We'll make our way to Prewitt's Station the next day, then take a big swing to the east and head for home in the Hickory Grove. We should be in our own bunks in seven or eight days."

"That will be nice," declared Ezekiel. "I'm ready to get back."

Walter nudged the young fellow with his elbow. "You're not still sweet on Captain Kyle's skinny little daughter, are you?" He could see the boy blushing, even in the darkness.

"Maddie is a nice girl."

"I know she is." Walter grinned. "You are well-suited for one another, though I doubt that your father would approve."

"He does not approve of much of anything, though, does he? So, what does it matter?"

"I suppose you are right about that." Walter paused. He announced guardedly, "We'll see your family and the others in a couple of days, you know."

Ezekiel gave a bit of a surprised start. "How? Where?"

"They have made a settlement near Lost Creek, on the Holston. A fellow by the name of John Mills has a cabin there."

"I remember Mr. Mills! He lived near us in Guilford County. He left three or four years ago to cross the mountains."

"Well, it seems your family and friends have discovered his location and joined him. I hear they've taken to calling the place, 'New Market.'"

"That was our meeting house back in Guilford County!" declared Ezekiel, somewhat in a state of disbelief.

"I know. I remember." Walter eyed the boy cautiously. "You understand that we *must* go there, don't you? It is our duty to check on all of the homesteads and settlements … even the Quaker ones."

Ezekiel nodded. "I do not mind. It will be good to see my brothers and sisters, and all of my old friends."

"But, what about your father and the other men?"

"I shall treat them cordially and with respect. How they choose to respond is entirely up to them."

"Good boy," affirmed Walter, patting his friend on the shoulder.

The two men sat in silence for the next several minutes, puffing their pipes and staring into the ravine. Both simultaneously caught sight of movement in the haunting glow of the dawn. It was just a brief tremble amongst the trees, well over a hundred yards away. They each tensed and grabbed their weapons. Their fears were allayed, however, when they saw the familiar flash of a furry, white tail. It was a deer feeding on the ample acorns that littered the forest floor.

Walter chuckled. "That doe certainly has her priorities in the right place." He glanced upward at the purplish-black sky. "The sun will be up full within the half-hour. Let us not allow the day to get away from us. We'll rouse Gabriel, get some bread and tea in our bellies, and then get moving. We need to get to Davidson's before nightfall."

Ezekiel tapped the smoldering remnants of ash from his pipe. "Let's just hope that Mrs. Davidson has some stew in her pot. I'm weary of hard bread and dried venison."

Four Days Later – Christmas, 1781

The three scouts were all anxious to reach their destination. They were traversing a particularly dangerous part of the trail that led to the Quaker village at New Market. The weather had taken a decidedly wetter and colder turn on the previous evening. Several inches of heavy, wet snow fell during the night, coating the tree limbs and forest floor with a beautiful, thick blanket of white. The limbs of the numerous pine trees hung low, weighted heavily by their snowy burdens. Several limbs had broken under the weight and fallen to the ground or hung shattered and suspended awkwardly from the trunks of the evergreen trees. The current weather did not bode well for the coming winter. It was relatively early in the season for such a significant snowfall.

"How much further?" whined Ezekiel. "I can no longer feel my feet!"

"It's about another mile, maybe a little more," responded Walter. "We must stay on the river trail. It will lead us right in."

"This ground is treacherous!" groaned Gabriel.

The Englishman had declared a grave understatement. A high hillside rose precipitously to their right. The slowly churning waters of the Holston River flowed to their left. The trail was no more than three feet in width at its widest point. Turning their horses or retreating back from whence they came was an impossibility. They had no other option than to continue northward.

The trail that hugged the bank of the Holston was not only narrow and snow-covered. It was also steep and rocky. The smooth coating of snow was deceptive, for it masked the uneven myriad of stones that populated the little-used trail. Walter's horse, Patches, clung precariously to the unsteady ground. She snorted nervously. Her hooves slipped repeatedly in the fresh snow. She was obviously not happy about her situation.

Walter was leading the group. He guided the animal around a small tree that crowded the trail. It marked a sharp turn in the river. Indeed, the change of direction along the trail was almost ninety degrees to their right. He was almost past the tree when a small rock gave way beneath one of Patches' rear feet. The animal lurched instinctively to her right … away from the water. The sudden move caused her to slam her right hip directly into the trunk of the tree. The horse's hind quarter bounced off of the tree and recoiled left. She dug furiously with her rear hooves in an effort to retain her footing, but the frantic thrashing only served to dislodge more loose dirt and rocks. Her back feet and legs began to slip down the bank of the river.

Gabriel screamed, "Walter! Jump off!"

But it was too late. Patches gave one final mighty push with her back legs and then tumbled backwards into the river. Walter plunged into the water first. He landed flat on his back. Gabriel and Ezekiel heard a deep, loud gasp as his warm flesh made contact with the icy water. Then … tragically and unimaginably … his horse landed upside-down on top of him, burying him in a thunderous geyser of water and spray.

20

SNOWED IN

January 1, 1782

Walter awakened with a start. He was lying flat on his back in a soft, warm bed. He sensed an overwhelming weight upon his chest. Indeed, the pressure was so overpowering that he felt he could scarcely breathe. His body ached from hunger and thirst. Walter needed water ... desperately. Panicked and disoriented, he searched his surroundings in an attempt to discern his whereabouts. There was nothing near his bedside that offered any clue to his location. He tried to turn his head and see behind him, but his range of motion was limited by a stiff, sore neck.

Walter ceased his attempts at movement and instead focused upon listening. He heard the familiar crackling of a fireplace. There was a drone of human conversation nearby. It was a pleasant mixture of voices and laughter. The chattering of voices confused him even more. And there was the familiar high-pitch clinking sound made by silverware coming in contact with plates and dishes. It sounded as if someone was having dinner in the room where he lay. He suddenly realized the smell of the food. It made his stomach twist into knots of envious pain.

Somewhere behind him and beyond his field of view a youngster's voice loudly proclaimed, "Look! He is moving! He hath awakened!"

The sounds of eating and conversation ended abruptly, and were replaced by the din of chairs scooting across a wooden floor. Walter heard the pounding of feet as several people darted across the room toward him. The first face he saw was that of his best friend and compatriot, Gabriel Blevins. A half-dozen other faces followed in quick succession. They were the members of the William Sumner family. Walter exhaled in relief. He was among friends.

"There you are! I say there, old chap! We thought that you were going to sleep until the spring time!" Gabriel grinned excitedly.

Walter stared pleadingly at Gabriel. He mumbled silently with parched mouth and lips, "Water."

"This man is thirsty! Fetch him some water!" urged Gabriel.

"That is certainly a good sign," declared another nearby male voice. The man's face popped into view. It was the Quaker leader and master of the house, William Sumner. He was smiling, as well.

Little Mary Sumner appeared at Walter's right side with a maple burl bowl of water and a large spoon cut from a small gourd. She sat authoritatively on his bedside. She carefully lifted his head with her left hand, supporting the weight of it, and then lovingly lifted a spoonful of the cool fluid to Walter's lips. He lapped voraciously, draining the spoon.

"More," he begged. His voice was louder this time.

"Just one more spoonful, Mary," urged Mr. Sumner. "There are a couple of ounces in that spoon. Tis not good to partake of an overabundance of fluids after such a long and tormenting fever."

"Yes, Father."

She carefully filled a second spoonful and lifted it carefully to Walter's lips. She did not waste a single drop. Once he was finished, she gently returned his head to his plush goose feather pillow. She wiped his forehead with a cool, damp cloth.

Mary declared, "Thou mayest have some more in just a short while, Mr. Billingsley. Meanwhile, I shall go and fix thee a bowl of broth whilst thou speaketh to Papa and Mr. Blevins. We have a broth of turkey bones simmering over the fire. Thou art hungry, I assume?"

He whispered, "Yes. Very. Thank you, Mary." He smiled.

Mary's cheeks flushed red. She beamed with a gigantic smile of pride and affection as she rose from his bedside and glided toward the fireplace. Gabriel and Mr. Sumner pulled chairs near to Walter and sat down. Both men grinned happily.

"We were quite concerned about you, Walter," Gabriel declared.

"I'm burning up," growled Walter. "Can you get some of these covers off of me? I can scarcely breathe."

"Another good sign!" declared Mrs. Eleanor Sumner, who quite suddenly appeared at Walter's side. She peeled back several layers of wool blankets and placed them on them on a cherry wood five-plank bench that sat beside the fireplace.

She explained, "Mr. Billingsley, we shall not uncover thee entirely. We do not want to cast thee back into a rigor." She barked at her daughter, "Abigail, hurry up with the broth. Mr. Billingsley must be famished."

Abigail Sumner's soft, bland voice echoed from the far side of the room, "Yes, Mother."

Walter's heart skipped at the mention of his favorite name. Yet, that female voice sounded nothing like the vibrant voice of his Abigail. The young woman across the room sounded empty and lifeless. Walter immediately wondered how Abigail Sumner had fared since the attack. Indeed, he could not quite fathom how any woman could recover from such a personal, invasive assault. He determined to speak to her later and inquire as to her well-being.

Mr. Sumner's voice invaded his searching thoughts. "Walter, thou hast been in a feverish rigor for most of thy time in this bed. There were some nights when we were compelled to add heated stones beside thee to keep thee warm. Thou hast experienced both soaking sweats and uncontrollable chatters. Thy fever finally broke and departed earlier this afternoon."

"How long?" Walter demanded, confused. "How long have I been down?"

"One week," responded Gabriel. "Today is January 1."

Walter stared at his friend with a gaze of shock and disbelief. He could scarcely comprehend the fact that he had just lost an entire week of his life. He had no memory, whatsoever, of those seven days. The notion of it appalled him.

"Dost thou remember what happened to thee?" Mr. Sumner inquired.

"I remember that we followed the Cherokee until their trail turned south, and then we made our way up along the Holston River. We were headed for New Market."

Gabriel waved his hand in the air. "Well, obviously, we reached New Market ... though you reached it several minutes before Ezekiel and I. Do you remember falling into the river?"

Walter closed his eyes and struggled to remember such an incident, but he could not. His final recollection was that of riding on the narrow trail near the river's edge. He had absolutely no memory of falling into the water. He shook his head.

"Well, the simple explanation is that your horse lost her footing and then bounced off of a tree. She tumbled backwards into the river and carried you with her. We never saw you surface, and had feared that you were dead. However, one of the Quaker boys discovered you a mile downstream, entangled in the brush on the eastern bank. He thought that you were dead, for certain, and was quite surprised to find that you were still breathing. He mobilized the entire village to your rescue and aid. Ezekiel and I arrived just as they were bringing you into Mr. Sumner's house. I was quite pleased, as well, to find that you were still breathing." He squeezed Walter's arm affectionately.

Mr. Sumner continued the story. "Thou hast experienced a fever and catarrh since the very moment of thy arrival in this house. The sickness crept deep into thy lungs. Thou hast coughed some blood." He paused. "And I suspect that thy regular use of rum and opium powder caused increased discomfort in thy members. Thou hast had tremors and shakes even when there was no fever. I have never seen anything like it. Thou shouted at visions and demons in the air and screamed about worms consuming thy flesh." He shuddered as he attempted to dispel the vision of it from his mind. "It was devilish and frightful, I assure thee."

Walter greatly desired to change the subject. "What about Patches?"

"Not to worry, Walter. Your mare swam safely to a shallow rock bar and pulled herself from the river. She is stabled comfortably inside Mr. Sumner's barn. His boys have taken most excellent care of her. I daresay you shall barely recognize her when the time comes to ride again. She is fat from generous helpings of oats and hay."

Walter was greatly relieved. He had sincere affection for his horse.

"And what of my guns and equipment?"

Gabriel shook his head. "Your pistol never left your belt. I managed to clean and preserve it. However, your rifle remains at the bottom of the river. Most of your other belongings were either lost or ruined beyond repair."

Walter nodded grimly in response. He lamented silently the loss of his fine Virginia rifle.

Mr. Sumner punched Walter's arm lightly and affectionately. "Rifles and powder horns can be replaced, Walter. Thy life has been spared. That is what is truly important. Surely, our Lord God hath great plans for thee."

Walter did not respond to the man's theological assessment of his life. He was thankful, sure enough, that he had survived the ordeal. However, he entertained no notions of any sort of divine scheme that might explain his accident or subsequent deliverance. His personal faith, which had once been a significant influence upon his life, had been all but extinguished after the death of Abigail and his unborn son. He held little regard for any "plans" of God. Indeed, Walter remained quite angry at the Almighty for the numerous cruel misfortunes that had so often and regularly visited his life up until the current moment. He wanted to dismiss such thoughts, lest he bring upon himself further judgement from above. He refocused his mind upon the matters of the moment.

"Where is Ezekiel?" demanded Walter, glancing around the room.

"He is visiting with his family. He has been ever since our arrival," Gabriel explained.

Walter was somewhat surprised. "Has his father welcomed him back, then?"

"Not quite," answered Mr. Sumner. "I would say that they are tolerating one another's presence for the sake of the younger children."

"There have been no more sermons and prayer meetings, then?"

Mr. Sumner smiled. "I assure thee that young Ezekiel hath been covered in prayer and supplication ever since his departure. Mr. Martin attempted one such Scriptural intervention shortly after Ezekiel's arrival, but I do believe that the young man made his sentiments clear. He returned to visit with family, not to theologize."

"Good for him," Walter growled.

"Perhaps," responded Mr. Sumner with a slight grimace. "Still, I pray that their relationship will one day be mended and restored. Fathers need their sons." He stared insightfully at Walter. "And sons need their fathers."

Walter nodded subtly. "As well I know, Mr. Sumner."

Mary arrived with a bowl of steaming, fragrant broth. She forced her way between the chairs occupied by her father and Gabriel and sat, once again, on the side of Walter's bed.

She chirped, "It's time for thy supper, Mr. Billingsley. Dost thou feel like sitting up?"

"I can try. But I'll need some help."

Gabriel and Mr. Sumner rose quickly. Gabriel went around to the other side of the bed in order to help reposition Walter. Each man took hold of one of Walter's arms and lifted him gently. They elevated him to a partially seated position. Mary placed a plush goose-feather pillow between Walter's back and the thick headboard of the bed.

"That is sufficient, I believe," declared Mr. Sumner. "Thou art elevated enough so that thou mayest enjoy thy broth without danger of choking. Dost thou agree, Mary?"

"Yes, Father. This is fine."

Mr. Sumner smiled proudly. "Walter, this crazy Englishman hath refused to leave thy side since thou arrived here. Thou hast a fine and faithful friend in this one." He slapped Gabriel soundly on the back.

"As well I know it," Walter affirmed. "A Carolina boy could do worse." He winked at his friend.

Mr. Sumner continued, "And Mary hath been quite the faithful nurse over these past several days, Walter. She hath invested much toil and effort in thy constant care."

"Has she, now? Well, then … I am most grateful, indeed, Mary Sumner."

Mary blushed yet again. "It is the least that I could do, Mr. Billingsley, after what thee did to save our family." She nodded to Gabriel and her father. "Now, if thou gentlemen wouldst give us a few moments in peace, I shall get Mr. Billingsley fed."

"As thou wisheth, Daughter." He tapped Gabriel on the arm. "Mr. Blevins, let us return to our supper."

Gabriel patted his friend on the shoulder. He leaned down and whispered, "It is, indeed, good to see you back amongst the living again, Walter." A tear glistened in his eye. He spun quickly and returned to the supper table.

Mary stretched a linen napkin across Walter's chest and tucked the edges inside the collar of his shirt. She fetched the soup bowl and spoon from the side table.

"There!" she declared. "Now, we shall get thee fed. Afterwards, Papa and Mr. Blevins shall help thee change into a fresh shirt. Thy current one hath become a bit musty."

"Are you inferring that I stink, Mary Sumner?"

"There is no inference intended, Mr. Billingsley. It is simply a matter of fact. Thy odor is pungent."

Walter laughed enthusiastically, but quickly lurched into a coughing spasm.

"Careful now, Mr. Billingsley," Mary cautioned. "Let us calm down and get some nourishment in thy belly."

"Yes ma'am. Your wish is my command."

Mary Sumner grinned broadly and proudly.

New Market – February 10, 1782

"I simply cannot believe this snow!" Walter declared as he stared through the milky, distorted glass of the small window.

"It has not abated since we arrived," responded Gabriel. "It snowed heavily the entire time you slept. I cannot remember a single day without some measure of snow."

"How much must there be?"

"I estimate three feet of accumulation on the ground now, though I am quite certain that much more has fallen," answered Gabriel. "Neither man nor beast can move about in such horrid conditions."

"It surely didn't keep the Sumner clan at home and away from their Sunday meeting," declared Walter sarcastically. The two non-Quakers were enjoying a few hours of solitude at the Sumner home while the family was attending their weekly worship service.

"They are a people of great faith, Walter. Besides, the boys have shoveled ample paths throughout the village. All they have to do is stay within the walls of snow, and they will be just fine."

"Well, I am sick of it all, and I shall be glad when it is gone. I need to get out of this house, lest I lose what little is left of my mind. I am anxious to return to the fort," Walter declared.

"Why, pray tell?" asked Gabriel. "I'm reasonably certain that the people there are snowed in, same as us. If we were inside that fort, we would be staring at the four bland walls of our tiny bunk-room. Here we have a comfortable, cheerful house, a warm fire, tasty and plentiful food, and excellent company."

Walter cut his eyes at Gabriel. "I've been keeping an eye on you and your 'excellent company.' I have seen the special attention that you've been paying to Miss Abigail. It's a bold, sinful man that you are, Gabriel Blevins." Walter grinned teasingly.

Gabriel frowned. "There is nothing sinful about my friendship with Abigail. I find her to be a beautiful and sweet young woman. I would be thrilled if she were interested in me romantically."

"But you must admit ... there are complications," Walter warned.

"I know. Her faith is much different from my Anglicanism. Likely, her father would not approve of any romance between us. I do not believe that they often marry outside their order. But, time will tell, I suppose."

"And then there's the other matter."

"What matter is that?" challenged Gabriel.

"You know."

"No, Walter, I do not know. Please enlighten me."

"The attack, Gabriel. An Indian raped her. You know that."

"Yes ... and ...?" Gabriel responded, defensively.

Walter stammered uncomfortably, "Well, Gabriel ... you know. It's just that ... well ... it changes things."

"Walter, I wish you would stop dancing around whatever notion is fomenting inside your mind and simply speak it. I can no longer tolerate the suspense."

"Damn it, Gabriel! She's been visited already. She's been spoiled. That Cherokee took her purity. Surely, you cannot claim that it does not bother you!"

Gabriel stared sullenly at the dancing flames of the fireplace. He felt an ire rising within his spirit. He wanted to choose his words very carefully and respond to his friend in a fair, but firm manner.

"No, Walter. In all honesty, it does not bother me ... not in the way that you seem to be thinking. It bothers me deeply that she was hurt. It bothers me greatly that she was ravaged and victimized instead of loved and cherished. And it bothers me even more that your regard of Abigail is lessened because of something that was entirely no fault of her own." He paused. His lip quivered. "I must confess ... I thought you were a better man than that."

Gabriel's words penetrated and stung. Walter suddenly felt very ashamed. He had judged Abigail Sumner for a crime that she had suffered, not for a sin that she had committed. That much was true. The realization of his insensitive unfairness overwhelmed him. In addition to his own shame, he was filled with admiration and love for his kindly British friend. He had no recourse but repentance.

"Of course. You are absolutely correct, Gabriel ... in every measure. Clearly, I judged that poor girl for an event over which she held no power or decision. I am truly sorry, and I sincerely beg your forgiveness."

"There is nothing for me to forgive. We all need adjustments in our thinking from time to time."

"Yes, but it seems like I need such adjustments more than most men." He cut a quick glance at Gabriel. His friend was staring at him and smiling warmly.

Gabriel pronounced, "I can find nothing in that statement with which to argue."

Walter reached over with his right hand and thumped his best friend in the head. Both men laughed.

"You *should* pursue Abigail," Walter encouraged. "She would make you a fine wife, indeed. But, she does seem very distant and sad. I wonder if she has been able to put the horrors of that night behind her."

"I shall endeavor to help her do so," Gabriel promised resolutely. "My heartfelt desire is to make her understand that she is most worthy of true love and affection."

Walter slapped his knee hopefully. "And you shall do just that, my friend. We only need to convince Mr. Sumner that you are worthy of the same ... from his daughter, I mean."

Gabriel grinned hopefully.

On the Banks of the Holston River
New Market - March 27, 1782

"Why must thou depart so soon?" begged Mary Sumner.

Walter shrugged. "We've been here over three months, Mary. It is time for us to go. The winter snows have broken. Springtime is upon us, and the Cherokee will, likely, resume their attacks and raids along the frontier. I must return to my duty at Captain Kyle's fort."

Mary grunted her obvious disapproval.

Walter and Mary were strolling along the trail that ran beside the Holston. Such times together, walking the hills and trails around the village, had become something of a daily ritual for them over the past week. Walter greatly enjoyed getting out of the house. His heart craved to be in the wilds of the outdoors. But, Mary only wanted to be with Walter. The young girl was smitten with the handsome frontiersman, and she made no secret about it. Her siblings teased her about her romantic aspirations. Her fellow Quaker villagers scorned and shamed her because of it. They were quite open and public with their sentiments of judgmental displeasure. It was evident in the cold stares and shaking heads that Walter and Mary endured as they walked together around the village of New Market.

But, Mary Sumner did not care. She loved Walter Billingsley … and she intended to have him.

Walter was actually flattered by the attention. He also realized that he owed the girl a great debt. She had cared faithfully for him during his weeks of illness and recuperation. She fed him, kept him comfortable, washed his clothing, emptied his chamber pot, and attended to his every need while he was confined to the bed. Indeed, she refused to allow anyone else in the household to assist her.

Walter was greatly indebted to the kind and faithful child. But, she was, after all, just that … a child. She was only twelve years old. He was a young man of twenty years. Walter knew that her affections toward him could never be realized. To think otherwise was simply an exercise in foolishness. Still, he saw no harm in enjoying her company and conversation during their daily walks. She was truly a delightful person, and a great joy to be around. She seemed wise and informed beyond her years.

Walter attempted to dismiss all notions of romance and focus his attention upon the awakening world around him. The Holston River was swollen to the very top of its banks by the rapidly melting snows. The forest was reviving with the newness and life of springtime. Tiny leaf buds filled the limbs of the trees. Wildflowers were peeking through the forest floor. Some of them even penetrated through the thin patches of snow that hid in the shadows of the mountains. Squirrels chattered, barked, and played in the tree tops. Thousands of blue jays squawked their obnoxious calls and battled over the handful of remaining acorns that remained unclaimed from the previous autumn.

Walter enjoyed discovering the signs of new life all around him. It had been a long, hard, confining winter. He appreciated his months with the Sumner family, but it was time to move on. He and his friends needed to get back to their work as scouts. The Sullivan County settlements needed their services. The Sumners needed back their privacy and space. And the Quakers of New Market village simply needed the invasive outsiders to be gone.

Yes, the presence of the two "non-believers" had been a growing source of gossip and consternation within the colony. But the budding romance between Gabriel and Mary's sister, Abigail, was the greatest scandal of all. She was old enough to marry, and it seemed clear that she had set her sights on this peculiar, one-legged Englishman. The women of the village were apoplectic. The gossip mill was in full operation. It surely would not be long before prayer meetings and Biblical interventions by the church elders would begin. Walter did not want William Sumner's name nor his reputation to be tarnished any more than it already had. He desired to leave as soon as was practicable.

The mismatched pair continued their stroll along the river. After several minutes of uncomfortable, thoughtful silence, Mary determined to resume their conversation.

"When shalt thou depart, then? I assume that thou hast set a date."

"We leave the day after tomorrow."

"So soon," Mary whispered with bitter disappointment. "It shall be treacherous. I do not know where thee shall find a safe place to cross the river. Surely, there are no fords available with the water running so high."

"We'll figure something out." Walter smiled.

"Just like thou figured out how to fall into the river on Christmas Day?" teased Mary, smiling.

"Something like that." Walter returned her affectionate smile.

"And what of Abigail and Mr. Blevins? What is to be done? She loves him deeply, you know."

"I know," Walter answered. "He greatly desires to marry."

"As does she."

Walter's head whipped toward Mary. "You are certain of this?"

She nodded. "It is all that my sister speaks of these days. All that remains is the asking. Mr. Blevins has helped breathe new life back into her spirit. She was so broken … so dead after that night." She stared uncomfortably at the trail in front of them.

"I know. I cannot imagine her pain and despair."

"And yet, she has been restored, thanks to Mr. Blevins."

"What do your parents say about it all?"

"Mother is very pleased. Father is, as well … though he would never admit it."

"Would they allow her to marry him?"

"I believe they would, but not here amongst us, unless Mr. Blevins were to submit to the order and convert. If he were baptized into our faith he would be accepted … eventually."

"I doubt that Gabriel would consent to such as that. He is an avowed Anglican."

"Thou art probably right. So, if they marry, they shall have to leave this place. Abigail would be outcast from our society, and forbidden to return."

"Is it truly that serious?"

"The men of the village have held conferences with Father in recent days."

"All because of Gabriel?"

"Because of the both of thee. They are demanding thy departure from our village posthaste. They consider thee a so-called 'worldly influence' amongst us, and a threat to our way of life."

"And what do you say about that, Mary Sumner?" teased Walter.

She paused and considered her words carefully. She stopped walking. Walter stopped, as well. She turned and faced him.

"Thou art not any form of 'worldly influence,' Mr. Billingsley. However, thou art, indeed, a significant influence. Especially upon me."

"Mary, I must stop you …"

"No, Mr. Billingsley. Thou shalt be silent and hear me out."

The little girl was feisty. She reminded him of his Abigail. He liked it.

"I am about to do a bold, sinful, and brazen thing, Mr. Billingsley."

"Please, Mary, call me Walter."

"I shan't call thee by thy given name until thou art my husband."

Walter sighed. He was horribly, terribly embarrassed. "Mary, please!"

"Thou wilt listen!" she chirped. Walter ceased his protests and stared into her eyes. She continued, "I know that thou considerest me a child. But I shall not always be a child. I am soon to become a woman. In just a few short years I shall be of the age of childbearing." She paused. "And I intend to bear thy children."

"Mary! You must not speak in such a way! It is scandalous! We cannot be married. You said it yourself. I am a grown man, and you are but a young lass. And there is also the matter of your religion. Surely, you know that you must marry within your order, lest you be cast out."

"I do not care about that. Marriage is ordained by God. What God joins together, no man may turn asunder."

"But, it is not just that. It is not just about your age, or my age, or even our religion."

"What is it about, then?" she demanded with conviction.

"Mary, I do not think that I shall ever take a wife. It is not for me."

"Why would thou proclaim such a silly thing?" Her determination and resolution did not seem to waver.

Walter stared, once again, into her eyes. They were kind, beautiful, thoughtful, blue eyes. He rather liked them.

"You see, Mary ... I was once pledged to be wed. Indeed, my marriage was to have occurred two summers ago."

"And what happened?"

"The war happened. I was taken into the army and eventually captured by Tories. I spent many months in a British prison."

"I know this already. Thou hast related the stories before. But what of thy fiancé?"

Walter felt his chest begin to heave. His heart was tortured. He could almost feel the muscle of it separating within his very body. He felt tears welling in his eyes. His hands began to tremble.

Mary reached out and caressed his left hand. "Oh, Mr. Billingsley. Whatever happened?" Tears of shared heartbreak flowed down her cheeks.

Walter inhaled a deep, heaving breath. "She died, Mary. Almost exactly one year ago. I discovered it when I went back to Camden after the battle at Guilford Courthouse. She was already dead and buried." He wept. He offered no further details. He did not mention the pregnancy, or his stillborn son.

"What was her name?"

"Abigail Hamer."

"Abigail," Mary repeated. "The same as my sister." She paused and stared deeply into Walter's eyes. Her gaze penetrated into the depths of his thoughts and soul. "Has my sister's name troubled thee? Has it rekindled thy grief?"

"Yes, Mary. Yes, it has. It is most difficult to hear that name repeated each day. It almost makes it impossible for me to allow her to go. Every time I hear one of you call your sister's name, my heart aches from sorrow and emptiness."

"Oh, Mr. Billingsley!"

She leaned into him and rested her head in the center of his chest. She wrapped her arms around him and hugged him close, weeping. Walter did not respond in kind. He felt uncomfortable enough having the girl clinging against him. He did not think it appropriate to hold her in similar fashion. He stood awkwardly, with his arms dangling loosely by his sides. She finally pulled away from him after the agonizingly long and intimate embrace. She wiped the tears from her eyes.

She declared, "Then it is that deep pain within thy heart that thou hast been attempting to drown with rum and whiskey and opium."

Walter wiped his cheeks with the sleeve of his wool coat. "That is what Gabriel keeps telling me. But I kept insisting that it was just my aching legs and back." He chuckled and smiled at her.

"But thou hast defeated that need." She declared with great satisfaction, "Thou hast not had a single drop since taking refuge in our home."

"Yes. That is true. I suppose that my time of unconsciousness helped me to subdue the addictions that had claimed me. My pleasant weeks with you and your family have been most encouraging, as well. Indeed, my time here has made all the difference."

Mary considered his statement. She glanced past him and stared at the swollen river. She then responded with a single word. "Time."

"What?" asked Walter, confused.

"Time, Mr. Billingsley! That is what we both need. Time for thy heart to heal, and time for my body to catch up with my heart."

"And you think it is just that simple, do you?"

She nodded convincingly. "Indeed, I do. One day soon thou shalt release thy memories of Abigail. They will no longer be a source of mourning and pain. They will become sweet and fond memories. Time heals all wounds, Mr. Billingsley. Even the deepest wounds of the heart. So, I shall wait for thee. One day thou will be able to lay Abigail Hamer to rest in thy broken heart. And I will be waiting. Then, I shall be thy wife and thou shalt be my husband."

Walter stared at the girl with a mixture of disbelief and admiration. She was so very bold and headstrong and confident. She was an enigma, especially among the Quakers. And her spirit was almost an exact reflection of that of his beloved Abigail. This girl knew what she wanted, and she pursued it. Just like Abigail.

As much as he wanted to fight against her logic and plans, little Mary Sumner was beginning to thaw the wounded, closed, icy heart of Walter Billingsley.

"So, it is like that, then?" he challenged. "That is your prophecy?" He grinned teasingly.

Her cheeks blushed red and the vessels in her temples pulsated. Clearly, this handsome young man thought that she was nothing but a silly little girl. Mary Sumner was embarrassed, but remained determined.

"Yes, Mr. Billingsley. I shall have thee for a husband, whether thou believest it or not!"

She spun quickly and stomped angrily up the trail toward the village.

21

A BITTER END

Encampment on Long Island, Holston River – July 11, 1782

"Damn, it's hot!" declared Walter, wiping the sweat from his face with a linen kerchief. Despite the nearing of dusk, the oppressive and humid heat of summer still smothered the militia camp.

Gabriel poked at his campfire with an extremely long stick. He desired desperately to remain as far away from the heat as possible. The smoldering coals revived and, once again, sent forth dancing flames. Above those flames the pink flesh of a large rabbit sizzled on an iron spit.

Walter growled with displeasure. "Don't stir it too much, Gabriel. We want to cook our supper, not ourselves. We do not require a great conflagration to roast a simple rabbit."

"But we do, indeed, desire to cook the beast, do we not?" retorted his British friend. "Summer heat or no, I have absolutely no desire to consume raw rabbit."

"Of course, we want it cooked! Nobody likes raw meat!"

"And have I ever failed you previously with my cooking skills?"

"No. You are a splendid cook. I'm half a mind to kidnap you and marry you, but it would break Abigail Sumner's heart." He chuckled good-naturedly, despite the intolerable heat.

"Then you should leave the supper preparations to me. If the heat of the cook fire bothers you that much, consider moving further away from it. Better yet, leave me in peace and go take a quick swim in the river."

"You know? That is not a bad idea!" Walter declared, rising to his feet. "The southern channel is nice and shallow." He stared longingly in the direction of the tantalizingly cool water.

"Go! Enjoy yourself. I know that I shall enjoy the solitude," Gabriel teased, smiling.

"Watch your mouth, you no-good Redcoat. Don't make me turn you over to Colonel Sevier."

"As if he would listen! He knows that I am a better scout than you. And, besides, he likes me. He merely tolerates you."

"Arse-kisser!" hissed Walter.

"Fartleberry!" retorted Gabriel.

Walter pulled a small towel from a nearby clothesline. "I shall return shortly."

"Take a bucket and fetch back some water when you return. Preferably, one with a little less mud than the last. I need to wash these dishes and a couple of my shirts. I have no doubt that Ezekiel will need to do some laundry, as well."

"Will there be anything else, General Blevins?" Walter growled sarcastically.

"If I think of anything, you shall be the first to know," retorted Gabriel. "Please do not disappear for hours. This rabbit shall be done shortly, and it will be dark soon."

"Yes, Mother. I shan't play outdoors for too long, Mother."

"Go and take that bath, you raggabrash. You stink."

Walter grabbed his personal bag and a wood bucket as he passed their lean-to. He called over his shoulder, "Tell Zeke not to shoot me when I come back from the river! The lad's been a bit jumpy lately."

"You will likely return before he. Colonel Sevier sent him down to Hickory Grove with a satchel full of dispatches. He may not return until morning."

"Well ... I don't want you to shoot me, either," responded Walter.

Gabriel smiled. "Don't give me any fresh ideas."

Walter grunted, feigning offense. He smiled affectionately as he turned toward the river. He enjoyed exchanging such sparring, playful insults with Gabriel. The former British soldier was a fine and loyal friend ... the best friend he had ever known.

Walter proceeded, barefooted, down the narrow deer trail that led to the southern branch of the Holston River. He could not wait to immerse his body in the luxurious, cool water.

Walter and Gabriel were part of a large force of militiamen encamped on Long Island, an enormous four-mile-long island on the Upper Holston River. Colonel John Sevier was in command of the force of roughly two hundred men. The call-up of the militia was in response to an outbreak of violence in the North Carolina mountains.

The British were all but gone from the United States. Their last remaining stronghold was Charlestown, South Carolina. But, even that city would be evacuated by year's end. Many Loyalists were departing with their British friends and relocating to islands in the Caribbean. Some elected to head north to British Canada. Most of the Tories who chose remain resolved to acclimate to the new political environment. They swore their oaths to the United States and resumed their lives, much as before the war.

There were a few, however, who remained steadfastly loyal to King George. Some of the more headstrong Loyalists fled over the mountains to seek refuge amongst their Cherokee allies and establish homes on the frontier. The influx of these troublesome Tories resulted in renewed tensions in the mountain settlements. There was an increase in the volume of raids, skirmishes, and murders. Most of the aggression came at the hands of a particularly bloodthirsty Cherokee war chief named Dragging Canoe. He was the leader of the Lower Cherokees, located along the Tennessee and Chickamauga Rivers.

Though the war was over on the eastern coast of America, the battle still raged on the distant, over-mountain frontier. But the mountain people longed for peace. They ached for the day when they might hunt, fish, plant and harvest their crops, and do commerce without the constant fear of ambush and violence.

Colonel Sevier and the other leaders of the mountain settlements decided to deal, once and for all, with the Cherokee and Tory raiders in the western counties. The culmination of their strategy was the current encampment of two hundred militiamen on Long Island. Their mission, as the colonel envisioned it, was quite simple. They would proceed southward in force and wipe out the Cherokee menace. First, however, they had to procure supplies for the armed expedition. Colonel Sevier remained resolute in his conviction that the North Carolina legislature should provide for the military protection of its western borders. But, thus far, the legislature had not responded to his entreaties. Colonel Sevier and his men were encamped on Long Island … and they were still waiting for food, lead, and powder from the state government at Hillsborough.

The Holston River was typical of most mountain rivers and streams. The waters flowed swift and crystal clear. It was entirely too dangerous to attempt any bathing in the churning waters of the main channel. Walter had to search for several minutes, but he soon found the perfect spot along the river's edge. It was a large, flat slab of rock that lay only a foot deep, just inside a small cut, and out of the swift flow of the channel. A small, circular eddy swirled gently in front of the large rock. He claimed the location and prepared to wash.

It was a gorgeous, clear mountain evening. The sun had just disappeared over the top of the lush, green peaks to the west. The sky to the east was slowly fading into a pale purple-pink hue, while the sky over the western mountains remained a dazzlingly clear blue. There were no clouds in any direction. The only thing in the vast expanse of sky was a lone eagle that circled lazily toward the southwest. The giant bird screeched its hunting call. Its head hung low and darted to and fro as it scanned the patches of tall grass along the edge of the river for its next meal.

Walter breathed a deep breath of satisfaction. He adored the beauty of the mountains. He also relished such rare moments of quiet solitude like the one he was about to enjoy. He scanned to his left and right. He saw three other men of his detachment lounging about and bathing in the waters of the river. All of them were completely naked, and seemed oblivious to his presence.

Walter's first order of business was his laundry. He stripped off his clothing and laid each of his garments in the tall grass. He removed a fresh bar of soap from his sack of toiletries and went to work on his hunting frock and breeches. He soaked both garments thoroughly in the cool water, then attacked them with the soap. Using small, round rocks from the riverbank, he pounded the cloth on the surface of a larger flat rock. He plunged, scrubbed, and rinsed until the level of cleanliness satisfied him. Once finished, he suspended both garments on nearby bushes to dry. He devoted equal efforts to two shirts and two particularly offensive pairs of wool stockings.

His next order of business was his own cleanliness. He felt of his face, which was prickly with almost a week's growth of beard. The ungentlemanly display of facial hair had to go. He placed a bar of cinnamon shaving soap in a small, wooden cup and took out his shaving brush. He whipped the soap into a thick lather and quickly coated his face. Finally, he removed one of his most precious possessions ... a tiny, two-inch looking glass suspended on a wooden paddle ... along with his oak-handled razor. He faced toward the west so that he might make the best use of the waning twilight and then proceeded to shave his ragged face. The deed was done in less than five minutes.

Finally, it was time for his bath. He removed the leather thong from his queue and walked out onto the large slab of submerged stone. He sat down carefully. The stone was quite slippery. The cold water felt especially soothing to his legs, which still bore the tender scars of his injuries at Guilford Courthouse. He then proceeded to scrub his tired, aching body with the luxuriously slick, oily soap.

Once all of his other parts were washed, Walter focused on his hair. He worked the bar of soap along his scalp and formed a thick lather that coated his entire head. It took several minutes of digging and pulling with his bull's horn comb to loosen the many rats and tangles that had invaded his customarily well-kept and orderly mane. Once he deemed his rather long hair sufficiently combed and cleansed, he lay back to rinse. He relaxed and floated on his back in the cool, gently rippling water. Only his nose and lips remained exposed in the hot, humid air that blanketed the river.

Walter's clean hair hovered loosely in the water around his head. The tips of the long hairs tickled his face, neck, and back. The pleasant sensation transported him back to that magical day when he met Abigail. It had been a hot summer day, much like this one, when his sister Clearanna had brought her husband's cousin home for a visit. Walter and Basil had plunged their heads into the refreshing water of the horse trough to cool themselves from the day's work. He remembered that moment when Basil slapped him on the back and screamed in celebration of the arriving visitors. And then he recalled seeing Abigail for the first time. He remembered falling in love the moment that his eyes met hers.

As he reclined lazily in the water, he thought, *"My God! That was six years ago! How can that be? It seems like someone else's life … and not my own."*

Walter was amazed. The pain in his heart remained, to be sure, but it was not as searing or debilitating as it had once been. Perhaps

Gabriel and Mary were right. Maybe time did, indeed, heal all wounds ... even the deep and painful scars of a broken heart.

The tranquility of Walter's bath was shattered by the crack of a gunshot and a frantic shout. He thrust himself up from the water and stared toward the southwest, in the direction of the report. The sun was almost gone. All that remained of the daylight was a dull glow over the western mountains. A horse and rider galloped across the shallow waters of the river channel, throwing a white spray high into the air. He heard a familiar voice yelling and urging his horse forward. It was Ezekiel Martin, his Quaker friend turned mountain scout. The boy was headed directly toward Colonel Sevier's headquarters.

Walter pulled himself from the water, gathered his clothes, and prepared to hike back to his camp. At the very last second, he caught sight of Gabriel's bucket near the water's edge. He grabbed the handle, plunged the bucket into the river to fill it, and then trotted naked up the trail toward the glow of his campfire.

Colonel John Sevier stood on a large rock in the center of the clearing. The orange-yellow glow of numerous campfires cast an eerie light upon his troubled face. His army of militiamen was gathered around him. Everyone had heard the gunshot of alarm and the ensuing commotion. The men were anxious for news.

"Gentlemen, Kelly's Fort has been hit. No one was killed, but all of the livestock were taken and the corn crop was destroyed. The defenders killed one savage. His war club bore the marks of the Chickamauga Cherokee. It was Dragging Canoe and his band of miscreants."

The gathering of militiamen murmured with a mixture of anger and excitement. If Dragging Canoe's men were roaming as far north at Kelly's Fort, it meant that none of their forts or homesteads were safe. There would be much blood spilled on the frontier before the snows of winter.

Sevier continued, "We can wait upon the politicians in Hillsborough no longer. The Cherokee menace must be addressed. Their raids have continued unabated, and they have become deadlier than ever. Runaway Tories continue to flood out of South Carolina into the Cherokee lands. They are rabble-rousers and agitators ... the whole lot of them. They will feed the Indians lies and whiskey and keep them stirred up for years to come. If we wait another season, the entire frontier could collapse. Our way of life will be destroyed."

"What about provisions, John?" asked his brother, Valentine Sevier. "The governor has promised to supply our coming campaign. Can't we wait a little while longer for his munitions and food?"

Colonel Sevier shook his head vigorously. "Val, we cannot be sure where Governor Martin is located at this time, or if the legislature is even meeting, anymore. They have been running scared ever since the Tories raided Hillsborough last autumn. They're most likely all back on the coast by now. No one knows when or where the legislature will convene again, or if they have even given our travails a moment's thought."

"What'll we do to eat, Colonel?" inquired one of the concerned militiamen.

John Sevier grinned affectionately at his men. "We'll eat what we always eat, boys. We shall take with us whatever provisions we already have. As we go, we will hunt and forage and live off of the land. We've survived for almost ten years now doing exactly that. Why should it be any different on this campaign? And we will also confiscate what we need from our enemies. The Cherokee villages will have livestock, corn in the ground, and smoked meat over their fires. There will be provisions and plunder for the taking."

The cluster of men nodded and mumbled their approval.

"This is it, fellows. The British will be out of Charlestown by year's end. All that remains between us and a permanent peace is Dragging Canoe and his thugs. We must wipe them out, once and for all. Are we in agreement?"

The men all cheered and waved their weapons high in the air. Some actually fired shots in celebration.

Colonel Sevier waved his arms and shouted, "Save that powder, boys! You're going to need every grain."

The crowd calmed somewhat.

"Now, eat your supper if you haven't already, and then get some sleep. We leave at dawn. We're going to Echota Town first and make sure that Chief Old Tassel isn't mixed up in all of this business." He pointed at Walter. "Billingsley and his scouts will lead us." He paused and savored a deep breath. "That's it, boys. Sleep well. We'll be moving hard and fast from here on out. Get your minds settled on what's ahead. Dismissed."

October 9, 1782 – Near the Hiwassee River

Walter and Ezekiel followed closely behind their Cherokee guide. He was a curious fellow who went by the name of John Watts. The scout's name definitely did not fit his appearance. The young man was every bit a Cherokee Indian. He sat majestically atop his horse and scanned the woods to the south with steely, focused eyes. Chief Old Tassel had provided this scout's services to Colonel Sevier after swearing an oath that his villages had not taken part in any recent raids. The evidence seemed to support the old chieftain's claims. The local Indians appeared to be completely occupied with the tasks of ordinary, daily life. They had also welcomed Sevier and his army with friendly, open arms.

John Watts had supposedly saved the army several days of travel time by taking them through previously unknown valleys and short cuts through the rugged mountains. However, the outcome of the army's raids on the Cherokee towns had been dubious, at best. The Eschota towns were freshly abandoned when they arrived. Fires still burned in their pits and the lodges were filled with food, clothing, and goods. But the people were all gone ... escaped into the dense mountain forests.

Sevier's men fell upon each of the abandoned villages and stocked up on plunder and supplies. After confiscating all that they could carry, they set torches to the homes and food stores. Even the cornfields, ready for harvest in only a matter of days, were set ablaze. The Cherokee residents of the Eschota towns, if they returned before winter, would find neither shelter nor food.

The result was the same in all of the villages that they approached, even the ones along the lower Chickamauga and Tennessee Rivers. Dragging Canoe was nowhere to be found. All that remained in the villages were women, old people, and children. Much to Walter's displeasure, Colonel Sevier had detained roughly twelve captives during the campaign. None of them were warriors. Walter did not see the point in taking any of them into custody. Indeed, why should they take any captives, at all? What did Colonel Sevier hope to accomplish by incarcerating a gaggle of women and children? Was it pride, coldheartedness, or simply frustration that compelled him to act with such vengeance against noncombatants?

Walter had grown quite disillusioned with this so-called "great expedition" against the Cherokee. The army had neither found a single enemy warrior nor fired a single shot in anger. All that they had accomplished was the burning of several dozen small, abandoned villages, along with all of their fields and crops. What the frontiersmen had not taken, they had simply destroyed. This was not the kind of warfare that Walter had envisioned for this campaign. He greatly desired to return to Kyle's Fort and secure his discharge from the army.

Finally, after weeks of frustration and wandering throughout the mountains, the men of the overmountain army were returning toward home. On the way northward, they decided to check the villages along the Hiwassee River and Shoemake Creek. Walter suspected that the results would be much the same as in all of their previous encounters. Indeed, his silent suspicions all focused upon their Cherokee guide, John Watts, as the true reason for their inability to locate and engage the enemy.

"I don't trust that Indian," Walter whispered quietly to Ezekiel.

Zeke shrugged. "He seems nice enough to me. He's saved us a lot of trouble with his short cuts and secret pathways."

"So says he," Walter answered. "And yet, everywhere we go, we find nothing but abandoned homes and fields. It's almost as if someone went ahead to warn them."

Ezekiel cut his eyes at Walter. "Dost thou truly believe that he is a spy sent to thwart our campaign?"

"The thought has crossed my mind," Walter growled. "We need to keep a close eye on him, for certain. We will talk with Gabriel about it when we return to the main camp."

"Why did he not come with us today?"

"He returned from courier duty during the middle of the night. I left him in his bedroll. The fellow deserves some extra sleep. He's been moving a bit slowly the last few days, and not just because of his missing leg. I'm afraid he might be getting sick."

"Gabriel will be just fine, Walter. Of that thou can rest assured. He just needs some rest. It was good of thee to leave him in his bed today."

"You and he are my only true friends, Zeke. It is my duty to take care of both of you." Walter grinned. The sunlight reflected off of his heavy growth of whiskers.

Ezekiel nodded and smiled back. The lad took a deep, pleasant breath and scanned their stunning surroundings. "Has thou ever seen land so beautiful as this?"

"No, Zeke, I have not. And that valley we crossed through yesterday was absolutely breathtaking."

Zeke nodded. "John Watts said that the Cherokee call that valley the Sequatchie. He says it goes in a straight line for a hundred miles to the southwest."

"That is difficult to believe," responded Walter.

"But would thou not like to find out if his claims were true?"

Walter grinned and nodded. He would, indeed, like to explore that long, narrow valley.

Walter pointed toward the southeast. "I think that someday I would like to settle over there amongst those rolling hills. The low, flat hilltops would make fine fields, once cleared. There is good water and ample timber for cabins. I could send for my brothers to come and join me. They would love this country."

"No one will settle here, Walter. These are Cherokee lands. North Carolina will never open them to settlements ... not as long as the Indians remain combative."

"Surely, this murdering and fighting will end someday," Walter declared wishfully.

"I pray so, my friend. And when it does, I shall settle this country with thee."

Walter patted his young compatriot on the shoulder. The Cherokee, John Watts, interrupted their sentimental conversation when he suddenly turned his horse and guided it in their direction.

"Didst thou see something that concerneth thee, Mr. Watts?" Ezekiel inquired.

The Indian stared at the Quaker lad, somewhat confused by his odd speech. He shook his head. "No. But we now close to Tellico River. Village at mouth of river. Very near."

"Are there Cherokee living there now?" Walter demanded.

Watts nodded. "For many, many years the people have lived there in peace."

Walter eyed the Cherokee scout suspiciously. "We must examine the town, as you well know."

"Of course. I will go alone. Make sure the way is safe."

"No," Walter declared adamantly. "We will go together."

"What is wrong? You no trust John Watts?" the Indian pleaded innocently.

Walter leaned forward and rested his elbow on the pommel of his saddle. He growled, "No. I do not trust you, Mr. Watts. We shall go together."

The Indian frowned slightly and then shrugged. "As you wish."

Without further response or comment, the Indian turned and headed downhill toward the Tellico village. Walter and Gabriel followed closely behind. Less than a half-mile down the trail, they emerged from the woods into an open, grassy field. John Watts stopped and stared straight ahead. Walter and Ezekiel pulled their horses alongside him. On the far side of the field there stood a cluster of twenty Cherokee lodges. Smoke drifted lazily from several cooking fires. About a dozen women and old men were busy nearby, tending their cornfields. The village appeared tranquil and untouched by war.

John Watts glanced at Walter, who nodded permission to proceed. Watts clucked at his horse and led the animal along a narrow dirt path through the tall stalks of corn toward the village. Moments later, a shout of alarm echoed across the field. The people scattered throughout the village. Most ran for the shelter of their homes, or into the adjacent forest. Within seconds, there was not a single soul visible anywhere within the entire village. There remained only livestock and dogs. Walter and his party rode confidently into the Cherokee town. But what greeted him there was beyond anything that he could have ever imagined. A shirtless white man stepped out of the door of one of the nearby Cherokee lodges. He was pale-skinned and had bright red hair. The fellow greeted them with a distinctly British voice.

"Good afternoon, gentlemen. I welcome you to the village of Tellico."

Walter drew his pistol and pulled back the hammer. He kept the weapon trained on the curious Englishman. The fellow looked hauntingly familiar.

"I am Walter Billingsley of the Sullivan County Militia, in the service of the United States. Identify yourself."

The fellow bowed slightly. "I am Samuel Jacocks, formerly of His Majesty's Army, at your service, sir."

"What regiment?" demanded Walter.

"Why does it matter? I deserted my post well over a year ago and have been living here amongst the Cherokee since. I have a wife and baby. This is my home now. I shall never leave the Colonies."

"The *United States,*" Walter corrected him, emphasizing the name of his country.

"Of course. Please pardon my political stumble." The fellow bowed again.

"Mr. Jacocks, we are going to have to question you. There have been British soldiers and Tories causing trouble amongst the Cherokees in this region ... stirring them up against the American settlements."

"Well, surely you can see that I am not one of those. Had I been such a troublemaker, I would have taken to the woods some time ago. I had ample time to depart. The people of the village have known of your approach for several hours."

"How is that?" demanded Walter.

"They have eyes in these woods."

Walter scanned the village. Dozens of faces peeked from the doorways of the lodges. "Where are all of the fighting men? All I see are old folk, women, and children."

"A few of the younger men have gone off to fight with Dragging Canoe. They are currently in hiding far to the southwest in a place the Choctaw call *Alibamu.* The remainder have hidden themselves in the forest until you depart."

"So, they just left their families here? Undefended?"

"They did so with the hope that you would not wage war against their families. I assured them that you would not." He paused and stated pleadingly at Walter. "You must understand, sir. They are afraid. They have heard about the destruction of the other villages."

"But you are not afraid?"

"I have nothing to fear from your army, sir. I have done nothing wrong. I live at peace here."

"You seem familiar to me, Mr. Jacocks. What was your regiment? Were you ever at Camden?"

The fellow eyed Walter suspiciously. "Yes. I served in the 7th Regiment of Foot, near Camden."

Walter could scarcely believe it. He knew that he had seen this man before! He was one of the Camden prison guards. He had seen this man in his crimson uniform dozens of times during his months inside the walled compound.

"I know who you are, Jacocks. You were one of the guards at the prison yard at Camden, under Colonel Beecham."

The man's jaw dropped. He stammered, "What? How? How could you possibly know this?"

Walter removed his hat and pulled his dirty, stringy hair back from his face. "Because I was one of the prisoners."

The man's eyes opened wide with a gaze of shock mixed with recognition. He exclaimed with his thick, British accent, "Oh, my God!"

Walter declared, "There's someone who would like to talk with you, Jacocks." He turned to John Watts. "Mr. Watts, ride back and fetch Corporal Gabriel Blevins. Tell him to get up here immediately. We have a British deserter that we need to interrogate."

The Cherokee scout nodded his understanding, spun his horse around in the clearing, and then galloped toward their encampment.

The two Englishmen laughed as they embraced.

"Blevins, I simply cannot believe that it is you! How did you get here?"

"The story is much too long to tell, Samuel. But, suffice it to say that I am considered a deserter, the same as you." He pointed at Walter. "Mr. Billingsley rescued me after the battle at Guilford Courthouse. His family gave me care. They are the reason that I am alive today."

"I suppose that we should be thankful that Lord Washington won," quipped Jacocks. "It would have been the hangman's rope for both of us, otherwise." He pointed to the wooden peg that substituted for Gabriel's leg. "Was that from Guilford?"

Gabriel nodded.

"And you actually serve in their army, now?" asked Jacocks, somewhat in disbelief.

"I do. I am a scout for the settlements here in the mountains. We have endeavored to protect the northern outposts from attacks by Cherokees and troublemaking Loyalists."

Jacocks nodded. "A handful of Loyalists from South Carolina have visited these villages before. They attempted to stir the people for war. But, most of the men here ignored them and eventually forced them to leave. The younger ones who were anxious to fight left and joined Dragging Canoe."

"When was that?"

"Back in the spring, right after winter's thaw."

Gabriel nodded. "That is good." He changed the subject to Jacocks' personal life. "When did you leave the army?"

"During that fiasco of last January … when that idiot Tarleton sacrificed our entire force."

"At the Cowpens?"

"Indeed," responded Jacocks. "Any fool could see what was going to happen. Well … allow me to rephrase that … any fool except Tarleton. I simply stole away into the forest during the confusion of the second charge. I worked my way westward during the snows of last winter. I was almost dead from hunger and cold when a hunting party from this very village found me. They brought me here and nursed me back to health. Last summer I married the eldest daughter of the man who hosted me." He grinned mischievously. "She was already carrying my child."

"So, you have a family, then?"

"I do. My wife is called Salali. My son of seven months is Wohali." He smiled proudly. "But I call him Charles, after my father. They are inside our lodge. Salali is afraid of all of you, despite my reassurances."

"Well, she has nothing to fear from us. That is certain. We shall go and make our report to Colonel Sevier, and then leave you in peace."

The sound of horses echoed across the clearing. A half-dozen men on horseback rode through the cornfield toward the village.

"What are they doing here?" Walter mused.

Gabriel frowned. "There was much interest in the camp when the Indian, John Watts, announced that you had found a British deserter. They are filled with questions, no doubt."

"It looks like Lieutenant Green is leading them," observed Ezekiel.

The militia officer led his men into the center of the village. They halted their horses and scanned the town. Each man remained in the saddle.

"Where is he?" demanded Green.

"Who do you seek, Levtenant?" inquired Blevins.

The officer sneered. "The British troublemaker. Is that him?" He pointed an accusing finger at Samuel Jacocks.

"This is no troublemaker, sir. He is a deserter from His Majesty's army and has lived here in this village for over a year. He has a fam …"

Gabriel's sentence was cut off by the explosive report of a pistol. A lead ball entered the left side of Jacocks' head and exited from his ear on the right side, splattering blood and brain matter onto the dry, dusty ground. He collapsed in a heap beside Gabriel, whose face and upper torso were covered with the man's blood spray. Gabriel, Walter, and Ezekiel stared at the spectacle in disbelief. They turned toward the militiamen and observed one of the older fellows holding a still-smoking pistol. He grinned savagely, revealing crooked, decayed, tobacco-stained teeth.

He declared victoriously, "Reckon I finally plugged me a Lobsterback!" He spat on the ground.

The other men in the militia entourage nodded in affirmation. One of the younger men patted him on the back in admiration.

Suddenly, a frantic scream emanated from the nearest hut. A young woman ran out of the door. She carried a huge war club, which she hurled awkwardly in the direction of Lieutenant Green. The club bounced along the ground and stopped harmlessly at the feet of his horse. The woman screamed again and ran toward the body that lay sprawled on the ground. She wailed, "Sam! Sam!" She knelt beside his body, quivering with fear and rage. It was Salali, the wife … the widow … of Samuel Jacocks.

Another pistol cracked. A projectile hit the back of her head, just below the crown, and ripped open the top of her skull. She collapsed across the still body of her dead husband, convulsed, and then died.

"What in God's Name?" demanded Walter. He stared hatefully at Lieutenant Green, who held a smoking pistol in his hand.

"The woman tried to kill me, Billingsley! You saw her! She is the enemy!"

"The enemy?" Walter's face flushed red. He seethed with rage. "One of your men just murdered her husband! And you just shot a helpless, unarmed woman in the back of the head!"

Lieutenant Green busied himself reloading his pistol. His demeanor was nonchalant, prideful, and aloof. "Sergeant Anderson executed an enemy of North Carolina, and I merely defended myself against that red-faced savage."

"You are a lying, cowardly son of a bitch!" growled Walter. He whipped his pistol from his belt and aimed it at the chest of Lieutenant Green.

Ezekiel Martin screamed, "No, Walter!"

Pistols and muskets clicked throughout the clearing as Walter drew his second pistol and aimed it at the murderer, Sergeant Anderson. Gabriel and Ezekiel drew their weapons, as well.

Throughout the central courtyard of the small village, militiamen yelled, threatened, cursed, and screamed at one another.

Then, unexpectedly, a pistol cracked near the edge of the woods to the northwest. Another group of approximately ten men rode into the village. The man at the head of the cluster of riders was their commander, Colonel John Sevier. He drew his horse to a stop beside the confused gaggle of red-faced, belligerent, pistol-pointing men.

"What in the hell is going on here? Have all of you lost your minds? Put your weapons away!" the colonel demanded.

Walter waved his pistol at the awkward pile of bodies on the ground beside him. "Lieutenant Green and his murderous lackeys just killed an unarmed, innocent man and his helpless wife. Blevins and I were speaking to the man when Sergeant Anderson summarily executed him. He drew his pistol and fired without warning. And then, moments, later, this arse-licker Green shot the woman in the back of the head."

Colonel Sevier growled, "All of you … lower your weapons! Now!"

The men hesitated.

"Now, damn it! Don't make me say it again, or I shall have the entire lot of you hanged!"

The men slowly and reluctantly returned their pistols to their belts.

Colonel Sevier stared at the lieutenant. "Green, you had better start explaining yourself."

"Sir, we came upon the scene and discovered Billingsley and his men interrogating that red-haired fellow. We knew that he was a British agitator. Sergeant Anderson thought that the man was making an aggressive move toward Billingsley, so he drew his weapon and fired."

"That is a damned lie!" screeched Walter. "There was no aggression. This dead man was known personally by both myself and Blevins!"

Lieutenant Green cleared his throat and continued, "Then … the woman ran out of the lodge wielding a war club. She hurled it at me. I barely had time to draw my weapon and fire a shot."

"My God!" boomed Walter. "You shot her in the back! And after she had knelt on the ground beside her murdered husband. Are you seriously going to lie in such a brazen fashion to your commanding officer?"

Green shot a steely glance of hate at Walter. He declared, "I stand by my report, sir."

Colonel Sevier stared at the young officer for a moment and then sighed. "Green, you and your men will leave immediately. I want you all back in camp. Now." He turned to the men who had accompanied him into the village. "Captain Mills, you and your men will return with them. I want to speak to my scouts … alone."

"But, sir!" protested Walter.

"Shut up, Billingsley." He turned once again to his men. "Now, git! All of you. I want the entire lot of you out of this village!"

Several of the men mumbled, "Yes, sir." They quickly turned their horses and trotted back along the trail through the cornfield. Only Colonel Sevier remained in the clearing with Walter, Gabriel, and Ezekiel. They watched until the last man entered the trees and disappeared from view. Within seconds, women and children began to emerge from the huts scattered throughout the village. Others came forth from the woods.

"Are you seriously going to let those men get away with murder?" Walter demanded.

The colonel grimaced. "This is a tenuous, confusing situation, Walter. You said, yourself, that this man was British."

"As am I," injected Gabriel.

"True … and yet, you have sworn your oath and now serve the United States."

Gabriel's nostrils flared. "But this man deserted the British army over a year ago, and was unarmed. We were in friendly discussions when your levtenant rode upon the scene and allowed his man to shoot this fellow down as if he were a stray dog. It is both inhuman and incomprehensible."

"And, still, my lieutenant claims that these two people were enemies of our army and acted aggressively."

"Obviously, he is lying," responded Walter. "He was merely thirsty for blood and saw this as an opportunity to satisfy his sick desire."

"Perhaps. Still, he is one of my officers, and has made his report. Absent any other evidence, I must accept that report."

"Then, our word is not considered as evidence?" asked Ezekiel in disbelief.

"I did not say that, Son," answered the colonel. He exhaled and seemed frustrated. "I'm simply trying to make the most of a bad situation. Sincerely, gentlemen. What are we talking about here, really?" He pointed at the two corpses. "Those are the bodies of a British deserter and a Cherokee woman. Both are enemies of the United States. It's best that we just leave things be and go home. In the end, what does it really matter?"

"It matters to me!" exclaimed Walter. "We have to be better men than this!"

Colonel Sevier sighed. "Sometimes even good men make mistakes."

Walter countered, "My biggest mistake was coming on this foolish expedition." He glanced at Gabriel and Ezekiel, then faced the colonel and snapped to attention. "Sir, I request my immediate discharge."

"As do I," added Gabriel.

"Me, too," chirped Ezekiel. Huge tears of despair trailed down the Quaker boy's dusty cheeks.

"Are you certain? We still have three days before we get back to the settlements."

"You all know the way, sir. You can make it just fine without us. Anyhow, I don't think it is a very good idea that we return to your camp. There might be trouble."

The colonel nodded understandingly. “Very well. Walter Billingsley, Gabriel Blevins, and Ezekiel Martin … you are all hereby discharged with honor. You have served your country admirably, and I am grateful.” He nudged his horse forward, leaned down, and shook each man’s hand. “Boys, I wish you all the best. And I am truly sorry how all of this turned out.”

“As am I, sir,” Walter responded coolly.

The colonel nodded, removed his cocked hat, and saluted the three men. He wheeled his horse about and galloped along the trail back toward the militia encampment.

Gabriel stared at the contorted, bloody bodies that lay on the ground beside him. He was angry and confused. “Well, what do we do now, fellows?”

“We bury these people and then we go home,” Walter answered. “Our war is over. I will not fight again.”

“But, where is home?” asked Ezekiel innocently.

Walter wrapped his arm around the lad’s shoulder. “Wherever we choose to make it, Ezekiel. I just hope that we make it together.”

The hollow, mournful cry of a baby echoed from inside the lodge of Samuel Jacocks. It grew in volume and intensity. The three men glanced at the dead couple on the ground beside them and then stared at one another. Their eyes reflected the confusion and pain in their souls.

Ezekiel muttered, “God, Almighty. Their baby!” His lip quivered.

Gabriel took a deep, sorrowful breath. “It appears that someone else will be needing a new home. I will go and fetch the child.” He turned and limped toward the Cherokee lodge.

Walter called after him, “Wait!”

Gabriel turned and stared curiously at his friend.

“I will get him. You fellows do something with these bodies.”

Gabriel nodded. “As you wish.”

Walter walked numbly toward the open door, stooped down, and stepped through the entrance. The inside of the hut was dark and smelled of smoke. It took a moment for his eyes to adjust to the dim light. He quickly spotted the infant. The little one was sitting on a blanket in the corner. Walter quickly recalled that Jacocks said the boy was seven months old. The lad wailed in fear when he spied the stranger inside his home.

Walter spoke quietly and soothingly to the child, "There, there, now. It's all right, little one. I won't hurt you. My name is Walter."

He cautiously approached the boy. Curiously, as Walter knelt beside the lad, the little fellow reached up with both arms and wrapped them around his neck. The sudden movement surprised Walter. It made him chuckle with delight.

The boy hugged Walter tightly. And his tiny hug felt so very good! The simple, pure affection of the child washed across Walter's spirit like a healing balm. The scars of anger, bitterness, and pain that had engulfed his broken heart melted away in an instant. He closed his eyes and took refuge the child's tender embrace. He allowed the baby's warm, innocent touch to penetrate deep into his soul. The child lingered, refusing to let go. Finally, Walter returned the loving embrace.

Walter wondered if this is how the embrace of his own son would have felt. He wept as he tried to imagine what his own child would have looked like, felt like, and sounded like. The boy would have been a little over a year old had he lived ... just a few months older than orphaned Charles Jacocks. Walter's sobs and tears increased in volume. His chest heaved as the deep pains of grief, loss, anger, and bitterness finally released their stranglehold upon his heart and spirit. Walter somehow found solace, and peace, and freedom in the arms of the little dark-skinned, red-haired baby boy. He had walked into the hut intending to rescue an orphaned child. Instead, that child rescued him.

After several minutes, Baby Charles released his hug and then stared intently at Walter's face. He grinned, revealing a row of tiny teeth. Walter's heart melted with love for the orphaned boy. He kissed the child on the forehead.

Walter declared, "It is time for us to go, Charles. I reckon you are going to be my boy from now on."

The little fellow wrapped his arms around Walter's neck again. Walter gathered all of the clothing and blankets that he could find and stuffed them clumsily into a leather sack. He pulled the sack on the ground behind him as he walked out of the shadowy lodge back into the brilliant sunlight of the afternoon. His friends were waiting outside. The bodies had been removed. All that remained were some dark spots of blood in the dust.

Walter lifted his face to the sun and allowed the light to warm his face. He took a deep, cleansing breath. He felt renewed. He felt alive. He felt like he had been reborn.

Walter Billingsley's war was, indeed, over. At long last, he had found peace. And he had discovered, through the powerful, healing hug of a tiny, orphaned child, that he really could love again.

EPILOGUE

Ninety-Six District Courthouse, South Carolina – June 1, 1787

Walter and his beautiful, beaming bride-to-be stood before the Ninety-Six District judge. They were not touching one another. Indeed, almost a foot of space separated them. Walter was clad in his finest navy breeches and wool coat. His long, brown hair was braided into a perfect queue and tied off with strips of black ribbon. The cuffs of his white shirt extended several inches beyond the sleeves of his coat. Likewise, his silk neck sock fluttered loosely over the top button of the garment. He wore a single yellow rose on his left breast. His future wife wore an elegant blue damask gown over a lighter blue petticoat. Her straw hat was decorated with a wide blue ribbon and numerous yellow flowers. Like her husband-to-be, she smiled with delight.

Walter glanced over his left shoulder to make sure that all of his friends and loved ones were close by. Gabriel Blevins and his family were seated in a row of chairs to the right of the door. Gabriel clung tightly to his bride, Abigail Sumner Blevins. Three-year-old Eleanor Blevins sat beside her mother. Abigail held their one-year-old son, Walter, in her arms. She smiled and playfully waved the baby boy's arm at the man for whom he was named. The little boy squealed with delight.

Walter winked at the little boy who sat to Gabriel's left. He was a handsome, but curious-looking lad of six years. His skin was very dark, but freckled, and he had blazing, curly red hair. He was Walter's adopted son, Charles Jacocks, the orphaned child of Samuel Jacocks and the Cherokee maiden, Salali. Charles smiled proudly and waved at his papa.

Another young couple sat in the row of chairs on the other side of the front door. They were Ezekiel and Maddie Kyle Martin. Maddie cuddled their baby girl and cooed to soothe the child. Ezekiel grinned with great joy.

The judge cleared his throat. "Shall we proceed, Mr. Billingsley?"

Walter winked at little Charles again, then turned to the officiant and nodded.

The old judge seemed very pleased with himself. He had not had the honor of performing a wedding ceremony in many months. He wanted to make the most of this one. His wife, who sat silently in the corner of the room, smiled and watched in silence. The old fellow's spectacles hung precariously onto the end of his nose as he attempted to focus upon the text in front of him. He glanced at Walter over the rims of the glasses as he read the words from his prayer book with great drama and eloquence.

"Walter ... wilt thou have this woman to be thy wedded wife, to live together after God's ordinance in the holy estate of matrimony? Wilt thou love her, comfort her, honor, and keep her, in sickness, and in health? And forsaking all others, keep thee only to her, so long as you both shall live?"

Walter lifted his chin high and proclaimed, "I will!"

The judge turned slightly to face the bride.

"And to you, Mary ... wilt thou have this man to be thy wedded husband, to live together after God's ordinance in the holy estate of matrimony? Wilt thou obey him and serve him, love, honor, and keep him, in sickness and in health? And forsaking all others, keep thee only to him so long as ye both shall live?"

She responded confidently, "I will."

The judge nodded to the couple. "You may now face one another, join your right hands, and say your vows."

Walter and Mary did as they were instructed. He accepted her tiny, warm hand into his own and stared lovingly into her perfect, dazzlingly blue eyes. He winked mischievously. She covered her mouth in embarrassment with her left hand.

Walter took a deep breath. "I, Walter Billingsley, take thee, Mary Sumner, to be my wedded wife, to have and to hold from this day forward; for better, for worse, for richer, for poorer, in sickness, and in health, to love and to cherish, till death us depart; according to God's holy ordinance, and thereto I pledge thee my troth."

Mary smiled warmly and responded, "I, Mary Sumner, take thee, Walter Billingsley, to be my wedded husband; to have and to hold, from this day forward, for better, for worse, for richer, for poorer, in sickness, and in health; to love, cherish, and to obey, till death us depart, according to God's holy ordinance, and thereto I pledge thee my troth."

The judge responded, "Excellent! Do you have a ring, Walter?"

Gabriel rose from his seat and stepped forward. He placed a simple gold band in Walter's palm. Walter gave his friend's hand an affectionate squeeze. Gabriel smiled. The happy bridegroom turned back to face the judge.

"Well, then! What are you waiting for? Place it on her finger!"

Everyone in the room laughed as Walter pushed the ring onto the fourth finger of Mary's left hand.

"Now, Walter … repeat after me …"

Walter paid little attention to the words of the ring ceremony. He simply repeated each short phrase as it was offered by the judge. He was too captivated by Mary's mesmerizing eyes and her perfect smile. The glow of the sunlight from the window behind her framed her head with a halo of radiance. She was the most beautiful vision that he had ever entertained. She never ceased smiling.

The judge suddenly raised his voice as he offered a prayer from his book. "Oh, eternal God, Creator and Preserver of all mankind,

Giver of all spiritual grace, the Author of everlasting life. Send thy blessing upon these thy servants, this man and this woman, whom we bless in thy name. That as Isaac and Rebecca lived faithfully together, so these persons may surely perform and keep the vow and covenant betwixt them made, whereof this ring given and received is a token and pledge, and may they ever remain in perfect love and peace together, and live according unto thy laws. Through Jesus Christ our Lord. Amen."

The judge took a deep breath and smiled.

"Now, those whom God hath joined together, let no man put asunder." He paused. "There are many other words written out in this prayer book, but I am no priest. Most of it is gibberish to me. Anyhow, I quite think that what we have done will suffice."

Walter and Mary stared expectantly at the judge.

"Well, Son, what are you waiting for? Kiss your bride!"

Walter surrounded the diminutive young woman with his strong arms and lifted her up off of the floor. Their faces converged in a warm, long-awaited, passionate kiss. It was the very first time that their lips had ever met. Gabriel cheered. Abigail wept. The judge laughed.

As Walter released Mary from his embrace and allowed her to stand once again, she whispered into his ear, "I told thee, did I not?"

"Told me what?" he asked, smiling.

She stepped back one step, planted both fists on her hips, and scolded him. It was loud enough for everyone in the room to hear. "I told thee that I would have thee for my husband! It was five years ago, on the bank of the Holston River. Thou dismissed me … and told me that I was nothing but a little girl."

Gabriel and Abigail could not help but laugh at the spectacle of the tiny girl chastising her tall husband.

Walter's eyes wandered down the young maiden's shapely body. He mumbled, "Well, you certainly are no longer a little girl. You are every bit a woman, and you are the only woman in this world for me, Mrs. Billingsley."

Mary stretched upward on her toes and kissed him a second time. Again, she whispered into his ear, "Thou must get me home, Walter. I am anxious to commence making little Billingsleys."

She grinned mischievously, grabbed Walter by the hand, and dragged him toward the door of the courthouse.

THE REAL WALTER BILLINGSLEY

Walter Billingsley was my fifth great-grandfather. He was a Patriot of the American Revolution and a frontiersman in the mountains of North Carolina and Tennessee. Most of the details in this novel regarding his service in the war were true. They came from his pension record. He enlisted in an unknown Virginia regiment early in 1780, marched toward Charleston, and was captured shortly after making his escape from the battlefield at the Waxhaws Massacre. He spent almost eight months in captivity in Camden, and was evacuated with the British Army in January, 1781, in the direction of the Battle of Cowpens.

Following the historic British loss at Cowpens, Walter and eighteen other prisoners were dragged by their captors through the forests and fields of North Carolina in the infamous "Race to the Dan River." He made his escape in March, 1781, just days before the Battle of Guilford Courthouse. He joined in with a group of North Carolina militiamen and actually took part as a combatant in that tremendous battle. Immediately after, he located his brother, James, who secured a furlough for him from General John Butler and then sent him home.

The details I included about his parents and siblings were largely true. James Billingsley was a Baptist "exhorter" and a protégé of the rather famous Baptist clergyman, the Rev. Shubal

Stearns. He preached as a lay-minister in fledgling Baptist churches in and around Guilford County, North Carolina. Two which contain his name in their records are the Sandy Creek and Abbott's Creek Baptist Churches. According to family legend, he was hanged by Tories in his yard in the spring of 1776. Walter, Basil, and Martha were living at home and experienced the event in person. I, of course, included his dramatic execution in my story. It was too amazing not to share, and provided me with the "Martyrs" portion of my title.

Unfortunately, since there is no official record or period documentation of the hanging of James Billingsley, I have been unable to have James Billingsley recognized as a Patriot by the Sons of the American Revolution. Indeed, despite having a chapter named after him in Texas, the Daughters of the American Revolution also refuse to accept the family chronicle as a testimony of his unfailing patriotism.

Walter's mother, Elizabeth Crabtree Billingsley lived to a ripe, old age. Indeed, according to family legend, she died while traveling from John's home near Bowling Green, Kentucky, back to Walter's home in the Bradly/McMinn County area in southeast Tennessee. The year of her death was recorded as 1839. If this is true, then she was roughly 110 years old!

On a very interesting note, I recently discovered a reference to a will that Elizabeth Billingsley swore in Randolph County, North Carolina, in 1782. In that will she bequeathed her whiskey still to her sons, Walter and Basil. This is the same liquor still that became such an important part of my story line. But, what is truly amazing to me is the Patriotic significance of the will. By a North Carolina statute adopted in 1777, all individuals who filed a will or legacy had to swear the "official" oath to North Carolina and the United States. Since the war was still, technically, ongoing in 1782, Elizabeth Billingsley had to swear that oath. Therefore, this will of legacy serves as an official document proving that she, too, was a Patriot of the American Revolution!

I recently received a copy of that will from the Randolph County Historical Society. I immediately filed a Supplemental Application with the SAR to have her "officially" recognized as a Patriot of the American Revolution. That application is now in the hands of the SAR genealogists and I am awaiting its approval. Female Patriots are rare and difficult to prove. Grandma Elizabeth will be the second one that I have discovered in my family tree.

Walter's brothers James, Samuel, and John all served in the militia of North Carolina during the war. Curiously, they served in regiments from different counties in the region. The three older brothers actually served in the Cherokee Campaign of 1776. Later in the war, James served in Rowan County as a Captain of a company of Rangers under Colonel Francis Locke. Samuel was a private in the same Rowan Regiment. John was a private in the Randolph County Regiment. It seems that all of the Billingsley boys were true Patriots.

It is interesting to me that Walter appears to have been the first of the Billingsley brothers to cross over the mountains and settle on the frontier. I am not certain what drew him to Sullivan County. One possibility is the presence of a Baptist preacher by the name of Tidence Lane. He was the first ordained minister and preacher in Tennessee. He and James Billingsley, Walter's father, learned to preach together under the guidance of Shubal Stearns at the Sandy Creek Baptist Church in Guilford County. Indeed, Walter's sister, Elizabeth, married a young man by the name of Lane. Though I cannot prove it, I believe that she may have been the first wife of Tidence Lane Jr. Family records show that she died in 1781. We know that the younger Tidence Lane married in Tennessee in 1783, so a previous marriage might have been possible.

But, whatever the circumstance, there may have been deep relational and familial connections between the Billingsleys and the Lanes, which may have led to Walter's pursuit of a life "over the mountains."

James and Samuel Billingsley later settled homesteads in the Sequatchie Valley in east Tennessee, not far from Walter. John Billingsley eventually settled on the frontier in Warren County, Kentucky, where he later applied for and received a pension for his service. His burial site is a little over an hour from my home. I was honored to visit his grave earlier this year.

I must confess, however, that the storyline surrounding Abigail Hamer is a complete fabrication of my imagination. The notion of an early love interest entered my mind and found its way into the novel early on in my planning. After that, the romance took on a life of its own. It seemed to be an emotionally moving and dramatic connection that could link Walter to Camden, and also provide a logical explanation for his rather strange, sudden, and unexplained foray over the mountains into Tennessee in late 1781.

Walter's friendships with Gabriel Tate, Thomas Whitlock, and Gabriel Blevins were also products of my imagination. However, the name Whitlock actually refers to a real person from Walter's life. In his pension statement, he describes how he discovered a "Virginian named Whitlock" in the woods following the battle of Waxhaws. I simply assigned the man a first name and kept him in my story.

Likewise, the culminating drama of the death of the British deserter, Samuel Jacocks, and his Cherokee wife was a fictionalization of some actual events. There is one record of the Cherokee expedition that describes the killing of a British deserter and a Cherokee woman. I merely gave them names and a location and wrote them into my story. And, as you can imagine, there was no little boy named Charles Jacocks. Walter did not have an adopted son. I simply thought that such a character, juxtaposed against the memory of a son that he never knew, could provide an uplifting ending to his otherwise dark and somewhat tragic wartime experiences.

According to family tradition, Walter did, indeed, marry in 1787 to a young woman named Mary. Her family and origins are unknown. Some family records claim that her last name was Sumner.

There may be confusion in those records, since there was, indeed, a Mary Sumner who married into the Billingsley family line back in Virginia.

I decided to go ahead and use Sumner for her last name in my account. Interestingly, in my research I discovered that the Quaker, William Sumner, was an early settler in east Tennessee. I also discovered that he was from the New Market Meeting House in Guilford County, North Carolina. This Quaker settlement was only a few miles from the Billingsley home place. Though I cannot be certain, a young woman named Mary Sumner could have been a member of that pioneer Quaker family. Anyhow, the possibility served me well in my story.

Walter and Mary rambled about throughout South Carolina and Tennessee after their marriage. Unfortunately, there is no governmental marriage record in existence for them. However, the fact that they were on the 1790 and 1800 U.S. censuses in Greenville and Pendleton Counties in South Carolina (both in the Ninety-Six District), leads me to believe that they were, most likely, married in South Carolina.

Walter and Mary Billingsley, according to all the records I could find, parented ten surviving children between the years 1789 and 1813. I descend from their third son, William, born in South Carolina in 1797.

Walter's name appears on land records further west in Jackson County, Tennessee, around 1802. His brother, John, is on records there, as well. He remained in Jackson County, near the Kentucky border, through at least the year 1817, as evidenced in land records. Walter appears to have lived out his later days in the former Cherokee lands of east Tennessee. He was named on the 1820 U.S. census in Franklin County, Tennessee. In 1830, he was in McMinn County, Tennessee. This was the last census in which his wife, Mary, appeared. He was on the 1840 census in Bradley County, Tennessee, in the home of his youngest son, Jesse. I believe that

Walter died sometime in the mid-1840's, right around the age of eighty.

In the early 1830's, shortly after his move to McMinn County, Walter Billingsley made application to the United States government for a pension for his Revolutionary War service. Despite multiple courtroom testimonies, and his spot-on accurate and vividly detailed recollections of the events in which he participated, he was denied receipt of a pension from the United States government. The reason cited for his rejection was, "*... insufficient proof of six months of actual military service in an embodied corps or organization ...*"

Despite over seven months of captivity in a British prison, he was denied a military pension because he failed to serve for six months in a "recognized" army unit. This was, in my opinion, an unimaginable injustice. Over the years, I have read scores of pension records in which men were awarded lifelong pensions based upon much less compelling testimony than Walter Billingsley's. This incident serves as proof positive of how unjust bodies of government officials can be in some instances. I quite imagine that, even then, such matters were not so much about "what you knew" as they were about "who you knew," or how politically connected you were.

Interestingly, and on a more positive note, local historians in Bradley County, Tennessee, recently located an unmarked grave in their county which lies near the home site of Jesse Billingsley. These historians, local residents, and researchers believe that this is the grave of Walter Billingsley. Earlier this year, I personally financed the purchase of a memorial headstone to place on that site. On Saturday, October 28, 2017, the Tennessee Society of the Sons of the American Revolution hosted a Patriot Grave Marking Ceremony at the tiny cemetery. I was honored to take part in that ceremony. My photo with his stone is included in the back of this book! You can also go to my web site, geoffbaggett.com, or my Facebook Author Page, and view other photos from the event.

I hope that my story has helped you connect, personally, to the life and history of another brave Patriot of the American Revolution. I am proud of Walter Billingsley, and grateful that he endured such a selfless life of sacrifice in order to help give birth to this great nation. I salute him with a heartfelt and enthusiastic, "Huzzah!"

Until we meet again,

Geoff Baggett – Cadiz, Kentucky

ABOUT THE AUTHOR

Geoff Baggett is a small-town pastor in rural Kentucky. Though his formal education and degrees are in the fields of chemistry, biology, and Christian theology, his hobbies and obsessions are genealogy and Revolutionary War history. He is an active member of the Sons of the American Revolution and the Descendants of Washington's Army at Valley Forge. He has discovered over twenty Patriot ancestors in his family tree from the states of Virginia, North and South Carolina, and Georgia.

Geoff is an avid living historian, appearing regularly in period uniform in classrooms, reenactments, and other Revolutionary War commemorative events throughout the southeastern United States. He lives on a small piece of land in rural Trigg County, Kentucky, with his amazing wife, Kim, a daughter and grandson, and a yard full of fruit trees and perpetually hungry chickens and goats.

THANK YOU FOR READING MY STORY!

I hope that you enjoyed my work of fiction. It was a pleasure preparing and writing it for you. I am just a simple "part-time" author, and I am grateful that you chose to read my book.

I would humbly ask that you help me spread the word about the books of my two series on the Revolutionary War. It's not easy for an independent writer to "break through" and find success in the overly-saturated book market. But you can help me in a number of ways!

Tell your friends! Word of mouth is always the best!

Mention my books on Facebook or in other social media. This is just a "high tech" form of word of mouth.

Write a review for me on Amazon.com! Reviews are so very important in marketing these days. I am grateful for every review that I receive and watch my titles daily in search of new reviews.

- **Connect with me and like my author page on Facebook @cockedhatpublishing, and follow me on Twitter @ GeoffBaggett.**
- **Use my student books in your school curriculum!** I currently have a teaching supplement for my first book for kids, ***Little Hornet***, and similar products are under development for my other children's titles. They are available for free

(PDF downloads) on my web site. If you are interested in a "class set" for your school, please contact me directly. I make copies available for classrooms at a very low price.

Book me for a presentation! I have several unique, engaging, and interesting Revolutionary War presentations available for groups or classes. I am a professional speaker and living historian. I will travel if I can have the opportunity to connect to readers and sell some books! Contact me through my web site, geoffbaggett.com, or through my Facebook author page, to arrange an event.

Thanks again! Please be on the lookout for my next novel in the series. This one will be about some of my wife's German ancestors from Pennsylvania and Virginia. From a research perspective, this will be my most adventurous book, by far. It will focus on the northern theater of the war, especially the battles and events leading up to the winter at Valley Forge. The working title is ***Immigrants and Patriots***. That may change ... but for now I think that this best describes the story that I have in mind. Look for it in the fall of 2018!

CPSIA information can be obtained
at www.ICGtesting.com
Printed in the USA
BVHW030302030820
585286BV00001BA/76

9 780997 383393